CAMILLA L

Born in 1974, Camilla Lackberg worked as an economist before a course in creative crime writing led to a drastic change of career. She is a household name in Sweden and all seven of her psychological thrillers featuring Erica Falck and Patrik Hedström are number one bestsellers across Europe. Camilla lives in Stockholm with her husband and three children.

By the same author

The Ice Princess
The Preacher
The Stonecutter
The Gallows Bird

CAMILLA LACKBERG

The Hidden Child

Translated by Tiina Nunnally

HARPER

This novel is entirely a work of fiction.
The names, characters and incidents portrayed in it are
the work of the author's imagination. Any resemblance to
actual persons, living or dead, events or localities is
entirely coincidental.

Harper
An imprint of HarperCollins*Publishers*
77–85 Fulham Palace Road,
Hammersmith, London W6 8JB

www.harpercollins.co.uk

Published by HarperCollins*Publishers* 2011

1

A catalogue record for this book is
available from the British Library

ISBN: 978-0-00-741947-0

Set in Meridien by Palimpsest Book Production Limited,
Falkirk, Stirlingshire

Printed and bound in Great Britain by
Clays Ltd, St Ives plc

Mixed Sources

Product group from well-managed
forests and other controlled sources
www.fsc.org Cert no. SW-COC-001806
© 1996 Forest Stewardship Council

FSC is a non-profit international organization established
to promote the responsible management of the world's forests.
Products carrying the FSC label are independently certified
to assure consumers that they come from forests that are managed
to meet the social, economic and ecological needs
of present and future generations.

Find out more about HarperCollins and the environment at
www.harpercollins.co.uk/green

To Wille & Meja

In the stillness of the room the only sound was from the flies. A constant buzzing from the frantic beating of their wings. The man in the chair didn't move, and he hadn't for a long time. He wasn't actually a man any more. Not if a man was defined as someone who lived, breathed, and felt. By now he'd been reduced to fodder. A haven for insects and maggots.

The flies buzzed in a great swarm around the motionless figure. Sometimes landing, their mandibles moving. Then flying off again in search of a new spot to land. Feeling their way and bumping into one another. The area around the wound in the man's head was of particular interest though the metallic odour of blood had long since vanished, replaced by a different smell that was mustier and sweeter.

The blood had coagulated. At first it had poured from the back of his head and down the chair, on to the floor where it formed a pool. Initially it was red, filled with living corpuscles. Now it had changed colour, turning black. The puddle was no longer recognizable as the viscous fluid that ran through a person's veins. Now it was merely a sticky black mass.

Some of the flies had had their fill. They had laid their eggs. Now, sated and satisfied, they simply wanted out. Their wings beat against the windowpane in their futile attempts to get past the invisible barrier, striking the glass with a faint clicking sound. Eventually they gave up. When their hunger returned, they went back to what had once been a man but was now nothing but meat.

All summer long Erica had circled around the thoughts that were always on her mind. Weighing the pros and cons, she would find herself tempted to go up there. But she never got further than the bottom of the stairs leading to the attic. She could blame it on the fact that the past few months had been so busy, with everything that had to be done after the wedding and the chaos in the house when Anna and her kids were still living with them. But that wasn't the whole truth. She was simply afraid. Afraid of what she might find. Afraid of rooting around and bringing things to the surface that she would have preferred not to acknowledge.

She knew that Patrik was wondering why she didn't want to read the notebooks they'd found up in the attic. Several times he had seemed on the verge of asking her about it, but he'd held back. If he had asked, she wouldn't have been able to answer. What scared her most was that she might have to change her view of reality. The image she'd always had of her mother – who she was as a person and how she'd treated her daughters – was not very positive. But it was Erica's, all the same. An image that was familiar, an unshakable truth that had held up through the years and had been something she could count on. Maybe it would be confirmed. Maybe it would even be reinforced. But what if it was undermined? What if she was forced to relate to a whole new reality? Up until now she hadn't been brave enough to find out.

Erica set her foot on the first step. From downstairs in the living room she heard Maja's happy laughter as Patrik played with her. The sound was comforting, and she put her

2

other foot on the stairs. Only five more steps to the top.

The dust swirled in the air when she pushed open the trap door and climbed up into the attic. She and Patrik had talked about remodelling the space sometime in the future, maybe as a cosy hideaway for Maja when she was older and wanted some privacy. But thus far it remained an unfinished attic with wide planks for the floor and a sloping ceiling with exposed beams. It was partially filled with clutter. Christmas decorations, clothes that Maja had outgrown, and boxes of items that were too ugly to have downstairs but too expensive or too fraught with memories to discard.

The chest stood way at the back, near the gable wall. It was old-fashioned, wood with metal fittings. Erica had a vague notion that it was what they called an 'America trunk'. She went over and sat down on the floor next to it, running her hand over the top. After taking a deep breath she gripped the latch and lifted the lid. A musty smell rose up, making her nose twitch. She wondered what created such a distinct, heavy odour of age. Probably mildew, she thought, noticing that her scalp was beginning to itch.

She could still recall the emotion that had overwhelmed her when she and Patrik first discovered the chest and went through its contents, slowly lifting each item out. Drawings that she and Anna had done when they were children, little things they had made at school. All of them saved by their mother Elsy. The mother who had never seemed interested when her young daughters had come home and eagerly presented her with their creations.

Erica did the same thing now, taking out one item after another and setting everything on the floor. What she was looking for was at the very bottom of the chest. Carefully she took out the piece of cloth, finally holding it in her hands again. The infant's shirt had once been white, but as she held it up to the light she could see how it had yellowed with age. And she couldn't take her eyes off the

3

small brown stains on the garment. At first she had assumed they were rust spots, but then she'd realized they must be dried blood. There was something so heartbreaking about finding spots of blood on the child's shirt. How had it ended up here in the attic? Whose was it? And why had her mother saved it?

Erica gently placed the shirt next to her on the floor. When she and Patrik first found the garment, an object had been wrapped inside, but it was no longer there. That was the only thing she had removed from the chest – a Nazi medal that had been hidden in the stained cloth. The emotions awakened in her when she first saw the medal had been surprising. Her heart had begun pounding, her mouth went dry, and images from old newsreels and documentaries about the Second World War flickered before her eyes. What was a Nazi medal doing here in Fjällbacka? In her own home and among her mother's possessions? The whole situation seemed absurd. She had wanted to put the medal back in the chest and close the lid, but Patrik had insisted that they take it to an expert to find out more. Reluctantly Erica had agreed, but she felt as if voices were whispering inside her; ominous voices, warning her to hide the medal away and forget all about it. But her curiosity had won out. In early June she'd taken it to an expert specializing in World War II artefacts, and with a little luck they would soon know more about the medal's origin.

But what interested Erica most was what they'd found at the very bottom of the chest. Four blue notebooks. She recognized her mother's handwriting on the covers. That elegant, right-slanted writing, but in a younger, rounder version. Now Erica removed the notebooks from the chest, running her index finger over the cover of the one on top. Each of them had been labelled 'Diary', a word that aroused mixed feelings in her. Curiosity, excitement, eagerness. But also fear, doubt, and a strong feeling that she was invading her mother's privacy. Did she have the right to read these notebooks? Did she have the right to delve into her mother's innermost thoughts and feelings? A diary was not intended for anyone else's eyes. Her mother hadn't written the books so that others might share the contents. Maybe she would have forbidden her daughter to read them. But Elsy was dead, and Erica couldn't ask for permission. She would have to decide for herself what to do with the notebooks.

'Erica?' Patrik's voice interrupted her thoughts.

'Yes?'

'The guests are arriving!'

Erica glanced at her watch. Oh lord, was it already three o'clock? Today was Maja's first birthday, and their closest friends and family members were coming over. Patrik must have thought she'd fallen asleep up here.

'I'm coming!' She brushed the dust off her clothes and, after a moment's hesitation, picked up the notebooks and the child's shirt before descending the steep attic stairs.

'Welcome!' Patrik stepped aside to let in the first of their guests. It was through Maja that they'd met Johan and Elisabeth, who had a son the same age. The boy loved Maja to bits, but sometimes he was a little too aggressive in showing it. Now, as soon as William caught sight of Maja in the hall, he bulldozed into her like an ice-hockey player. Unsurprisingly, Maja didn't particularly care for this, and his parents had to extricate the shrieking object of his affections from William's embrace.

'William, that's no way to behave! You have to be more careful with girls.' Johan gave his son an admonishing look as he tried to restrain him.

'I think his pickup technique is about the same as the one you used to use,' Elisabeth said with a laugh, but her husband was clearly not amused.

'There, there, sweetheart, it wasn't that bad,' Patrik said

5

to Maja. 'Upsy-daisy.' He picked up his sobbing daughter and hugged her until her cries dwindled to whimpers. Then he set her down again and gave her a gentle push in William's direction. 'Look what William has brought for you. A present!'

The magic word had the intended effect. Maja's tears evaporated as William tottered across to hand her a present tied with ribbon. With Patrik's help she got the package open and pulled out a cuddly grey elephant, which was an instant success. She hugged it to her chest, wrapping her arms around the soft body and stamping her feet in delight, but William's attempt to pat the elephant was repelled with a look of defiance. Rising to the challenge, her little admirer immediately redoubled his efforts.

'Let's go through to the living room,' said Patrik, scooping his daughter up in his arms to prevent further conflict. William's parents followed, and when the boy was placed in front of the big toy box, peace was restored. At least temporarily.

'Hi, everybody!' said Erica as she came downstairs. She gave their guests a hug and patted William on the head.

'Who wants coffee?' Patrik called from the kitchen. All three said 'I do' in unison.

'So how is life as a married woman?' asked Johan with a smile, putting his arm around Elisabeth as they sat on the sofa.

'About the same. Except that Patrik keeps calling me "the missus". Any tips on how I can get him to stop?' Erica turned to Elisabeth and winked.

'You might as well give up trying. It won't be long before he'll stop talking about the "missus" and go on and on about the government instead, so make the most of it. Where's Anna, by the way?'

'She's over at Dan's house. They've already moved in together.' Erica raised an eyebrow significantly.

6

'Oh, really? That was fast.' Elisabeth's eyebrow went up too.

They were interrupted by the sound of the doorbell, and Erica jumped up. 'That's probably them now. Or Kristina.' The latter name was spoken with ice cubes audibly clinking between the syllables. Since the wedding, Erica's relationship with her mother-in-law had grown even frostier. This was mostly due to Kristina's zealous campaign to convince Patrik that it wouldn't be right for a real man to take four months' paternity leave. To her great dismay, he had refused to budge an inch. In fact, he was the one who had insisted on taking care of Maja through the autumn.

'Hello, is there a birthday girl here?' Anna could be heard asking from the front hall. Erica couldn't help shivering with contentment every time she heard how happy her little sister sounded. For so many years there had been no joy in her voice, but now it was back. Anna sounded strong and happy and in love.

At first Anna had been worried that Erica might be upset that she and Dan had taken up with each other. But Erica had merely laughed at her concern. It seemed an eternity since she and Dan had been a couple. And even if she had found it a bit awkward, she would have set aside her own feelings just to see Anna happy again.

'Where's my favourite girl?' Dan, big, blond and boisterous, came in and looked around for Maja. The two of them had a special rapport, and she immediately came toddling towards him, holding out her arms. 'Present?' she asked, now that she'd started to understand the whole concept of a birthday.

'Of course we have a present for you, sweetie,' said Dan. He nodded to Anna, who held out a big package wrapped in pink paper with a silver ribbon. Maja pulled out of Dan's arms and began struggling to open the present. This time Erica helped her, and together they took out a big doll with eyes that opened and closed.

'Dolly,' said Maja gleefully, giving the present another of her bear hugs. Then she set off to show William her latest treasure.

The doorbell rang again, and a second later Kristina came into the room. Erica couldn't help gritting her teeth. She hated the way her mother-in-law would press the doorbell in what was largely a symbolic gesture before barging into the house.

The presentation and unwrapping of a gift was repeated, but this time it wasn't such a hit. Maja hesitantly held up the undershirts that she found inside the package, then searched the wrapping paper again to make sure that she hadn't overlooked a toy. Then she stared at her grandmother, wide-eyed.

'Last time I was here I noticed that she'd almost outgrown the undershirt she was wearing, and since Lindex had a three-for-the-price-of-two sale on, I bought her a few. I'm sure they'll come in handy.' Kristina smiled with satisfaction and seemed completely oblivious to Maja's disappointed expression.

Erica fought back the urge to say how stupid she thought it was to buy clothes for a child's first birthday. Besides the fact that Maja was clearly disappointed, Kristina had also managed to slip in one of her customary barbs. Apparently Erica and Patrik were incapable of properly clothing their daughter.

'Time for cake,' called Patrik, who had an infallible knack for knowing the exact moment to distract everyone from an awkward situation. Swallowing her annoyance, Erica joined the blowing-out-the-candles ceremony. Maja's attempts to blow out the solitary candle succeeded only in spraying the cake with saliva. Patrik discreetly extinguished the tiny flame, and then everyone sang happy birthday and shouted 'Hurrah'. Over Maja's blonde head, Erica caught her husband's eye. A lump formed in her throat, and she saw that Patrik was equally moved by the occasion. One year. Their baby was a year old. A little girl who toddled around on her own, who clapped her hands whenever she heard the theme music for *Bolibompa*, who could feed herself, who doled out the softest kisses in all of northern Europe, and who loved the whole world. Erica smiled at Patrik. He smiled back. At that particular moment, life was perfect.

Bertil Mellberg sighed heavily. That was something he did frequently these days. The setback from last spring was still making him depressed. But he wasn't surprised. He'd allowed himself to lose control, allowed himself merely to be, to feel. And that sort of thing never went unpunished. He should have known better. It might even be said that he deserved what had happened to him. Well, he'd learned his lesson, and he wasn't the sort to make the same mistake twice; that much was certain.

'Bertil?' Annika called urgently from the reception area. With a practised gesture, Mellberg pushed back the lock of hair that had slipped down from his nearly bald pate and reluctantly got up. There were very few females from whom he was willing to take orders, but Annika Jansson belonged to the exclusive club. Over the years he'd even developed a reluctant respect for her, and he couldn't think of another woman of whom he could say that. The disastrous consequences of hiring that female officer last spring had only served to reinforce his view. And now they were going to have another woman join the team. He sighed again. Was it so hard to find male officers? Why did they insist on sending girls to replace Ernst Lundgren? It was a miserable situation.

He frowned when he heard a dog barking out in the reception area. Had Annika brought one of her dogs to work? She knew what he thought about mutts. He'd have to have a talk with her about that.

9

But it was not one of Annika's Labradors paying a visit. Instead he was confronted by a mangy-looking mongrel of indeterminate colour and breed, tugging at a lead held by a short, dark-haired woman.

'I found him outside the station,' she said with a broad Stockholm accent.

'So what's he doing in here?' asked Bertil crossly, turning to go back to his office.

'This is Paula Morales,' Annika hastened to say, prompting Mellberg to turn around again. Jesus. Now he remembered that the bird who was supposed to be joining had a Spanish-sounding name. She was certainly small. Short and slender. Although the gaze she fixed on him was anything but weak. She held out her hand.

'Nice to meet you. The dog was running around loose outside. And judging by the shape he's in, he doesn't belong to anyone. At least not to anyone who's capable of taking care of him.'

Her words had a demanding tone, and Bertil wondered what she had in mind.

'Well, take him somewhere then.'

'There isn't any place for lost dogs. Annika already told me that.'

'There isn't?' said Mellberg.

Annika shook her head.

'So, I suppose you'll just have to take him home with you then,' he said, swatting away the dog, which was pressing itself against his trouser leg. Ignoring his efforts, the dog sat down on Mellberg's right foot.

'I can't. We already have a dog, and she wouldn't like a companion,' replied Paula calmly, giving him the same penetrating stare.

'So what about you, Annika? He could . . . keep company with your dogs, couldn't he?' said Mellberg, beginning to sound resigned. Why did he always have to deal with

10

such trivial matters? He was the boss here, for God's sake!

But Annika shook her head. 'They're not used to other dogs. It wouldn't go down too well.'

'You'll have to take him,' said Paula, handing the lead to Mellberg. Stunned by her boldness, he took the lead, and the dog reacted by pressing even harder against his leg and uttering a whimper.

'See, he likes you,' said Annika.

'But I can't . . . I can't . . .' Mellberg stammered.

'You don't have any other pets at home. I promise I'll ask around to see if he belongs to anyone. Otherwise we'll just have to find somebody to adopt him. We can't let him out to run loose; he'll get hit by a car.'

Against his will, Mellberg felt himself yielding. He looked down at the dog. The dog looked up at him, its eyes moist and plaintive.

'Okay, okay, I'll take the damn dog. But only for a couple of days. And you're going to have to wash him off before I take him home.' He shook his finger at Annika, who looked relieved.

'No problem, I'll give him a bath here at the station,' she said eagerly. Then she added, 'Thanks so much, Bertil.'

Mellberg grunted. 'Just make sure that the next time I see that dog, he's squeaky clean! Otherwise he's not setting foot in my place!'

He stomped angrily down the corridor and slammed the door to his office behind him.

Annika and Paula smiled at each other. The dog whimpered and happily thumped his tail against the floor.

'Have a good day,' said Erica, waving at Maja, who ignored her mother. She was sitting on the floor in front of the TV, watching *Teletubbies*.

'We're going to have a cosy time together,' said Patrik,

11

giving Erica a kiss. 'This little girl and I will be just fine for the next few months.'

'You make it sound as if I'm going to be off sailing the seven seas,' said Erica with a laugh. 'But I'll be coming downstairs for lunch.'

'Do you think this will work out, you staying in the house to work?'

'We can at least give it a try. Just pretend I'm not here.'

'No problem. As soon as you close the door to your work-room, you no longer exist for me.' Patrik gave her a wink.

'Hmm. Well, we'll see,' replied Erica and headed upstairs. 'But it'll be worth it if I can avoid having to rent office space.'

She went into her workroom and closed the door with mixed feelings. In the twelve months she'd been at home taking care of Maja, she'd found herself longing for the day she could pass the baton to Patrik and devote herself to grown-up matters again. She'd grown sick and tired of play-grounds, sandboxes, and children's TV programmes. Making the perfect sand pie didn't exactly qualify as intellectual stimulation, and no matter how much she loved her daughter if she was forced to sing 'Itsy-bitsy Spider' one more time she'd go crazy. Now it was Patrik's turn to look after the child.

With a certain feeling of reverence, Erica sat down in front of the computer, pressed the 'on' button, and listened with pleasure to the familiar hum. The deadline for the new book in her true crime series was February, but she'd already managed to do some of the research over the summer, so she felt ready to get started. She opened the Word document she'd dubbed 'Elias', since that was the name of the murderer's first victim, and placed her fingers on the keyboard. A discreet knock on the door interrupted her.

'Sorry for disturbing you . . .' Patrik opened the door and peered at Erica from under the shock of hair that fell over

12

his forehead '. . . but I was wondering where you put Maja's zip suit.'

'In the drier.'

Patrik nodded and closed the door.

Again she placed her fingers on the keyboard and took a deep breath. Another knock.

'I'm sorry, I promise to leave you alone, but I just need to ask what sort of clothes Maja should wear today. It's really chilly outside, but she always gets overheated, and then it might be easier for her to catch cold . . .' Patrik smiled sheepishly.

'All she needs is a thin shirt and trousers under the zip suit. And she usually wears the thin cotton cap.'

'Thanks,' said Patrik and shut the door again. Erica was just about to type the first sentence when she heard cries from downstairs. They quickly rose to a crescendo, and after listening for two minutes, she pushed back her chair and went downstairs.

'I'll give you a hand. It's hopeless trying to get her dressed.'

'Yeah, I can see that,' said Patrik, sweat dripping from his brow after the struggle to shoehorn a complaining and resistant Maja into her outdoor clothing.

Five minutes later she was still sulky but fully dressed, and Erica gave both daughter and husband a kiss on the lips before she hustled them out the door.

'Take a long walk so Mamma can have some peace and quiet to work,' she said. Patrik looked embarrassed.

'I'm sorry. I guess it will take a few days to get into the swing of things, but then you should have all the peace and quiet you want. I promise.'

'That'll be nice,' said Erica and firmly closed the door after them. She poured herself a big mug of coffee and went back upstairs to her workroom. Finally she could get started.

'Shh . . . Stop making such a damn racket.'

'What's the problem? My mother says that they're both

away. Nobody has bothered to take in the post all summer. They must have forgotten to get it redirected, so she's been emptying their letter box since June. Take it easy, we can make as much noise as we want.' Mattias laughed, but Adam still looked sceptical. There was something creepy about the old house. And there was something creepy about those old men too, no matter what Mattias said. He wasn't taking any chances.

'So how do we get in?' He hated the fact that his fear made his voice go up a notch, but he couldn't help it. He often wished that he was more like Mattias. Brave and fearless, sometimes bordering on reckless. But he was also the one who got all the girls.

'We'll see. There's bound to be some way for us to get inside.'

'And you're speaking from your vast experience breaking into houses?' Adam laughed, but he still made sure to keep his voice down.

'Hey, I've done a lot of things you don't know about,' said Mattias loudly.

Oh, right, thought Adam, but he didn't dare contradict his friend. Sometimes Mattias liked to play the tough guy, and Adam let him do it. He knew better than to get into that sort of discussion with Mattias.

'What do you think he's got inside there?' Mattias's eyes were shining as they slowly made their way around the house, looking for a window or a hatch, anything that might allow them access.

'No idea,' said Adam, looking over his shoulder anxiously. He was feeling less happy about the situation with each passing second.

'Maybe some cool Nazi souvenirs. What if he has uniforms and stuff like that?' There was no mistaking the enthusiasm in Mattias's voice. Ever since they'd done a class project on the SS, he'd been obsessed, reading everything he could find

14

about World War II and Nazism. Everyone knew that the neighbour down the road was some sort of expert on Germany and the Nazis, so Mattias had felt an irresistible urge to find out what he had in his possession.

'But maybe he doesn't keep anything like that in his house,' Adam attempted to object, even though he knew it was hopeless. 'Pappa said he was a history teacher before he retired, so he probably just has a lot of books and things like that. It doesn't mean he has any cool stuff.'

'We'll see soon enough.' Mattias's eyes flashed triumphantly as he pointed at a window. 'Look. That window is open a crack.'

Adam noted with dismay that Mattias was right. He'd been quietly hoping that it would turn out to be impossible to get inside the house.

'We just need something to push up the window with.' Mattias glanced around. He settled on a window latch that had come off and landed on the ground.

'Okay, let's see now.' Mattias held the latch overhead and poked one end into a corner of the window. The window didn't budge. 'Shit! This has to work.' Sticking out his tongue in concentration, he had another go. It wasn't easy to hold the latch overhead and apply force at the same time, and he was breathing hard from the effort. Finally he managed to insert the latch another half an inch.

'They're going to notice that someone broke in!' Adam protested weakly, but Mattias didn't seem to hear him.

'I'm going to make this fucking window open!' Sweat rolling down his face, he gave it one last prod, and the window swung up.

'Yes!' Mattias clenched his fist in a gesture of victory and then turned in excitement to Adam.

'Give me a leg-up.'

'But maybe there's something we can use to climb up on, a ladder or . . .'

15

'Forget it, just give me a boost, and then I'll pull you up afterwards.'

Obediently Adam moved close to the wall, lacing his fingers to form a step for Mattias. He winced as Mattias's shoe dug into the palms of his hands, but he ignored the pain and lifted his friend upwards.

Mattias caught hold of the window ledge and managed to hoist himself so that he could plant first one foot and then the other on the sill. He wrinkled his nose. God, what a smell! The place stank. He moved aside the blind and peered into the room. It looked like it might be a library, but all the blinds were down, so the room was wrapped in shadow.

'Hey, it smells like shit in here.' Holding his nose, he turned to look at Adam.

'Then let's forget it,' said Adam with a hopeful glint in his eye.

'No way! Not now we're finally in. This is where the fun begins! Here, take my hand.' Letting go of his nose, he gripped the window ledge with his left hand as he reached out his right to Adam. 'Come on, you're not chicken, are you?'

By way of response Adam grabbed his hand, and Mattias began pulling with all his might. For a moment it looked as though he wasn't going to make it, but then Adam caught hold of the window sill, and Mattias hopped down on to the floor to make room for him. There was a strange crackling sound as he landed. He looked down at the floor. Something covered the surface, but in the dim light he couldn't tell what it was. Probably just some dried leaves.

'What the –?' said Adam as he too jumped down on to the floor. But he couldn't identify what the crunching sound came from. 'Shit, it really smells in here,' he said, looking as if he might gag from the stench.

'That's what I told you,' said Mattias. He was growing

16

accustomed to the smell, and it didn't bother him as much any more.

'Let's see what the old man's got in here. Pull up the blind.'

'But what if somebody sees us?'

'Who's going to see? Pull up the fucking blind.'

Adam did as he was told. The blind rolled up with a swishing sound, letting light pour into the room.

'Cool room,' said Mattias, looking around with awe. All the walls were covered with bookshelves, floor to ceiling. In one corner stood two leather armchairs on either side of a small table. Presiding over the far end of the room was an enormous desk and an old-fashioned chair, turned halfway round so the high back was facing them. Adam took a step closer, but the crunching noise under his feet made him look down again. This time he saw what they were walking on.

'What the . . .' The floor was covered with flies. Disgusting black flies, all of them dead. The windowsill, too, was covered in flies, and without thinking Adam and Mattias both wiped their hands on their trousers.

'Shit, that's disgusting.' Mattias grimaced.

'Where did all these flies come from?' Adam stared at the floor in amazement. Then his *CSI*-indoctrinated brain put two and two together. Dead flies. A revolting stench . . . He tried to push the thought away, but his eyes were drawn inexorably to the desk chair.

'Mattias?'

'What?' his friend replied, sounding annoyed. He looking for somewhere to put his feet where he wouldn't be stepping on dead flies.

Adam didn't answer. Instead he slowly moved towards the chair. He had a feeling that he should turn round, leave the way they'd come, and run until he couldn't run any more. But curiosity got the better of him, and his feet seemed to move of their own accord, taking him to the chair.

'Well, what is it?' Mattias said, but then he fell silent when he saw Adam moving forward, tense and alert.

He was still a half-metre from the chair when he reached out his hand. He noticed that it was shaking. Inch by inch, Adam moved his hand towards the back of the chair. The only sound in the room was the crunching under his feet. The leather of the chair felt cool to his fingertips. He pressed harder, shoving the chair to the left so that it began to rotate. He took a step back. Slowly the chair turned, gradually revealing what it held. Behind him Adam heard Mattias throw up.

The eyes watching his every move were big and moist. Mellberg tried to ignore the animal, but with only partial success. The dog remained practically plastered to his side, looking at him with adoration. Finally Mellberg relented. He pulled out the bottom desk drawer, took out a coconut marshmallow and tossed it on the floor. In two seconds it was gone, and for a moment Mellberg thought the dog was smiling. Pure fantasy, no doubt. At least his fur was clean. Annika had done a good job of shampooing and rinsing him off. Even so, Bertil had found it a bit distasteful to wake up this morning and discover that during the night the dog had hopped up on the bed and stretched out next to him. He wasn't convinced shampoo would get rid of fleas and the like. What if the animal's fur was full of tiny vermin that wanted nothing more than to hop on to Mellberg's ample body? But a close examination hadn't revealed anything lurking in the fur, and Annika had sworn that she hadn't found any fleas when she washed the dog. But he was damned if he'd allow the mutt to sleep on the bed again. There had to be a limit.

'So, what are we going to call you?' said Mellberg, instantly feeling foolish for talking to a creature who walked on all fours. But the dog needed a name. He thought it over as he

18

looked about for something that might inspire him, but only stupid dog names whirled through his mind: Fido, Spot . . . No, that wouldn't do. Then he gave a chuckle. He'd just had a brilliant idea. In all honesty he'd missed Ernst Lundgren, not much but at least a little, ever since he'd been forced to fire the man. So why not call the dog Ernst? There was a certain humour in the choice. He chuckled again.

'Ernst. What do you say to that, old boy? Is that good, or what?' He pulled out the desk drawer again and took out another marshmallow. Of course Ernst should have another one. It wasn't his problem if the dog got fat. In a few days Annika would probably find somebody to take him, so it really made no difference if he got a marshmallow or two in the meantime.

The shrill ring of the phone startled them both.

'Bertil Mellberg.' At first he couldn't hear what the voice on the phone was saying, it was so high-pitched and hysterical.

'Excuse me, but you'll have to talk slower. What did you say?' He listened hard and then raised his eyebrows when he finally understood.

'A body, you say? Where?' He sat up straighter in his chair. Ernst sat up too, pricking his ears. Mellberg wrote down an address on the notepad in front of him, ended the conversation by saying, 'Stay where you are,' and then jumped to his feet. The dog followed at his heels.

'Stay here.' Mellberg's voice had taken on an unusually authoritative tone and, to his great surprise, he saw the dog come to an abrupt halt to await further instructions. 'Stay!' Mellberg ventured, pointing to the dog basket that Annika had put in a corner of the office. Ernst obeyed reluctantly, slinking over to the basket and lying down with his head resting on his paws, casting a hurt look at his temporary master. Energized by the novelty of someone actually

19

acceding to his authority, Bertil Mellberg rushed down the hall shouting to everyone and no one: 'We've had a report of a body.'

Three heads poked out from three different doorways: one red, belonging to Martin Molin, one grey, belonging to Gösta Flygare, and one raven-black, belonging to Paula Morales.

'A body?' said Martin, emerging into the corridor. Now even Annika appeared from the reception area.

'A teenage boy just rang to report it. Apparently he and a mate were larking about and decided to break into a house between Fjällbacka and Hamburgsund. Inside they found a body.'

'The owner of the house?' asked Gösta.

Mellberg shrugged. 'That's all I know. I told the boys to stay there. We'll drive over right now. Martin, you and Paula take one car; Gösta and I will take the other.'

'Shouldn't we call Patrik?' asked Gösta cautiously.

'Who's Patrik?' asked Paula, looking from Gösta to Mellberg.

'Patrik Hedström,' explained Martin. 'He works here too, but he's on paternity leave, starting today.'

'Why on earth should we ring Hedström?' said Mellberg with a scornful snort. 'I'm here,' he added pompously, setting off at a trot towards the garage.

'Yippee,' muttered Martin when Mellberg was out of earshot. Paula raised her eyebrows quizzically. 'Oh, never mind,' said Martin apologetically, but he couldn't resist adding, 'You'll understand soon enough.'

Paula was still looking bewildered, but she let it go. She'd suss out the workplace dynamics soon enough.

Erica sighed. It was quiet in the house now. Too quiet. For a year her ears had been attuned to the slightest whimper or cry. But now it was totally and completely quiet. The

20

cursor was blinking in her Word document. In half an hour she hadn't typed a single letter. Her brain was becalmed. So far she'd paged through her notes and looked at the articles that she'd copied during the summer. After sending several letters, she'd finally managed to get an appointment with the central figure in the case – the murderer – but that was still three weeks away. Until then she'd have to make do with the archival material. The problem was, she couldn't think how to begin. The words weren't exactly tumbling into place, and now doubt had set in. The doubt that authors always had to contend with. Were there any words left? Had she written her last sentence, used up her quota? Did she have any more books in her at all? Logic told her that she almost always felt this way on starting a new book, but that didn't help. It was a form of torture, a process that she had to go through each time. Almost like giving birth. But today she felt especially sluggish.

She absently popped a Dumlekola chocolate caramel in her mouth to console herself as she eyed the notebooks lying on the desk next to the computer. Her mother's fluid script was clamouring for her attention. She was torn between fear of looking at what her mother had written and curiosity about what she might find. Slowly she reached for the first notebook. She weighed it in her hand. It was thin, rather like the small notebooks used in elementary school. Erica ran her fingers over the cover. The name had been written with a pen, but the years had made the blue ink fade considerably. *Elsy Moström.* That was her mother's maiden name. She'd taken the surname Falck when she married Erica's father. Slowly Erica opened the notebook. The pages had thin blue lines. At the top was the date: 3 September 1943. She read the first sentence:

Will this war never end?

21

FJÄLLBACKA 1943

Will this war never end?

Elsy chewed the end of her pen, wondering what to write next. How could she put into words her thoughts on this war that didn't involve her own country and yet did? It felt strange to be writing a diary. She didn't know where she'd got the idea, but it was as if she felt the need to formulate all her thoughts about the life she was living, which was both familiar and unfamiliar.

In some ways she could hardly remember a time before the war. She was thirteen, soon to be fourteen; she'd been only nine when war broke out. During the first years, they hadn't noticed much difference, although the grown-ups seemed to pay more attention to things, developing a sudden interest in the news, both in the papers and on the radio. When they sat listening to the radio in the living room, they seemed nervous, scared, but also oddly excited. In spite of everything, what was happening in the world was exciting – menacing, but exciting. Otherwise life seemed much the same. The boats went out to sea and came back home again. Sometimes the catch was good. Sometimes it wasn't. On land, the women went about their daily chores – the same chores that their mothers had tended to, and their grand-mothers too. Children had to be born, clothes had to be

22

washed, and houses had to be cleaned. It was a never-ending cycle, but the war was now threatening to upset these familiar routines and their everyday reality. Ever since she was a child, she'd been aware of this underlying tension. And now the war was almost upon them.

'Elsy?' She heard her mother calling from downstairs. Quickly she closed her notebook and put it in the top drawer of her little desk next to the window. She'd spent so many hours sitting there and doing her homework, but now her school days were over, and she really had no need for the desk any more. She got up, smoothed the skirt of her dress, and went down to find her mother.

'Elsy, could you help me get water?' Her mother's face looked tired and grey. They'd spent the whole summer living in the small room in the basement while they rented out the rest of the house to summer visitors. In return for the rent payments, they had to clean, cook, and wait on their lodgers – a lawyer from Göteborg, with his wife and three rambunctious children – and they'd been very demanding. Elsy's mother, Hilma, had been kept running all day and well into the evening, doing the laundry, packing picnic baskets for their boating excursions, and tidying up after them in the house. At the same time, she'd had her own household chores to do.

'Sit down and rest for a moment, Mamma,' said Elsy gently, hesitantly placing her hand on her mother's shoulder. Hilma flinched at the touch. Neither of them was used to any sort of physical contact, but after a slight pause, she put her own hand over her daughter's and gratefully sank down on to a chair.

'It was certainly about time for them to leave. I've never met such demanding people. "Hilma, would you please . . . Hilma, would you mind . . . Hilma, could you possibly . . ."' She mimicked their cultured tones but then put her hand over her mouth in alarm. It wasn't customary to show such disrespect for wealthy people. It was important to know one's place.

'I can understand why you're tired. They weren't easy to deal with.' Elsy poured the last of the water into a saucepan and set it on the stove. When the water boiled, she stirred in some coffee substitute and put a cup on the table for Hilma and one for herself.

'I'll get more water in a minute, Mamma, but first we're going to have some coffee.'

'You're a good girl.' Hilma took a sip of the wretched ersatz brew. On special occasions she liked to drink her coffee from the saucer, holding a lump of sugar between her teeth. But nowadays sugar was scarce, and besides, it wasn't really the same thing with ersatz coffee.

'Did Pappa say when he'd be back?' Elsy lowered her eyes. In wartime this question was more charged than it used to be. It wasn't long ago that the *Öckerö* had been torpedoed and sunk with the entire crew on board. Since that incident, a fateful tone had slipped into the farewells before every new departure. But the work had to be done. No one had a choice. Cargo had to be delivered, and fish had to be caught. That was their life, whether there was a war on or not. They should be grateful at least that the cargo-boat traffic back and forth to Norway had been allowed to continue. It was also considered safer than the safe-conduct traffic that was carried on outside of the blockade. The boats from Fjällbacka could continue fishing, and even though the catch was smaller than before, they could supplement their income with transports to and from the Norwegian harbours. Elsy's father often brought home ice from Norway; if he was lucky, he also carried cargo on his way over there.

'I just wish . . .' Hilma fell silent, but then went on. 'I just wish that he'd be a little more cautious.'

'Who? Pappa?' said Elsy, even though she knew quite well who her mother was talking about.

'Yes.' Hilma grimaced as she took another sip of the coffee. 'He has the doctor's son with him on this trip, and . . . well, it's bound to end badly, that's all I can say.'

'Axel is a brave boy; he'll do what he can. And I'm sure Pappa will help out as best he can.'

'But the risks,' said Hilma, shaking her head. 'The risks he takes when that boy and his friends are along . . . I can't help thinking that he's going to drag your father and the others into some sort of danger.'

'We have to do what we can to help the Norwegians,' said Elsy quietly. 'Just think if we'd ended up in their position. Then we'd be the ones needing help from them. Axel and his friends are doing a lot of good.'

'Let's not talk about it any more. Are you ever going to get the water?' Hilma sounded cross as she stood up and went over to the sink to rinse out her coffee cup. But Elsy wasn't offended. She knew that her mother was acting annoyed because she was so worried.

With one last look at her mother's back, prematurely stooped, Elsy picked up the bucket and went out to get water from the well.

To his surprise, Patrik enjoyed taking walks. He hadn't had much time for working out the past few years, but if he could take a long walk every day while he was on paternity leave, he might be able to rid himself of the paunch he was starting to get. The fact that Erica had cut back on sweets at home was also having its effect, helping him to shed a few pounds.

He passed the petrol station and continued at a brisk pace along the road heading south. Maja was sitting in her push-chair, facing forward and babbling happily. She loved being outside and greeted everyone they met with a gleeful 'Hi' and a big smile. She was truly a little sunbeam, although she could also show a real mischievous streak when she set her mind to it. She must get that from Erica's side of the family, thought Patrik.

As they continued along the road, he felt more and more satisfied with his life. He was looking forward to a new daily routine, and it was good to have the house to themselves at last. Not that he didn't like Anna and her kids, but it had been rather trying to live under the same roof month after month. Now there remained only the issue of his mother to contend with. He always felt caught in the middle between Erica and his mother. Of course he understood Erica's irritation at his mother's habit of rattling off criticisms about their parenting skills every time she came to visit. Still, he wished Erica would do as he did and just turn a deaf ear to whatever his mother said. She could also show a little sympathy; Kristina lived alone, after all, with little to occupy her time other than her son and his family. His sister Lotta lived in Göteborg and even though that wasn't so far away, it was still easier for Kristina to visit Patrik and Erica. And she was actually a big help sometimes. He and Erica had been able to go out to dinner on a couple of occasions while Kristina babysat, and. . . well, he just wished that Erica could see the positive side more often.

'Look, look!' said Maja excitedly, pointing her finger as they passed the Rimfaxe horses grazing in the pasture. They stopped a moment to watch; Patrik wasn't particularly fond of the creatures, but he had to admit that Fjord horses actually were quite lovely, and they looked relatively harmless. He reminded himself to bring some apples and carrots next time. After Maja had seen her fill of the horses, they set off on the last leg of their route to the mill, where they would turn to go back towards Fjällbacka.

As they came in sight of the church tower looming over the crest of the hill, he suddenly caught sight of a familiar car. No blue lights flashing or siren wailing, so it couldn't be an emergency situation, but he still felt his pulse quicken. No sooner had the first police car come over the hill than he saw the second one close behind. Patrik frowned. Both vehicles; that meant it must be something serious. He started waving when the first car was about a hundred metres away. It slowed down, and Patrik went over to talk to Martin, who was sitting behind the wheel. Maja eagerly waved both arms. In her world, it was always fun when something happened.

'Hi, Hedström. Out for a walk?' said Martin, waving to Maja.

'Well, a guy has to keep in shape . . . What's going on?' The second police car came up behind and stopped. Patrik waved to Bertil and Gösta.

'Hi, I'm Paula Morales.' Only now did Patrik notice the woman in the police uniform sitting next to Martin. He shook hands with her and introduced himself, and then Martin answered his question.

'We've had a report of a dead body. Right near here.'

'Do you suspect foul play?' Patrik asked with a frown.

Martin shrugged. 'We don't know anything yet. Two kids found the body and called us.' The police car behind them honked, which made Maja jump in her pushchair.

'Hey, Patrik,' said Martin hastily. 'Couldn't you hop in and come along? I'm not feeling very comfortable with . . . you know who.' Martin motioned towards the other car.

'I don't know if that's such a good idea,' said Patrik. 'I've got my little girl with me . . . and officially I'm on leave, you know.'

'Please,' said Martin, tilting his head. 'Just come along and take a look. I'll run you home afterwards. There's room for the pushchair in the boot.'

'But you don't have an infant seat in the car.'

'Oh, you're right. Well, how about if you walk over to the place? It's just around the corner. The first street to the right, second house on the left-hand side. It says "Frankel" on the letter box.'

Patrik hesitated, but another honk from the second police car prompted him to make up his mind.

'Okay, I'll wander over, just to take a look. But you'll have to watch Maja while I go inside. And not a word to Erica about this. She'd be furious if she found out that I took Maja to a possible crime scene.'

'I promise,' said Martin, winking. He waved to Bertil and Gösta and shifted into first. 'See you there.'

'Okay,' said Patrik, with a strong feeling that this was something he was going to regret. But curiosity won out over his instinct for self-preservation; he turned the pushchair around and began swiftly heading for Hamburgsund.

'Everything made of pine has to go!' Anna was standing with her hands on her hips, trying for as stern an expression as she could muster.

'What's wrong with pine?' said Dan, scratching his head.

'It's ugly! How can you even ask such a question?' said Anna, but she couldn't help laughing. 'Don't look so scared, love . . . But I really am going to have to insist. There's nothing uglier than furniture made of pine. And that bed is the worst of all. Besides, I don't want to go on sleeping in the same bed that you shared with Pernilla. I can live in the same house, but I can't sleep in the same bed.'

'That's something I can understand. But it's going to be expensive to buy a lot of new furniture.' He looked worried. When he and Anna became a couple, he'd abandoned plans to sell the house, but it was still proving difficult to make ends meet.

'I have the cash that I got from Erica when she bought my share of our parents' house. Let's use some of it to buy new things. We can do it together, or you can give me free rein – if you dare.'

'Believe me, I'd rather not make decisions about furniture,' said Dan. 'As long as it's not too outrageous, you can buy whatever the heck you want. Enough talk, come over here and give me a hug.'

As usual, things started to get hot and heavy, and Dan was just unhooking Anna's bra when someone pulled open the front door and came in. Since there was a good view of the kitchen from the hall, there was no question of what was going on.

'Jesus, how disgusting! I can't believe you're actually making out in the kitchen!' Belinda stormed past and made for her room, her face bright red with fury. At the top of the stairs she stopped and shouted:

'I'm going back to live with Mamma as soon as I can – do you hear me? At least there I won't have to watch the two of you sticking your tongues down each other's throats all the time! It's gross! Do you hear me?'

Bang! The door to Belinda's room slammed shut, and they heard the key turn. A second later the music started up, so loud that it made the plates on the counter jump and clatter to the beat.

'Oops,' said Dan with a wry expression as he looked up at the ceiling.

'Yes, "oops" is the right word for it,' Anna said, pulling out of his arms. 'This really isn't easy for her.' She picked up the clinking plates and put them in the sink.

'I know, but she's just going to have to accept that I have a new woman in my life,' said Dan, sounding annoyed.

'Just try and put yourself in her position. First you and Pernilla get divorced, then a whole lot of . . .' – she weighed her words carefully – 'girlfriends come waltzing through here, and then I appear on the scene and move in with two little kids. Belinda is barely seventeen, which is tough enough, without having to get used to three strangers moving in.'

'You're right, I know that,' said Dan with a sigh. 'But I have no idea how to deal with a teenager. I mean, should I just leave her alone, or will that make her feel neglected? Or should I insist on talking to her and then risk having her think I'm pressuring her? There should be a manual for situations like this.'

Anna laughed. 'I think they forgot about handing out manuals back in the maternity ward. But you could try talking to her. If she slams the door in your face, at least you've given it a try. And then you should try again. And again. She's afraid of losing you. She's afraid of losing the right to be a child. She's afraid that we're going to take over

30

everything now that we've moved in. And that's perfectly understandable.'

'What did I do to deserve such a wise woman?' said Dan, pulling Anna close again.

'I don't know,' said Anna, smiling as she burrowed her face into his chest. 'Mind you, I'm not particularly wise. It just seems that way, compared to your previous conquests.'

'Hey, watch out,' said Dan with a laugh as he wrapped his arms tighter around her. 'If you keep that up, I might decide to hang on to the pine bed after all.'

'So do you want me to stay here or not?'

'Okay. You win. Consider it gone.'

They both laughed. And kissed. Overhead the pop music continued to pound, turned up to a deafening volume.

Martin saw the boys as soon as he turned on to the drive in front of the house. They were standing off to the side, both of them hugging their arms to their bodies and shivering. Their faces were pale, and they looked visibly relieved when they caught sight of the police cars.

'Martin Molin,' he said, shaking the hand of the first boy, who introduced himself as Adam Andersson, mumbling the name. The other boy waved his right hand, offering an apology with an embarrassed expression.

'I threw up and wiped it off with my . . . Well, I don't think I should shake hands.'

Martin nodded sympathetically. 'All right, so what exactly happened here?' He turned to Adam, who seemed more composed. He was shorter than his friend, with shaggy blond hair and an angry outbreak of acne on his cheeks.

'Well, the thing is, we . . .' Adam glanced over at Mattias, who merely shrugged, so he went on. 'Well, we were thinking of going inside the house to have a look around, since it looked like the old guys had gone away.'

'Old guys?' said Martin. 'So two people live here?'

31

Mattias replied, 'Two brothers. I don't know what their first names are, but my mother probably does. She's been taking in their post since the beginning of June. One of the brothers always goes away during the summer, but not the other one. Except this time no one was taking in the post from the letter box, so we thought that . . .' He left the rest of the sentence unspoken and looked down at his feet. A dead fly was still lying on one shoe. He kicked out in disgust, trying to knock it off. 'Is he the one who's dead inside the house?' he said then, looking up.

'At the moment you know more than we do,' said Martin. 'But go on. You were thinking of going inside, and then what happened?'

'Mattias found a window that was open, and he climbed in first,' said Adam. 'Seems funny now, because when we came out we discovered that the front door was unlocked. So we could just as well have walked right in. Anyway, Mattias climbed in through the window and pulled me up after him. When we jumped down on to the floor, we noticed something crunching under our feet, but we didn't see what it was because it was too dark.'

'Dark?' Martin interrupted him. 'Why was it dark?' Out of the corner of his eye he saw that Gösta, Paula and Bertil were now standing behind him, listening.

'All the blinds were down,' Adam explained patiently. 'But we rolled up the blind of the window we'd come through. And then we saw that the floor was covered with dead flies. And the smell was horrible.'

'Really awful,' Mattias chimed in, looking as if he was fighting off another wave of nausea.

'Then what?' Martin said, in an effort to keep them on track.

'Then we went further into the room, and the chair behind the desk was turned so the back was facing us, and we couldn't tell what was there. But I had a feeling that . . . well, I've seen *CSI*, and with such an awful smell and all those

32

dead flies . . . you don't have to be Einstein to figure out that something had died in there. So I went over to the chair and turned it around. And there he was!'

Apparently the scene was still all too vivid for Mattias; he turned and threw up on the grass. He wiped off his mouth and whispered, 'Sorry.'

'That's okay,' said Martin. 'We've all done the same thing at some point when we've seen a dead body.'

'Not me,' said Mellberg arrogantly.

'Me neither,' said Gösta laconically.

'I never have either,' Paula added.

Martin glanced over his shoulder and gave them all a stern look.

'He looked really gross,' Adam told them. In spite of the shock, he seemed to be taking a certain pleasure in the situation. Behind him Mattias had doubled over and was retching again, but he seemed to have nothing more in his stomach.

'Could someone take the boys home?' said Martin, turning to face his colleagues. At first no one answered, but then Gösta said:

'I'll take them. Come on, lads, hop in the car.'

'We only live a few hundred metres from here,' said Mattias weakly.

'Then I'll walk you home,' said Gösta, gesturing for them to follow. They slunk after him in their typical teenage way – Mattias with a grateful expression, while Adam was obviously disappointed to miss out on what was going to happen next.

Martin watched until they were out of sight round the bend in the road and then said, without any hint of anticipation, 'Well, let's see what we have here.'

Bertil Mellberg cleared his throat. 'I have no problem with dead bodies and the like – absolutely none; I've seen quite a few in my day. But somebody ought to check . . . the surrounding area too. Maybe it'd be best if I took on that

33

assignment, since I'm the boss and the most experienced officer here.' Again he cleared his throat.

Martin and Paula exchanged amused glances, but before replying, Martin was careful to put on a serious expression.

'You're got a point there, Bertil. It'd be best for someone with your experience to make a careful inspection of the site. Paula and I can go inside and take a look.'

'Right . . . exactly. I think that would be best.' Mellberg rocked back on his heels for a moment before sauntering off across the lawn.

'Shall we go in?' said Martin.

Paula merely nodded.

'Careful now,' Martin told her as he opened the door. 'We don't want to disturb any evidence in case it turns out that this was not a death from natural causes. We'll just have a quick look around before the techs get here.'

'I have five years' experience in the violent crimes division with Regional Criminal Investigation in Stockholm. I know how to handle a potential crime scene,' Paula replied good-naturedly.

'Oh, sorry, I didn't know that,' said Martin, embarrassed, but then he focused his attention on the task at hand.

An uncanny silence reigned inside the house, broken only by their footsteps on the hall floor. Martin wondered if the silence would have seemed as creepy if they hadn't known there was a corpse on the premises; he decided it wouldn't have.

'In there,' he whispered, but then realized there was no reason to whisper. So in his normal voice he repeated the words, the sound bouncing off the walls.

Paula followed close behind as Martin took a couple more steps towards the room that was presumably the library and opened the door. The strange smell that they'd noticed as soon as they entered the house got stronger. The boys were right. There were flies all over the floor. Their feet made a crunching sound as he and Paula went in. The smell was intensely sweet, but by now it was only a fraction of what it must have been in the beginning.

'There's no doubt that someone died here a good while ago,' said Paula, and then she and Martin both caught sight of what was seated at the far end of the room.

'No doubt about it,' said Martin. There was an unpleasant taste in his mouth. He steeled himself and cautiously headed across the room to the body sitting in the chair.

'Stay there.' He raised a hand to warn off Paula, who obediently stayed near the door. She wasn't offended. The fewer police treading through the room, the better.

'It doesn't look like he died of natural causes,' said Martin as the bile rose up in his throat. He swallowed over and over, fending off the urge to vomit as he concentrated on the job. In spite of the pitiful condition of the body, there was no doubt at all. A big contusion on one side of the victim's head spoke volumes. The person seated in the chair had been the victim of a brutal assault.

Carefully Martin turned around and exited the room. Paula followed. After taking a few deep breaths of fresh air, the urge to throw up faded. At that moment he saw Patrik turn the corner and make his way down the gravel path.

'It's murder,' said Martin as soon as Patrik was within earshot. 'Torbjörn and his team will have to come out and get to work. There's nothing more we can do right now.'

'Okay,' said Patrik, his expression grim. 'Could I just . . .' He stopped and glanced at Maja sitting in her pushchair.

'Go in and take a look. I'll watch Maja,' said Martin eagerly. He went over and picked her up. 'Come on, sweetie, let's go and look at the flowers over there.'

'Flowers,' said Maja, pointing at the flower bed.

'Did you go inside?' Patrik asked Paula.

She nodded. 'Not a pretty sight. Looks like he's been sitting there all summer. That's my opinion, at least.'

'I suppose you saw your share of things during your years in Stockholm.'

'Not too many bodies in that state, but a few nasty ones.'

'Well, I'm going in to have a quick look. I'm actually on paternity leave, but . . .'

Paula smiled. 'It's hard to stay away, isn't it? I understand. But Martin seems to have a good handle on things.' With a smile she looked over at the flower bed where Martin was squatting down with Maja to admire the blooms.

'He's a rock. In every sense of the word,' said Patrik as he started walking towards the house. A few minutes later he returned.

'I agree with Martin. Not much doubt about it, given that massive contusion on the victim's head.'

'No trace of a suspect.' Mellberg was huffing and puffing as he came round the corner. 'So, how does it look? Have you been inside, Hedström?' he demanded. Patrik nodded.

'Yes, there's little doubt that it's murder. Are you going to call in the techs?'

'Of course,' said Mellberg pompously. 'I'm the boss of this madhouse. And by the way, what are you doing here? You insisted on taking paternity leave, and now that you've got it, you pop up here like a jack-in-the-box.' Mellberg turned to Paula: 'I really don't understand the modern generation – men staying home to change nappies and women running about in uniform.' Abruptly he turned away and stomped back to the police car to summon the techs.

'Welcome to Tanumshede,' said Patrik drily, receiving an amused smile in reply.

'Don't worry, I'm not insulted. I've come across his kind before. If I let all the dinosaurs in uniform bother me, I would have thrown in the towel long ago.'

'I'm glad you see it that way,' Patrik said. 'And the one advantage with Mellberg is that at least he's consistent – he discriminates against everybody and everything.'

36

'That's comforting to know,' said Paula with a laugh.

'What's so funny?' asked Martin, who was still holding Maja.

'Mellberg,' said Patrik and Paula in unison.

'What did he say now?'

'Oh, the usual,' said Patrik, reaching for Maja. 'But Paula seems able to handle it, so things should be okay. Right now this little lady and I need to go home. Wave goodbye, sweetheart.'

Maja waved and grinned at Martin, whose face lit up.

'What, are you leaving me, my girl? I thought we had something special going, you and me.' He stuck out his lower lip in a pout and pretended to look sad.

'Maja is never going to be interested in any man but her pappa. Right, sweetie?' Patrik rubbed his nose against Maja's neck, making her shriek with laughter. Then he put her in the pushchair and waved to his colleagues. Part of him was relieved that he could walk away. But another part would have liked nothing better than to stay.

She was confused. Was it Monday? Or was it already Tuesday? Britta nervously paced the living room. It was so . . . frustrating. It felt as if the more she struggled to catch hold of something, the faster it evaded her grasp. In more lucid moments, a voice inside told her that she ought be able to control things through sheer force of will. She should be able to make her brain obey her. At the same time, she knew that her brain was changing, breaking down, losing its ability to remember, to hold on to moments, facts, information, faces.

Monday. It was Monday. Of course. Yesterday her daughters and their families had come over for Sunday dinner. Yesterday. So today was Monday. Definitely. With relief, Britta stopped in mid-stride. It felt like a small victory. At least she knew what day it was.

Tears welled up in her eyes, and she sat down at one end of the sofa. The Josef Frank upholstery was nice and familiar.

37

She and Herman had bought the fabric together. Or rather, she'd chosen it and he had agreed with her choice. Anything to make her happy. He would have gladly accepted an orange sofa with green spots if that was what she wanted. Herman, yes . . . Where was he? She started picking at the sofa's floral pattern uneasily. She did know where he was. She really did. In her mind she pictured his lips moving as he explained where he was going. She even remembered that he'd repeated it several times. But just as she'd suddenly forgotten what day it was, that little scrap of information now slipped away too, baffling her, taunting her. She gripped the armrest in frustration. She ought to be able to remember, if only she concentrated hard enough.

A feeling of panic overtook her. Where was Herman? Was he going to be away for long? He hadn't gone off on a trip, had he? Leaving her here? Maybe even leaving her for good? Was that what his lips had said in the vague memory that had crossed her mind? She needed to make sure that wasn't the case. She had to go look and make sure his things were still here. Britta sprang from the sofa and dashed upstairs. Panic pounded in her ears like a tidal wave. What exactly had Herman said? A glance in the wardrobe reassured her. All his things were there: jackets, sweaters, shirts. Everything was there. But she still didn't know where he was.

Britta threw herself on to the bed, curled up like a little child, and wept. Inside her brain, things kept on disappearing. Second by second, minute by minute, the hard-disk of her life was being erased. And there was nothing she could do about it.

'Hi! That was quite a walk the two of you took. You've been gone a long time.' Erica came to greet Patrik and Maja, who gave her mother a sloppy kiss.

'Uh-huh. Shouldn't you be working?' Patrik avoided looking Erica in the eye.

'Yes, well . . .' Erica sighed. 'I'm having trouble getting started. I sit and stare at the screen, eating chocolates. If this keeps up, I'll weigh fourteen stone by the time the book is finished.' She helped Patrik take off Maja's outer garments. 'I couldn't resist having a look at Mamma's diaries.'

'Anything interesting?' asked Patrik, relieved that he wasn't going to have to answer any more questions about why they'd taken such a long walk.

'Not really. It's mostly about day-to-day life. But I only read a few pages. I need to take it in small doses.'

Erica went out to the kitchen and, as if to change the subject, she said, 'Shall we have some tea?'

'That'd be great,' said Patrik, hanging up his coat and Maja's. He followed Erica out to the kitchen, watching her as she busied herself putting on the water and getting out the teabags and cups. They could hear Maja playing with her toys in the living room. After a few minutes Erica set two steaming cups of tea on the kitchen table, and they sat down across from each other.

'Okay, let's hear it,' she said, studying Patrik. She knew him so well. The expression in his eyes under the shock of hair, the nervous drumming of his fingers; there was something he either didn't want to tell her or didn't dare.

'What do you mean?' he asked, trying to look innocent.

'Don't you go blinking those baby blue eyes at me. What aren't you telling me?' She took a sip of the hot tea and waited with amusement for him to stop squirming and get to the point.

'Well . . .'

'Yes?' said Erica helpfully, acknowledging that part of her was taking a sadistic delight in his obvious discomfort.

'Well, something happened while Maja and I were out on our walk.'

'Really? You're both back home in one piece, so what could it be?'

'Er . . .' Patrik sipped his tea to buy some time as he pondered how best to explain. 'We were walking over towards Lersten's mill, and then Martin and the team turned up to check out a call they'd received.' He gave Erica a cautious look. She raised one eyebrow and waited for him to go on.

'Someone had phoned in a report of a dead body in a house on the road to Hamburgsund, so they were heading over there to take a look.'

'I see. But you're on paternity leave, so that really has nothing to do with you.' Suddenly she gave a start, her cup halfway to her lips. 'You don't mean that you . . .' She stared at him in disbelief.

'Yes,' said Patrik, his voice sounding a bit shrill and his eyes fixed on the table.

'Don't tell me you took Maja to a place where a dead body was found?' Her gaze was riveted on him.

'Um, yes, but Martin watched her while I went inside to have a look. He took her over to see the flower bed.' He ventured a slightly conciliatory smile but received only an icy glare in return.

'Inside to have a look?' The ice cubes in her voice were clinking mercilessly. 'You're on paternity leave. The key words here are "on leave", not to mention "paternity"! How hard can it be to say "I'm not working right now"?'

'I just went inside to take a look,' said Patrik lamely, but he knew Erica was right. He was on leave. Paternity leave. His colleagues could run the show. And he shouldn't have taken Maja anywhere near a crime scene.

At that instant he realized that there was one more detail Erica didn't know about. He felt a nervous twitch on his face as he swallowed hard and added:

'It turned out to be murder, by the way.'

'Murder!' Erica's voice rose to falsetto. 'It's not enough that you take Maja to a house where a body was discovered

40

– it turns out to be homicide.' She shook her head. The rest of the words she wanted to say seemed to have stuck in her throat.

'I won't do it ever again.' Patrik threw out his hands. 'The team will just have to solve the case on their own. I'm on leave until January, and they know that. I'm going to devote myself one hundred per cent to Maja. Word of honour!'

'You better mean that,' snarled Erica. She was so angry that she wanted to lean across the table and shake him. Then curiosity overcame her:

'Where did it happen? Have they found out who the victim was?'

'I've no idea. It was a big white house a few hundred metres down the road on the left-hand side, on the first turnoff to the right after the mill.'

Erica gave him a strange look. Then she said, 'A big white house with grey trim?'

Patrik thought for a moment and then nodded. 'Yes, I think that's right. It said "Frankel" on the letter box.'

'I know who lives there. Axel and Erik Frankel. You know, the Erik Frankel that I went to see about the Nazi medal.'

Patrik looked at her, dumbstruck. How could he have forgotten that? Frankel wasn't exactly the most common name in Sweden.

From the living room they could hear Maja babbling happily.

It was late afternoon by the time they finally made it back to the station. Torbjörn Ruud, head of the crime tech division, and his team had arrived, made a thorough job of it, and then left. The body had also been removed and was on its way to the forensics lab where it would undergo every imaginable and unimaginable examination.

'Well, that was a hell of a Monday,' said Mellberg with a sigh as Gösta parked the car.

41

'Sure was,' said Gösta, never one to waste words.

As they entered the station, Mellberg barely had time to register something approaching at high speed before a shaggy form jumped on him and he felt a wet tongue licking his face.

'Hey! Hey! Cut that out!' Mellberg pushed the dog away in disgust. Ears drooping, the disappointed animal shambled over to Annika, knowing that at least there he would be welcome.

Gösta fought the urge to laugh as Mellberg wiped off the dog spit with the back of his hand and fussily restored his comb-over to its rightful place, muttering irritably all the while.

Shoulders heaving with mirth, Gösta was turning into his office when the cry of 'Ernst! Ernst! Come here, now!' stopped him in his tracks. It had been quite a while since his colleague Ernst Lundgren had been given the axe, and there'd been no talk of him returning to the force.

Gösta stepped out into the corridor and saw Mellberg, his face beet red, pointing at something on the floor. 'Ernst, what's this?'

As the dog slunk into view, head hanging with shame, Mellberg bellowed for Annika, who arrived a moment later.

'Oops, it looks like we've had a little accident here.' She cast a sympathetic look at the dog, who gratefully moved closer to her.

'A little accident? Ernst has shit on my floor.'

'What's going on?' asked Martin, entering with Paula close behind.

Gösta, who by this time had completely lost the battle to contain his laughter, could barely get out the words: 'Ernst . . . has shit on the floor.'

Martin looked from the little pile on Mellberg's floor to the dog pressed close to Annika's leg. 'Don't tell me you named the dog Ernst?' he said, and then he too dissolved into giggles.

'All right, all right,' said Mellberg. 'Get this cleaned up,

Annika, so we can all go back to work.' He stomped over to his desk and sat down. The dog looked from Annika to Bertil then, having decided that the worst was over, wagged his tail and went over to join his new master.

The others exchanged surprised glances, wondering what the dog saw in Bertil Mellberg that they had apparently missed.

Erica couldn't stop thinking about Erik Frankel. She hadn't known him well, but he and his brother Axel had always been an integral part of Fjällbacka. 'The doctor's sons', they were called, even though it had been fifty years since their father had practised medicine in Fjällbacka, and forty years since he'd died.

She recalled her visit to the house which had once belonged to their parents and had become home to both brothers. It had been her only visit. The elderly bachelors shared a fascination with Germany and Nazism, each in his own way. Erik, a former history teacher, collected artefacts from the Nazi era. Axel, the older brother, had some sort of association with the Simon Wiesenthal Centre, if Erica remembered correctly, and she also had a vague memory that he'd run into some sort of trouble during the war.

She'd phoned Erik and told him what she'd found, describing the medal to him. She'd asked if he could help by researching its origins and maybe explain how it might have ended up among her mother's possessions. His immediate reaction had been silence. She'd said 'Hello' several times, thinking he might have hung up on her. Finally, he told her in a strange-sounding voice to bring over the medal and he'd have a look at it. His long silence and odd tone of voice had bothered her, but she hadn't mentioned anything about it to Patrik. She convinced herself that she must have been imagining things. And when she went over to the brothers' house, she didn't notice anything odd. Erik received her politely and ushered her into the library. With a guarded

43

expression, he had taken the medal from her and studied it carefully. Then he asked whether he might keep it for a while in order to do some research. Erica had agreed.

He'd gone on to show her his collection. With a mixture of dread and interest, she'd looked at the artefacts so intimately connected with that dark, evil period. She couldn't resist asking why someone like him, who was so opposed to everything that Nazism had stood for, would collect and surround himself with things that would remind him of that awful time. Erik had hesitated before answering. He'd picked up a cap bearing the SS emblem and held it in his hand as he formulated his reply.

'I don't trust people to remember,' he'd said at last. 'Without having things that we can see and touch, we so easily forget what we don't want to remember. I collect things that will serve as reminders. And part of me probably also wants to keep these things out of the hands of people who might see them with other eyes. Regard them with admiration.'

Erica had nodded. She sort of understood, and yet she didn't. Then they shook hands and she'd left.

And now he was dead. Murdered. Maybe not long after her visit. According to what Patrik had told her, Erik had been sitting in the house, dead, all summer long.

Again she thought about the strange tone of Erik's voice when she'd told him about the medal. She turned to Patrik, who was sitting next to her on the sofa, channel surfing.

'Do you know if the medal is still there?'

Patrik gave her a surprised look. 'I have no idea. It didn't even occur to me. But there weren't any indications that he'd been murdered as a result of a robbery. Besides, who would be interested in an old Nazi medal? They're not exactly rare. It seems to me there are quite a lot of them . . .'

'Yes, I know, but . . .' Erica said. Something was still bothering her. 'Could you ring your colleagues tomorrow and ask them to check on the medal?'

44

'I don't know about that,' said Patrik. 'I think they've got better things to do than spend time looking for an old medal. We can talk to Erik's brother later on. Ask him to find it for us. It's probably still in the house somewhere.'

'Oh right, Axel. Where is he? Why didn't he discover his brother's body?'

Patrik shrugged. 'I'm on paternity leave, remember? You'll have to ring Mellberg yourself and ask him.'

'Ha ha, very funny,' said Erica. But she still felt uneasy. 'Don't you think it's odd that Axel didn't find him?'

'Sure, but didn't you say he was off somewhere when you went over to their house?'

'Well, yes. Erik told me that his brother was abroad. But that was back in June.'

'Why are you worrying about this?' Patrik shifted his gaze back to the TV. *Home at Last* was just about to start.

'I don't really know,' Erica said, staring blankly at the TV screen. She couldn't explain even to herself why this feeling of anxiety had come over her. But she could still remember Erik's silence on the phone and hear that slight catch in his voice when he asked her to bring over the medal. He had reacted to something. Something having to do with the medal.

She tried to put it from her mind and focus on Martin Timell's woodcarvings instead.

'Grandpa, you should have seen it. That black bastard went to cut in line and – Pow! One kick and he keeled over like a tree. Then I kicked him in the nuts and he lay there whimpering for at least fifteen minutes.'

'And what good did it do, Per? Aside from the fact that you could be charged with assault and sent off to a juvenile institution, you're not going to win any sympathy that way. You'll just have everybody ganging up on you even more. And instead of helping our cause, it's going to end with you mobilizing even more opposition.' Frans stared at his grandson. Sometimes

45

he didn't know how he was going to curb all the teenage hormones surging through the boy. And he knew so little. In spite of his tough demeanour, with his army camouflage trousers, heavy boots, and shaved head, he was nothing more than a fearful child of fifteen. He knew nothing. He had no idea how the world operated. He didn't know how to channel the destructive impulses so that they could be used like a spear point to pierce right through the structure of society.

The boy hung his head in shame as he sat next to him on the stairs. Frans knew that his harsh words had got through. His grandson was always trying to impress him. But he would be doing Per a disservice if he didn't show him how the world worked. The world was cold and hard and relentless, and only the strongest would emerge victorious.

At the same time, he loved the boy and wanted to protect him from evil. Frans put his arm around his grandson's shoulders, struck by how bony they were. Per had inherited his own physique. Tall and gangly, with narrow shoulders. All the gym workouts in the world wouldn't change that.

'You just need to stop and think,' said Frans, his voice gentler now. 'Think before you act. Use words instead of your fists. Violence is not the first tool you should use. It's the last.' He tightened his hold on the boy's shoulders. For a second Per leaned against him, as he'd done when he was a child. Then he remembered that he was trying to be a man. That the most important thing in the world was that he make his grandfather proud. Per sat up straight.

'I know, Grandpa. I just got so angry when he pushed in. Because that's what they always do. They push their way in everywhere. They think they own the world, that they own Sweden. It made me so . . . furious.'

'I know,' said Frans, removing his arm from around his grandson's shoulders and patting the boy's knee instead. 'But please stop and think. You'll be no use to me if you end up in prison.'

46

KRISTIANSAND 1943

He had battled seasickness all the way to Norway, although it hadn't seemed to affect the others. They were used to sailing, had grown up going to sea. They had their sea legs, as his father used to say; they rolled with the swells and had no trouble walking on deck. And they seemed immune to the nausea that spread from his stomach up to his throat. Axel leaned heavily against the rail. All he wanted to do was lean over the side and vomit, but he refused to give into such degrading behaviour. He knew the taunts from the others wouldn't be mean-spirited, but he was too proud to be the subject of their derision. Soon they'd be arriving, and the minute he went ashore, the nausea would vanish like magic. He knew this from experience, for he'd made this trip many times before.

'Land ho!' shouted Elof, the ship's captain. 'We'll dock in ten minutes.' Elof cast a glance at Axel, who had come to join him at the helm. The captain's face was tanned and weatherbeaten, his skin like creased leather from years of exposure to the elements.

'Is everything in order?' he asked in a low voice, looking around. In the harbour at Kristiansand they could see all the German boats lined up, a clear reminder of the occupation. So far Sweden had been spared Norway's fate, but nobody knew how much longer their luck would last. Until then the Swedes were keeping an anxious eye on their neighbour to the west, and for that matter on the Germans' advance throughout the rest of Europe.

'Take care of your own affairs, and I'll take care of mine,' said Axel. It sounded harsher than he'd intended, but it troubled him that he was involving the ship's crew in risks that should have been his alone. Still, he wasn't coercing anyone. Elof had agreed without hesitation when Axel asked if he might sail with him once in a while, bringing certain . . . goods along. He'd never needed to explain what he was transporting, and Elof and the other crew members on the *Elfrida* had never asked.

They put into port and took out the documents they would need to present. The Germans were punctilious when it came to paperwork, and only when the formalities were out of the way would the Swedes be allowed to unload the machine parts that comprised their official cargo. The Norwegians took delivery of the goods while the Germans grimly oversaw the procedure with guns at the ready. Axel bided his time until evening. His cargo couldn't come ashore until after dark. Most often it was foodstuffs. Food and information. That was what he had this time as well.

After eating supper in tense silence, Axel sat down to wait restlessly for the appointed hour. A cautious knock on the windowpane made him and everybody else jump. Axel quickly leaned forward, lifted up a section of the floorboards, and began taking out wooden crates. Hands reached in, quietly and carefully, to receive the crates, which were then passed to someone on the dock. All the while they could hear the Germans talking amongst themselves in the barracks just a short distance away. By that time of night, they were on to the strong liquor, which allowed the dangerous activity on board ship to go unnoticed. Drunken Germans were significantly easier to fool than sober Germans.

With a whispered 'thank you' in Norwegian, the last of the cargo vanished into the darkness. Another delivery had gone smoothly. Giddy with relief, Axel went back down to the forecastle. Three pairs of eyes met his gaze, but no one said a word. Elof merely nodded and then turned away to fill his pipe. Axel felt an overwhelming sense of gratitude towards these men who defied both storms and Nazis with the same composure. Having long since accepted that they had no control over the twists and turns of life and fate, they simply got on with trying to live the best life they could. The rest was in God's hands.

Exhausted, Axel lay down in his bunk, rocked by the slight swaying of the boat and the lapping of the water against the hull. In the barracks up on the dock, the voices of the Germans rose and fell. After a while they began to sing. But by then Axel was sound asleep.

'Okay, what do we know so far?' asked Mellberg, looking around the break room. The coffee was made, there were buns on the table, and everyone was present.

Paula cleared her throat. 'I've been in contact with the brother – Axel. Apparently he works in Paris and always spends the summer there. But he's on his way home now. Seemed upset when I told him about his brother's death.'

'Do we know when he left Sweden?' Martin turned to Paula. She consulted the notebook lying in front of her.

'The third of June, he says. Of course I'll be checking that out.'

Martin nodded.

'Have we received a preliminary report from Torbjörn and his team?' Mellberg moved his feet cautiously. Ernst had settled the whole weight of his body on top of his feet and he was getting pins and needles, but for some reason Mellberg couldn't bring himself to push the dog away.

'Not yet,' said Gösta, reaching for a bun. 'But I talked to him this morning, and we might have something tomorrow.'

'Good, bright and early, let's hope,' said Mellberg, again shifting his feet, but Ernst simply moved too.

'Any suspects? Possible enemies? Threats? Anything?'

Martin shook his head. 'No reports on our files, at any

rate. But he was a controversial figure. Nazism always rouses strong feelings.'

'We could go out to his house and take a look. See if there are any threatening letters or such like in the drawers.'

Everyone turned to stare at Gösta in surprise. His colleagues were all of the opinion that Gösta Flygare only came to life on the golf course. It was rare for him to show any initiative on the job.

'Take Martin with you, and go out there after the meeting,' said Mellberg with a pleased smile. Gösta nodded and quickly resumed his usual lethargic stance.

'Paula, find out when the brother – Axel, was it? – is due to arrive. Since we don't yet know when Erik died, it's possible that Axel was the one who bashed his head in and then fled the country. We need to get hold of him as soon as he sets foot on Swedish soil.'

Paula looked up from her notebook. 'He's arriving at Landvetter airport at nine fifteen tomorrow morning.'

'Good. Make sure that he comes here first, before he does anything else.' Now Mellberg was forced to move his feet, which were starting to go numb. Ernst got up, gave him an offended look, and set off for Mellberg's office and the comfort of his basket.

'Looks like true love,' remarked Annika, laughing as she watched the dog exit.

'Hmm, well . . .' Mellberg cleared his throat. 'I've been meaning to ask you about that. When is somebody going to come and get that mongrel?'

'You know, it's not that easy,' said Annika, putting on her most innocent expression. 'I've phoned around, but nobody seems able to take a dog of his size, so if you could just take care of him for a few more days . . .' She gazed at him with her big blue eyes.

He grunted. 'Oh, all right, I should be able to stand the

mutt for a few more days. But then he'll have to go back out on the street if you can't find a home for him.'

'Thanks, Bertil. That's nice of you. And I'll pull out all the stops.' As Mellberg turned away, Annika winked at the others. Realizing what she was up to, they struggled not to laugh. She had Bertil sussed; no question about it.

'Fine, fine,' said Mellberg. 'Now let's get back to work.' He lumbered out of the break room.

'Okay, you heard the chief,' said Martin, getting to his feet. 'Shall we go, Gösta?'

Gösta looked as though he was already regretting making a suggestion which would entail more work for himself, but he nodded wearily and followed Martin out the door. It was just a matter of making it through the work week. Come the weekend he'd be out on the golf course by seven in the morning, both Saturday and Sunday. Until then, he was just treading water.

Thoughts of Erik Frankel and the medal continued to haunt Erica. She managed to put it out of her mind for a couple of hours and make a start on her manuscript, but as soon as her concentration faltered she began to replay the brief meeting that she'd had with Erik. He had seemed a gentle, courteous man, eager to share his knowledge of the subject that interested him most: Nazism.

Admitting defeat, she closed her manuscript file and Googled 'Erik Frankel'. A number of hits turned up, some clearly referring to other individuals with the same name. But there was no shortage of information on the correct Erik Frankel, and she spent nearly an hour clicking through the links. Born in 1930 in Fjällbacka, he had one sibling: a brother named Axel who was four years older. His father had been a doctor in Fjällbacka from 1935 to 1954. Many of the links led to blogs about Nazism, but she found nothing to indicate that he was some sort of Nazi sympathizer. On the contrary. Though some of the blogs betrayed a reluctant admiration for aspects of Nazism, it seemed that Erik's interest was motivated by pure fascination with the subject.

She had just shut down the Internet browser, reminding herself that she really didn't have time for this, when there was a cautious knock on the door behind her.

'Sorry, am I bothering you?' Patrik opened the door and poked his head in.

'No, don't worry.' She spun round in her desk chair to face him.

'I just came up to tell you that Maja is asleep and I need to nip out on a little errand. Could you keep this in here while I'm out?' He handed her the baby monitor so she'd be able to hear if Maja woke up.

'Er . . . I really should be working.' Erica sighed. 'Why do you need to go out?'

'I have to go to the bank, and we're out of Nezeril so I thought I'd call in at the pharmacy, and then I might as well get a lottery ticket and a few groceries too.'

Erica suddenly felt very tired. She thought about all the errands she'd done during the past year, always with Maja sitting in the pushchair or in her arms. More often than not she'd been soaked with sweat by the time she was done. There'd never been anyone to watch Maja while she waltzed off to the shops. But she put these thoughts out of her mind; she didn't want to seem petty or cranky.

'Of course I can look after her while you're out,' she said with a smile, summoning some enthusiasm. 'I can keep working while she's asleep.'

'That's great,' said Patrik, giving her a kiss on the cheek before he shut the door behind him.

'That's great, all right,' said Erica to herself, opening her manuscript document and preparing to put all thought of Erik Frankel out of her mind.

She had no sooner set her fingers on the keyboard when

a crackling noise issued from the baby monitor. Erica froze. It was probably nothing. Maja was just moving around in her cot; sometimes the monitor was overly sensitive. She heard the sound of a car starting up, and then Patrik drove off. As she moved her eyes back to the screen, struggling to think of the next sentence, she heard the crackling noise again. She looked at the baby monitor as if she could will it to stay quiet, but her efforts were rewarded with an audible 'Waaaaaa.' Followed by a shrill 'Mammaaaa . . . Pappaaaa . . .'

Feeling resigned, she pushed back her chair and got up. How typical. She went down the hall to Maja's room and opened the door. Her daughter was standing up, crying angrily.

'But Maja, sweetheart, you're supposed to be sleeping.'

Maja shook her head.

'Yes, it's time for your nap,' said Erica firmly, setting her daughter down in the cot, but Maja sprang up as she were made of rubber.

'Mammaaaa!' she cried with a voice that could break glass. Erica felt fury gathering in her chest. How many times had she done this? How many days had she spent feeding, carrying, playing with Maja and then putting her down for a nap? She loved her daughter, but she had a desperate need for some respite from the responsibility. To rediscover what it was to be a grown-up and do grown-up things – exactly the way Patrik had been able to during the whole year that she'd been home with Maja.

No sooner did she put Maja down in the cot than she clambered back up, even more furious.

'You need to sleep now,' said Erica, backing out of the room and closing the door. Anger surging in her chest, she picked up the phone and punched in the number for Patrik's mobile, pressing the buttons a little too hard. She heard the first ringtone and then gave a start when she realized it was

54

coming from downstairs. Patrik's mobile was on the kitchen counter.

'Bloody hell!' She slammed down the receiver, angry tears welling up in her eyes. She took a couple of deep breaths and told herself it wasn't the end of the world if she had to jump in for a little while, even though it might feel like it. She realized this whole thing was about the fact that she felt unable to let go, unable to trust Patrik with the baton she had passed him.

But there was nothing she could do about it. And the most important thing was not to take out her feelings on Maja. It wasn't her fault, after all. Erica took another deep breath and went back to her daughter's room. Maja was wailing, her face bright red. And an unmistakable odour had started to spread through the room. The mystery was solved. That was why Maja didn't want to sleep. Feeling a bit guilty and extremely inadequate, Erica tenderly picked up her daughter and comforted her, pressing the little downy head against her breast. 'There, there, sweetie, Mamma is going to change the nasty nappy. There, there.' Maja sniffled as she pressed closer. Downstairs in the kitchen, Patrik's mobile was ringing shrilly.

'It feels . . . creepy.' Martin was still standing in the entry hall, listening to the sounds characteristic of all old houses. Small creaks and squeaks, faint sounds of protest when the wind picked up.

Gösta nodded. There was definitely something creepy about the atmosphere in this house, but he thought it was because they knew what had happened here, rather than anything inherent in the house itself.

'So you said Torbjörn's given the all-clear to go in, right?' Martin turned to look at Gösta.

'Yes, Forensics are done with the place.' Gösta nodded his head towards the library, where traces of fingerprint powder were clearly visible. Black, sooty particles that disturbed the image of an otherwise beautiful room.

'Okay, then.' Martin wiped his shoes on the doormat and headed for the library. 'Shall we start in here?'

'Might as well,' said Gösta with a sigh.

'I'll take the desk while you go through the file folders and ring binders.'

'Sure.' Gösta sighed again, but Martin paid no attention. Gösta always sighed when confronted with an assignment.

Martin cautiously approached the big desk. It was a huge piece of furniture made of dark wood, ornately carved, that looked as if it belonged in some English manor house. The desktop was very neat, with only a pen and a box of paper clips, aligned in perfect symmetry. A little blood had stained a notepad that was covered in scribbles, and Martin leaned closer to see what had been scrawled there. *'Ignoto militi'* it said over and over. The words meant nothing to him. He carefully began pulling out one desk drawer after another, methodically going through the contents. Nothing piqued his interest. The only thing he could tell was that Erik and his brother seemed to have shared the work area, and they also seemed to share a fondness for neatness and order.

'Doesn't this border on the obsessive?' Gösta held up a binder and showed Martin the neatly arranged documents inside, complete with a table of contents on which Erik and Axel had meticulously detailed what each scrap of paper was about.

'It's not what my files look like, I can tell you that.' Martin laughed.

'I've always thought there's something wrong with people who are this neat. It probably has to do with deficient toilet training or something like that.'

'Well, that's one theory.' Martin smiled. 'Have you found anything? There's nothing of interest here.' He closed the last drawer that he'd been looking through.

'Nope, nothing yet. Mostly bills, invoices, stuff like that. Do you realize they've saved every single electricity bill since time immemorial? Arranged by date.' Gösta shook his head. 'Here, take one of these files.' From the bookshelf behind the desk he pulled out a big, thick binder with a black spine and handed it to his colleague.

Martin took it over to one of the armchairs and sat down to read. Gösta was right. Everything was systematically arranged. He went over each item, and was despairing of finding anything significant when he came to the letter 'S'. A quick glance showed that 'S' stood for 'Sweden's Friends'. Curious, he started leafing through the papers, which proved to be letters. Each one bore a printed logo in the upper right-hand corner showing a crown against a billowing Swedish flag. They had all been written by the same person: Frans Ringholm.

'Listen to this –' Martin began reading aloud from one of the first letters, which according to the date was among the most recent:

'In spite of our shared history, I can no longer ignore the fact that you are actively working against the goals and aims of Sweden's Friends, and this will inevitably lead to consequences. I've done my best for the sake of old friendship, but there are powerful forces within the organization that do not look upon this kindly, and there will come a time when I can no longer offer you protection . . .'

Martin raised one eyebrow. 'And it goes on in the same vein.' He quickly leafed through the other letters and saw that there were four more.

'It looks as if Erik Frankel managed to upset some neo-Nazi group, but paradoxically enough, someone in that very organization was shielding him.'

'A protector who ultimately failed.'

57

'So it seems. Let's go through the rest of the documents and see if we can find out anything else. But there's no doubt we need to have a talk with this Frans Ringholm.'

'Ringholm . . .' Gösta stared straight ahead as he thought. 'I recognize that name.' He frowned as he racked his brain to come up with a connection, but in vain. He was still looking pensive as they silently combed through the rest of the binders.

After nearly an hour, Martin closed the last one and said, 'Well, I didn't find anything of interest. How about you?'

Gösta shook his head. 'No, and there aren't any other references to that group called Sweden's Friends.'

They left the library and searched the rest of the house. Erik Frankel's fascination with Germany and the Second World War was evident throughout, but nothing caught their attention. It was a beautiful house, but it appeared that the brothers had left the place pretty much as it was when they'd inherited it. The parents' presence was palpable: black-and-white photographs of them, along with other relatives, hung on the walls or were displayed in heavy frames set on top of bureaus and sideboards. The furnishings were rather outmoded, and had begun to show signs of wear; the whole place had a feeling of age. A thin layer of dust was the only thing disturbing the order.

'I wonder if they did the dusting themselves or if they had someone come in to clean?' said Martin, running a finger over the surface of the chest of drawers in one of the three bedrooms upstairs.

'I have a hard time picturing two men in their late seventies doing the dusting,' said Gösta as he opened the door to the wardrobe. 'What do you think? Is this Erik's or Axel's room?' He looked at the row of brown jackets and white shirts hanging inside the wardrobe.

'Erik's,' said Martin. He'd picked up a book lying on the bedside table and now held it up to show the title page where a name had been written in pencil: *Erik Frankel*. It was a biography of Albert Speer. 'Hitler's architect,' Martin read aloud from the back cover before he put the book back where he'd found it.

'He spent twenty years in Spandau prison after the war,' murmured Gösta, and Martin gave him a look of surprise.

'How do you know that?'

'The Frankels aren't the only ones interested in the Second World War. I've read a lot about it over the years. And seen some documentaries on the Discovery channel and the like.'

'Is that so?' said Martin, still looking surprised. In all the years they'd worked together this was the first time he'd heard Gösta show an interest in anything besides golf.

They spent another hour searching the house but found nothing more. Yet Martin felt pleased with their efforts as he drove back to the station. The name Frans Ringholm gave them something to go on.

The supermarket wasn't too busy, and Patrik took his time strolling down the aisles. It was a relief to get out of the house for a while, a relief to have some time to himself. This was only the second day of his paternity leave, but while part of him rejoiced in the opportunity to stay home with Maja another part was having a hard time adjusting. Not because he didn't have enough to do during the day – he'd quickly realized that he had his hands full taking care of a one-year-old. He was ashamed to admit that the problem was, he didn't find it particularly . . . stimulating. And it was unbelievable how restricted he felt. He couldn't even go to the toilet in peace, since Maja had got into the habit of standing outside and crying 'Pappa, Pappa, Pappa, Pappa' as she banged on the door with her tiny fists until he relented and let her in. Then she'd stand there and stare at him with curiosity as he did what he'd always done before in much greater privacy.

He felt slightly guilty about leaving Erica to take over while he went out to do errands. But Maja was asleep, so she could carry on working. Maybe he should ring home and check, though, just to be sure. He stuck his hand in his pocket to get his mobile phone, then realized that he'd left it on the kitchen counter. Damn! Never mind, it was probably okay.

Finding himself in the baby-food section, he started reading the labels: *Beef stew with cream gravy, fish in dill sauce.* Hmm . . . *Spaghetti with meat* sounded much better. He took five jars. Maybe he should really start cooking food for Maja at home. That's a great idea, he thought, and put back three of the jars. He could be the big chef, and Maja could sit next to him, and . . .

'Let me guess. You're making the typical rookie mistake of thinking you could cook these things yourself.'

The voice was familiar but somehow seemed out of place. Patrik turned around.

'Karin? Hi! What are you doing here?' Patrik hadn't expected to bump into his ex-wife in the Konsum super-market in Fjällbacka. They hadn't seen each other since she moved out of their terraced house in Tanumshede and moved in with the man she'd been in bed with when Patrik discovered them together. An image of that scene flitted through his mind but quickly vanished. It was all so long ago. Water under the bridge, so to speak.

'Leif and I have bought a house here in Fjällbacka. In the Basket district.'

'Oh, really?' said Patrik, trying not to look surprised.

'Yes, we wanted to move closer to Leif's parents now that we have Ludde.' She pointed to her shopping cart, and only now did Patrik notice the little boy sitting there, grinning from ear to ear.

'How about that for timing,' said Patrik. 'I've got a little girl at home, about the same age. Her name is Maja.'

60

'I'd heard rumours to that effect,' said Karin, laughing. 'You're married to Erica Falck, right? Tell her that I love her books!'

'I'll do that,' said Patrik, waving to Ludde.

'But what are you doing now?' he asked Karin. 'Last I heard, you were working for an accounting firm.'

'Oh, that was a while back. I quit three years ago. Right now I'm on maternity leave from a consulting company that handles financial services.'

'Is that right? This is actually my second day on paternity leave,' said Patrik with a certain pride.

'What fun! But where's . . . ?' Karin looked past him, and Patrik smiled a bit sheepishly.

'Erica is looking after her at the moment. I had to go out to do some errands.'

'Uh-huh. Well, I'm very familiar with the phenomenon.' Karin gave him a wink. 'The male lack of ability to multitask seems to be universal.'

'I suppose it is,' said Patrik, embarrassed.

'But why don't we get together with our kids sometime? It's not that easy to keep them occupied on their own, plus then you and I would have a chance to talk to another grown-up. And that's always a plus!' She rolled her eyes and gave Patrik an enquiring look.

'Sure, that'd be great. When and where?'

'I usually take a long walk with Ludde every morning around ten. You're welcome to join us. We could meet outside the pharmacy, at about ten fifteen. How's that?'

'Sounds good. By the way, do you know what time it is? I left my mobile at home, and I use it as my clock too.'

Karin glanced at her watch. 'Two fifteen.'

'Shit! I should have been home two hours ago!' He raced off towards the cashier, pushing the cart in front of him. 'See you tomorrow!'

'Ten fifteen. Outside the pharmacy. And don't show up

61

fifteen minutes late, like you used to,' Karin called after him.

'I won't,' Patrik shouted back as he began putting his groceries on the check-out belt. He sincerely hoped that Maja was still sleeping.

There was a thick layer of morning fog outside the window as the plane began its descent towards Göteborg. The landing gear whirred as it was deployed. Axel leaned back in his seat and closed his eyes. That was a mistake. The images again appeared, as they had so many times in past years. Wearily he opened his eyes. He hadn't got much sleep last night. He'd mostly lain awake in bed in his Paris flat, tossing and turning.

The woman on the phone had told him the news about Erik in a tone of voice that was both sympathetic and distant. He could tell from her manner that this was not the first time she'd notified someone about a death.

His head swam as he thought how many times such news had been delivered throughout history. Conversations with the police, a pastor standing on the doorstep, an envelope with a military seal. All those millions and millions of people who had died. And each time someone must have conveyed the news.

Axel tugged at his earlobe. Over the years this had become an unconscious habit. He was practically deaf in his left ear, and touching it seemed to calm the constant rushing sound.

He shifted his gaze to look out the window but saw only his own reflection. The grey, furrowed face of a man in his eighties, with sorrowful, deep-set eyes. He touched his face. For a moment he imagined that he was looking at Erik instead.

With a thud the wheels touched down. He had arrived.

Wary of another 'accident' in his office, Mellberg took down the dog lead that he'd hung on a hook and attached it to Ernst's collar.

'Come on, let's get this over with,' he grunted, and Ernst scampered joyfully towards the front door, moving at a speed that forced Bertil to trot after him.

'You're supposed to be walking the dog, not vice versa,' remarked Annika with amusement as they rushed past.

'I'd be happy to let you take him out,' snapped Mellberg, but he continued towards the door.

Stupid mutt. His arms were aching from holding the dog back. But once Ernst had lifted his leg to a bush the sense of urgency dissipated and they were able to continue on their walk at a more sedate pace. Mellberg even found himself whistling. This isn't so bad after all, he thought. Some fresh air and a little exercise might do him good. And Ernst had settled into sniffing at the wooded path they were walking along, calm as could be. Just like a person, he could sense when someone with a firm hand was in control. There shouldn't be any problem training the mutt properly.

At that moment Ernst stopped, his ears pricked forward and every muscle tensed in his sinewy body. Then he exploded into motion.

'Ernst? What the –?' Mellberg was yanked forward so fast that he almost fell on his face, but at the last second he managed to keep his footing and hung on as the dog set off at a gallop.

'Ernst! Ernst! Stop! Stop right now! Heel!' Mellberg was panting from the unaccustomed physical effort, and that made it hard for him to shout. The dog ignored his commands. As they came flying around a corner, Mellberg saw what it was that had precipitated their flight. Ernst threw himself at a big, light-coloured dog that looked to be of a similar breed, and the two began romping around each other while their owners tugged at the leads.

'Señorita! Stop that! Sit!' The short, dark-haired woman spoke in a harsh tone, and her dog obediently backed away from Ernst, who continued to ignore Mellberg's remonstrations. 'Bad dog, Señorita! You shouldn't be carrying on like that.' Looking suitably abashed, Señorita peered up at her owner from under a shaggy fringe.

'I . . . I . . . must apologize,' Mellberg stammered, tugging at the lead to prevent Ernst launching himself at the other dog who, judging by the name, must be female.

'You clearly have no control over your dog.' Her sharp tone of voice had him fighting back the urge to stand to attention. She had a slight accent and this, together with her flashing dark eyes, gave him the impression she must come from some southern country.

'Well, it's not really my dog. I'm just taking care of him until . . .' Mellberg heard himself stammering like a teenager. He cleared his throat and attempted to sound a bit more authoritative. 'I'm not used to dogs. And he's not mine anyway.'

'He seems to have a different opinion about that.' She pointed to Ernst who was pressed close to Mellberg's leg, looking up at him with adoring eyes.

'Er, well . . .' said Mellberg, embarrassed.

'Shall we continue walking the dogs together? My name is Rita.' She held out her hand, and after a slight hesitation, he shook it.

'I've had dogs all my life, so I'm sure I can give you a few tips. Besides, it's much more pleasant to walk with somebody to keep me company.' She didn't wait for a reply before starting off along the path. Without knowing how it had happened, Mellberg found himself keeping step with her, as if his feet had a will of their own. And Ernst had no objections. He fell in beside Señorita, wagging his tail vigorously.

FJÄLLBACKA 1943

'Erik? Frans?' Britta and Elsy cautiously stepped inside. They'd knocked but received no answer. They glanced around nervously. The doctor and his wife probably wouldn't be pleased to find two girls coming over to visit their son while they were away. Usually they met in Fjällbacka, but on bold impulse Erik had suggested that the girls come to the house since his parents would be out all day.

'Erik?' Elsy called a little louder and then jumped when she heard someone say 'Shhh' from the room directly in front of them. Erik appeared in the doorway and motioned for them to come in.

'Axel is upstairs asleep. He came back this morning.'

'Oh, he's so brave,' said Britta with a sigh, but her face lit up when she saw Frans.

'Hi!'

'Hi,' said Frans but he was looking past her. 'Hi, Elsy.'

'Hi, Frans,' replied Elsy, but then she headed straight for the bookshelves.

'My, what a lot of books you have!' She ran her fingers over the spines.

'You can borrow some if you like,' said Erik generously, although he added, 'But only on condition that you take good care of them. Pappa is very particular about his books.'

65

'Of course,' said Elsy happily, devouring the rows of books with her eyes. She loved to read. Frans didn't take his eyes off her for even a second.

'Books are a waste of time,' said Britta. 'It's much better to experience things yourself rather than just reading about other people's experiences. Don't you agree, Frans?' She sat down in the chair next to him, tilting her head to look into his eyes.

'One doesn't necessarily have to exclude the other,' he said gruffly but without meeting her gaze. He was still staring at Elsy. A furrow appeared on Britta's forehead, and she jumped up from the chair.

'Are any of you going to the dance on Saturday?' She took a few dance steps across the floor.

'I don't think Mamma and Pappa will let me go,' said Elsy in a low voice, still engrossed in the books.

'Who do you think will be there?' said Britta, dancing some more. She tried to pull Frans to his feet, but he resisted and managed to stay seated in the armchair.

'Stop fooling around.' His tone of voice was brusque, but then he couldn't help laughing. 'Britta, you're crazy, do you know that?'

'Don't you like crazy girls? If not, I can be serious too.' She put on a stern expression. 'Or happy.' She laughed so loud that the sound echoed off the walls.

'Shhh,' said Erik, glancing up at the ceiling.

'Or I can be very quiet,' whispered Britta melodramatically, and Frans laughed again, pulling her down on to his lap.

'Crazy will do just fine.'

A voice from the doorway interrupted them.

'What a ruckus you're making.' There stood Axel, leaning against the door jamb and smiling tiredly.

'Sorry, we didn't mean to wake you.' Erik's voice was brimming with the awe that he felt towards his brother, but he also looked worried.

'It doesn't matter, Erik. I can take a nap later.' Axel folded his arms and said, 'So, looks like you're taking advantage of our parents going out to visit the Axelssons by having a few ladies over.'

'Er, I don't know if I'd call it that,' muttered Erik.

Frans laughed, still with Britta perched on his lap. 'Do you see ladies anywhere? There isn't a lady in sight. Just two saucy little girls.'

'Shut up, why don't you!' Britta punched Frans in the chest. She did not look amused.

'And Elsy is so busy looking at the books that she hasn't even said hello.'

Elsy turned around, embarrassed. 'I'm sorry. Hello, Axel.'

'I was just kidding you. Go back to the books. Did Erik tell you that you could borrow some if you like?'

'Yes, he did.' Still blushing, she quickly turned her attention back to the bookshelves.

'How'd it go yesterday?' Erik was looking at his brother as if hungry for every word.

Axel's cheerful, open expression shut down at once. 'Fine,' he said curtly. 'It went fine.' Then he turned on his heel. 'I'm going to lie down again for a while. Please try to keep the noise level to a minimum, okay?'

Erik watched his brother go. Besides the awe and pride that he felt, there was also a certain amount of envy.

But Frans was filled with nothing but admiration. 'Your brother is so courageous . . . I wish I could help too. If only I were a few years older.'

'And what would you do then?' asked Britta, still sulking because he'd ridiculed her in front of Axel. 'You'd never dare. And what would your father say? From what I've heard, it's the Germans he'd rather lend a helping hand to.'

'Cut it out,' said Frans crossly, shoving Britta off his lap. 'People say so many things. I didn't think you listened to crap like that.'

Erik, who always played the role of mediator in the group, abruptly stood up and said, 'We can listen to my father's records for a while, if you want. He has Count Basie.'

He hurried over to the gramophone to put on the record. He didn't like it when people argued. He really didn't.

She'd always loved airports: the planes landing and taking off, the travellers with eyes full of anticipation as they set off on holiday or on a business trip, and all the coming and going, with people reuniting or saying their farewells. She remembered an airport from a long, long time ago. The crush of people, the smells, the colours, the hum of voices. The tension that she sensed rather than saw in her mother's face and the way she held Paula's hand in a tight grip. The suitcase that she'd packed and repacked and then packed again. Everything had to be right, because this was going to be a trip with no return. She remembered too the heat, and then the chill when they arrived. She would never have believed it possible to be so cold. And the airport where they landed was different. Quieter, with cold grey paint. No one spoke loudly, no one waved their hands around. Everybody seemed locked inside their own little bubbles. No one looked them in the eye. Their documents were stamped and then they were sent on their way by a strange-sounding voice in a strange-sounding language. And her mother had kept a tight grip on her hand the whole time.

'Is that him?' Martin pointed at a man in his eighties who had just exited the passport control area. He was tall, with grey hair, and he wore a beige trench coat. Very stylish, thought Paula immediately.

'Let's find out.' She led the way. 'Axel Frankel?'

The man nodded. 'You're from the police? I thought I was supposed to come and see you at the station.' He looked tired.

'We thought we might as well come out here to meet you.' Martin gave him a friendly nod, introducing himself and his colleague.

'I see. Well, in that case, I thank you for offering to give me a lift. I usually have to make do with public transport, so this will be a treat.'

'Do you have a suitcase?' Paula cast a glance at the luggage belt.

'No, no, this is all I brought.' He gestured towards the carry-on bag he was pulling behind him. 'I always travel light.'

'An art I've never mastered,' said Paula with a laugh. The weariness on the man's face vanished for a moment as he laughed too.

They chatted about the weather until they all got into the car and Martin began driving towards Fjällbacka.

'Have you . . . have you found out anything more?' Axel's voice quavered and he had to stop talking in order to pull himself together.

Paula, who was sitting next to him on the back seat, shook her head. 'No, unfortunately. We were hoping that you could help us. For example, we need to know whether your brother had any enemies. Is there anyone who might have wanted to harm him?'

Axel shook his head. 'No, no, not really. My brother was the most peaceful and placid man, and . . . no, it's absurd to think that anyone would want to harm Erik.'

'What do you know about his involvement with a group called Sweden's Friends?' Martin tossed out the question from his place in the driver's seat, meeting Axel's eyes in the rear-view mirror.

'So you've gone through Erik's correspondence with Frans Ringholm.' Axel rubbed the bridge of his nose before he said anything more. Paula and Martin waited patiently.

'It's a complicated story that started a very long time ago.'

'We have plenty of time,' said Paula, making it clear that she was expecting him to answer the question.

'Frans is a childhood friend of mine and Erik's. We've known each other all our lives. But . . . how should I put it? We chose one path and Frans chose another.'

'Frans is a right-wing extremist?' Again Martin met Axel's gaze in the mirror.

Axel nodded. 'Yes, I don't really know in what way or to what extent, but all through his adult life he's mixed in those circles, and he even helped to start that group called Sweden's Friends. He probably picked up a lot of his views from home, although back when I knew him he never showed any such sympathies. But people change.' Axel shook his head.

'Why would this organization feel threatened by Erik? From what I understand, he wasn't politically active. He was a historian specializing in the Second World War, right?'

Axel sighed. 'It's not that easy to remain neutral. You can't research Nazism and at the same time remain, or be viewed as, apolitical. For instance, many neo-Nazi organizations dispute that the concentration camps existed, and all attempts to describe the camps and investigate what happened are regarded as a threat or an attack on their group. As I said, it's complicated.'

'What about your own involvement in the issue? Have you ever received any threats?' Paula studied him closely.

'Of course I have. To a much greater extent than Erik. My life's mission has been working with the Simon Wiesenthal Center.'

'And what exactly does the Center do?' asked Martin.

'The organization tracks down Nazis who have fled and gone underground. And it sees that they're brought to justice,' Paula explained.

Axel nodded. 'That's right, among other things. So yes, I've received my share of threats.'

'Do you still have any of the actual letters?' Martin asked.

'The Center has them. Those of us who work for the Center send in any letters we get so they can be kept in the archives. If you contact them they'll give you access to everything.' He handed his business card to Paula, who put it in her jacket pocket.

'And Sweden's Friends? Have you received any threats from them?'

'No . . . I don't think so. No, not that I can recall. But as I said, you should check with the Center. They have everything.'

'Frans Ringholm. How does he fit into the picture? You said he was a childhood friend?' Martin enquired.

'To be precise, he was Erik's childhood friend. I was a couple of years older, so we didn't really have the same circle of friends.'

'But Erik knew Frans well?' Paula's brown eyes again studied Axel intently.

'Yes, but that was ages ago. We're going back sixty years here.' Axel didn't seem very comfortable with the topic of conversation. He kept shifting position on the back seat. 'Even without dementia, the old memory starts to get a bit murky.' He smiled wryly as he tapped his head.

'But there's been more recent contact, judging by the letters we found. Frans has been in touch with your brother repeatedly, at least by letter.'

Axel ran his hand through his hair in a gesture of frustration. 'I've lived my life, and my brother has lived his. And it was only three years ago that we both settled in Fjällbacka

72

permanently – well, semi-permanently, in my case. Erik had a flat in Göteborg during all the years he worked there, and I've spent my time more or less travelling around the world. Of course we've always had the house here as our base, and if anyone asks me where I live, I tell them Fjällbacka. But in the summertime I always flee to my flat in Paris. I can't take all the hustle and bustle that comes with the tourists. For the most part we live a rather quiet and isolated life, my brother and I. The cleaning lady is the only one who ever visits us. We prefer . . . preferred it that way.' Axel's voice broke.

Paula caught Martin's eye, and he shook his head slightly before returning his gaze to the motorway. Neither of them could think of anything else to ask. They spent the rest of the drive to Fjällbacka chatting tensely about trivial matters. Axel looked as if he might fall apart at any moment, and he seemed visibly relieved when they finally pulled up in front of his house.

'Do you have any problem with . . . staying here now?' Paula asked.

Axel stood in silence for a moment, his eyes fixed on the big white house, his carry-on bag in his hand. Finally he said:

'No. This is my home, and Erik's. We belong here. Both of us.' He smiled sadly and shook hands with them before heading for the front door. To Paula, gazing after him, it seemed that he exuded loneliness.

'So, did she rake you over the coals when you got home yesterday?' Karin laughed as she pushed Ludde in his push-chair. She was walking at a brisk pace, and Patrik was panting with the effort of keeping up.

'You might say that.' He winced at the thought of the reception he'd had when he got home. Erica had not been in the sunniest mood. And to some extent, he could understand why. He was supposed to be taking responsibility for Maja during the daytime so that Erica could work. At the same time, he couldn't help feeling that she'd over-reacted. He hadn't been out on some fun expedition; he was busy doing household errands. And how could he know that Maja wasn't going to take her nap the way she usually did? It had seemed a bit unfair that he ended up in the doghouse for the rest of the day. But the good thing about Erica was that she never held a grudge for long, so this morning she'd given him a kiss, as usual, and the events of yesterday seemed forgotten. Although he hadn't dared tell her that he was going to have company on his walk today. Of course he planned to tell her eventually; he was just putting it off for the moment. Even though Erica wasn't a particularly jealous person, taking a walk with his ex-wife was not a subject that Patrik wanted to broach while he was already in the doghouse. As if Karin could read his mind, she said:

'Is Erica okay with the idea that we spend time together? It's years ago that we got divorced, but some people are a little more . . . sensitive.'

'Sure, of course it's okay,' said Patrik, unwilling to admit to his cowardice. 'It's fine. Erica has no problem with it.'

'That's great. I mean, it's nice to have company, but not if it causes problems on the home front.'

'What about Leif?' asked Patrik, eager to change the subject. He leaned over the pushchair to straighten his daughter's cap, which was sitting askew. Maja didn't pay any attention because she was fully occupied communicating with Ludde in the pushchair moving alongside her own.

'Leif?' Karin snorted. 'You might say it's a miracle that Ludde even knows who Leif is. He's always out on the road.'

Patrik nodded sympathetically. Karin's new husband was a singer with a dance band called Leffes. He could see how it might be a strain to be a dance band 'widow'.

'No serious problems between the two of you, I hope.'

74

'No, we see each other too seldom for any problems to arise,' replied Karin, laughing. But the laugh sounded bitter and hollow. Patrik sensed that she wasn't telling the whole truth, and he didn't know what to say. It felt a little strange to be discussing relationship problems with his ex-wife. Thankfully the ringing of his mobile saved him.

'Patrik Hedström.'

'Hi, it's Pedersen. I'm ringing with the post-mortem results for Erik Frankel. We've faxed over the report, as usual, but I thought you'd want to hear the main points on the phone.'

'Sure, of course,' Patrik said hesitantly, casting a glance at Karin, who had slowed her pace to wait for him. 'But the thing is, I'm actually on paternity leave at the moment.'

'Is that right? Congratulations! Oh, you've got a wonderful time ahead of you. I stayed home for six months with both of my children, and those were the best months of my life.'

Patrik felt his jaw drop. He would never have believed that of the super-efficient, reserved, and rather cold medical examiner at the forensics lab. He suddenly pictured Pedersen, wearing his doctor's lab coat, sitting in a sandbox where he was slowly and meticulously, with the greatest precision, making the perfect sand pies. Patrik couldn't stop himself from laughing, which prompted a brusque 'What's so funny?' in reply.

'Nothing,' said Patrik, as he motioned to Karin, who was looking surprised, that he'd explain later. 'Would you mind giving me a brief summary?' he went on in a more serious tone of voice. 'I was at the crime scene the day before yesterday, and I'd like to keep up-to-date on what's happening.'

'Of course,' said Pedersen, still sounding miffed. 'It's quite straightforward. Erik Frankel received a blow to the head from a heavy object. Probably something made of stone, because there are tiny fragments of stone in the wound, indicating that the substance in question had to be very porous. He died instantly since the blow struck him above his left temple and caused massive bleeding in the brain.'

'Do you have any idea from which direction the blow was delivered? From behind? In front?'

'In my opinion, the perpetrator was standing directly in front of the victim. And in all likelihood, the perp is right-handed. It's more natural for someone who is right-handed to strike from the right. It would be extremely awkward for a left-handed person to do that.'

'And the object that was used, any ideas as to what it might be?' Patrik was aware of the eagerness in his own voice.

'That's for you to determine. A heavy object made of stone. Although it doesn't look as if the victim's skull was struck by any sort of sharp edge. The wound looks more like a contusion.'

'Okay, that at least gives us a little to go on.'

'Us?' said Pedersen with a slightly sarcastic tone. 'Didn't you say you're on paternity leave?'

'Er, yes,' said Patrik and paused for a second before he continued. 'Well, I assume that you'll ring the station and give them all the information.'

'I supposed I'd better do that, under the circumstances,' said Pedersen in amusement. 'Shall I take the bull by the horns and ring Mellberg? Or do you have another suggestion?'

'Martin,' said Patrik instinctively, and Pedersen chuckled. 'I'd already decided to do that, but thanks for the tip anyway. I'm surprised at you though: don't you want to ask me when Frankel died?'

'Oh, that's right. When did he die?' Patrik's voice regained its eager tone. He cast another glance at Karin.

'Impossible to say exactly. His body has been lying there in the heat for too long. But my best estimate is between two and three months ago. So that takes us to sometime in June or July.'

'And you can't be more specific than that?' Patrik knew the answer to his question even before he asked it.

'We're not magicians over here. We have no crystal balls. June. That's the best answer you're going to get in this situation. I'm basing it partly on the type of flies that were found, partly on how many generations of flies and larva were present. Taking all of that into consideration, plus the body's state of decay, I can say that he probably died in June. It's your job to determine a more precise date of death. Or rather – it's your colleagues' job.' Pedersen laughed.

Patrik couldn't remember ever hearing him laugh before. And yet it had now happened several times during this phone conversation. All at Patrik's expense. But maybe that's what it took to get Pedersen to laugh. Patrik offered the usual words of thanks and then ended the call.

'Work?' Karin enquired.

'Yes, an investigation that we're doing at the moment.'

'The old man who was found dead on Monday?'

'I see that the gossip mill is as effective as ever,' said Patrik. Karin had picked up the pace again, and he had to jog to catch up.

A red car passed them. After about a hundred metres, it slowed down, and the driver seemed to be glancing in the rear-view mirror. Then the car swiftly backed up, and Patrik swore to himself. Only now did he realize that the car belonged to his mother.

'What's this, are the two of you out for a walk together?' asked Kristina. Having rolled down the window, she looked in surprise at Patrik and Karin.

'Hi, Kristina! How nice to see you!' Karin leaned towards the open window. 'I've moved back to Fjällbacka and happened to run into Patrik. We discovered that we're both on leave from our jobs and in need of company. I have a little boy named Ludvig.' Karin pointed to the pushchair, and Kristina leaned forward, uttering the appropriate cooing sounds at the sight of the one-year-old.

'Oh, how nice,' said Kristina in a tone of voice that made Patrik's stomach clench. Then a thought occurred to him that made his stomach hurt even more. Without wanting to know the answer, he asked his mother, 'And where are you off to right now?'

'I was on my way to your house. It's been a while since I dropped by. I've brought some baked goods with me.' She pointed happily to a bag of buns and sponge cake on the seat next to her.

'Erica's working . . .' Patrik ventured lamely, but he knew it was pointless.

Kristina shifted into first gear. 'That's good. Then she'll be happy to take a little coffee break. And you'll be home soon too, won't you?' She waved to Maja, who merrily waved back.

'Sure, of course,' said Patrik, trying frantically to come up with a way to ask his mother not to mention who he'd been walking with. But his brain was completely blank, and in resignation he raised his hand to wave goodbye. With his stomach in knots, he watched his mother race off towards Sälvik. He was going to have to do quite a bit of explaining.

The work on her book was going well. She'd written four pages this morning, and now she stretched with satisfaction as she sat at her desk. Her anger from yesterday had faded, and in hindsight she thought that she might have over-reacted. She would make it up to Patrik tonight by cooking something extra good for dinner. Before the wedding they'd both made an effort to lose a few pounds, but now they were back to their daily routines. And it was important to treat themselves once in a while. Maybe fillet of pork with gorgonzola sauce. Patrik liked that.

Erica stopped thinking about dinner and reached for

her mother's diaries. She really ought to sit down and read through all of them at once, but she just couldn't bring herself to do that. She'd have to do it in small doses. Little glances into her mother's world. She propped her feet up on the desk and began the laborious task of trying to decipher the old-fashioned, ornate handwriting. So far she'd mostly read about daily life in her mother's home, the chores she'd helped out with, minor meditations about the future, their worry about Elsy's father who spent all his time out at sea, even on the weekends. The descriptions of life were filled with the naïveté and innocence of a teenager, and Erica had a hard time associating the girlish voice evident in the text with the mother she remembered. She had seemed so remote, so stern and forbidding; Erica and Anna had never known her to speak a tender word or display any affection for them.

After reading partway down the second page, Erica suddenly sat up straight. A familiar name had appeared. Or rather, two names. Elsy wrote that she'd been over to Erik and Axel's house while their parents were away. The text was mostly a lyrical description of their father's library, which had impressed Elsy enormously, but Erica saw only the two names: Erik and Axel. It had to be Erik and Axel Frankel. Eagerly she read through the whole passage about the visit, realizing from the tone that they must have spent a lot of time together, Elsy and Erik, and two other youths named Britta and Frans. Erica searched her memory. No, she'd never heard her mother mention any of them. She was quite sure about that. And Axel was depicted in Elsy's diary as almost a mythical, heroic figure. Elsy described him as 'infinitely brave, and nearly as stylish as Errol Flynn'. Had her mother been in love with Axel Frankel? No, that wasn't the feeling Erica got from reading her words; it was more as if Elsy had harboured a deep admiration for him.

Erica set the diary on her lap as she brooded over what

she'd just read. Why hadn't Erik Frankel mentioned that he'd known her mother when they were young? Erica had told him where she'd found the Nazi medal, and who it had belonged to. Yet he hadn't said a word. Again Erica recalled the strange silence that had ensued. She was right. There was something that he'd been keeping from her.

The shrill sound of the doorbell interrupted her thoughts. With a sigh she swung her legs down from the desk and pushed back her chair. Who could that be? Her question was immediately answered by someone calling 'Hello?' in the hall. Erica sighed again, now with even greater emphasis. Kristina. Her mother-in-law. She took a deep breath, opened the door, and went over to the staircase. 'Hello?' she heard again, the tone of voice even more insistent, and Erica felt herself clenching her jaw with annoyance.

'Hello,' she said, as cheerfully as she could manage, although she was aware how false it sounded. Thank goodness Kristina was not particularly attuned to nuances.

'Just popped into say hello!' replied her mother-in-law happily as she hung up her jacket. 'I brought along some cookies for coffee. Baked them myself. Thought you'd appreciate it, since you career girls don't have time for such things.'

Erica was gnashing her teeth. Kristina had an unbelievable talent for issuing veiled criticisms. Was she born that way or was it something she'd perfected through long years of practice?

'Oh, that sounds nice,' she said politely as she went into the kitchen where Kristina was already making coffee, as if it were her house and not Erica's.

'Sit down. I'll fix the coffee,' she said. 'I know where everything is.'

'You certainly do,' said Erica, knowing that Kristina wouldn't pick up on the sarcasm.

'Patrik and Maja are out taking a walk. They probably

won't be back for a while,' she said, hoping that might make her mother-in-law cut her visit short.

'I know,' said Kristina as she measured out scoops of coffee. 'Two, three, four . . .' She put the scoop back in the tin and then turned her attention to Erica. 'They'll be home any minute. I drove past them on the way over. It's so nice that Karin has moved back, and that Patrik has some company in the daytime. It's boring to go out walking all alone, especially for someone like Patrik, who's used to working and being productive. It looked as though they were enjoying each other's company.'

Struggling to process this information, Erica stared at Kristina. What was she on about? Karin? Karin who?

The moment Patrik stepped through the door, a light went on in Erica's head. Oh, *that* Karin.

Patrik smiled sheepishly, and after a strained pause he said, 'How nice – coffee.'

They'd gathered in the kitchen for a run-through of the case. It was getting close to lunchtime, and Mellberg's stomach was growling loudly.

'Okay then, what do we have so far?' He reached for one of the buns that Annika had set out on a platter. Just a little appetizer before lunch. 'Paula and Martin? You talked to the victim's brother this morning – did you find out anything interesting?' He chewed on the bun as he talked, dropping crumbs on to the table.

'That's right, we picked him up at Landvetter airport,' said Paula. 'But he doesn't seem to know very much. We asked him about the letters from Sweden's Friends, but the only thing he was able to clarify was that Frans Ringholm was apparently one of Erik's childhood friends. Axel didn't know about any specific threats from that organization; it seems that threats were something of an occupational hazard, given the work that he and Erik did.'

'Axel received threats?' asked Mellberg, spraying more crumbs across the table.

'Quite a few, from what he said,' said Martin. 'They're all on file with the organization that he works for.'

'Had he received any from Sweden's Friends?'

Paula shook her head. 'He couldn't tell us whether he had or not. And I can understand that. He must get so much of that junk in the post, why would he pay any attention to it?'

'What was your impression of him? I've heard that he was something of a hero in his youth.' Annika gave Martin and Paula an inquisitive look.

'Stylish, distinguished . . .' said Paula, 'but very subdued, which is only natural in the circumstances. He definitely seemed upset by his brother's death. Did you have the same impression?' She turned to Martin, who nodded.

'Yes, I thought so too.'

'I assume that you're going to question him again,' said Mellberg, looking at Martin. 'And I understand you've been in touch with Pedersen, is that right?' He cleared his throat. 'A bit odd that he didn't want to talk to me.'

Martin coughed. 'I think you must have been out walking the dog when he called. I'm sure you were at the top of his list.'

'Hmm, well, you're probably right. Okay, go on. What did he say?'

Martin summarized Pedersen's findings. Then he told them: 'Apparently Pedersen rang Patrik first. Sounds as though he isn't entirely happy about being a stay-at-home father: he got Pedersen to give him a full report. Considering how easy it was to entice him over to the crime scene, I bet we'll be seeing him and Maja here at the station very soon.'

Annika laughed. 'Yes, I talked to him yesterday. He was trying to be diplomatic, saying that it would probably take him some time to get adjusted.'

'I believe it,' snorted Mellberg. 'What a stupid idea: grown men changing nappies and making baby food! My generation didn't have to put up with that sort of rubbish. We could devote ourselves to things we were better suited for, while the women took care of the kids.'

'I would have gladly changed nappies,' said Gösta quietly, looking down at the table.

Patrik and Annika glanced at him; they'd only recently found out that Gösta and his late wife had had a son who died shortly after birth. There had been no other children. Everyone sat in silence for a moment and avoided looking at Gösta. Then Annika said:

'Well, I happen to think it's a good thing. You men get to find out how much work is involved. I don't have any of my own' – now it was Annika's turn to look sad – 'but all my women friends have children, and it's not like they lie around eating bonbons all day long because they're at home with the kids. So this will probably be good for Patrik.'

'You'll never convince me of that,' said Mellberg. Then he frowned impatiently and peered down at the papers lying on the table in front of him. Brushing off all the crumbs, he read a few sentences before he spoke again.

'Okay, here's the report from Torbjörn and his boys . . .'

'And girls,' added Annika. Mellberg sighed loudly.

'And girls. You're certainly on some sort of feminist warpath today! Shall we get on with this investigation, or should we just sing "Kumbaya" and debate the feminist agenda?' He shook his head before proceeding:

'As I said, I have here the report from Torbjörn and his *team*. And I can sum it up in two words: "no surprises". They found a number of shoe prints and fingerprints, and of course we'll have to follow up on those. Gösta, make sure that we get the boys' prints so we can eliminate them, and the brothers' too. By the way' – he hesitated as he read a few lines to himself again – 'it seems they've established that the victim received a blow to the head, delivered by some kind of blunt instrument.'

'So, no other injuries? Just the one blow to the head?' said Paula.

'Uh, yes, that's right: one blow. I asked Torbjörn that very question, and apparently it's possible to tell by analysing the blood spatter on the walls. At any rate, the conclusion is quite clear: a powerful blow to the head.'

'That agrees with the post-mortem results,' said Martin, nodding. 'What about the weapon? Pedersen thought it was a heavy object made of stone.'

'Exactly!' said Mellberg triumphantly, jabbing his finger at the middle of the document. 'Under the desk they found a heavy stone bust. It had traces of blood and hair and brain matter on it, and I'm convinced that the stone fragments embedded in the wound will match the stone that the bust is made of.'

'So we have the murder weapon. At least that's something,' said Gösta gloomily, taking a gulp of his coffee, which had gone cold.

Mellberg glanced at his subordinates sitting around the table. 'Any suggestions as to how we should proceed?' He made it sound as if the question were merely a formality and that he had already devised a long list of suitable investigative measures. Which was not the case.

'I think we should talk to Frans Ringholm. Find out more about those threats.'

'And talk to the people who live in the neighbourhood, to see if anyone noticed anything around the time of the murder,' Paula added.

Annika looked up from her notebook. 'Somebody should also interview the cleaning woman who worked for the brothers. Find out when she was last there, whether she spoke to Erik, and why she hasn't been over to clean all summer.'

'Good.' Mellberg nodded. 'So, why are you all sitting here? Let's get to work!' He glared at the officers and continued to do so until they trooped out of the room. Then he reached for another bun.

Delegation. That was the mark of a good leader.

They had all agreed that it was a total waste of time to go to classes, so they only showed up sporadically, whenever the spirit happened to move them. Which wasn't very often. Today they'd gathered around ten o'clock. There wasn't much to do in Tanumshede. They mostly sat around, talking. And smoking.

'Did you hear about that old fart in Fjällbacka?' Nicke took a drag on his cigarette and laughed. 'It was probably your grandfather and his pal who killed him.'

Vanessa giggled.

'Hey,' said Per crossly, though not without a certain pride. 'Grandpa had nothing to do with that. He wouldn't risk prison time just to kill some geriatric fossil. Sweden's Friends has better things to do, and bigger goals in mind.'

'Have you talked to the old guy yet? About letting us come to a meeting?' Nicke had stopped laughing, an eager expression now on his face.

'Not yet,' said Per reluctantly. He enjoyed a special status in the group because he was the grandson of Frans Ringholm, and in a weak moment he'd promised the others that he'd get them into one of the Friends' meetings in Uddevalla. But he hadn't found the right occasion to bring it up with his grandfather. Besides, he knew what Frans would say. They were too young. They needed a couple more years to 'develop their full potential'. What that meant, he had no idea. He and his friends understood the issues just as well as the older people did, the ones who had already been accepted. It was simple, after all. What was there to misunderstand?

And that was what appealed to him: the fact that it was simple. Black and white. No grey areas. Per couldn't understand why people had to complicate matters, to study things first from one angle and then from another, when the whole thing was so very, very simple. It was us versus them – that's all there was to it. Us and them. If they'd only keep to their own kind, there wouldn't be a problem. But they would insist on forcing their way into territory that didn't belong to them, crossing boundaries that ought to be obvious. The differences couldn't be any clearer. White or yellow. White or brown. White or that disgusting blue-black skin of the ones who came from the darkest jungles of Africa. So bloody simple. Until they started mixing and jumbling everything up until it was one great muddy mess. He looked at his friends listlessly slumped on the bench next to him. Did he really know what their bloodlines were? Who knew what the whores in their family had been up to? Maybe impure blood ran through them too. Per shuddered.

Nicke gave him a questioning look. 'What's the matter with you? You look like you've swallowed something nasty.'

Per snorted. 'It's nothing.' But the thought and the feeling of revulsion wouldn't leave him. He stubbed out his cigarette.

'Come on, let's go get some coffee. It's making me depressed, just sitting here.' He cocked his head towards the school building and then set off at a brisk pace without waiting to see whether the others followed. He knew they would.

For a moment he thought about the murdered man. Then he shrugged. The old boy wasn't important.

FJÄLLBACKA 1943

The cutlery clinked against their plates as they ate. All three of them tried not to look at the empty chair at the dining-room table, but they couldn't help themselves.

'I can't believe he had to leave again so soon.' Gertrud frowned as she handed the bowl to Erik, and he put yet another potato on his plate, even though it was already full. It was easier to do that, otherwise his mother would keep urging him to take more food until he gave in. But when he looked down at his brimming plate, he wondered how on earth he was ever going to eat it all. Food didn't interest him. He ate only because he was forced to do so. And because his mother kept saying that she was ashamed at how skinny he was. She said that people were going to think she was starving him.

Axel, on the other hand, ate everything with a healthy appetite. Erik cast a glance at the empty chair as he reluctantly raised the fork to his lips. The food seemed to swell in his mouth. The gravy transformed the potatoes into a soft mush, and he chewed mechanically to get rid of what was in his mouth as quickly as possible.

'He has to do his part.' Hugo Frankel gave his wife a stern look. But he too glanced at the empty chair.

'I just thought he could have a few days of peace and quiet here at home.'

'That's up to him. Nobody can tell Axel what to do, except Axel himself.' Hugo's voice swelled with pride, and Erik felt a stab of pain in his chest, as he did whenever his mother and father talked about Axel. Sometimes Erik felt as if he were almost invisible, a mere shadow of the dazzling Axel, who was always the focal point, even though he wasn't trying to be. Erik stuffed another forkful into his mouth. If only dinner would be over so he could go to his room and read. Mostly he read history books. There was something about all the facts, the names and dates and places, that he loved. Those things didn't change; they were something he could rely on, depend on.

Axel had never been very interested in books, but he'd still managed to pass all his school exams with the highest marks. Erik got good marks too, but he had to work hard for them. And no one ever patted him on the back or beamed with pride as they boasted about him to friends and acquaintances. Nobody bragged about Erik.

Yet he still couldn't bring himself to resent his brother. Sometimes he wished that he could. Wished he could hate him, despise him, wash away that stabbing pain in his chest. But the truth was that he loved Axel – more than anyone else. Axel was the strongest and bravest; he was the one worth bragging about. Not Erik. That was a fact. Like in the history books. Just as much a fact as the date of the Battle of Hastings. He couldn't question it, argue about it, or change it. That's just how things were.

Erik looked down at his plate. To his surprise, it was empty.

'Father, may I be excused?' His voice was filled with hope.

'Have you already finished eating? Well, look at that . . . All right, you can go. Your mother and I will sit here a while longer.'

As Erik went upstairs to his room, he heard his parents talking in the dining room.

'Don't you think Axel is taking too many risks?'

'Gertrud, you have to stop coddling him. He's nineteen years old, after all . . . We should be glad to have such a . . .'

Their voices faded as Erik closed the door behind him. He threw himself down on the bed and picked up the book on top of the pile, the one about Alexander the Great. He'd been brave too. Just like Axel.

'All I'm saying is that you might have mentioned it. I stood there looking like an idiot when Kristina said that you and Karin were out taking a walk together.'

'Er, uh . . . okay, I know.' Patrik hung his head. The hour that Kristina had spent drinking coffee with them had been filled with undercurrents and surreptitious glances, and no sooner had she closed the front door behind her than Erica had exploded.

'It's not the fact that you're out walking with your ex-wife that bothers me. I'm not the jealous type, and you know it. But why didn't you tell me? That's what upsets me.'

'Sure, I can understand that . . .' Patrik avoided looking Erica in the eye.

'Understand! Is that all you can say? No explanation? I mean, I thought we could tell each other everything!' Erica could sense that she was approaching the borderline of what might be considered an extreme over-reaction. But all the frustration of the past few days had now found an outlet, and she couldn't stop herself.

'And I thought the division of labour between us was clear! You were going to take paternity leave, and I was going to work. Instead you keep interrupting me, running upstairs to my workroom as if it has a revolving door, and yesterday you even had the nerve to leave the house for two hours and leave me to look after Maja. How do you think I handled things during the year I was home alone with her? Do you think I had some bloody maid who could step in whenever I needed to run out to do errands? Or someone who could tell me where Maja's mittens were? Do you?' Erica could hear how shrill her voice was, and she wondered whether it was really possible for her to sound like that. She cut herself off in mid-flow and then said in a more muted tone:

'I'm sorry, I didn't mean . . . You know what? I think I'll go for a walk. I need to get out of the house for a while.'

'Do that,' said Patrik, peering from under his fringe like a turtle cautiously sticking its head out to see if the coast was clear. 'And I'm sorry that I didn't . . .' He gave her a pleading look.

'Oh, don't give me that look,' said Erica, smiling faintly. The white flag had been hoisted. She regretted flying off the handle, but they'd have to talk later. Right now she needed some fresh air.

She walked through town at a brisk pace. Fjällbacka seemed strangely deserted now that summer was over and the tourists had gone home. It was like a living room on the morning after a party: dirty glasses holding the dregs of wine and beer, a crumpled banner in the corner, a party hat perched askew on the head of a guest who had passed out on the sofa. But Erica actually preferred this time of year. Summertime was so intense, so intrusive. Right now a calm had settled over Ingrid Bergman Square. Maria and Mats would keep the Centrum kiosk open for a few more days and then close it up and return to their business in Sälen, just as they did every year. And that was what Erica loved so much about Fjällbacka: the predictability of it all. Each year the same thing, the same cycles. Exactly as it had been the year before.

Erica said hi to everyone she met as she walked past Ingrid Bergman Square and up Galärbacken. She knew, or knew of, almost everybody in town. But she picked up speed as soon as anyone seemed inclined to stop for a chat. She just wasn't in the mood.

It was only as she passed the petrol station that she realized where she was heading.

'Three cases of assault, two bank robberies, plus a few miscellaneous charges. But no convictions for agitating against ethnic groups,' said Paula, closing the passenger-side door of the police vehicle. 'I also came across a file on a guy named Per Ringholm, but only minor offences.'

'That's his grandson,' said Martin, closing the door on the driver's side. They had driven to Grebbestad, where Frans Ringholm lived in a flat next door to the Gästis Hotel.

'I've had my share of drunken nights in that place,' said Martin, nodding in the direction of Gästis.

'I can imagine. But those days are over, right?'

'You can say that again. I haven't seen the inside of a dance hall in more than a year.' He didn't sound particularly unhappy about it. These days he was so in love with Pia that he never wanted to leave the flat they shared unless it was absolutely necessary. But before he found his princess he'd had to kiss quite a number of frogs, or rather toads.

'What about you?' Martin looked at Paula.

'What about me?' She pretended not to understand the question. And before he could pursue it any further they reached the door to Frans's flat. Martin knocked loudly and was rewarded with the sound of footsteps approaching from inside.

'Yes?' A man with silvery grey hair, cropped so short that it was no more than stubble, opened the door. He was wearing jeans and a checked shirt, the type that the Swedish author Jan Guillou always wore, displaying a complete lack of interest in fashion trends.

'Frans Ringholm?' Martin studied him with open curiosity.

The man was well known in the area – and beyond, as Martin had discovered after searching the Internet at home. Apparently Ringholm was a founder of one of Sweden's fastest growing anti-foreigner organizations, and according to the chatter in various online forums, the group was starting to become a major force.

'That's right. What can I do for' – he looked Martin and Paula up and down – 'you officers?'

'We have a few questions we'd like to ask you. May we come in?'

Frans stepped aside without comment, merely raising one eyebrow. Martin looked around the flat in surprise. He didn't know what he was expecting; something dirtier and messier, perhaps. Instead the flat was so tidy that it made his own place seem like a junkie's den.

'Have a seat.' Frans motioned towards a couple of sofas in the living room to the right of the entry hall. 'I just put on a fresh pot of coffee. Milk? Sugar?' His voice was calm and courteous, and Martin and Paula exchanged slightly disconcerted looks.

'None of the above, thanks,' replied Martin.

'Just milk, no sugar,' said Paula as she entered the living room ahead of Martin. They sat down next to each other on the white sofa and looked around. The room was bright and airy, with big windows facing the sea. The flat didn't seem overly fastidious, just comfortable and well-kept.

'Here, have some coffee.' Frans came in carrying a heavily loaded tray. He set down three cups of steaming coffee, and then a big plate of biscuits.

'Go ahead and help yourselves.' He gestured towards the coffee table and then picked up one of the cups before leaning back in a big armchair. 'So, how can I be of service?'

Paula took a sip of coffee. Then she said, 'I'm sure you've heard about the man who was found dead just outside of Fjällbacka.'

'Erik, yes,' said Frans, nodding sadly before sipping his coffee. 'Yes, I was very upset when I heard the news. It's awful for Axel. This must be a terrible time for him.'

'Er, yes, well . . .' Martin cleared his throat. He'd been caught off guard by the man's friendliness, and by the fact that Ringholm was the complete opposite of what he'd expected. But he pulled himself together and said: 'The reason that we'd like to talk to you is that we found some letters from you in the house, addressed to Erik Frankel.'

'Oh, so he saved those letters,' said Frans, chuckling as he reached for a biscuit. 'Erik loved to collect things. You young people probably think it's extremely old-fashioned to send letters. But those of us who belong to the older genera-tion have a hard time giving up old habits.' He gave Paula a friendly wink. She almost smiled back but reminded herself that the man sitting in front of her had devoted his whole life to trying to thwart and combat people like herself.

'In your letters you talk about a threat . . .' She put on a stern expression.

'Well, I wouldn't exactly call it a threat.' Frans regarded her calmly, again leaning back in his chair. He crossed one leg over the other before going on. 'I just thought I ought to mention to Erik that there existed certain . . . forces within the organization that didn't always behave – how shall I put it? – sensibly.'

'And you felt compelled to inform Erik of this because . . .?'

'Erik and I had been friends since we were boys, though I'll openly admit that we'd drifted apart, and there hadn't been any real friendship between us for years. We . . . chose rather different paths in life.' Frans smiled. 'But I didn't wish Erik any harm, so when I had the chance to warn him, I did. Some people have a hard time understanding that resorting to physical force isn't always the best solution.'

'You yourself haven't been a stranger to . . . resorting to physical force,' said Martin. 'Three convictions for assault,

94

several for bank robbery, and from what I understand you didn't exactly serve out your time like some sort of Dalai Lama.'

Far from taking offence, Frans merely smiled at Martin's comments in a manner reminiscent of the Dalai Lama. 'To everything there is a season. Prison has its own rules, and only one language is understood. I've also heard that wisdom comes with age, and I've learned my lesson along the way.'

'Has your grandson learned his lesson yet?' Martin reached for a biscuit as he asked the question. In a flash Frans's hand shot out and grabbed Martin's wrist in an iron grip.

Fixing his eyes on the police officer, Frans snarled: 'My grandson has nothing to do with this. Do you understand?'

Martin held his gaze for a long time before tearing his hand away. 'Don't do that again,' he said in a low voice, resisting the urge to massage his sore wrist.

Frans laughed and leaned back. He was again his friendly, avuncular self. But for a few seconds the façade had cracked to show rage lurking behind the outward calm. The question was whether Erik had borne the brunt of that rage.

Ernst tugged eagerly at the lead, unable to understand why his master suddenly insisted on taking baby steps and pausing to look around him all the while. The more Mellberg fought to restrain the animal, the more Ernst strained against the lead, determined to pick up the pace.

They had walked almost the entire route before Mellberg was rewarded for his efforts. He was on the verge of giving up when he heard the sound of footsteps behind him and Ernst started prancing with joy at the approach of a playmate.

'So you're out for a walk too.' Rita's voice sounded as cheerful as Mellberg remembered, and he felt a smile appear on his lips.

'Yes, we are. Out for a walk, I mean.' Mellberg felt like kicking himself. What kind of stupid answer was that? And he was usually so suave with the ladies. But here he was, sounding like a complete idiot. Assuming his most authoritative voice, he said, 'I understand that it's important for dogs to get some exercise. So I try to walk Ernst for at least an hour every day.'

'And it's not just the dogs that benefit from a little exercise. You and I could use some too.' Rita giggled and patted her round stomach. Mellberg found this highly liberating. Finally a woman who understood that a bit of meat on the bone wasn't necessarily a bad thing.

'Indeed,' he said, patting his own capacious paunch. 'It's important to maintain a certain gravitas.'

'Heavens, yes.' Rita laughed. The slightly old-fashioned exclamation sounded enchanting in combination with her accent. 'That's why I always see about charging the batteries.' She paused outside a block of flats, and Señorita began pulling towards one of the entrances. 'May I offer you some coffee? And coffee cake?'

It was all Mellberg could do to stop himself from leaping with joy, but he paused as if considering the offer before responding, 'Yes, thanks, that would be nice. I can't be away from my work for very long, but . . .'

'All right then.' She punched in the door code and led the way inside. Ernst, lacking his master's self-control, bounded forward with delight at the prospect of accompanying Señorita into her home.

The first word that occurred to Mellberg when he entered Rita's flat was 'comfortable'. It didn't have that minimalist coldness that Swedes tended to favour; her place literally sparkled with colour and warmth. He unfastened the lead, and Ernst raced off after Señorita. Mellberg hung up his jacket, removed his shoes and set them neatly on the shoe rack before following Rita's voice out to the kitchen.

'They seem to like each other.'

'Who?' said Mellberg stupidly, his brain preoccupied with the sight of Rita's marvellously ample behind, which was turned towards him as she stood at the counter measuring the coffee into the coffee-maker.

'Señorita and Ernst, of course.' She turned around and laughed.

Mellberg laughed with embarrassment. 'Oh, yes, of course. They do seem to like each other, don't they?' A glance towards the living room confirmed this: Ernst was in the process of sniffing under Señorita's tail.

'Do you like buns?' asked Rita.

'Does Dolly Parton sleep on her back?' asked Mellberg rhetorically, immediately regretting his choice of words. Rita turned towards him, a quizzical look on her face.

'I don't know. Does she? Well, with those breasts, I suppose she does.'

Mellberg laughed. 'It's just an expression. What I mean is, I love buns.'

He watched with surprise as she set three cups and three plates on the kitchen table. The mystery was solved when Rita turned to the room next to the kitchen and called: 'Johanna, time for coffee!'

'Coming!' they heard from the other room, and a second later a ravishing blonde with an enormous stomach came into the kitchen.

'This is my daughter-in-law, Johanna,' said Rita, gesturing at the very pregnant young woman. 'And this is Bertil. He's the owner of Ernst. I met him walking in the woods,' she said with a giggle. Mellberg held out his hand to introduce himself, and the next instant almost fell to his knees in pain. He'd shaken hands with a few tough customers over the years but never experienced a handshake as powerful as Johanna's.

'That's quite a grip you have,' he squeaked as she released his hand.

Johanna regarded him with amusement before sitting down at the kitchen table. It took her a moment to find a position that allowed her to reach both her cup and the plate holding the buns, but then she launched into the refreshments with gusto.

'When are you due?' asked Mellberg politely.

'Three weeks,' she replied curtly, intent on finishing every last crumb. Then she reached for another bun.

'I see that you're eating for two,' said Mellberg and laughed, but a surly look from Johanna silenced him. Not an easy chick to flirt with, he realized.

'It's my first grandchild,' said Rita proudly, patting Johanna's stomach tenderly. Johanna's face lit up when she looked at her mother-in-law, and she placed her own hand on top of Rita's belly.

'Do you have any grandchildren?' asked Rita after filling the coffee cups and joining them at the table.

'No, not yet. But I do have a son. His name is Simon, and he's seventeen,' Mellberg said proudly. The son had arrived late in his life, and the news of his existence was not something that he'd received with much enthusiasm. But they'd gradually grown accustomed to each other, and now he was constantly amazed by his feelings for Simon. He was a good lad.

'Seventeen? Well, there's no rush, then. But let me tell you, grandchildren are life's dessert.' She patted Johanna's stomach again.

They drank their coffee and chatted pleasantly while the dogs padded about the flat. Mellberg was fascinated by the pure and genuine joy he felt just sitting in Rita's kitchen. After all the disappointments he'd suffered in recent years, he thought he'd never want to see another woman. Yet here he was. And he was enjoying himself.

'So, what do you think?' Rita was staring at him, and he realized that he'd missed the question that now demanded an answer.

'Sorry?'

'I was asking whether you'd like to come to my salsa class tonight. It's for beginners. Not difficult at all. At eight o'clock.'

Mellberg looked at her in disbelief. Salsa class? Him? What a perfectly ridiculous idea. But then he happened to look a little too deep into Rita's dark eyes, and to his astonishment he heard himself saying:

'Salsa class? Eight o'clock? Great.'

Erica was already starting to regret her decision as she walked up the gravel path towards the house belonging to Erik and Axel. It no longer seemed such a good idea, and it was with much hesitation that she raised her fist to knock on the door. At first there was no response, and she was relieved to think that nobody was at home. Then she heard footsteps inside, and her heart sank as the door opened.

'Yes?' Axel Frankel looked worn out. He gave her a puzzled look.

'Hi, I'm Erica Falck, and I . . .' She paused, not knowing how to go on.

'Elsy's daughter.' Axel's weariness seemed to disappear as he studied her with an odd look in his eyes. 'Yes, I can see it now. You're very much alike, you and your mother.'

'We are?' said Erica, surprised. No one had ever said that before.

'Yes, there's something about your eyes. And your mouth.' He tilted his head and seemed to take in every detail of her appearance. Then he stepped aside. 'Come in.'

Erica went into the entry hall and stopped.

'Come this way – we'll go and sit on the veranda.' He strode off, apparently expecting Erica to follow. She hung up her coat and hurried to catch up. He motioned her to a sofa in a beautiful glassed-in veranda similar to the one that she and Patrik had in their home.

'Have a seat.'

They sat there for a while in silence. Realizing that he wasn't going to offer her coffee, Erica cleared her throat and said: 'Well, the reason that I . . .' She started over. 'The reason that I stopped by was that I left a medal with Erik.' She could hear how brusque that sounded and added: 'Oh, of course I wanted to offer you my condolences. I . . .' Growing more uncomfortable by the mintue, she fidgeted as she searched for a way to continue.

Axel dismissed her obvious embarrassment with a wave of his hand and said in a friendly voice: 'You were saying something about a medal.'

'Yes, that's right,' said Erica, grateful that he'd taken charge. 'This past spring I found a medal among my mother's belongings. A Nazi medal. I didn't know why she'd kept it and I was curious. And since I knew that your brother . . .' She shrugged.

'Was Erik able to help you?'

'I don't know. That is, we spoke on the phone in the spring, but then I got really busy and, well . . . I was planning to contact him again, but . . .' Her words faded away.

'And now you're wondering if it's still here?'

Erica nodded. 'Yes. I'm sorry. It sounds so awful that I'm bothering you about it right now when . . . But my mother hadn't kept very many things, so . . .' She fidgeted again. She really should have phoned instead. This felt so cold-blooded.

'I understand. I really do understand. Believe me, I of all people know how important it is to have ties to the past. Even if those ties are based on inanimate objects. And Erik would definitely have understood, considering all the things he collected, all the facts. For him they weren't dead. They were alive, told a story, taught us something . . .' He stared through the glass panes and for a moment seemed to be somewhere far away. Then he turned to Erica again.

'Of course I'll look for it. But first tell me a little more about your mother. What was she like? What was her life like?'

Erica found these questions rather strange. But seeing Axel's pleading eyes she tried her best to answer.

'Hmm . . . what was my mother like? To be honest, I don't really know. Mamma was older when she had me and my sister, and . . . I don't know . . . we never had a very good relationship with her. As for her life . . .' Erica was confused by the question. Partly because she didn't fully understand what he wanted to know, and partly because she didn't know what to say.

'I think she had rather a hard time of it. With life, I mean. She was always so reserved. To me, she never seemed . . . happy.' Erica struggled to find a better way to explain, but that was as close to the truth as she could get. She couldn't recall ever seeing her mother happy.

'I'm sorry to hear that.' Axel again gazed out of the window, as if he couldn't bear to look at Erica. She wondered why he was asking her these questions.

'What was my mother like when you knew her?' Erica couldn't disguise the eagerness in her voice.

Axel turned towards her, and his face seemed to soften. 'It was actually my brother who was friends with Elsy, since they were about the same age. But they were part of a four-some: Erik, Elsy, Frans, and Britta. A real four-leaf clover.' He laughed, a strangely joyless laugh.

'Yes, she wrote about them in the diaries that I found. I know about your brother, but who were Frans and Britta?'

'Diaries?' Axel gave a start of surprise, but it came and went so quickly that a second later Erica thought she must have imagined his reaction. 'Frans Ringholm and Britta . . .' Axel snapped his fingers. 'Now what was Britta's last name?' He closed his eyes as if searching the dark recesses of his memory but shook his head, unable to find the information. 'Anyway, I think she still lives here in Fjällbacka. She has daughters – two or three, I'm not sure – but they're quite

101

a bit older than you. Hmm . . . it's on the tip of my tongue, but . . . She probably changed her name when she got married. Wait, now I remember. Her last name was Johansson, and she married a man also named Johansson, so she didn't have to change her name after all.'

'So I should be able to find her. But you didn't answer my question. What was my mother like? Back then.'

Axel was silent for a long time, then he said: 'She was a quiet girl. Contemplative, but never gloomy. Not the way you describe her. She had a quiet joy about her that came from inside. Nothing like Britta.' He snorted.

'So what was Britta like?'

'I never really liked her. I couldn't understand why my brother wanted to spend time with such a . . . silly goose.' Axel shook his head. 'No, your mother was a very different sort of girl. Britta was shallow and superficial, and she kept running after Frans in a way that . . . girls just didn't do back then. Those were different times, you know.' He gave Erica a wry smile and winked.

'So what about Frans?' Erica was staring at Axel open-mouthed, ready to take in all the information that he had about her mother. The more she found out, the more she realized how little she'd known her mother.

'Frans Ringholm was someone else I didn't think my brother should spend time with. A fierce temper, a mean streak, and . . . no, he's not the sort you should be friends with. Then or now.'

'What does he do now?'

'He lives in Grebbestad. And you might say that he and I have taken different paths in life.' Axel's tone of voice was filled with contempt.

'How do you mean?'

'I mean that I've devoted my life to fighting Nazism, while Frans would like to see history repeat itself, and preferably here on Swedish soil.'

102

'So how does the Nazi medal that I found come into the picture?' In her eagerness, Erica leaned towards Axel, but it was as if his face suddenly closed.

'Ah, that's right, the medal . . .' he said, getting to his feet and moving quickly towards the door. 'I think we should go and look for it.'

As she followed, Erica wondered what she'd said to make him shut down like that, but she decided it wasn't the right time to ask. Out in the hall she saw that Axel had stopped in front of a door that she hadn't noticed before. The door was closed, and he hesitated, his hand on the knob.

'I think I'd better go in alone,' he said, his voice quavering slightly. Erica realized they must be standing outside the library, the room where Erik had died.

'We can do this some other time,' she said, again feeling guilty for disturbing Axel in his bereavement.

'No, we'll do it now,' he said brusquely. Then he repeated his words, this time in a gentler tone, as if to show that he hadn't meant to sound so harsh.

'I'll be right back.' He opened the door, stepped inside, and then closed the door behind him. Erica stayed in the hall, listening to Axel rummaging about inside. It sounded as though he was pulling out drawers, and he must have found what he was looking for very quickly because it took only a minute or two before he came out.

'Here it is.' With an inscrutable expression, he put the medal in Erica's outstretched hand.

'Thank you. I . . .' At a loss for words, she simply closed her fingers around the medal and repeated 'Thanks.'

As she walked along the gravel path with the medal in her pocket, she could feel Axel's eyes watching her. For a moment she considered going back to apologize for bothering him, but then she heard the sound of the front door closing.

FJÄLLBACKA 1943

'I don't understand how Per Albin Hansson can be such a coward!' Vilgot Ringholm slammed his fist on the table, making the cognac decanter jump. He'd told Bodil to bring out the supper-time snacks, and he wondered what was taking her so long. How typical of the woman, dawdling like that. Nothing ever got done properly unless he did it himself.

'Bodil!' he shouted in the direction of the kitchen, but there was no response. He knocked the ash from his cigar and shouted again, bellowing at the top of his lungs, 'Bodillll!'

'Did the missus lose her way out in the kitchen?' joked Egon Rudgren, and Hjalmar Bengtsson joined in the laughter. That made Vilgot even angrier. Now the woman was making him look a fool in front of his presumptive business partner. Something had to be done. But just as he was about to get up and find out what was going on, his wife came in from the kitchen, carrying a fully laden tray in her hands.

'I'm sorry it took so long,' she said, her eyes lowered as she placed the tray on the table in front of them. 'Frans, could you . . .?' She motioned towards the kitchen, but Vilgot waved the boy back.

'I won't have Frans in the kitchen, fussing with women's work. He's a big boy now, and he can stay here with us and learn a thing or two.' He winked at his son, who sat up straight in the armchair across from him. This was the first time he'd been allowed to linger on in the room after one of his father's business dinners. Usually he was expected to excuse himself as soon as they finished eating and retreat to his room, but today his father had insisted that he stay. Pride swelled his chest until it seemed the buttons would fly off his shirt and scatter in every direction. And the evening was about to get even better.

'All right, my boy, how about tasting a few drops of cognac? What do you gentlemen think? He turned thirteen this week. Isn't it about time the boy tasted his first cognac?'

'About time?' laughed Hjalmar. 'I'd say it was long overdue. My boys got their first taste when they were eleven, and it did them good, let me tell you.'

'Vilgot, do you really think . . .' Bodil watched disconsolately as her husband deliberately poured a big glass of cognac and handed it to Frans, who started coughing at the first swallow.

'All right, lad, take it easy – it should be sipped, not gulped.'

'Vilgot . . .' said Bodil again.

'Why are you still here?' snarled Vilgot, his face darkening. 'Don't you have things to clean up in the kitchen?'

For a moment it looked as if Bodil meant to say something. She turned to Frans, but he merely raised his glass triumphantly and said with a smile: '*Skål*, my dear mother.'

To the sound of roaring laughter she went back to the kitchen, closing the door behind her.

'Now where was I?' said Vilgot, motioning for his guests to help themselves to the herring sandwiches on the silver tray. 'Oh, right, what can Prime Minister Per Albin be thinking? Of course we must offer Germany our support!'

Egon and Hjalmar nodded. Naturally, they were in full agreement.

'It's deplorable,' said Hjalmar, 'that in these difficult times

Sweden can't stand tall and uphold Swedish ideals. It almost makes me ashamed to be Swedish.'

All the men nodded and sipped their cognac.

'What am I thinking? We can't sit here drinking cognac with the herring. Frans, go downstairs and fetch us some cold pilsners.'

Five minutes later order was restored, and the herring sandwiches could be washed down with big gulps of Tuborg beer, chilled from the cellar. Frans was again sitting in the armchair across from his father, and he smiled from ear to ear when Vilgot, without comment, opened one of the bottles and handed it to him.

'I've contributed a krona or two to support the good cause. And I'd suggest that you gentlemen do the same. Hitler needs all the good men that he can get on his side right now.'

'Business is certainly booming,' said Hjalmar, raising his bottle. 'We can hardly keep up with the export demand for all the ore. Say what you like about the war, from a business perspective, it's not a bad idea.'

'You're right about that. And if we can get rid of those miserable Jews at the same time, so much the better.' Egon reached for another herring sandwich. By now there were only a few left. He took a bite and then turned to Frans, who was listening intently to everything that was said. 'You should be proud of your father, boy. There aren't many like him in Sweden these days.'

'Yes, sir,' mumbled Frans, suddenly embarrassed by the attention directed at him.

'Listen to what your father says, and ignore all those morons who condemn the Germans and the war. Most of them are mixed-breeds, you know. There are a lot of gypsies and Walloons hereabouts, and naturally they're out to twist the facts. But your father, he knows what's what. And we do too. We've all seen how the Jews and the foreigners have

106

tried to take over, doing their damnedest to destroy what's Swedish and pure. No, Hitler is on the right track, you mark my words.' Egon was all fired up, breadcrumbs flying out of his mouth. Frans was spellbound.

'I think we should talk business now, gentlemen.' Vilgot set his bottle of beer down on the table with a bang and all eyes turned to him.

Frans sat there listening to the men for another twenty minutes. Then he stood up unsteadily and went to bed. It felt as if the whole room was spinning as he lay down, fully clothed. From the parlour he could hear the low drone of the men talking. As Frans drifted off to sleep, he was blissfully unaware of how he was going to feel when he woke up.

Gösta sighed deeply. Summer was about to be replaced by autumn, and in practical terms this meant that his rounds of golf would soon be drastically curtailed. It was still quite warm, and in theory he had about a month's worth of playing. But he knew from bitter experience how it would go. A couple of games would be rained out. Another couple would be cancelled due to thunderstorms. And then from one day to the next the temperature would plunge from pleasant to intolerable. That was the disadvantage of living in Sweden. And he couldn't see too many advantages that made up for it, aside from the availability of *surströmming*, the fermented Baltic herring that was his favourite delicacy. But if he moved abroad he could just take a couple of jars in his suitcase. Then he'd have the best of both worlds.

At least things were calm at the police station. Mellberg was out taking Ernst for a walk, and Martin and Paula had gone to Grebbestad to interview Frans Ringholm. Gösta wondered again why the name seemed so familiar, and to his great relief, something clicked in his brain. He snatched up that day's edition of *Bohusläningen* from his desk and looked through it until he triumphantly set his finger on the name – Kjell Ringholm. The newspaper's irascible columnist was the scourge of local politicians and anyone else in power. Could be a coincidence, but it wasn't a common surname. Frans's son perhaps? Gösta filed away the information in his mind, in case it might prove useful later on.

For the moment, he had more pressing things to deal with. He sighed again. Over the years he'd made sighing into an art form. Maybe he should wait until Martin came back, that way he'd be able to share the workload. Better still, it would give him an hour to himself, maybe two if Martin and Paula decided to stop for lunch before heading back to the station.

But on second thought he decided it might be better to get it out of the way instead of having it hanging over him. Gösta grabbed his jacket, told Annika where he was off to, took one of the cars from the garage, and headed for Fjällbacka.

Not until he rang the doorbell did it occur to him what a stupid decision he'd made. It was just past noon: the boys would be in school. He was just about to leave when the door opened and a snuffling Adam appeared, his nose red and his eyes glazed.

'Are you sick?' Gösta asked.

The boy nodded, and as if corroboration were necessary, he sneezed loudly and then blew his nose on the handkerchief he was holding. 'I've got a cold,' he said, in a voice that clearly demonstrated how stuffed up his nose was.

'May I come in?'

Adam stepped aside. 'Okay, but it's at your own risk,' he said, sneezing again.

Gösta felt a light shower of virus-bearing saliva strike his hand, which he calmly wiped on the sleeve of his shirt. A couple of days sick leave wouldn't be so bad. He'd gladly suffer a runny nose if he could stretch out on the sofa at home and watch a DVD of the latest Masters tournament. He had been waiting for a chance to study Tiger's swing in slow motion.

'Babba isn't 'obe,' Adam snuffled.

Gösta frowned as he followed the boy into the kitchen. Then he worked it out. Adam must have meant to say 'Mamma isn't home.' It crossed Gösta's mind that he shouldn't really be interviewing a minor without a legal guardian present, but he quickly dismissed the thought. Had Ernst been here, he would have given Gösta his full support – as in Ernst his former colleague, rather than the dog. Gösta chuckled at that, drawing a puzzled look from Adam.

They sat down at the kitchen table, which still bore traces of that morning's breakfast: breadcrumbs, dabs of butter, and a little puddle of O'Boy chocolate drink.

'So,' said Gösta, drumming his fingers on the table and instantly regretting it when his fingers came away covered in sticky crumbs. He wiped them on his trousers and started again.

'So. How . . . are you taking this whole thing?' The question sounded odd even to him. He wasn't particularly good at talking with kids or with so-called traumatized people. Not that he really went along with any of that nonsense. Good Lord, the old man was dead when they found him, so how bad could it have been? He'd seen a few stiffs in his years on the force, and it had never made him feel traumatized.

Adam blew his nose and then straightened his shoulders. 'Er, okay, I suppose. Everybody at school thinks it's cool.'

'How did the two of you happen to go there in the first place?'

'It was Mattias's idea.' Adam mumbled the name, but by now Gösta was used to the way the boy's cold was affecting his speech, and he could decipher what he said.

'Everybody around here knows that those old guys are weirdos who are obsessed with World War II and stuff like that, and somebody at school said they had a load of cool stuff at their house, so Mattias thought we should go in and check it out . . .' His torrent of words was suddenly cut off by such a big sneeze that Gösta actually jumped.

'So it was Mattias who thought you should break in?' said Gösta, giving Adam a stern look.

'I don't know if I'd call it "breaking in" . . .' Adam squirmed. 'We weren't going to steal anything, we just wanted to take a look. And we thought they were both away, so they probably wouldn't even notice that we'd been there.'

'Well, I suppose I'll have to take your word for it,' said Gösta. 'Had you ever been inside their house before?'

'No, word of honour,' said Adam earnestly. 'That was the first time we went there.'

'I'm going to need to take your fingerprints so I can verify what you're telling me. And so we can rule out your prints. Do you have a problem with that?'

'No, not at all,' said Adam, his eyes shining. 'I always watch *CSI*. I know how important that is – to rule someone out. And then they put all the fingerprints in the computer to find out who else has been inside.'

'Exactly. That's exactly how we work,' said Gösta with a solemn expression. Inside, he was having a good laugh. Put all the fingerprints in the computer. Oh, sure.

He got out the equipment he needed to take Adam's fingerprints: an ink pad and a card with ten squares in which he carefully pressed the boy's fingers, one after the other.

'That's it,' he said with satisfaction. 'We're done.'

'Do you scan them in, or how do you do it?' asked Adam.

'Right, we scan them in,' said Gösta, 'and then we run them through the database you were talking about. We have every Swedish citizen over eighteen in the database. And a number of foreigners too. Via Interpol, you know. We're connected with them. Interpol, I mean. Via a direct link. And with the FBI and CIA, too.'

'Awesome!' said Adam, looking at Gösta with admiration.

Gösta laughed all the way back to Tanumshede.

He set the table with great care, using the yellow tablecloth that he knew Britta liked so much. The white china with the raised pattern. The candleholders they'd received as a wedding gift. And a few flowers in a vase. No matter what the time of year, Britta had always had flowers in the house. She was a regular customer at the florist's, or at least she used to be. These days it was usually Herman who bought the flowers. He wanted everything to be the way it had always been. Maybe if everything around her remained unchanged the downward spiral might at least be slowed, even if it couldn't be stopped altogether.

The worst was in the beginning. Before they received the diagnosis. Britta had always been so meticulous about things. None of the family could understand why she suddenly couldn't find her car keys, or why she would call a grandchild by the wrong name, or find it impossible to remember the phone numbers of friends she'd known most of her life. They'd blamed it on fatigue and stress. She'd started taking multivitamins and drinking *Blutsaft*, thinking it would combat whatever nutritional deficiency she was suffering from. But there came a point when they could no longer close their eyes to the fact that something was seriously wrong.

The diagnosis had rendered them both speechless. Then Britta had let out a sob. That was all: one sob. She'd given Herman's hand a squeeze, and he'd squeezed back. They both knew what it meant. The life that they'd shared for fifty-five years was about to change inexorably. The disease was slowly going to break down her mind, cause her to lose more and more of herself: her memories, her personality. The abyss gaped wide and deep before them.

A year had passed since then. The good moments were

now few and far between. Herman's hands shook as he folded the paper napkins. Britta had always formed them into fans, but even though he'd watched her countless times he couldn't manage it himself. After the fourth attempt, anger and frustration surged up inside him, and he tore the napkin to shreds that floated down on to the plate. He sat down on a chair and tried to pull himself together as he wiped a tear from his eye.

They'd had fifty-five years together. Good years. Happy years. Of course they'd had their ups and downs, just like in every marriage. But the foundation had always remained solid. They'd become adults together, he and Britta. Especially after they'd had Anna-Greta. He'd been so proud of Britta. Before their daughter was born, he had to admit that he'd sometimes found his wife to be rather shallow and superficial. But from the first day she held Anna-Greta in her arms, she'd changed. It was as if becoming a mother had given her a foundation that she'd lacked until then. They'd had three daughters. Three blessed daughters. And his love for his wife had grown with each birth.

He felt a hand on his shoulder. 'Pappa? What's wrong? You didn't answer when I knocked, so I decided to come in.'

Herman quickly wiped his eyes and put on a smile when he saw the worried expression on his eldest daughter's face. But he couldn't fool her. She wrapped her arms around him and pressed her cheek against his.

'Is this one of the bad days, Pappa?'

He nodded and for a moment allowed himself to feel like a child in his daughter's arms. They'd brought her up well, he and Britta. Anna-Greta was a warm and considerate person, and a loving grandmother to two of their great-grandchildren. Sometimes he couldn't understand how things had happened so fast. How could this grey-haired woman in her fifties be the daughter who had toddled about the house and wrapped him around her little finger?

'Time passes, Anna-Greta,' he said at last, patting her arm as it lay across his chest.

'Yes, Pappa, time passes,' she said, hugging him even harder. She gave him an extra little squeeze and then let him go.

'I'll fold the napkins while you get the knives and forks. I think that would be best, judging by what I see here.' She pointed to the scraps of napkin lying like confetti on the table and gave him a wink.

'You're right, that would probably be best,' he said, smiling at his daughter gratefully. 'That would probably be best.'

'When are they supposed to get here?' called Patrik from the bedroom where, at Erica's request, he was changing into something more appropriate than jeans and a T-shirt. His protests – 'But it's just your sister and Dan coming to dinner . . .' – had got him nowhere. Having guests over for dinner apparently required something more than casual attire. End of story.

Erica opened the oven door to take a look at the baked fillet of pork. She had been feeling guilty ever since she yelled at Patrik the day before, so to make up for it she was cooking one of his favourite dishes: fillet of pork baked in puff pastry, with a port wine sauce and mashed potatoes. It was what she'd cooked for him the first time she invited him over. The first night that they'd . . . She laughed to herself and shut the oven door. It seemed so long ago, even though it was only a few years back. Much as she loved Patrik, it was strange how quickly the daily routines and the demands of child-care could kill off any desire to make love five times in a row, the way they had on that first night. Nowadays the mere thought of it left her feeling worn out. Once a week seemed a real achievement.

'They'll be here in half an hour,' she shouted upstairs and then began making the sauce. She'd already changed into black trousers and a lilac blouse – one of her favourites from

114

the years when she'd lived in Stockholm and still had a decent number of shops to choose from. Just to be on the safe side, she'd put on an apron, and Patrik whistled appreciatively when he came into the kitchen.

'What do my weary eyes see here? A revelation. A divinely glamorous creature, but with a touch of homespun chic and culinariness.'

'There's no such word as "culinariness",' said Erica with a laugh as Patrik kissed the back of her neck.

'There is now,' he said, winking. Then he took a step back and did a pirouette in the middle of the kitchen. 'So? Will I do? Or do I need to go back upstairs and change into something else?'

'Stop it, you make it sound like I'm a real nag.' Erica looked him up and down with a stern expression but then laughed and said: 'Very nice. You're a sight for sore eyes. Now, if you can just set the table, maybe I'll start to remember why I married you.'

'Set the table? Consider it done!'

Half an hour later, at precisely seven o'clock when the doorbell rang, the food was ready and the table was set. Anna and Dan appeared at the door, along with Emma and Adrian, who came right in, calling for Maja. Their little cousin was very popular.

'Who is that cute guy, Erica?' said Anna. 'And what have you done with Patrik? It's about time you traded him in for a fancier model.'

Patrik gave Anna a hug. 'Nice to see you too, my dear sister-in-law. So, how are the turtle doves doing? Erica and I are honoured that you can tear yourselves away from the bedroom long enough to drop by and see us in our humble abode.'

'Cut it out,' said Anna, blushing as she batted Patrik in the chest. But the look that she gave Dan showed that Patrik actually had a point.

They spent a very pleasant evening together. Emma and Adrian were happy to keep Maja entertained until it was time to put her to bed, and then the two of them fell asleep at opposite ends of the sofa. The food received the praise that it deserved, the wine was excellent and quickly disappeared from the bottles, and Erica enjoyed having her sister and Dan at the table for a nice dinner without any dark clouds on the horizon, without thinking about everything that had happened in the past. Just pleasant conversation and good-natured banter.

The mood was suddenly shattered by the urgent ringing of Dan's mobile.

'Sorry, I just need to see who could be calling me at this time of night,' said Dan. He went out and retrieved his mobile from his jacket pocket, frowning at the display as if he didn't recognize the number.

'Hello? This is Dan,' he said. 'Who's this? Sorry, but I can't hear what you're . . . Belinda? Where? What? But I've been drinking wine, and I can't . . . Put her in a taxi and send her over here. Right now! Yes, I'll pay the driver when she arrives. Just make sure she gets here.' He rattled off Patrik and Erica's address and hung up. 'I don't believe it!'

'What's going on?' asked Anna, worried.

'It's Belinda. Apparently she went to some party and now she's drunk. That was one of her friends. They're going to send her here in a cab.'

'But I thought she was staying with Pernilla in Munkedal.'

'So did I, but clearly that's not where she went. Her friend was calling from Grebbestad.'

Dan began punching numbers on his mobile. It sounded as if he'd interrupted his ex-wife's beauty sleep. He went into the kitchen, and they could hear only bits and pieces of the conversation, but it didn't sound particularly friendly. A few minutes later he came back to the dining room and sat down at the table shaking his head in frustration.

116

'Apparently Belinda told her mother she was going to spend the night with a friend. And the friend most likely said that she was going to spend the night with Belinda. Instead, the two of them went to some party in Grebbestad. Damnit! I thought I could count on her to keep an eye on the girl!'

'You mean Pernilla?' said Anna, stroking his arm to calm him down. 'It's not that easy, Dan. It's the oldest trick in the book, but even you could have been taken in by it.'

'No, I wouldn't!' replied Dan angrily. 'I would have phoned her friend's parents during the evening to hear how things were going. I would never trust a seventeen-year-old. How stupid can anyone be? Shouldn't I be able to rely on her to take care of the kids?'

'Calm down,' said Anna sternly. 'The most important thing right now is to look after Belinda when she gets here.' Dan opened his mouth to say something but she stopped him before he could speak. 'And we're not going to yell at her tonight. We'll save that conversation for the morning, after she's sober. Okay?' Everyone at the table, including Dan, could tell that this was non-negotiable. He nodded.

'I'll go make up the guest room,' said Erica, getting up from the table.

'And I'll get a bucket,' said Patrik, fervently hoping that he wouldn't find himself saying the same thing when Maja was a teenager.

A few minutes later they heard a car pull up outside, and Dan and Anna hurried to the front door. Anna paid the driver while Dan lifted Belinda out of the car. She'd been lying across the back seat like a rag doll.

'Pappa . . .' she said, slurring the word. Then she put her arms around his neck and pressed her face against his chest. The smell of vomit made Dan feel sick, but at the same time he felt a tremendous tenderness for his daughter, who suddenly seemed so small and fragile. It had been years since he'd carried her in his arms.

A retching sound from Belinda made him instinctively move her head, turning it away from his chest. A stinking, reddish sludge poured out on to Erica and Patrik's front steps. Clearly red wine had been her drink of choice.

'Bring her inside. Don't worry about the mess, we'll hose it off later,' said Erica, motioning for Dan and Anna to come in. 'Put her in the shower. Anna and I will rinse her off and give her some clean clothes to wear.'

In the shower Belinda started to cry. The sound was heartbreaking. Anna stroked her hair as Erica carefully rubbed her dry with a towel.

'Shhh, everything's going to be fine, don't worry,' said Anna, pulling a dry T-shirt over Belinda's head.

'Kim was supposed to be there . . . And I thought that . . . But he told Linda he thought I was . . . ugly . . .' She could barely get the words out between sobs.

Anna looked at Erica over Belinda's head. Neither of them would have wanted to trade places with the girl for anything in the world. There was nothing so painful as a teenaged broken heart. They'd both been through it and understood why, in the circumstances, she'd sought to drown her sorrows in red wine. But that was only a temporary respite. Tomorrow Belinda would feel even worse, if that was possible – this was something else the sisters knew from personal experience. But all they could do was put her to bed. They'd deal with the rest in the morning.

Mellberg stood with his hand on the doorknob, weighing the pros and cons. It was undeniable that the 'cons' were going to win by some distance. But he had come, nonetheless, and there were two reasons for that. First, he had nothing better to do with his evening. Second, he kept seeing Rita's dark eyes in his mind. He was still wondering whether these two factors were sufficient cause for him to do something as absurd as attend a salsa class. The place would probably be full of desperate women, women who thought they could snag a guy by going to a dance class. How pathetic. For a moment he considered turning on his heel and going over to the petrol station to buy a packet of crisps before heading home to watch his favourite sitcom, *Full Freezer with Stefan and Christer*. The mere thought made him laugh. Those two were such a riot.

Mellberg had no sooner made up his mind to opt for Plan B than the door opened in front of him.

'Bertil! How nice to see you! Come in. We're just about to start.' And before he knew it, Rita had grabbed his hand and pulled him inside the gym. Latin-American music was blaring from a portable stereo on the floor, and four couples looked at him with interest as he came in. An equal number of men and women, Mellberg noted with surprise, and his image of himself as a meaty bone that would be torn apart by a gang of voracious bitches in heat instantly faded.

'You'll have to dance with me. You can help me demonstrate the moves,' said Rita, leading him to the centre of the floor. She positioned herself in front of him, took one of his hands in hers and put his other arm around her waist. Mellberg had to restrain an urge to grab hold of her lovely plump body. He simply couldn't understand men who preferred skinny women.

'All right, Bertil, pay attention now,' said Rita sternly, and he stood up straight. 'Watch what Bertil and I do,' said Rita to the other couples. 'For the ladies: right foot forward, shift your weight to your left foot, and right foot back. For the men: the same move except using the opposite foot; left foot forward, weight on your right foot, then left foot back. We'll keep doing the sequence until everybody gets it.'

Mellberg fought to master the steps. At first it was as if his brain was determined to erase even the most basic information, such as which was his right foot and which was his left. But Rita was a good teacher. She firmly led the way, making him move his feet forward and back, and it wasn't long before he started to get the hang of it.

'And now . . . we'll start moving our hips,' said Rita, giving her students an encouraging look. 'We Swedes are so stiff. But salsa is all about movement, sensuality, and softness.'

She demonstrated what she meant by swaying her hips to the music, making it look as if they were ebbing back and forth, like a wave. Mellberg watched with fascination as Rita moved her body. It looked so easy when she did it. Determined to impress her, he set about mimicking her movements as he moved his feet forward and back in the pattern that he thought he'd memorized. But nothing worked any more. His hips felt wooden, and all attempts to coordinate the movement of his hips with his feet resulted in a total short circuit. He stopped abruptly, a frustrated expression on his face. And to make matters worse, his hair chose that moment to slip down over his left ear. Quickly he pushed it back into place, hoping that no one had noticed. But a stifled giggle from one of the other couples crushed any illusions on that score.

'I know it's difficult, Bertil. It just takes practice,' said Rita, urging him to have another go. 'Listen to the music, Bertil, listen. And then let your body follow the beat. But don't look at your feet, look at me. In salsa you always look the woman in the eye. It's a dance of love, a dance of passion.'

She fixed her gaze on him, and with great effort he managed to look at her instead of at his feet. At first it seemed hopeless. But after a while, under Rita's gentle tutelage, he felt something happening. Only now did his body truly seem to hear the music. His hips began moving softly and sensually. He looked deeper into Rita's eyes. And as the Latin American rhythms pulsed from the stereo, he could feel himself falling.

KRISTIANSAND 1943

It wasn't that Axel enjoyed taking risks, nor was he particularly brave. Of course he was afraid. He'd be a fool not to be scared. But it was simply something that he felt he had to do. He couldn't just sit back and allow evil to take over without lifting a finger.

He stood at the rail, feeling the wind whip at his face. He loved the smell of salt water. He'd always been envious of the fishermen, out on the sea from early morning until late in the evening, letting their boats take them where the fish were plentiful. Axel kept his envy to himself; he knew that they would only laugh at him. They wouldn't believe that he, the doctor's son, who was supposed to continue his studies and become something grand, would be jealous of them. Envious of the blisters on their hands, the smell of fish that never left their clothes, the uncertainty about whether they would return home each time they went out. They would find it both absurd and presumptuous that he should wish to live the life of a fisherman. They would never understand. But he felt in every fibre of his being that this was the sort of life he was actually destined for. Of course he had a good head for studying, but he never felt as comfortable with books and learning as he did out here, on the rolling deck of a boat, with the wind gusting through his hair and the smell of fish in his nostrils.

Erik, on the other hand, loved the world of books. A happy glow suffused him as he sat on his bed in the evening, his eyes racing over the pages of some book that was much too old and thick to prompt any kind of enthusiasm in anyone else. He devoured information, he revelled in acquiring knowledge, gorging on facts, dates, names, and places. Axel was fascinated by this, but it also made him sad. They were so different, the two brothers. Maybe it was the age gap. Because he was four years older, they'd never played together, never shared toys. Moreover their parents treated them so differently. They put Axel on a pedestal in a way that upset the balance in the family, turning him into something he wasn't and diminishing Erik. But how could he stop them? He could only do what he was meant to do.

'We'll be entering the harbour any minute now.'

Axel jumped at the sound of Elof's dry voice behind him. He hadn't heard him approach.

'I'll slip ashore as soon as we dock. I'll be gone about an hour.'

Elof nodded. 'Be careful, boy,' he said, giving Axel one last look before he went astern to take over the helm.

Ten minutes later Axel took a good look around before he climbed up on to the wharf. He caught a glimpse of German uniforms in all directions on shore, but most of the soldiers seemed to be busy checking the boats. He felt his pulse quicken but forced himself to assume the same nonchalant air as the seamen who were going about their business loading and unloading the ships. He wasn't carrying anything this time. The purpose of this trip was to pick something up. Axel didn't know what was in the document that he'd been asked to smuggle back to Sweden. And he didn't want to know. All he knew was the name of the recipient.

His instructions were quite clear. The man he was looking

for would be standing at the far end of the harbour, wearing a blue cap and brown shirt. Keeping an alert eye on his surroundings, Axel approached the corner of the harbour where the man was supposed to be. So far it was all going to plan; he passed among the fishermen unnoticed by the Germans until he caught sight of a man who fit the description. He was stacking crates and seemed completely focused on the job. Axel headed towards him, careful not to shift his gaze or cast furtive glances – that would be like painting a target on his chest.

When he was almost level with the man, who appeared not to have spotted him, Axel picked up the closest crate and added it to a stack. Out of the corner of his eye he saw his contact drop something on the ground next to the crates. Leaning down to pick up a crate, Axel first snatched up the rolled paper and stuffed it into his pocket. The handover had been successfully made, even though he and the man hadn't yet exchanged a single glance.

Relief flooded through his veins. The handover was always the most critical moment. Once that was accomplished, there was much less risk that . . .

'Halt! Hände hoch!'

The German commands came out of nowhere. Axel cast a surprised look at the man next to him, whose shamefaced expression told him what was going on. It was a trap. Either the entire assignment had been staged in order to capture him, or else the Germans had come across information about what was in play and forced those involved to help them set the trap. The Gestapo had probably been watching him from the moment he stepped ashore until the delivery was completed. And the document was now burning a hole in his pocket. He raised his hands in a gesture of surrender. The game was up.

A loud knock on the door interrupted his morning ritual. Each morning the same routine. First shower. Then shave. Then he'd make breakfast, consisting of two eggs, a slice of rye bread with butter and cheese, and a big cup of coffee. Always the same breakfast, which he would eat in front of the TV. Another knock on the door. Annoyed, Frans got up and went to open it.

'Hi, Frans.' His son was standing on the doorstep with that harsh look in his eye that had become so familiar.

Frans could no longer remember a time when everything had been different. But he had to accept what he couldn't change, and this was one of those things. Only in his dreams would he feel that small hand holding his; a faint memory from a time long, long ago.

With a barely audible sigh he moved aside to let his son come in.

'Hi, Kjell,' he said. 'What brings you here today to visit your old father?'

'Erik Frankel,' said Kjell coldly, glaring at his father as if expecting a particular reaction.

'I'm in the middle of breakfast. Come on in.'

Kjell followed him into the living room, taking a good look around. He'd never been inside the flat before.

Frans didn't bother to offer his son coffee. He knew in advance what his response would be.

'So, what's this about Erik Frankel?'

'I suppose you know he's dead.' It was a statement, not a question.

Frans nodded. 'Yes, I heard that old Erik was dead. It's a shame.'

'Is that your sincere opinion? That it's a shame?' Kjell stared at his father, and Frans knew full well what was in his mind. He hadn't come over as a son but as a journalist.

Frans took his time before answering. There was so much roiling below the surface. So many memories. But these were things he would never tell his son. Kjell wouldn't understand. He'd condemned his father long ago, and now they stood on opposite sides of a wall so high that it was impossible to peer over the top. Frans knew he was largely the one to blame. Kjell hadn't seen much of his father, the old jailbird, when he was a child. His mother had brought him along to the prison a few times, but the sight of that little face, filled with questions, in the cold, inhospitable visitors' room had made Frans harden his heart and forbid any more visits. He'd thought he was doing what was best for the boy. Maybe he'd been wrong, but it was too late to do anything about it now.

'Yes, I'm sorry that Erik's dead. We knew each other when we were young, and I have only good memories of Erik. Later we went our separate ways . . .' Frans threw out his hands. He didn't need to explain to Kjell. The two of them knew all there was to know about taking separate paths.

'But that's not true. According to my source, you had contact with Erik later on. And Sweden's Friends have shown an interest in the Frankel brothers. You don't mind if I take notes, do you?' Kjell made a show of setting his notepad on the table, giving his father a defiant look as he put pen to paper.

Frans shrugged and waved his hand dismissively. He didn't feel like playing this game any more. There was so much anger inside Kjell, and he could feel every ounce of it. It was the same all-consuming rage that had afflicted Frans ever since he could remember, landing him in trouble and destroying the things he held dear. His son had found a way to channel his anger, venting it upon politicians and leaders of industry in the newspaper column which bore his byline. Though they'd chosen opposite sides of the political spectrum, father and son had much in common. They shared the same capacity to hate, the same burning anger. That was what had made Frans feel so at home with the prison's Nazi sympathizers during his first jail sentence. He'd understood the hatred that drove them. And they'd welcomed him because they viewed his anger as an asset, proof of his strength. Plus he was good at debating the issues – thanks to his father, who had schooled him in rhetoric. Belonging to the jail's Nazi gang had given him status and power; by the time he left prison he'd grown into the role. It was no longer possible to differentiate him from his opinions. His politics defined him. He had a feeling that the same was true of Kjell.

'Where were we?' Kjell glanced down at his notepad, which was still blank. 'Oh, right. Apparently you've been in contact with Erik.'

'Only for the sake of our old friendship. Nothing significant. And nothing that could be linked to his death.'

'So you say,' replied Kjell, 'but it's up to others to determine whether it's true or not. What sort of contact did you have? Did you threaten him?'

Frans snorted. 'I don't know where you got your information from, but I never threatened Erik Frankel. You've written enough about people who share my views to know that there are always a few . . . hotheads who can't think rationally. All I did was to warn Erik about the risks.'

126

'People who share your views,' said Kjell with a scorn that verged on loathing. 'You mean those lunatic throwbacks who think they can seal Sweden's borders.'

'Call them what you will,' said Frans wearily. 'But I didn't threaten Erik Frankel. And now I'd appreciate it if you'd leave.'

For a brief moment it looked as if Kjell might refuse. Then he stood up, leaned over his father, and fixed his eyes on him.

'You were no father to me, and I can live with that. But I swear if you drag my son any deeper into this than you've already done, I'll . . .' He clenched his hands into fists.

Frans glanced up at him, calmly meeting his gaze. 'I haven't dragged your son into anything. He's old enough to think for himself. He makes his own choices.'

'Same way you did?' spat Kjell and then stormed out, as if he could no longer stand to be in the same room with his father.

Frans didn't move, feeling his heart pounding in his chest. As he listened to the front door slam, he thought about fathers and sons. And about the choices that were made for them, whether they liked it or not.

'Did you have a nice weekend?' Paula directed her question at both Martin and Gösta as she added coffee to the coffee-maker. Her colleagues merely nodded gloomily. Neither of them was particularly fond of Monday mornings. Besides, Martin hadn't slept well all weekend.

Lately he'd started lying awake at night, worrying about the baby that was due to arrive in a couple of months. Not about whether the child was wanted. Because it was. Very much so. But it had only just dawned on him what a huge responsibility he was taking on. He would have to protect, raise, and take care of a tiny life, this little person, on all possible levels. It was this that kept him awake at night, staring up at the ceiling, while Pia's big belly rose and fell in time with her gentle breathing. What he saw in the future was bullying and guns and drugs and sexual abuse and sorrows and misfortunes. When he thought about it, there was no end to all the terrible things that might befall their child. And for the first time he wondered whether he was really up to the task. But it was a bit late to be worrying about that now. In a couple of months the baby would be here.

'What a cheerful pair you are.' Paula sat down and rested her arms on the table as she regarded Gösta and Martin with a smile.

'It should be against the law to be so cheerful on a Monday morning,' said Gösta, getting up to refill his coffee cup. The water hadn't finishing running through yet, so when he pulled out the pot, coffee dribbled on to the hotplate. Gösta didn't even notice as he set the pot back in place after filling his cup.

'Gösta,' said Paula sternly as he turned his back on the mess he'd made and sat down at the table again. 'You can't just leave it like that. You need to wipe up the coffee you spilled.'

Gösta cast a glance over his shoulder at the puddle of coffee he'd left on the counter. 'Oh, sorry,' he said morosely, and went over to clean it up.

Martin laughed. 'Good to see that somebody knows how to keep you in line.'

'Oh, right, typical woman. They always have to be so damned finicky.'

Paula was about to say something scathing when they heard a sound out in the corridor. A sound that didn't belong to the normal noises of the station. The merry prattling of a child.

Martin craned his neck, an eager look on his face. 'That must be . . .' he began. Before he could finish the sentence Patrik appeared in the doorway, holding Maja in his arms.

128

'Hi, everybody!'

'Hi!' said Martin happily. 'I see you just couldn't stay away any longer.'

Patrik smiled. 'Nope, the little lady and I thought we'd just stop by to see that you're actually working. Right, sweetie?' Maja gurgled happily, waving her arms about. Then she started squirming to show that she wanted to get down. Patrik complied, and she instantly set off on her wobbly legs, heading straight for Martin.

'Hi, Maja. So you recognize your Uncle Martin, huh? Remember how we looked at the flowers together? You know what, Uncle Martin is going to go find a box of toys for you.' He trotted off to get the box that they kept at the station for those occasions when someone came in with a child who needed to be kept busy for a while. Maja was overjoyed with the treasure chest that appeared in the kitchen a few minutes later.

'Thanks, Martin,' said Patrik. He poured himself a cup of coffee and sat down at the table. 'So, how are things going?' he asked, grimacing as he took his first sip. It had taken him only a week to forget how terrible station coffee was.

'A bit slow,' said Martin, 'but we do have a number of leads.' He told Patrik about the conversations they'd had with Frans Ringholm and Axel Frankel. Patrik nodded with interest.

'And Gösta collected the fingerprints and shoe prints from one of the boys. We just need to get the same from the other boy and then we can eliminate their prints from the investigation.'

'What did the boy say?' asked Patrik. 'Did they see anything of interest? Why did they decide to break into the house in the first place? Did you come up with any leads worth pursuing?'

'No, I didn't get anything useful out of the boy,' said Gösta sullenly. He felt as if Patrik was questioning how he did his job, and he didn't appreciate it. At the same time, Patrik's questions had sparked something in his brain. Something was stirring there, something that he knew he ought to bring up to the surface. Or maybe it was just his imagination. Either way, it would only set Patrik off again if he mentioned it. 'The only thing we've turned up that's of real interest is the link to Sweden's Friends. Erik Frankel doesn't seem to have had any enemies, and we haven't found any other possible motives.'

'Have you checked his bank accounts? You might find something interesting there,' said Patrik, thinking out loud.

Martin shook his head, annoyed that he hadn't thought of doing that himself. 'We'll do that ASAP,' he said. 'And we also need to ask Axel whether Erik had a woman in his life. Or man, for that matter. Somebody he might have confided to. Another thing we need to do today is have a talk with the woman who cleaned house for Erik and Axel.'

'Good,' said Patrik, nodding. 'Maybe then you'll find out why she hasn't cleaned their house all summer. Which would explain why Erik's body wasn't found earlier.'

Paula stood up. 'I think I'm going to ring Axel right now and find out about any possible love interests Erik might have had.' She left the room.

'Do you have the letters that Frans sent to Erik?' asked Patrik.

Martin got up. 'I'll go and get them, since I assume you'd like to have a look at them, right?'

Patrik shrugged, feigning nonchalance. 'Well, since I'm here anyway . . .'

Martin laughed. 'A leopard can't change its spots. But aren't you on paternity leave?'

'Okay, okay, just wait until you're in the same position. There are only a certain amount of hours you can spend in the sandbox. And Erica is working at home, so she's only too happy if we stay out of her hair for a while.'

'She knows your little expedition with Maja was heading for the police station?' Martin's eyes twinkled.

'Well, maybe not, but I'm just dropping by for a moment. To see how you're all holding up.'

'Then I suppose I'd better fetch the letters, since you're just dropping by.'

A few minutes later Martin returned with the five letters, which had now been inserted in plastic sleeves. Maja glanced up from her toy-box, stretching her hand out towards the papers Martin was holding, but he handed them to Patrik. 'Sorry, sweetheart, these aren't for you to play with.' Maja responded with a slightly offended expression but then went back to exploring what was in the box on the floor.

Patrik placed the letters next to each other on the table. He read them in silence, deep furrows on his brow.

'There's nothing specific. He mostly just repeats the same things. Says that Erik should lie low because he can't protect him any longer. And that there are forces within Sweden's Friends that don't think before they act.' Patrik continued reading. 'And here I get the impression that Erik has replied, because Frans writes:

'I think what you say is wrong. You talk about consequences. About responsibility. I'm talking about burying the
past. About looking forward. We have different opinions,
different points of view, you and I. But our point of
departure is the same. At the bottom is the same monster,
lurking. Unlike you, I think it would be unwise to waken
the old monster to life. Certain bones should remain
untouched. I already gave you my opinion about what
happened in my previous letter, and I won't speak of it
again. I recommend that you do the same. Right now I've
chosen to act in a protective capacity, but if the situation
changes, if the monster is brought out into the open, I may
feel differently.'

131

Patrik looked up at Martin. 'Did you ask Frans what he meant by this? What's this "old monster" that he talks about?'

'We haven't had a chance to ask him yet. But we'll be conducting several more interviews with him.'

Paula appeared in the doorway.

'I've managed to discover a woman in Erik's life. I did as Patrik suggested and phoned Axel. And he said that for the past four years Erik has had a "good friend", as he put it, by the name of Viola Ellmander. And I've already talked to her. We can go see her this morning.'

'That was fast work,' said Patrik, giving Paula an appreciative smile.

'Want to come along?' asked Martin impulsively. But then he cast an eye at Maja, who was intently studying the eyes of a doll and added, 'No, of course that wouldn't work.'

'Sure it would. You can leave her here with me,' they heard Annika say from the doorway. She gave Patrik a hopeful look as she smiled at Maja, and was immediately rewarded with a smile in return. Since she had no children of her own, Annika was happy to have an opportunity to borrow one.

'Hmm . . .' said Patrik hesitantly.

'Don't you think I can handle it?' asked Annika. She folded her arms, pretending to take offence.

'It's not that,' said Patrik, still hesitant. But then his sense of curiosity won out and he nodded. 'Okay, let's do it. I'll tag along for a while, so long as I'm back before lunch. But call me if you have any problems. And she needs to eat around ten thirty, and she still prefers mashed food, but I think I have a jar of meat sauce you can warm up in the microwave, and she usually gets tired after eating, but all you have to do is put her in the pushchair and wheel it around a bit, and don't forget her dummy and she wants her teddy bear next to her when she sleeps and –'

'Stop, stop,' said Annika, holding up her hands with a

laugh. 'We'll be fine, don't worry. I'll make sure she doesn't starve to death in my care, and we'll manage the nap too.'

'Thanks, Annika,' said Patrik, getting to his feet. Then he squatted down next to his daughter and stroked her blonde hair. 'Pappa is leaving for a little while, but you're going to stay here with Annika. Okay?' Maja looked up at him, wide-eyed, for a moment but then shifted her attention back to pulling out the doll's eyelashes. Slightly miffed, Patrik stood up and said, 'Well, you can see how indispensable I am. Have a nice time.'

He gave Annika a hug and then went out to the garage. There was a surge of elation as he got behind the wheel of the police car while Martin climbed into the passenger seat next to him. Then Patrik backed the vehicle out of the garage and headed for Fjällbacka. It was all he could do to stop himself bursting into song.

Axel slowly replaced the receiver. Suddenly everything seemed so unreal. It was as if he was still lying in bed, dreaming. The house was so empty without Erik. They'd been careful about giving each other space, eating their meals at different times and keeping to their rooms in separate parts of the house, not wanting to intrude on each other's privacy. Sometimes several days would pass without them even speaking to one another. But that shouldn't be interpreted as meaning they weren't close. They were. Or they had been, Axel corrected himself. Now a different kind of silence filled the house. A silence that was not the same as when Erik used to sit in the library, reading. Back then they'd always been able to break the silence by exchanging a few words, if they felt like it. This silence was all-encompassing and endless.

Erik had never brought Viola home with him. Nor had he ever spoken about her. The only contact Axel ever had with her was if he happened to answer the phone when she rang. These calls would usually be followed by Erik disappearing for a couple of days. He'd pack a small bag with just the essentials, say a brief goodbye, and leave. Occasionally Axel would feel jealous. He'd never been able to form a lasting romantic relationship. There had been women, of course, but they never stuck around for long. His fault, not theirs. Love couldn't compete with his other, all-consuming passion. Over the years his work had become a demanding mistress that left no room for anything else. It was his life, his identity, his innermost core. He didn't really know when that had happened. No, that was a lie – he did.

In the silent house, Axel sat down on the overstuffed chair next to the bureau in the hall. And for the first time since his brother died, he wept.

Erica was enjoying the silence in the house. She could even leave the door open to her workroom without being disturbed by any outside noise. She propped her feet up on the desk and thought about the conversation she'd had with Erik Frankel's brother. It had opened some sort of floodgate for her, provoking a tremendous, insatiable curiosity about aspects of her mother's life that she'd known nothing about, or even suspected. She sensed that Axel Frankel had told only a fraction of what he knew about her mother. But why was he holding back? What was there in Elsy's background that he wanted to hide from her? Erica reached for the diaries and started reading from where she'd left off a couple of days ago. But they offered no clue as to what might have prompted that odd tone in Axel's voice when he spoke of her mother.

Erica kept on reading, searching the pages for anything that might quell the uneasiness she was feeling. But it wasn't until she reached the final pages of the third book that she found something that might have a plausible link to Axel.

All of a sudden she knew what to do. She swung her legs

134

down from the desk, picked up the diaries and carefully slipped them into her handbag. After opening the front door to check on the temperature, she put on a light jacket and set off at a brisk pace.

She climbed the steep stairs to Badis, pausing at the top, sweating from exertion. The old restaurant looked deserted and abandoned now that the summer rush was over, but its popularity had been waning the past few years and even in the height of summer it was rarely busy. And yet it occupied a prime location on a hillside offering unobstructed views of the Fjällbacka archipelago. Sadly the building had fallen into disrepair over the years, and presumably it would require a major investment to make something of Badis.

The house she was looking for was located a bit beyond the restaurant, and she was hoping that the person she sought would be at home.

A pair of lively eyes looked at her when the door opened. 'Yes?' the woman said.

'My name is Erica Falck.' She hesitated for a moment. 'I'm the daughter of Elsy Moström.'

Something glittered in Britta's eyes. For a moment she just stood there, unmoving and without saying a word. Then she suddenly smiled and stepped aside.

'Yes, of course. Elsy's daughter. I can see it now. Come in.'

The house was bright and pleasant, and Erica's inquisitive gaze took in the scores of photos – children and grand-children, and maybe even a few great-grandchildren – that covered the walls. 'How many children do you have, ma'am?' she asked, studying the pictures.

'Three daughters. And for God's sake don't call me ma'am. It makes me feel so old. Not that I'm exactly young. But there's no reason a person has to feel old. Age is just a number, after all.'

'How true,' said Erica with a laugh. She liked this old lady.

'Come in and sit down,' said Britta, touching Erica's elbow lightly. After taking off her shoes and jacket, Erica followed her into the living room.

'You have such a nice home.'

'We've lived here for fifty-five years,' said Britta. Her face looked gentle and sunny whenever she smiled. She sat down on the big sofa with the floral upholstery and patted the cushion next to her. 'Sit here, so we can have a little chat. It's so nice to meet you. Elsy and I . . . we spent a lot of time together when we were young.'

For a moment Erica thought she heard the same odd undertone in Britta's voice that had crept into Axel's when he talked of her mother, but the next second it was gone, and Britta was smiling her gentle smile again.

'Well, I found a few things that my mother left behind when I was clearing out the attic and . . . well, they made me curious. I don't really know much about my mother's past. For instance, how did the two of you get to know each other?'

'We were classmates, Elsy and I. We always sat next to each other from our very first day at school.'

'And you were friends with Erik and Axel too?'

'More with Erik than Axel. Erik's brother was a few years older, and he probably thought us too childish. But he was a terribly handsome boy, that Axel.'

'Yes, that's what I heard,' laughed Erica. 'By the way, he's still handsome.'

'I'm inclined to agree with you, but don't tell my husband,' Britta whispered melodramatically.

'I promise I won't.' Erica was warming more and more to her mother's old friend. 'What about Frans? From what I understand, Frans Ringholm was also part of your little group. Is that right?'

Britta stiffened. 'Frans? Yes, well, Frans was also in our group.'

136

'It sounds as though you weren't too keen on Frans.'

'Not keen on him? Oh, but I was. I was terribly in love with him. But the feeling wasn't mutual. He only had eyes for . . . someone else.'

'Oh? And who was that?' asked Erica, even though she thought she knew the answer.

'Your mother. He followed her around like a puppy. Not that it did any good. Elsy would never have fallen for someone like Frans. Only a silly goose like me would make that mistake, because all I cared about then was how a boy looked. And he was definitely attractive. In that slightly dangerous way that seems so enticing to teenage girls but terrifying when they get older.'

'Oh, I don't know about that,' said Erica. 'Dangerous men seem to be enticing even to older women.'

'You're probably right,' said Britta, looking out the window. 'But, as luck would have it, I grew out of that phase. And grew out of liking Frans. He . . . he wasn't the sort of man I wanted in my life. Not like my Herman.'

'Aren't you judging yourself a bit harshly? You don't seem like a silly goose to me.'

'No, not now. But I might as well admit it – until I met Herman and had my first child . . . No, I was not a nice girl.'

Britta's candour surprised Erica. That was quite a harsh opinion she had of herself.

'What about Erik? What was he like?'

Again Britta turned her gaze to the window. She seemed to be considering how to answer. Then her expression softened. 'Erik was like a little old man even as a child. But I don't mean that in a negative way. He just seemed old for his age. And sensible, in an adult sort of way. He was always thinking about things. And reading. His nose was always in some book or other. Frans used to tease him about that. But Erik was probably a bit odd because of who his brother was.'

137

'I understand that Axel was very popular.'

'Axel was a hero. And the person who admired him most was Erik. He worshipped the ground his brother walked on. In Erik's eyes, Axel could do no wrong.' Britta patted Erica's leg and then stood up abruptly. 'You know what? I'm going to put on some coffee. Elsy's daughter. How nice. So very nice.'

Erica stayed where she was while Britta disappeared into the kitchen. She heard the clattering of china and trickling of water. Then not another sound. Erica waited calmly, sitting on the sofa and enjoying the view that stretched out in front of her. But after a few more minutes of silence, she started to smell something burning. 'Britta?' she called. 'Is everything all right?' No answer. She got up and went out to the kitchen to look for her hostess.

Britta was sitting at the kitchen table, staring into space. One of the burners on the stove was glowing a fiery red. An empty coffee pot stood on it, and it had just started to smoke. Erica rushed over to pull the pot off the stove. 'Damn!' she cried as she burned her hand. To quell the pain, she stuck her hand under running water. Then she turned to Britta.

'Britta?' she said gently. The woman's face had taken on such a vacant expression that for a moment Erica was afraid she must have suffered some sort of seizure. But then Britta turned to look at her.

'To think that you finally came over to say hello to me, Elsy.'

Erica gave her a puzzled look. She said, 'Britta, I'm Erica, Elsy's daughter.'

The words didn't seem to register with the old woman. 'Oh, Elsy,' she said, 'I've wanted to talk to you for a long time, to explain. But I just couldn't . . .'

'What couldn't you explain? What did you want to talk to Elsy about?' Erica sat down across from Britta, her heart

138

racing. For the first time she felt as if she were on the verge of discovering whatever secret it was that Erik and Axel had tried to hide from her.

But Britta just looked at her in confusion. Resisting the urge to shake her, force her to say what had been on the tip of her tongue, Erica repeated the question: 'What couldn't you explain? Something about my mother? What is it?'

Britta waved her hand dismissively but then leaned forward across the table. In a voice that was almost a whisper she hissed: 'Wanted to talk to you. But old bones. Must. Rest in peace. Will serve no purpose to . . . Erik said that . . . unknown soldier . . .' Her voice faded into a murmur and she stared into space again.

'What bones? What are you talking about? What did Erik say?' Without being aware of it, Erica was raising her voice. In the silence of the kitchen it sounded almost like a shriek. Britta clasped her hands over her ears and began babbling something incoherent, the way children do when they don't want to listen to someone scolding them.

'What's going on here? Who are you?' An angry male voice behind Erica made her spin round. A tall man with grey hair encircling a bald pate had appeared in the doorway clutching two Konsum grocery bags. Erica realized he must be Herman. She stood up.

'I'm sorry, I . . . My name is Erica Falck. Britta knew my mother when they were young, and I just wanted to ask her a few questions. It seemed harmless enough at first . . . but then . . . And she'd turned on the stove.' Erica could hear that she wasn't making any sense, but nothing about the situation seemed to make sense. Behind her, Britta's childish babble continued unabated.

'My wife has Alzheimer's,' said Herman, setting down the bags. Hearing the sorrow in his voice, Erica felt a pang of guilt. Alzheimer's – she should have guessed, given the rapid shift between perfect clarity and utter confusion. She'd read somewhere that the brains of Alzheimer's patients forced them into a kind of borderland where, in the end, only fog remained.

Herman went over to his wife and gently removed her hands from her ears. 'Britta, dear. I just had to go out to do the shopping. I'm back now. Shhh, it's all right, everything is fine.' He rocked her in his arms, and gradually the babbling stopped. He looked up at Erica. 'It's best if you leave now. And I'd prefer it if you didn't come back.'

'But your wife mentioned something about . . . I need to know . . .' Erica stumbled over her words, attempting to find the right thing to say, but Herman merely glared at her and said firmly:

'Don't come back.'

Feeling like an intruder, Erica slipped out of the house. Behind her she heard Herman speaking in a soothing tone to his wife. But in her head Britta's confused words about old bones still echoed. What could she have meant?

The geraniums were unusually splendid this summer. Viola walked around, lovingly plucking the withered petals. Dead-heading was a necessity if she wanted them to stay beautiful. By now her geranium beds were quite impressive. Each year she took cuttings and carefully planted them in small pots. As soon they'd grown big enough she would transfer them to a larger pot. Her favourite was the Mårbacka geranium. Nothing could match its beauty. There was something about the combination of the gossamer pink blossoms and the slightly ungainly and straggly stems that moved her beyond words. But the rose pelargonium was lovely too.

There were lots of geranium afficionados out there. Since her son had initiated her into the splendours of the Internet, she'd become a member of three different geranium forums and subscribed to four newsletters. But she found the most joy in exchanging emails with Lasse Anrell. If there was anyone who loved geraniums more than she did, it was him. They'd been corresponding by email ever since she attended one of his lectures. She'd had many questions to ask him that evening and he'd signed a copy of his book on geraniums for her. They'd taken a liking to each other, and now she looked forward to the emails that regularly appeared in her inbox. Erik used to tease her about that, saying she must be having an affair with Lasse Anrell behind his back, and that all the talk about geraniums was just a code for more amorous activities. Eric had his own theory as to what each term might mean; 'rose pelargonium' had a particular fascination for him, and he'd taken to calling her Rose Pelargonium . . . Viola blushed at the thought, but the crimson quickly disappeared from her face to be replaced by tears. For the thousandth time in the past few days, she was confronted with the realization that Erik was gone.

The soil eagerly soaked up the water as she cautiously poured a little into each saucer. It was important not to over-water geraniums. The soil should dry out properly in between waterings. In many ways, that was an appropriate metaphor for the relationship that she'd had with Erik. They were like two plants whose soil had been parched when they'd met, and they were fearful of over-watering. Thus they continued to live apart, they maintained their separate lives and saw each other only when they both felt like getting together. Early on, they'd made a promise that their relationship would be a mutual exchange of tenderness, love, and good conversation. Whenever the spirit moved them. The trivialities of daily life would never be allowed to weigh it down.

Hearing the knock on the door, Viola set down the watering can and wiped the tears on the sleeve of her blouse. She took a deep breath, cast one last glance at her geraniums to give herself strength, and went to open the door.

141

FJÄLLBACKA 1943

'Britta, calm down. What happened? Is he drunk again?' Elsy stroked her friend's back to soothe her as they sat on her bed. Britta nodded. She tried to say something, but it came out as a sob. Elsy pulled her close, still stroking her back.

'Shhh . . . Soon you'll be able to move out. Get a job somewhere. Get away from all the misery at home.'

'I'm never . . . I'm never coming back,' sobbed Britta, leaning against her friend.

Elsy could feel her blouse getting wet from Britta's tears, but she didn't care.

'Was he mean to your mother again?'

Britta nodded. 'He slapped her face. I didn't see any more after that. I took off. Oh, if only I were a boy, I would have punched him until he was black and blue.'

'It would be such a waste of a pretty face if you were a boy,' said Elsy, hugging Britta and laughing. She knew her friend well enough to realize that a little flattery could always brighten her mood.

'Very funny,' said Britta, her sobs subsiding. 'But I feel sorry for my little brothers and sister.'

'There's not much you can do about that,' said Elsy, picturing Britta's three younger siblings. Her throat tightened with anger when she thought of how miserable their father had made things for his family. Tord Johansson was notorious in Fjällbacka as an evil-tempered drunk. Several times a week he would beat his wife Ruth, a frightened creature who would hide the bruises on her face behind a kerchief if she was forced to show herself outside the house after a beating. Sometimes the children, too, suffered the brunt of his anger, but so far the beatings had been reserved for Britta's two younger brothers. He hadn't yet raised a hand to Britta and her younger sister.

'If only he'd just die. Fall in the sea and drown when he's drunk,' whispered Britta.

Elsy hugged her closer. 'Shhh. You shouldn't say things like that, Britta. With God's providence, I'm sure it will all work out, one way or other. And without you having to commit a sin by wishing him dead.'

'God?' said Britta bitterly. 'He's never found His way to our house. And yet my mother still sits at home every Sunday, praying. A lot of good that's done her! It's easy for you to talk about God. Your parents are so nice, and you don't have any brothers or sisters to compete with or take care of.' Britta couldn't keep the bitterness out of her voice.

Elsy let go of her friend. In a friendly but slightly sharp tone she said: 'Things aren't always that easy for us, either. Mamma worries so much about my father that she's getting thinner and thinner by the day. Ever since the *Öckerö* was torpedoed, she thinks that every trip my father makes in his boat will be his last. Sometimes I find her standing at the window staring out at the sea, as if she's pleading with it to bring my father back home.'

'Well, I don't think that's the same thing at all,' said Britta, sniffing pitifully.

'Of course it's not the same thing. I just meant . . . oh, never mind.' Elsy knew it was useless to continue the conversation. She loved her friend for all the good that she knew was inside her, but sometimes Britta could be incredibly self-centred.

They heard someone coming up the stairs, and Britta immediately sat up and began frantically wiping the tears from her face.

'You've got visitors,' said Hilma. Behind her Frans and Erik appeared on the stairs.

'Hi!'

Elsy could tell that her mother wasn't pleased, but she left them alone after saying: 'Elsy, don't forget that you need to deliver the laundry that I've done for the Östermans. You've got ten minutes until you have to go. And remember your father is due home any minute.'

When she had gone, Frans and Erik made themselves comfortable on the floor in Elsy's room since there was nowhere else to sit.

'It doesn't sound like she wants us to come over here,' said Frans.

'My mother doesn't believe people from different social classes should mix,' said Elsy. 'The two of you are upper class, though I don't really know why anyone would think so.' She gave them a mischievous smile, and Frans stuck out his tongue in reply. Erik was looking at Britta.

'How's it going, Britta?' he said quietly. 'It looks like you're feeling bad about something.'

'None of your business,' she snapped, holding her head high.

'Probably just a girl's problem,' said Frans with a laugh.

Britta gave him an adoring look and a big smile. But her eyes were still red-rimmed.

'Why do you always think everything is so funny, Frans?' asked Elsy, clasping her hands in her lap. 'Some people have a hard time, you know. Not everybody is like you and Erik. The war has brought hardships to so many families. You ought to think about that once in a while.'

'How did I get dragged into this?' asked Erik, offended. 'We all know that Frans is an ignorant fool, but to accuse me of not being aware that people are suffering . . .' He gave Elsy an insulted look but then jumped and yelled 'Ow' when Frans punched him in the arm.

'Ignorant fool? I beg to differ. The fools are the ones who talk about "not being aware that people are suffering". You sound like you're eighty years old. At least. All those books you read aren't good for your health. They're making you weird up here.' Frans tapped his finger on his temple.

'Oh, don't pay any attention to him,' said Elsy wearily. Sometimes the boys' constant squabbling got her down. They were so childish.

A sound from downstairs made her face light up. 'Pappa's home!' She smiled happily at her three friends and headed downstairs to see him. But halfway down she stopped, realizing that the cheerful tones that she usually heard when her father came home were missing entirely. Instead their voices rose and fell, sounding upset. As soon as she saw him, she knew that something was terribly wrong. His face was ashen, and he was running one hand over his hair, the way he always did when he was especially worried.

'Pappa?' she said hesitantly, feeling her heart pounding. What could have happened? She tried to catch his eye, but she saw that his gaze was fixed on Erik, who had come down behind her. He opened his mouth several times to speak, but then closed it again, unable to utter a word. Finally he managed to say, 'Erik, I think you should go home. Your mother and father . . . are going to need you.'

'Why? What's happened?' Then Erik clapped his hand over his mouth as he realized that Elsy's father was about to give him bad news. 'Axel? Is he . . .?' He couldn't finish the sentence, but kept swallowing hard as if to make the lump in his throat go away. An image of Axel's lifeless body raced through his mind. How could he face his mother and father? How could he . . .?

'He's not dead,' said Elof, when he realized what the boy was thinking. 'He's not dead,' he repeated. 'But the Germans have him.'

Erik's expression turned to bewilderment. The relief and joy he had felt upon hearing that Axel wasn't dead were quickly replaced by worry and dismay at the thought of his brother in the hands of the enemy.

'Come on, I'll walk you home,' said Elof. His whole body seemed weighed down by the responsibility of telling Axel's parents that their son wasn't coming back this time.

Paula smiled contentedly as she sat in the back seat. There was something so pleasant and familiar about the way Patrik and Martin were bickering with each other in the front seat. At the moment Martin was in the middle of a long diatribe about Patrik's driving; putting up with it was not something he'd missed. But it was obvious that the two men were fond of each other, and already she had formed a great respect for Patrik.

Thus far, Tanumshede seemed to have been a good move. From the moment she arrived, it felt as if she'd come home. She had lived in Stockholm for so many years that she'd forgotten what it was like to live in a small town. Maybe Tanumshede in some way reminded her of the little town in Chile where she'd spent her early years. She couldn't find any other explanation for why she'd so quickly adapted to the place. There was nothing she missed about Stockholm. Perhaps that wasn't Stockholm's fault; as a police officer, she'd seen the worst of the worst, and that had tainted her view of the city. But in truth she'd never felt at home there, even as a child. She and her mother had been part of an early wave of immigrants; they were assigned a tiny flat on the outskirts of Stockholm, in a neighbourhood where their dark eyes and black hair set them apart. She was the only one in her class who hadn't been born in Sweden. And she'd had to pay for that. Every day, every minute, she'd paid for the fact that she'd been born in a different country. It didn't help that after only a year she could speak perfect Swedish, without a trace of an accent. She was an outsider.

Contrary to popular belief, racism on the police force had ceased to be a problem by the time she joined. Swedes had finally grown used to people from other countries, and she wasn't really considered an immigrant any more. Partly because she'd lived so many years in Sweden, partly because, with her South American background, she didn't fall into the same category as refugees from the Middle East and Africa. She'd often thought it absurd that she'd lost her immigrant status by virtue of seeming less foreign than the more recent refugees.

She found men like Frans Ringholm frightening. They didn't see nuances, didn't see variations. After only a second's glance they were ready to target someone on the basis of their appearance. It was the same kind of indiscriminate prejudice that had forced her and her mother to flee Chile. Centuries-old beliefs that decreed only one way, only one type of person was the right one and everything else was anathema, a threat to their world order. People like Ringholm had always existed. People who believed that they possessed the intelligence or the power or the force to determine the norm.

'What number did you say it was?' Martin turned to Paula, interrupting her thoughts. She glanced down at the slip of paper in her hand.

'Number seven.'

'Over there,' said Martin, pointing to the building. Patrik turned in and parked. They were in the Kullen district, in front of a block of flats right across from the sports field.

The usual sign on the door had been replaced with a much more personal sign made of wood, with the name Viola

Pettersson elegantly printed inside a circle of hand-painted flowers. And the woman who opened the door matched the sign. Viola was plump but well-proportioned, and her face radiated warmth. When Paula saw her romantic, floral-print dress, she thought that a straw hat would suit her perfectly, perched atop the grey hair that was pinned up in a bun.

'Come in,' said Viola, stepping aside. Paula glanced appreciatively at the entry hall. The flat was very different to her own, but she liked it. She'd never been to Provence, but this was how she thought it must look. Rustic country furniture combined with fabric and paintings with flower motifs. She peered into the living room, and saw that the same style prevailed.

'I've made us some coffee,' said Viola, leading the way. On the coffee table stood a delicate pink-floral coffee service, with biscuits arranged on a plate.

'Thank you,' said Patrik, perching cautiously on the sofa. After the introductions were out of the way, Viola poured everyone coffee and then seemed to be waiting for them to go on.

'How do you get those geraniums to look so beautiful?' Paula found herself asking as she sipped the coffee. Patrik and Martin glanced at her in surprise. 'Mine always seem to rot away or dry up,' she explained. Patrik and Martin raised their eyebrows even higher.

'Oh, it's not really that hard,' said Viola proudly. 'Just make sure that the soil dries out properly between waterings; you must never over-water them. I got a marvellous tip from Lasse Anrell. He told me to fertilize them with a bit of urine every once in a while. That does the trick if they're giving you any trouble.'

'Lasse Anrell?' said Martin. 'Isn't he the sports writer for *Aftonbladet*? What does he have to do with geraniums?'

Viola looked as if she could hardly be bothered to answer such a silly question. For her, Lasse was first and foremost an expert on geraniums; the fact that he was also a sports writer and TV personality had barely entered her consciousness.

Patrik cleared his throat. 'From what we understand, you and Erik Frankel saw each other fairly regularly.' He paused but then went on. 'I'm . . . I'm very sorry for your loss.'

'Thank you,' said Viola, looking down at her coffee cup. 'Yes, we used to see each other. Erik sometimes stayed here, maybe twice a month.'

'How did you meet?' asked Paula. It was difficult to imagine how these two people had come together, seeing how different their homes were.

Viola smiled. Paula noted that she had two charming dimples.

'Erik gave a lecture at the library a few years ago. When was it exactly? Four years . . .? It was a talk about Bohuslän and the Second World War, as I recall. Afterwards we got to talking and, well . . . one thing led to another.' She smiled at the memory.

'You never met at his house?' Martin reached for a biscuit.

'No. Erik thought it was easier to meet here. He shares . . . shared the house with his brother, you know, and even though Axel was gone a lot . . . No, Erik preferred to come here.'

'Did he ever mention receiving threats?' asked Patrik.

Viola shook her head vigorously. 'No, never. I can't even imagine . . . I mean, why would anyone want to threaten Erik, a retired history teacher? It's absurd even to think such a thing.'

'But the fact of the matter is that he did receive threats, at least indirectly, because of his interest in the Second World War and Nazism. Certain organizations don't appreciate it when people paint a picture of history that they don't agree with.'

'Erik didn't "paint a picture", as you so carelessly express

150

it,' said Viola, anger suddenly flashing in her eyes. 'He was a dedicated historian, meticulous about facts and extremely finicky about portraying the truth as it really was, not the way he or anyone else would have liked it to be. Erik didn't paint. He pieced together puzzles. Ever so slowly, piece by piece, he would work out how things would have looked in the past. A piece of blue sky here, a piece of green meadow there, until at last he could show the results to the rest of us. Not that he was ever really finished,' she said. The gentle look had returned to her eyes. 'There are always more facts, more reality to uncover.'

'Why was he so passionate about the Second World War?' asked Paula.

'Why is anyone interested in anything? Why do I love geraniums? Why not roses?' Viola threw out her hands, but at the same time her expression turned pensive. 'In Erik's case, you don't have to be Einstein to figure it out. What happened to his brother during the war marked him. He never talked to me about it, or at least, only once – and that was also the only time I ever saw Erik drunk. It was the last time we saw each other.' Her voice broke, and it took a few minutes for Viola to pull herself together enough to go on. 'Erik showed up here without telling me he was coming. That alone was unusual, but he'd obviously had too much to drink, and that was unheard of. The first thing he did when he came in was to go to the drinks cabinet and pour himself a big whisky. Then he sat down here on the sofa and started talking as he gulped down his drink. I didn't understand much of what he was saying; it sounded like drunken ramblings to me. But I did understand that it had to do with Axel. And what he'd been through when he was a prisoner. How it had affected the family.'

'You said that was the last time you saw Erik. Why was that? Why didn't you see each other during the summer? Didn't you wonder where he was?'

151

Viola's face contorted as she fought back the tears. Finally, in a husky voice she said, 'Because Erik said goodbye. He walked out of here around midnight – staggered might be a better description – and the last thing he said was that we would have to say goodbye. He thanked me for our time together and kissed me on the cheek. Then he left. I thought it was just drunken nonsense. I behaved like a real fool the next day, sitting and staring at the telephone all day long, waiting for him to ring and explain, or to apologize, or . . . whatever . . . But I didn't hear from him. And because of my stupid, stupid pride, I refused to call him. If I had, he might not have been left alone there . . .' Sobs took over, preventing her from finishing her sentence.

But Paula understood. She put her hand over Viola's and said gently, 'There was nothing you could have done. How could you have known?'

Viola nodded reluctantly and wiped away the tears with the back of her hand.

'Do you remember what day he was here?' asked Patrik.

'I'll check the calendar,' said Viola and got up, grateful for the distraction. 'I always make notes for each day, so I should be able to find out for you.' She left the room and was gone for a while.

'It was June fifteenth,' she said when she returned. 'I remember I'd been to the dentist in the afternoon, so I'm positive that was the day.'

'Okay, thanks,' said Patrik, standing up.

After they'd said goodbye to Viola and were back out on the street, they all had the same thought. What happened on 15 June that made Erik, quite uncharacteristically, get drunk and then end his relationship with Viola? What could have happened?

'She obviously has no control over her!'

'But, Dan, you're being unfair! How can you be so sure

152

that you wouldn't have fallen for the same thing?' Anna was leaning on the counter with her arms folded, glaring at him.

'Oh, no. Absolutely not!' Dan's blond hair stood on end because he kept running his hands through it out of sheer frustration.

'Right. And you're the one who seriously thought that someone had broken in during the night and eaten all the chocolate in the pantry. If I hadn't found the chocolate wrappers under Lina's pillow, you'd still be out there looking for a thief with smears of chocolate around his mouth.' Anna choked back a laugh and felt some of her anger fade. Looking at her, Dan felt a smile tugging at his own lips.

'You have to admit she was awfully convincing when she assured me that she was innocent.'

'She certainly was. That kid is going to get an Oscar when she grows up. But keep in mind that Belinda can be just as convincing. It's not surprising that Pernilla believed her. You can't honestly swear that you wouldn't have done the same.'

'Okay, okay,' said Dan sullenly. 'But Pernilla should have phoned the friend's mother to double check. That's what I would have done.'

'Yes, you probably would have. And from now on, Pernilla will, too.'

'Why are you talking about Mamma?' Belinda came down the stairs, still wearing her nightgown and with her hair sticking out all over. She'd refused to get out of bed ever since they'd brought her home from Erica and Patrik's on Saturday morning, hung over and apparently filled with remorse. Most of the remorse had since vanished, replaced by even more of the anger that had become her constant companion.

'We're not talking specifically about your mother,' said Dan wearily, sensing that another row was imminent.

'Are you talking shit about my mother again?' snarled Belinda, turning on Anna.

Casting a resigned look in Dan's direction, Anna said calmly, 'I've never said anything bad about your mother – and you know it. So don't speak to me in that tone of voice.'

'I'll use whatever tone of voice I like!' yelled Belinda. 'This is my house, not yours! So you can just take your fucking kids and get out of here!'

Dan took a step forward, his eyes flashing.

'Don't talk that way to Anna! This is her home too. The same goes for Adrian and Emma. And if you don't like it . . .' The words were no sooner out of his mouth than he realized it was the worst thing he could have said.

'No, I don't like it! I'm going to pack my bags and go home to Mamma! And that's where I'm going to stay until that woman and her kids move out!' Belinda turned on her heel and rushed upstairs. Both Dan and Anna gave a start when the door to her room slammed shut.

'Maybe she's right, Dan,' said Anna faintly. 'Maybe everything has gone a little too fast. I mean, she didn't have much time to get used to the idea before we turned up and invaded her home and her life.'

'She's seventeen, for God's sake. And she's behaving like a five-year-old.'

'You have to understand Belinda's point of view. It can't have been easy for her. She was a sensitive age when you and Pernilla separated, and . . .'

'Oh, thank you very much. As if I need that whole guilt trip on my shoulders again. I know it was my fault that we got divorced, so you don't have to stand there and throw it in my face.'

With that he walked brusquely past Anna and out the front door. For the second time a door slammed so loudly that the windowpanes rattled. For several seconds Anna stood motionless at the kitchen counter. Then she sank down on to the floor and cried.

154

FJÄLLBACKA 1943

'I hear the Germans finally got their mitts on the doctor's boy.'

Vilgot chuckled with glee as he hung his coat on the hook in the hallway. He handed his briefcase to Frans, who set it in its usual place, leaning against a chair.

'It's about time. Treason, I call it, what he's been up to, but people are like sheep. They just follow the crowd and bleat on command. Only somebody like me, who dares to think independently, can see things the way they really are. And trust me, Axel Frankel was a traitor. I hope they'll make short work of him.'

Vilgot went into the parlour and sank into his favourite armchair. Frans followed on his heels, and Vilgot looked up at him.

'Hey, where's my drink? Why are you so slow about it today?' He sounded cross, and Frans hurried over to the drinks cabinet to pour a shot for his father. It had been their routine ever since he was a little boy. His mother hadn't liked the fact that Frans was asked to handle liquor at such a young age, but as usual, she hadn't had much say in the matter.

'Sit down, boy, sit down.' Gripping his glass firmly, Vilgot magnanimously motioned towards the armchair next to him.

155

Frans caught a waft of alcohol as he sat down. The drink he'd poured for his father was most likely not the first he'd had that day.

'Your father has made an excellent deal today, let me tell you.' Vilgot leaned forward, and the alcoholic fumes filled Frans's nostrils. 'I've signed a contract with a German company. An exclusive contract. I'm going to be their sole supplier in Sweden. They said they were having a hard time finding business partners, and I believe it.' Vilgot chuckled, his large belly shaking. He downed his drink and held out the glass to Frans. 'Pour me another.' His eyes were glazed from the alcohol. Frans's hand shook slightly as he took the glass. It was still shaking as he poured the aromatic spirit, spilling a few drops.

'Pour one for yourself,' said Vilgot. It sounded more like a command than an invitation. Which it was. Frans set down his father's full glass and reached for an empty one for himself. His hand was no longer shaking as he filled it to the brim. Focusing all his attention on the effort, he carried the two glasses over to his father. Vilgot raised his glass as Frans sat down again. 'Bottoms up, lad.'

Frans felt the liquid burning his throat, all the way down to his stomach, where it settled like a warm lump. His father smiled. A trickle of alcohol was dribbling down his chin.

'Where's your mother?' Vilgot asked in a low voice.

Frans stared at a spot on the wall. 'She's visiting Grandma and won't be home until late.' His voice sounded muffled and tinny, as if it were coming from somebody else. Someone outside.

'Great. So the two of us can talk in peace. Go ahead, son – have another.'

Frans was conscious of his father's eyes on him as he went to refill his glass. This time he didn't leave the bottle in the cabinet but brought it back with him. Vilgot smiled appreciatively and held up his glass for more.

'You're a good lad, Frans.'

Again the alcohol seared his throat before transforming itself into a pleasant feeling somewhere in his midriff. The contours of everything around him began to dissolve. He felt he was floating in limbo, between reality and unreality.

Vilgot's voice grew softer. 'I can earn thousands of *riksdaler* on this deal, just in the next few years. And if the Germans keep increasing their demand for armaments, I stand to make significantly more. Maybe even millions. They've promised to put me in touch with other companies that have a need for our services. Now that I've got my foot in the door . . .' Vilgot's eyes gleamed in the dim light. He licked his lips. 'It's going to be a successful business that you take over one day, Frans.' He reached out to place his hand on his son's leg. 'The day will come when you can tell everybody in Fjällbacka to take a flying leap. After the Germans take power, we'll be in charge. Then we'll have more money than those idiots could ever dream of. So have a drink with your father, and let's toast the bright future!' Vilgot raised his glass and clinked it against Frans's, which he'd again filled to the brim.

The feeling of well-being continued to spread through Frans's chest as he drank another toast with his father.

Gösta had just started a round of golf on his computer when he heard Mellberg's footsteps in the corridor. He quickly turned off the game and picked up a report, trying to look as though he was deeply immersed in reading it. Mellberg's steps came closer, but there was something different about them. And what was that strange grumbling sound? Gösta rolled back his desk chair so he could stick his head out into the hall. The first thing he saw was Ernst, padding along in front of Mellberg with his long tongue hanging out, as usual. Behind him came an oddly hunched figure who was laboriously shuffling forward. He looked a lot like Mellberg, and yet he didn't.

'What the hell are you staring at?'

The voice and tone definitely belonged to his boss.

'What happened to you?' asked Gösta. By now Annika was peering out from the kitchen where she was busy feeding Maja.

Mellberg muttered something inaudible.

'What?' said Annika. 'What did you say? I missed it.'

Mellberg glowered at her and then said, 'I've been taking salsa lessons. Anything wrong with that?'

Gösta and Annika looked at each other in astonishment. Then they struggled to keep a straight face.

158

'Well?' shouted Mellberg. 'Any funny remarks? Anyone? Because there's plenty of opportunity to cut salaries here at the station.' Then he slammed the door to his office.

For several seconds Annika and Gösta stared at the closed door, but then they could restrain themselves no longer. The pair of them laughed until they cried, but they did it as quietly as possible.

Having checked that Mellberg's door was still closed, Gösta slipped over to the kitchen and whispered to Annika: 'Did he say he'd been taking salsa lessons? Did he really say that?'

'I'm afraid so,' said Annika, wiping the tears on the sleeve of her sweater. Maja stared at them in fascination as she sat at the table with a plate in front of her.

'But why? What on earth's got into him?' said Gösta incredulously as he pictured the scene in his mind.

'Well, it's the first I've heard about it, at any rate.' Still laughing, Annika shook her head and then sat down to carry on feeding Maja.

'Did you see how stiff he was? He looked like that creature in *Lord of the Rings*. Gollum. Isn't that his name?' Gösta did his best to imitate how Mellberg was moving, and Annika put her hand over her mouth to keep from howling with laughter.

'Salsa! That must have given Mellberg's body a real shock. He hasn't done any exercise in . . . well, ever. It's a mystery to me how he ever passed the physical part of the police training.'

'For all we know, he might have been a great athlete in his younger days.' Annika thought about what she'd just said and then shook her head. 'But I don't think so. Good Lord, this is the entertainment highlight of the day. Mellberg at a salsa class! Whatever next?' She lifted a spoonful of food to Maja's mouth, but the child stubbornly turned her head away. 'This little one doesn't want to eat anything. But if I don't get her to take at least a few spoonfuls, they'll never trust me with her again,' she sighed and made another attempt, but Maja's mouth remained as impenetrable as Fort Knox.

'Shall I try?' asked Gösta, reaching for the spoon. Annika looked at him in surprise.

'You? Okay, go ahead. But don't get your hopes up.'

Gösta didn't reply as he changed places with Annika, sitting down next to Maja. He dumped off half of the huge mound of food that Annika had put on the spoon and then raised it in the air. 'Vroom, vroom, vroom, here comes the airplane.' He sailed the spoon around like a plane and was rewarded with Maja's undivided attention. 'Vroom, vroom, vroom, here comes the airplane, flying straight into your . . .' Maja's mouth opened as if on cue, and the plane with its load of spaghetti and meat sauce went in for a landing.

'Mmm . . . that was good,' said Gösta, putting a little more food on the spoon. 'Chugga, chugga, chug, now it's a train coming. Chugga, chugga, chug and straight into the tunnel.' Maja's mouth opened again and the spaghetti entered the tunnel.

'I can't believe it!' said Annika, gaping. 'Where did you learn to do that?'

'Oh, it's nothing,' said Gösta modestly. But he smiled proudly as a race car drove in with spoon number three.

Annika sat down at the kitchen table and watched as Gösta slowly emptied the plate in front of Maja, who swallowed every bite.

'You know what, Gösta?' said Annika. 'Life is so unfair sometimes.'

'Have the two of you thought about adopting?' asked Gösta without looking at her. 'In my day it wasn't very common. But today I wouldn't hesitate. Seems like every other kid is adopted.'

'We've talked about it,' said Annika, drawing circles on the tablecloth with the tip of her finger. 'But nothing has ever come of it. We've done our best to fill our lives with things other than children . . . but . . .'

'It's not too late,' said Gösta. 'If you start now, it might not take too long. And the colour of the child's skin doesn't matter, so choose the country with the shortest waiting list. There are so many kids who need a home. If I was a child, I'd thank my lucky stars if you and Lennart adopted me.'

Annika swallowed hard and looked down at her finger moving over the tablecloth. Gösta's words had awakened something inside of her, something that she and Lennart had somehow suppressed the past few years. Maybe they were afraid. After all the miscarriages, all the hopes that had been shattered again and again. But maybe they were strong enough now. Maybe they could do it, maybe they dared. Because the sense of longing was still there, as strong as ever. Nothing seemed to suppress that longing to hold a child in their arms, to have a child to love.

'Well, I'd better see about doing some work,' said Gösta, getting to his feet without looking at her. He patted Maja on the head. 'At least she ate something, so Patrik won't have to worry that she's starving when he leaves her here with us next time.'

He was just about to leave the kitchen when Annika said quietly, 'Thanks, Gösta.'

He nodded, embarrassed. Then he disappeared into his office and closed the door behind him. He sat down in front of his computer, staring at the screen without seeing it. Instead he saw Maj-Britt's face. And the boy who had lived only a few days. So many years had passed since then. An eternity. Almost an entire lifetime. But he could still feel the tiny hand grasping his finger.

With a sigh, Gösta clicked open the golf game.

For three hours Erica managed to push aside all thoughts of the disastrous visit with Britta. And during that time she wrote five pages of her new book. Then her mind returned to Britta, and she gave up trying to write anything more.

She'd felt deeply ashamed when she left Britta's home. It was hard for her to shake off the memory of Herman's expression when he saw her sitting there at the kitchen table next to his wife, who was in a state of collapse. Erica understood his reaction. It had been terribly insensitive of her not to recognize the signals. But at the same time, she didn't really regret visiting Britta. Slowly she was starting to gather more pieces of the puzzle. They were diffuse and vague, but they were beginning to form a picture of her mother that was more complete than the one she'd had before.

It was odd that she'd never even heard the names Erik, Britta, or Frans. At one time in her mother's life they must have been very important to her. But none of them seemed to have remained in contact with the others after they'd grown up, even though they'd gone on living in little Fjällbacka.

Both Axel and Britta had portrayed Elsy as a warm and thoughtful young woman, something she found hard to reconcile with her own memories of her mother. She wouldn't have said that her mother was a mean person, but she'd been so reserved, so closed off, that it was as if any warmth she might once have possessed had been extinguished long before Erica and Anna were born. Erica was suddenly overwhelmed by sorrow as she thought of all the things she'd missed out on. Things that she would never be able to reclaim. Her mother was gone, dead in a car accident four years ago, along with Tore – Erica and Anna's father. There was nothing that Erica could revive, nothing she could demand compensation for, nothing she could plead or beg for, no accusations that she could level against her mother. The only thing she could hope to find was clarity. What had happened to the Elsy Axel and Britta had known? What had happened to the warm, tender-hearted Elsy?

A knock on the front door interrupted Erica's thoughts, and she got up to open it.

'Anna? Come in.' With the keen eyes of an older sister, she immediately observed Anna's red-rimmed eyes. 'What's the matter?' she asked, sounding more concerned than she'd intended. Anna had been through so much during the past few years; Erica had never been able to relinquish the maternal role that she'd taken on when they were growing up.

'Just problems with trying to merge two separate families,' said Anna, with a feeble laugh. 'Nothing I can't handle, but it would be great to talk about it.'

'Then let's talk,' said Erica. 'I'll pour you a cup of coffee, and if I dig around in the cupboard I can probably find some treat we can have to console ourselves.'

'Does that mean you've given up on the diet now that you're a married woman?' said Anna.

'Don't even get into that,' sighed Erica, heading for the kitchen. 'After spending a week sitting at my desk, I'm going to have to buy new trousers pretty soon. These ones are starting to feel as tight as a sausage skin.'

'I know exactly what you mean,' said Anna, sitting down at the table. 'Since moving in with Dan, it feels like I've put on pounds. And it doesn't help matters that Dan seems able to eat everything in sight without gaining so much as an ounce.'

'It's easy to resent him for that,' said Erica, putting some buns on a plate. 'Does he still eat cinnamon rolls for breakfast?'

'You mean he was already doing that back when the two of you were together?' laughed Anna. 'Just imagine how hard it is to convince the kids that a healthy breakfast is important when Dan sits there dipping cinnamon rolls in hot chocolate right in front of their eyes.'

'Patrik dips his lumpfish caviar sandwiches with cheese

163

in hot chocolate too, and that's not much better. So, tell me, what's been going on. Is Belinda making trouble again?'

'Uh-huh, that's the crux of the matter, all right, but every-thing is getting so unpleasant. Today Dan and I started fighting because of it and . . .' Anna looked unhappy as she took a bun from the plate. 'It's not really Belinda's fault – that's what I've been trying to explain to Dan. She's reacting to a situation that's new for her, one that's not of her own choosing. And she's right. She didn't ask to have me and a couple of kids foisted on her.'

'I suppose that's true, but she should still behave in a civilized manner. And that's Dan's job. Dr Phil says that a step-parent should never discipline a child her age.'

'Dr Phil?' Anna laughed so hard that a crumb got stuck in her throat and she started coughing. 'Erica, I can see that it's high time you emerged from your maternity leave. Dr Phil?'

'If you must know, I've learned a lot by watching Dr Phil,' said Erica, sounding offended. Nobody got away with joking about her idol. Dr Phil's TV show had been the highpoint of her days the past year, and lately she'd even considered taking a lunch break from her writing so she could watch him.

'But I suppose he does have a point,' Anna admitted begrudgingly. 'I feel like Dan either doesn't take things seri-ously enough, or else he takes them too seriously. Since Friday I've had the worst time keeping him from fighting with Pernilla over how to raise the children. He started going on about how he couldn't trust her to take care of them and . . . Well, he got really angry. And in the middle of everything, Belinda came downstairs and then it all really went to hell. Now Belinda doesn't want to live with us any more, so Dan put her on a bus to Munkedal.'

'How are Emma and Adrian coping?' Erica took another bun from the plate. She'd go back on her diet next week.

Definitely. She just needed this week to get into a regular writing routine, and then . . .

'So far so good, knock on wood.' Anna tapped the kitchen table. 'They idolize Dan and the girls and think it's great to have big sisters. So, for the time being, there's no trouble on that front.'

'What about Malin and Lisen? How are they handling it?' Erica was referring to Belinda's younger sisters, who were eleven and eight.

'They're doing fine too. They like playing with Emma and Adrian and seem to tolerate me, at least. No, it's mostly Belinda who's having a hard time. But she's at that age, you know, when things are difficult.' Anna sighed and then reached for another bun too. 'What about you? How are things going here? Are you making progress on the book?'

'It's going okay, I suppose. It's always slow in the beginning. I have a lot of research material to process, plus I've also booked a lot of interviews. Everything's starting to take shape. But . . .' Erica hesitated. She had a deeply rooted instinct to protect her sister, but she decided that Anna had a right to know what had been preoccupying her lately. She started from the beginning and quickly told her sister about the medal and the other things she'd found in Elsy's chest, about the diaries and the fact that she'd talked to several people about their mother's past.

'Why didn't you tell me about this before?' asked Anna.

Erica shifted position uneasily. 'Er, well, I know I should have, but . . . Does it really matter? I'm telling you now, right?'

Anna seemed to be considering whether to argue the point, but then she apparently decided to let it pass.

'I'd like to see all of it,' she said curtly. Erica quickly got up, relieved that her sister wasn't going to yell at her for neglecting to share what she'd discovered.

'Of course. I'll go get everything.' Erica ran upstairs to

165

her workroom. When she came back, she set the items on the kitchen table: the diaries, the child's shirt, and the medal.

Anna stared. 'How on earth did she come by this?' she said, picking up the medal and holding it in the palm of her hand as she studied it intently. 'And this – who did this belong to?' She held up the little stained shirt. 'Is that rust?' She leaned closer to examine the patches that covered a good deal of the cloth.

'Patrik thinks it's blood,' said Erica, which made Anna sit up with a start.

'Blood? Why would Mamma keep a child's shirt covered with blood in an old chest in the attic?' With a look of disgust, she dropped the shirt on the table and picked up the diaries.

'Anything not meant for children in these?' asked Anna, waving the blue diaries. 'Any sex stories that will traumatize me for life if I read them?'

'No,' said Erica, laughing. 'Don't look so worried. Nothing X-rated. There's actually not much at all. Just some meaningless descriptions of daily life. But there is one thing that I've been wondering about . . .' For the first time Erica felt able to put into words the thought that had been hovering on the edge of her consciousness for a while.

'What is it?' asked Anna as she paged through the diaries.

'Well, I wonder if there are more of these somewhere. The ones in the chest stop in May 1944, when the fourth book was completely filled. And that's it. Of course, Mamma may have got tired of keeping a diary. But if that was the case, would she have bothered to complete the fourth book? It just seems odd.'

'So you think there might be more? But what else would they tell you, other than what you've already read? I mean, it's not as if Mamma had a particularly exciting life. She was born and raised here, she met Pappa, we were born, and then, well . . . What more is there?'

166

'Don't say that,' replied Erica. She wondered how much she should tell her sister. She didn't have anything concrete, but intuition told her that the medal and the blood-stained shirt would lead to other discoveries, maybe even reveal whatever it was that had cast such a shadow over their lives – hers and Anna's.

She took a deep breath and recounted in detail the conversations that she'd had with Erik and Axel and Britta.

'So you went over to Axel Frankel's house and asked him for the medal only a couple of days after his brother was found dead? My God, he must have thought you were a real vulture,' said Anna, with the cruel honesty that only a younger sister was capable of.

'Do you want to hear what they said or not?' asked Erica indignantly, even though she was inclined to agree with Anna. It hadn't been very sensitive of her.

When Erica had finished her story, Anna sat staring at her with a frown on her face. 'It sounds as if they knew a completely different person. What did Britta say about the medal? Did she know why Mamma had a Nazi medal in her possession?'

Erica shook her head. 'I didn't have time to ask her. She has Alzheimer's and after a while she started getting confused, and then her husband came home and he was really upset and . . .' Erica cleared her throat. 'Well, he asked me to leave.'

'Erica!' cried Anna. 'Are you telling me that you tried to interrogate a confused old woman? No wonder her husband threw you out! Don't you think you're getting a bit too carried away with this?'

'Okay, but aren't you in the least curious? Why did Mamma keep all these things hidden away? And why do people who knew her then describe someone who bears no resemblance to the mother we grew up with? Somewhere along the way something happened . . . Britta was just

167

starting to tell me when she got confused. She said something about old bones and . . . oh, I can't remember, but it seemed to me that she was using that as a metaphor for a secret that's been buried away and . . . Maybe I'm just imagining things, but . . .' The phone rang, and Erica stopped mid-sentence and got up to answer it.

'This is Erica. Oh, hi, Karin.' Erica turned to face Anna, rolling her eyes. 'Yes, everything's fine. Yes, it's nice to finally have a chance to talk with you too.' She grimaced at Anna, who hadn't a clue what it was all about. 'Patrik? No, he's not at home right now. He and Maja went over to the station to say hi and then I don't really know where they were going. I see. Uh-huh. Yes, I'm sure they'd love to go out for a walk with you and Ludde tomorrow. Ten o'clock. At the pharmacy. Okay, I'll tell him. He'll have to let you know if he has other plans, but I don't think he does. Uh-huh. Thanks. I'm sure we'll talk again. Thanks. You too.'

'What was that all about?' asked Anna in surprise. 'Who's Karin? And what's Patrik doing with her at the pharmacy tomorrow morning?'

Erica sat down at the kitchen table. After a long pause she said, 'Karin is Patrik's ex-wife. She and her second husband recently moved to Fjällbacka. And it just so happens that, like Patrik, she's on leave from her job to take care of the baby, so they're going to take a walk together tomorrow.'

Anna laughed. 'Did you just set up a date between Patrik and his ex-wife? Good Lord, I can't believe it. Does he have any ex-girlfriends you could phone to see if they'd like to go along too? We wouldn't want him to be bored while he's on paternity leave, the poor guy.'

Erica glared at her little sister. 'In case you didn't notice, she was the one who phoned me. And what's so strange about that, anyway? They're divorced. Have been for years. And they're both at home all day with a toddler. No, I don't think it's so strange. I really don't have a problem with it.'

168

'Oh, right!' Anna snorted. 'I can tell that you don't have a problem with it, not at all . . . Your nose is growing longer and longer by the second.'

For a moment Erica considered flinging a bun at her sister, but decided to refrain. Anna could think what she liked; she was *not* jealous.

'How about paying the cleaning woman a visit next?' asked Martin. Patrik hesitated, then took out his mobile phone.

'I just need to check that everything is okay with Maja.'

After listening to Annika's report, he put his mobile back in his pocket and nodded.

'Okay, everything's fine. Maja has just fallen asleep in her pushchair.' He turned to Paula: 'Do you have the address?'

'Yes, I do.' Paula looked through her notebook and then read the address aloud. 'Her name is Laila Valthers. She said she'd be at home all day. Do you know where the place is?'

'It's one of those yellow buildings near the roundabout on the southern edge of Fjällbacka,' Martin said. 'Turn right up ahead at the school.'

They were there in a matter of minutes, and Laila was at home, as she'd said. She looked a bit frightened when she opened the door and seemed unwilling to let them come in, but it wasn't as if they had many questions for her so they remained standing in the entry hall while they carried out the interview.

'You do house-cleaning for the Frankel brothers, is that right?' Patrik's voice was calm and soothing in an effort to make their presence as unthreatening as possible.

'Yes, but I'm not going to get in trouble because of that, am I?' said Laila, her voice nearly a whisper. She was short and wore comfortable brown clothing of some sort of soft fabric, perfectly suited to spending the whole day at home. Her hair was a mousy grey, cut short in a style that was undoubtedly practical but not particularly attractive. She

169

shifted her weight nervously from one foot to the other as she stood there with her arms folded. She seemed very anxious to hear their response to her question. Patrik thought he knew what was bothering her.

'Do you mean because you didn't declare your earnings? I can assure you that we've no interest in that side of things, and we don't plan to report you for it. We're conducting a murder investigation, so our focus is on completely different issues.' He ventured a reassuring smile, and Laila rewarded him by stopping her nervous shifting from one foot to the other.

'It's true. They would put an envelope with money for me on the hall bureau every other week. We had agreed that I should come in and clean every Wednesday.'

'Did you have your own key?'

Laila shook her head. 'No, they always put the key under the doormat, and I put it back when I was done.'

'Why didn't you clean their house all summer?' Paula asked. It was the question they most wanted to have answered.

'I thought I would be doing cleaning for them in the summer. At least, we hadn't discussed any change in the arrangement. But when I went over there, the key wasn't in the usual place. I knocked, but no one answered. So then I tried phoning, to see if there'd been some misunderstanding. But nobody answered. I knew that the older brother, Axel, was going to be away all summer. That's what he's done every year since I've been cleaning for them. So when I couldn't get an answer, I just assumed that the younger brother was gone for the summer too. I did think it was rather rude of them not to tell me, but now I understand why . . .' She looked down at the floor.

'And you didn't see anything that struck you as out of the ordinary?' asked Martin.

Laila shook her head vigorously. 'No, I can't say that I did. No, nothing comes to mind.'

'Do you know what day it was when you went over there but couldn't get in?' said Patrik.

'Yes, I do, because it was my birthday. And I thought it was very unlucky that I wasn't going to do any cleaning that day. I'd planned to buy myself a present with the money I made.' She fell silent, and Patrik asked her tactfully:

'So what was the date? When is your birthday?'

'Oh, how stupid of me,' she said. 'It was the seventeenth of June. I'm positive about that. June seventeenth. I went over there two more times to have a look, but nobody was home and there was still no key under the doormat. So then I assumed that they'd forgotten to tell me that they wouldn't be home all summer.' She shrugged to show that she was used to the fact that people forgot to tell her things.

'Thank you, that's extremely helpful.' Patrik held out his hand, shuddering slightly at her limp handshake. It felt as if someone had stuck a dead fish in his hand.

'So, what do you think?' he asked when they were back in the car and heading for the station.

'I think we can be pretty certain that Erik Frankel was murdered sometime between the fifteenth and the seventeenth of June,' said Paula.

'Yes, I'm inclined to agree,' said Patrik, nodding as he took the tight bend before Anrås a little too fast and came within a hair's breadth of colliding with a refuse vehicle. Leif the rubbish man shook his fist at him, and a terrified Martin gripped the handle above the door.

'Did you get your driving licence as a Christmas present?' asked Paula from the back seat, apparently unfazed by their near-death experience.

'What do you mean? I'm an excellent driver!' said Patrik, offended, glancing at Martin for support.

'Right,' Martin jeered. Then he turned to look at Paula. 'I put him forward for that programme, *Sweden's Worst Drivers*, but they must have thought he was overqualified.

171

It would be no contest if Patrik was one of the participants.'

Paula laughed and Patrik snorted to show he was insulted. 'I don't know what you're talking about, considering all the time that you and I have spent driving around together – have I ever crashed or had any sort of accident? No, I've an unblemished driving record, so what you're saying is pure slander.' He snorted again as he glared at Martin, which almost caused him to rear-end the Saab in front of them, and he had to brake hard.

'I rest my case,' said Martin, holding up his hands as Paula doubled over with laughter.

Patrik sulked the rest of the way back to the station. But at least he obeyed the speed limit.

Kjell was still riled after the encounter with his father. Frans had always had that effect on him. No, actually that wasn't true. Not always. When he was a boy, disappointment had been the predominant feeling. Disappointment mixed with love, which over the years had been transformed into a solid core of hatred and anger. He realized that he'd allowed these feelings to guide all the choices he'd made, and in that sense he'd practically let his father steer his life. But he was utterly powerless to do anything about it. Just as he'd been power-less to resist when his mother had dragged him along on her innumerable trips to see Frans in prison. The cold, grey visitors' room, completely impersonal, soulless. His father's awkward attempts to talk to him, pretending that he was actually part of his life and not just a stranger observing it from a distance. From behind bars.

It had been years since his father had served his last prison sentence, but that didn't mean he was a reformed character. He'd simply grown smarter. He'd chosen a different path. And as a consequence, Kjell had chosen the exact opposite. He'd written about the anti-foreigner

172

organizations with a vehemence and passion that had won him a name and reputation that extended far beyond the readership of the *Bohusläningen* newspaper. He was a frequent guest on national TV, whenever they needed an authority on the destructive forces of neo-Nazism and how society could best deal with them. Unlike many others, who in the conciliatory spirit of the times wanted to invite the neo-Nazi organizations into the public forum for an open discussion, Kjell had taken a hard line. They were simply not to be tolerated. They should be combatted every step of the way, opposed in whatever context they chose to speak out, and be literally shown the door, as the unwelcome monsters that they were.

He parked in front of his ex-wife's house. This time he hadn't bothered to phone ahead. Sometimes she contrived to leave before he arrived, but this time he'd made sure that she was at home. He'd been sitting in his car a short distance away, waiting to catch sight of her. After an hour she'd driven up to the house and parked in front. It looked as though she'd been shopping, because she took a couple of supermarket bags out of the car. Kjell waited until she was inside and then drove the last hundred metres up to the house. He got out and knocked. Carina's shoulders visibly slumped when she saw who was standing on the doorstep.

'So it's you, is it? What do you want?' she asked.

Why did she always have to look so . . . crushed? Still. After ten years. His sense of guilt only exacerbated his irritation. Why couldn't she understand the seriousness of the situation? Realize that it was time for them to take a tough approach?

'We need to talk. About Per.' He pushed past her and began taking off his shoes and hanging up his jacket. For a moment Carina looked as if she might object, but then she shrugged and went into the kitchen. She stood with her back leaned against the counter and her arms folded across her chest, as if preparing for a fight.

'What is it now?' She shook her head so the dark strands of her fringe fell into her eyes and she had to push them aside. He'd seen that same gesture so many times. It was one of the things he'd loved about her when they first met, before the daily grind and sorrow had taken their toll, before their love had faded and made him choose a different path. He still didn't know whether he'd made the right choice or not.

Kjell pulled out one of the kitchen chairs and sat down. 'We have to do something. This isn't something that's going resolve itself. Once a kid gets in with that type of crowd . . .'

Carina interrupted him by raising her hand. 'When did I say that it will resolve itself? I just have a different opinion as to what should be done. Sending Per away is not the solution. You should be able to see that too.'

'What you don't realize is that he needs to get away from this environment!' He angrily ran his hand through his hair.

'And I take it that by "this environment" you mean your father.' Carina's voice was dripping with contempt. 'I think you should see about solving your own problems with your father before you get Per involved.'

'What problems?' Kjell was aware of his voice rising, so he forced himself to take several deep breaths to calm down. 'First of all, it's not just my father that I'm talking about when I say that Per needs to get away from here. Don't you think I can see what's going on? Don't you think I know that you've got bottles hidden away in every cupboard and drawer?' He motioned towards the kitchen cabinets. Carina was about to protest, but he held up his hand to stop her. 'And there's nothing to be resolved between me and Frans,' he said through clenched teeth. 'As far as I'm concerned, I'd prefer not to have anything to do with the man, and I have no intention whatsoever of allowing him to have any

174

influence over Per. But since we can't keep watch over the boy every minute of the day, and you don't seem particularly interested in dealing with him, I can't see any other solution but to send him away. We need to find a boarding school where the staff know how to handle this sort of situation.'

'And just how do you think that's going to be arranged?' Carina snapped. 'They don't just send teenagers off to those sorts of schools for no reason. They have to have done something first –'

'Breaking and entering,' Kjell cut her off. 'He was caught breaking into somebody's house.'

'What are you talking about? He's never –'

'In early June. The homeowner caught him red-handed and phoned me. I went over and collected Per. He got in through a basement window and was in the middle of gathering things in the house when he got caught. The owner threatened to ring the police if he didn't cough up his parents' phone number. And so Per gave him my number – not yours.' He couldn't resist feeling smug when he saw how upset and disappointed Carina looked.

'He gave him your number? But why?'

Kjell shrugged. 'Who knows? I guess a father is always a father.'

'Whose house did he break into?' Carina still seemed to be having a hard time accepting the fact that Per had asked the man to call Kjell.

He hesitated for a couple of seconds before replying. Then he said, 'That old man they found dead in Fjällbacka last week. Erik Frankel. It was his house.'

'But why?' She shook her head.

'That's what I'm trying to tell you! Erik Frankel was an expert on the Second World War. He had tons of stuff from that period, and Per probably wanted to impress his friends by showing them some genuine Nazi memorabilia.'

'Do the police know about this?'

175

'Not yet,' he said coldly. 'It just depends on whether –'

'Would you do that to your own son? Report him for breaking and entering?' whispered Carina, horrified.

Kjell felt a hard knot in his stomach. He pictured her as she'd looked the first time they met. At a party at the journalism school. She'd come with a friend who was studying there, but the girl had gone off with some guy right after they arrived, so Carina had ended up sitting on a sofa feeling lonely and neglected. He'd fallen in love with her the moment he saw her. She had on a yellow dress with a yellow ribbon in her hair, which was just as dark as it was now but without the strands of grey that were becoming visible. There was something about her that had made him want to take care of her, protect her, love her. He thought about their wedding. The dress that would nowadays be regarded as a relic from the eighties, with its voluminous skirt and puffed sleeves. He, at any rate, had thought she was a vision in that dress. And then another image surfaced in his mind: Carina exhausted, without make-up, wearing an ugly hospital gown and holding their son in her arms. When she had looked up at him and smiled, he'd felt as if he could slay dragons or fight off an entire army for his wife and son.

As they stood in the little kitchen, two combatants facing each other down, each caught a fleeting glimpse of the way they had once been, the times they had laughed together, made love to each other. Back in the days before their love turned into something fragile and brittle. Making him vulnerable. The knot in his stomach hardened even more.

Kjell pushed away these thoughts. 'If I have to, I'll see to it that the police are given this information,' he said. 'Either we make arrangements to get Per out of this environment, or I let the police do the job for us.'

'You bastard!' cried Carina, her voice thick with tears and disappointment.

Kjell got up. His voice was cold as he said, 'That's how

it's going to be. And I have a suggestion as to where we can send Per. I'll email it to you and you can have a look at it. But under no circumstances is he to have any contact with my father. Understand?'

Carina didn't reply, just bowed her head as a sign of surrender. It had been a long time since she'd had the energy to fight Kjell. The day when he gave up on her, on them, she had given up on herself.

When Kjell was back in his car, he drove a few hundred metres and then parked. He pressed his forehead on the steering wheel and closed his eyes. Images of Erik Frankel flickered through his mind. He thought about what he'd found out about the man. The question was: what should he do with the information?

GRINI, OUTSIDE OSLO, 1943

The worst part was the cold. Never being able to get warm.
The damp that sucked up any warmth and wrapped around
his body like an icy, wet blanket. Axel curled up on the
bunk. The days were so long in his solitary cell, but he
preferred the gloominess to the frequent interruptions. The
beatings, interrogations, all the questions pummelling him
like a steady downpour that refused to stop. How could he
give them answers when he knew so little? And whatever
he did know, he would never tell them. They'd have to kill
him first.

Axel ran his hand over his scalp. There was only stubble
there now, and it felt rough under his palm. They had given
all the prisoners a shower and shaved their heads as soon
as they arrived. Then they were dressed in uniforms of the
Norwegian Guard. When he was caught, Axel knew at once
that this was where he'd end up: in the prison located twelve
kilometres outside of Oslo. But no one could have prepared
him for what life was like here – the unfathomable terror
that filled all hours of the day, the tedium, and the pain.

'Food.' There was a clattering outside his cell, and the
young guard set down a tray outside the bars.

'What day is it today?' asked Axel in Norwegian. He and
Erik had spent nearly all their summer holidays with their

maternal grandparents in Norway, and he spoke the language fluently. He saw this guard every day and always tried to engage him in conversation, for he craved human contact. But usually he received only the briefest of answers. Just like today.

'Wednesday.'

'Thanks.' Axel forced himself to smile. The boy turned to leave. Dreading the moment he would be left once again to his solitude and the cold, Axel attempted to detain the guard by tossing out another question:

'What's the weather like outside?'

The boy stopped. Hesitated. He glanced around, then he came back to Axel's cell.

'It's overcast. Really cold,' he said. Axel was struck by how young the boy looked. He must have been about the same age as Axel, maybe a couple of years younger, but given how Axel was feeling these days, he assumed that he looked considerably older – just as old on the outside as on the inside.

The boy again took a few steps away.

'Cold for this time of year, isn't it?' His voice broke, making the innocuous remark sound very strange. There was a time when he'd looked upon such meaningless chit-chat as a waste of time. Right now it was a lifeline, a reminder of the outside world that seemed more and more distant.

'Yes, you might say that. But it can get really cold in Oslo this time of year.'

'Are you from around here?' Axel hurried to ask the question before the guard decided to leave.

The boy hesitated, uncertain whether to reply. He glanced around again, but no one was in sight or within earshot.

'We've only been here a couple of years.'

Axel decided on another question. 'How long have I been here? It feels like an eternity.' He laughed but was startled by how harsh and unfamiliar his laugh sounded.

It had been a long time since he'd had anything to laugh about.

'I don't know if I should . . .' The guard tugged at his uniform collar. He seemed not to feel comfortable yet in the compulsory attire. Over time he'd get used to it, Axel thought. He would learn to accept both the uniform and the way the prisoners were treated. It was human nature.

'What difference will it make if you tell me how long I've been here?' coaxed Axel. There was something extremely upsetting about being in this timeless state. Without clocks, dates, or weekdays around which he could order his life.

'About two months. I'm not really sure.'

'About two months. And this is Wednesday. With overcast skies. That's good enough for me.' Axel smiled at the boy and received a cautious smile in return.

When the guard was gone, Axel sank down on his bunk with the tray on his lap. The food left a lot to be desired. The same slop every day. Potatoes fit for pigs, and disgusting stews. But that was undoubtedly part of their strategy to break down the prisoners. Listlessly he dipped the spoon into the grey mess in the bowl, but his hunger finally forced him to lift it to his mouth. He tried to pretend that he was eating his mother's beef stew, but that just made matters worse, since his thoughts then strayed to things that he'd forbidden himself to think about: his home and his family, his mother and father and Erik. Suddenly even his hunger wasn't strong enough; nothing could make him eat. He dropped the spoon in the bowl and leaned his head back against the rough wall. He could see them all quite clearly: his father with the big grey moustache that he meticulously combed every night before going to bed; his mother with her long hair pulled back into a bun at the nape of her neck, and with her glasses perched on the very tip of her nose as she sat crocheting in the light from the reading lamp in the evenings. And Erik. Probably in his room with his nose in

180

a book. What were they all doing? Were they thinking about him right now? How had his parents reacted to the news that he'd been taken prisoner? And Erik, who was so often silent, keeping his thoughts to himself. His brilliant intellect could analyse texts and facts with impressive speed, but he had a hard time showing his emotions. Once in a while, out of sheer cussedness, Axel would give his brother a big bear hug, just to feel his body go rigid with discomfort at being touched. But after a moment Erik would always relent; there would be a few seconds where he would relax and give in before snarling 'Let me go', and tearing himself away. Axel knew his brother so well. Much better than Erik would ever believe. He knew that Erik sometimes felt like an outsider in the family, that he thought he couldn't compete with Axel. And now things were probably going to be even worse for him. Axel knew that concern for him was going to affect Erik's daily life, that his brother's place in the family was going to be even more diminished. He didn't even dare think about how things would be for Erik if he died.

'Hi, we're home!' Patrik closed the door and set Maja down on the floor in the hall. She immediately headed off, so he had to grab her jacket to stop her.

'Just a minute, sweetie. We have to take off your shoes and jacket before you go running to see Mamma.' He got her undressed and then let her go.

'Erica? We're home!' he shouted. No reply, but when he stopped to listen, he heard a clacking sound from upstairs. He picked up Maja and went up to Erica's workroom, setting the little girl down on the floor.

'Hi. So this is where you are.'

'Yes, I've rattled off quite a few pages today. And then Anna came over and we had coffee.' Erica smiled at Maja and held out her arms to her daughter. Maja toddled over to press a wet kiss on Erica's lips.

'Hi, sweetheart. What have you and Pappa been doing today?' She rubbed her nose against Maja's, and the little girl gurgled with delight. Eskimo kisses were their speciality. 'You've been gone a long time,' said Erica, shifting her attention back to Patrik.

'Well, I had to jump in and do a little work,' he said enthusiastically. 'The new officer seems great, but they hadn't really thought through all the angles, so I drove over to

Fjällbacka with them to make a house call, which gave us a lead so we were able to pinpoint the two-day time frame when Erik Frankel was most likely murdered . . .' He trailed off mid-sentence when he saw Erica's expression, realizing that he should have given it more thought before he opened his mouth.

'And where was Maja while you "jumped in to do a little work"?' asked Erica with ice in her voice.

Patrik squirmed. This would be a good time for the smoke alarm to go off. But no such luck. He took a deep breath and launched right in.

'Annika took care of her for a while. At the station.' He couldn't understand why it sounded so bad when he said it out loud. Until now it hadn't even occurred to him that it might not be such a good idea.

'So Annika took care of our daughter at the police station while you drove out on a job for a couple of hours? Am I understanding this correctly?'

'Er . . . yes,' said Patrik, searching frantically for a way to turn the situation to his advantage. 'She had a great time. She had a big lunch, and then Annika went for a walk with her so she fell asleep in the pushchair.'

'I'm sure that Annika did a super job as the babysitter. That's not the point. What makes me upset is the fact that we agreed you would take care of Maja while I worked. It's not that I expect you to spend every minute with her until January; of course we'll need babysitters once in a while. But I think it's a bit much to start leaving Maja with the station secretary so you can run off on a job after only one week of paternity leave. What do you think?'

Patrik wondered for a second whether Erica's question was purely rhetorical, but when she seemed to be waiting for him to answer, he realized that wasn't the case.

'Well, now that you put it that way, I . . . okay, it was a stupid thing to do. But they hadn't even checked to see if

Erik had . . . and I got so involved that . . . All right, it was stupid!' he concluded his confused excuse. He ran his hand through his hair, making it stick straight up.

'From now on. No working. Promise me. Just you and Maja. Now give me a thumbs up.' He stuck up both thumbs, trying to look as trustworthy as he could.

Erica let out a big sigh and got up from her chair. 'Okay, sweetie, it doesn't look as if you've suffered any. Shall we forgive Pappa and go downstairs to fix dinner?' Maja nodded. 'Pappa can cook carbonara for us, to make up for today,' said Erica, heading downstairs, balancing Maja on her hip. Maja nodded eagerly. Pappa's carbonara was one of her favourite dishes.

'So did you reach any conclusions?' asked Erica later as she sat at the kitchen table watching Patrik fry bacon and boil water for the spaghetti. Maja was installed in front of the TV watching *Bolibompa*, so the adults had some peace and quiet to themselves.

'He most likely died sometime between the fifteenth and the seventeenth of June.' Patrik moved the bacon around in the pan. 'Damn it!' Some of the grease spattered his arm. 'That hurts! Good thing I don't fry bacon naked.'

'You know what, darling? I agree. It's a good thing you don't fry bacon naked.' Erica gave him a wink, and he went over to kiss her on the lips.

'So I'm your "darling" again, eh? Does that mean I'm out of the doghouse?'

Erica pretended to think about it for a moment. 'I wouldn't go that far, but you might be soon. If the carbonara is really good, I might reconsider.'

'So how was your day?' asked Patrik, returning to his cooking. He cautiously lifted out the pieces of bacon and placed them on a paper towel to absorb the grease. The trick to making a good carbonara was really crisp bacon; there was nothing worse than limp bacon.

'Where should I begin?' said Erica, sighing. First she told him about Anna's visit and her problems as the stepmother to a teenager. Then she recounted what had happened when she went to see Britta. Patrik put down the spatula and stared at her in surprise.

'You went over to her house to ask her questions? And the old woman has Alzheimer's? No wonder her husband yelled at you. I would have too.'

'Oh, thanks a lot. Anna said the same thing, so I've heard enough criticism about that, thank you very much.' Erica sulked. 'I didn't actually know about her condition when I went over there.'

'So what did she say?' asked Patrik, putting spaghetti into the boiling water.

'You realize that's enough for a small army, right?' Erica said when she saw that he'd put almost two-thirds of the packet into the pot.

'Am I cooking dinner or are you?' said Patrik, pointing the spatula at her. 'Okay, so what did she say?'

'Well, first of all it seems that they spent a lot of time together when they were young, Britta and my mother. Apparently they were a close-knit group, the two of them and Erik Frankel and somebody named Frans.'

'Frans Ringholm?' asked Patrik as he stirred the spaghetti.

'Yes, I think that's his name. Frans Ringholm. Why? Do you know him?' Erica gave him a quizzical look, but Patrik just shrugged.

'Did she say anything else? Has she had any contact with Erik or Frans? Or Axel, for that matter?'

'I don't think so,' said Erica. 'It didn't seem as though any of them had kept in touch with each other, but I could be wrong.' She frowned, rerunning the conversation in her mind. 'There was something . . .' she said hesitantly.

Patrik stopped stirring as he waited for her to go on.

'She said something . . . something about Erik and "old

185

bones". About how they should be left in peace. And that Erik had said . . . No, then she slipped into a fog and I couldn't understand anything else. She was really confused, so I don't know how much weight to attach to what she said. It was probably just nonsense.'

'Not necessarily,' said Patrik. 'Not necessarily. That's the second time today I've heard those words in connection with Erik Frankel. Old bones . . . I wonder what it could mean?'

And as Patrik pondered, the pasta water started to boil over.

Frans had carefully prepared before the meeting. The board convened once a month, and there were numerous issues they needed to discuss. It would soon be an election year, and their biggest challenge lay ahead of them.

'Is everyone here?' He glanced around the table, silently surveying the other five board members. They were all men. Equality between the sexes hadn't yet reached the neo-Nazi organizations. And presumably it never would.

The premises in Uddevalla had been leased from Bertolf Svensson, and they were now seated in the basement room of the block of flats that he owned. The space was otherwise used as a community hall, and there were still traces of the party that one of the tenants had held over the weekend. The group also had access to an office in the same building, but it was small and ill-suited to board meetings.

'They haven't cleaned up properly. I'm going to have a talk with them when we're done here,' muttered Bertolf, kicking an empty beer bottle and sending it rolling across the floor.

'Let's call this meeting to order,' said Frans sternly. They didn't have time for superfluous chatter. 'How far along are we with the preparations?'

Frans turned to Peter Lindgren, the youngest member of the board. In spite of Frans's loudly voiced objections, he'd been chosen to coordinate the campaign efforts. He simply didn't trust the man. Only last summer Lindgren had been in jail for assaulting a Somali at the marketplace in Grebbestad, and Frans didn't believe he'd be able to maintain his composure to the degree that would now be necessary.

As if to confirm Frans's suspicions, Peter evaded the question and said instead: 'Have you heard what happened in Fjällbacka?' He laughed. 'Someone apparently decided to do away with Frankel – that fucking traitor to his race.'

'Since I assume that none of us had anything to do with that, I suggest we get back to the agenda at hand,' said Frans, fixing his eyes on Peter. For a moment the two men fought a silent battle for power.

Then Peter looked away. 'We're making good progress. We've brought in some new recruits, and we've made sure that everyone, new and old, is prepared to do some of the footwork to spread our message over a wide area leading up to the election.'

'Good,' said Frans curtly. 'What about the registration of the party? Has that been done? And the ballots?'

'All under control.' Peter drummed his fingers on the table, clearly annoyed at being interrogated like a schoolboy. Unable to resist a dig at Frans, he added: 'So it looks as though you couldn't protect your old pal. What was so important about that old guy that you thought it was worth sticking your neck out for him? People have been talking about it, you know. Questioning your loyalty.'

Frans stood up and glared at Peter. Werner Hermansson, who was sitting on the other side of Frans, took hold of his arm. 'Don't listen to him, Frans. And for God's sake, Peter, take it easy. This is ridiculous. We should be talking about how to proceed, not sitting here flinging shit at each other. Okay now, shake hands.' Werner looked first at Peter, then at Frans. Aside from Frans, he was the longest-serving member of Sweden's Friends; he'd also known Frans longer than any of the others. It was Peter's welfare and not Frans's that he was looking out for now. He'd seen what Frans was capable of.

For a moment everything hung in the balance. Then Frans sat down.

'At the risk of sounding repetitive, I will again suggest that we return to the agenda. Any objections? Are there any other extraneous subjects that we need to waste time on? Well?' He stared at each of the board members until they looked away. Then he went on:

'It seems that most of the practical matters are falling into place. That being the case, shall we move on and talk about the issues that should form the party platform? I've been listening to what people have to say here in town, and I really think we can win a seat on the municipal council this time around. People realize how lax the national government and the county have been with regard to immigration issues. They can see how their jobs are going to non-Swedes. They can see how the municipal finances are being squandered on social services handouts to that same group. There is widespread dissatisfaction about how things are being run at local level, and that's what we need to exploit.'

Frans's mobile rang shrilly in his trouser pocket. 'Shit! Sorry, I forgot to switch it off. Just a second.' He took out the phone and glanced at the display. He recognized the number. Axel's home phone. He turned off his mobile without answering.

'Sorry. Okay, now where were we? Oh, right. We have a fantastic opportunity to exploit the ignorance that the town has demonstrated with regard to the refugee problem.'

Frans continued to talk as everyone around the table looked at him attentively. But his thoughts were racing in a completely different direction.

The decision to skip his maths class was a no-brainer. If there was one subject he never even considered showing up for, it was maths. There was something about numbers and all that stuff that made his skin crawl. He just didn't get it. His mind turned to mush the minute he tried to add or subtract. And what good was arithmetic to him anyway? He was never going to become one of those finance guys, so it would be a complete waste of time.

Per lit another cigarette as he surveyed the school playground. The others had left for Hedemyr's for a spot of shoplifting, but he hadn't felt like going along. He'd stayed over at Tomas's place last night, and they'd played Tomb Raider until five in the morning. His mother kept ringing his mobile until finally he switched it off. He would have preferred to stay in bed, but Tomas's mother had thrown him out when she left for work, so they'd come over here to the school, for want of a better idea.

Right now he was feeling really, really bored. Maybe he should have gone with the rest of the gang after all. He got up from the bench to saunter after them, but then sat down again when he saw Mattias come out of the school with that stupid bird in tow, the one everybody was always running after for some reason. He'd never understood why they thought Mia was so hot. He didn't go for that innocent-looking blonde type.

He pricked up his ears to listen in on what they were saying. Mattias was doing most of the talking, and it must be something interesting because Mia was hanging on every word, looking at him with those eyes of hers, baby-blue behind all the make-up. As they came closer, Per could hear bits and pieces of their conversation. He sat very still. Mattias was so focused on getting into Mia's knickers that he didn't even notice Per.

'You should have seen how white Adam went when he saw him. But I realized immediately what had to be done and told Adam to back out of there so we wouldn't disturb any evidence.'

'Wow,' said Mia admiringly.

Per laughed to himself. Jesus, Mattias was really laying it on thick to get her in the sack. Her knickers were probably wet.

'. . . And the cool thing is that nobody else dared go over there. Some of the others talked about it, but we all know it's one thing to talk about something, and another to actually do it.'

Per had heard enough. He leapt up from the bench and ran towards Mattias. Before Mattias knew what was happening, Per had flung himself at the boy from behind and knocked him to the ground. Per sat on his back, twisting his arm up until Mattias screamed with pain, and then he grabbed hold of his hair. That pathetic surfer hairstyle was made to be yanked. Then Per very deliberately lifted Mattias's head and slammed it against the asphalt. He ignored the fact that Mia was screaming a few metres away. As she ran off to the school for help, Per slammed Mattias's head against the hard surface again.

'What kind of shit are you going around spouting! You're such a wanker –don't think I'm going to let you keep doing that, you fucking little wimp.' Per was so furious that everything went black before his eyes, and the rest of the world disappeared. The only thing he was aware of was his hand holding on to Mattias's hair, and the jolt that went through his fingers every time the boy's head struck the pavement. The only thing he saw was the blood that started to colour the black surface under Mattias's head. He was filled with satisfaction when he saw those patches of red. He felt it deep inside his chest, tasted it, savoured it. He felt a calm that he'd rarely felt before. He made no attempt to resist the rage – he just let it fill him, surrendering to it, relishing the feeling of something primitive that pushed aside all else, everything that was complicated, sad, small. He didn't want to stop, couldn't stop. He kept on shouting and hitting, kept on seeing that patch of red, all sticky and wet, every time he lifted Mattias's head, until he felt someone grabbing him from behind and yanking him away.

'What are you doing?' Per turned around with a real sense of surprise to see the angry expression on the maths teacher's face. Up in the school building there were faces peering from every window, and a small flock of curious bystanders had gathered in the playground. Per stared without emotion at Mattias's still form, and without resisting allowed himself to be dragged several metres away from his victim.

'My God, are you out of your mind?' The maths teacher's face was only an inch away. He was shouting loudly, but Per turned his head, feeling nothing.

For a moment he had felt so fantastic. Now there was only emptiness.

He stood in the hallway staring at the pictures on the wall for a long time. So many happy times. So much love. The black-and-white photos from their marriage, when he and Britta looked more solemn than they actually felt. Britta holding Anna-Greta in her arms as he took their picture. If he remembered correctly, he'd put down the camera after taking the photo and held his daughter in his arms for the first time. Britta had nervously reminded him to support the baby's head, but it was as if he instinctively knew how to hold her. And he'd always taken an active role in caring for their babies, to a much greater degree than was expected of a husband back then. Many times his mother-in-law had admonished him, saying that it wasn't a man's job to change nappies or give babies a bath. But he couldn't stay away. It had felt so natural to him, and he didn't think it was fair for Britta to carry the whole load and mind the three girls that they'd had, so close in age.

Actually, he would have liked to have more children, but after the third birth, which had been ten times more

191

complicated than the first two put together, the doctor had taken him aside and said that Britta's body probably wouldn't survive another pregnancy. And Britta had wept. Bowed her head without looking at him and with tears running down her face, she'd apologized for not being able to give him a son. He had stared at her in surprise. It had never occurred to Herman to wish for anything other than what he'd been given. Surrounded by his wife and three girls, he felt richer than he'd ever dreamed possible. It had taken him a while to convince her of this, but when Britta realized that he meant what he said, she stopped crying, and then they focused all their attention on the girls that they'd brought into the world.

Now there were so many to love. The girls had their own children, whom Herman and Britta loved dearly, and he'd once again demonstrated his skill in changing nappies whenever they went over to help out their daughters. It was so hard for them nowadays, trying to handle everything at once, a job, a home, and a family. But he and Britta had been happy and grateful that there was room for them, that there was someone they could help, someone they could love. And now a few of their grandchildren had children. His fingers were certainly stiffer now, but with those new fancy 'up-and-go' nappies, he could still change one now and again. He shook his head. Where had all the years gone?

He went upstairs to the bedroom and sat down on the edge of the bed. Britta was taking her afternoon nap. It had been a bad day. A few times she hadn't recognized him, thinking that she was back in her parents' home. She'd asked for her mother. And then for her father, with fear clearly audible in her voice. And he had stroked her hair, assuring her again and again that her father had been gone for many years. That he could no longer do her any harm.

He caressed her hand as it lay on top of the crocheted coverlet. Her skin was wrinkled, with the same age spots as he had on his own hands. But her fingers were still long and elegant. And he smiled to himself when he saw her pink nail polish. She'd always been a bit vain; she still was. But he had never complained. She'd always been a beautiful wife, and during fifty-five years of marriage, he'd never so much as cast a glance at another woman.

Her eyelids fluttered. She was dreaming about something. He wished that he could get inside her dreams. Live inside them with her, and pretend that everything was the way it used to be.

Today, in her confusion, she'd talked about the thing they'd agreed never to mention. But as her brain disintegrated and crumbled, the dams were bursting, the walls that they'd built up over the years to contain their secret. They'd shared it for so long that it had somehow disappeared inside the fabric of their life, until it was invisible. He'd allowed himself to relax, to forget about it.

It hadn't been a good idea for Erik to visit her. Not at all. That was what had created the crack in the wall that was now growing bigger. If it couldn't be plugged, a deluge was going to come pouring out and drag all of them under.

But at least he didn't have to worry about Erik any more. They didn't need to worry about Erik any more.

He kept on patting her hand.

'Oh, I forgot to tell you: Karin phoned. You have a date to meet for a walk at ten o'clock. At the pharmacy.'

Patrik stopped in mid-stride. 'Karin? Today? In' – he glanced at his watch – 'half an hour?'

'Sorry,' said Erica, although her tone of voice indicated that she wasn't the least bit sorry. Then she relented. 'I was thinking of running over to the library to do some research, so if you and Maja could be ready in twenty minutes, you can catch a ride with me.'

'Is that . . .' Patrik hesitated. 'Is that all right with you?'

Erica went over and gave him a kiss. 'Compared with using a police station as a day-care centre for our daughter, a date to take a walk with your ex-wife is nothing.'

'Ha, ha, very funny,' said Patrik sullenly, even though he knew Erica was right. What he'd done yesterday was pretty stupid.

'So don't just stand there! Go and get dressed! I would definitely object if you went off to meet your ex-wife looking like that.' Erica laughed, looking her husband up and down as he stood in the bedroom, clad only in his underwear and a pair of tube socks.

'What, I don't look hunky enough like this?' said Patrik, striking a bodybuilder pose. Erica laughed so hard she had to sit down on the bed.

'Oh, God, stop it.'

'For your information,' said Patrik, pretending to be insulted, 'I'm so disgustingly buff that I have a hard time achieving this look, but it's important to lull the crooks into a false sense of security.' He patted his stomach, which quivered a bit more that it should have if he'd touched nothing but muscle. Marriage hadn't made his waistline dwindle to any significant degree.

'Stop!' hooted Erica. 'I'll never be able to have sex with you again if you don't stop it.' Patrik responded by flinging himself on the bed with his best beast-like howl as he started tickling her.

'Take that back! Are you going to take that back? Are you?'

'Yes, yes, I take it back! Now stop!' cried Erica, who was terribly ticklish.

'Mamma! Pappa!' Maja was standing in the doorway, clapping her hands delightedly at the show. She'd been enticed out of her room by all the interesting sounds coming from her parents' room.

'Come over here and let Pappa tickle you too,' said Patrik,

lifting Maja on to the bed. The next second both mother and daughter were howling with laughter. Afterwards all three of them lay on the bed, drained and snuggled up next to each other, until Erica abruptly sat up. 'The two of you better hurry. I can dress Maja while you make yourself decent.'

Twenty minutes later Erica pulled up in front of the municipal building, which also housed the pharmacy and library. This would be the first time she'd met Karin, even though she'd heard a fair bit about her, of course. She wasn't sure what to expect; Patrik had been rather tight-lipped when it came to the subject of his first marriage.

She parked the car, helped Patrik lift the pushchair out of the boot, and then went with him to meet Karin. Taking a deep breath, she held out her hand.

'Hi, I'm Erica,' she said. 'We spoke on the phone yesterday.'

'How nice to meet you!' said Karin, and Erica realized to her surprise that she instantly liked this woman standing in front of her. Out of the corner of her eye she saw how uncomfortable Patrik looked, rocking back and forth, and she couldn't help enjoying the situation. It was actually quite funny.

She studied his ex-wife with curiosity. Karin was thinner than she was and a bit shorter. Her dark hair was gathered up in a simple ponytail. She had delicate features, wore no make-up, and looked rather . . . tired. No doubt from taking care of a toddler, thought Erica, realizing that she herself wouldn't have stood up to close inspection before they'd managed to get Maja to sleep through the night.

They chatted for a while, but then Erica waved goodbye and headed for the library. It came as a relief to finally put a face to the woman who had been such a major part of Patrik's life for eight years. She hadn't even seen a picture of her before. But considering the circumstances that had caused them to split up, it was understandable that Patrik wouldn't have wanted to keep any photographic evidence of the time they'd spent together.

The library was as calm as always. She'd spent many hours here, and there was something about libraries that gave her a tremendous sense of satisfaction.

'Hi, Christian!'

The librarian glanced up and smiled when he saw Erica.

'Hi, Erica. How nice to see you again! What can I help you with today?' His Småland accent sounded so pleasant. Erica wondered why people from Småland always seemed so likable the minute they opened their mouths. In Christian's case, the first impression held true. He was always cordial and helpful, as well as good at his job. There had been many occasions when he'd helped Erica find information that she'd only the faintest hope of being able to locate.

'Do you need to know more about the same case that you were researching last time?' he asked, giving her a hopeful glance. Erica's research questions were always a welcome diversion from the rather monotonous routine of his job, which mainly consisted of looking up information about fish, sailboats, and the fauna of Bohuslän.

'No, not today,' she said, sitting down on a chair across from him in front of the information desk. 'Today I need some facts about people here in Fjällbacka. And certain events.'

'People and events. Could you possibly be a little more specific?' he said with a wink.

'I'll try.' Erica quickly rattled off a list of names: 'Britta Johansson, Frans Ringholm, Axel Frankel, Elsy Falck – or rather, Moström – and . . .' she hesitated a few seconds before adding, 'Erik Frankel.'

Christian gave a start. 'Isn't he the man who was found murdered?'

'That's right,' said Erica.

'And Elsy? Is that your . . .?'

196

'My mother, yes. I need some information about all of these people, from around the time of the Second World War. In fact, let's limit the search to the war years.'

'In other words, 1939 to 1945.'

Erica nodded and watched expectantly as Christian typed the desired request into his computer. 'How's it going with your own project, by the way?'

A cloud seemed to pass over the librarian's face. Then it was gone, and he answered her question. 'I'm about halfway done. Thanks for asking. And it's largely because of the advice you've given me that I've made it this far.'

'Oh, it was nothing,' said Erica, looking embarrassed. 'Just let me know if you need any more writing tips, or if you'd like me to have a look at your manuscript. By the way, have you chosen a working title?'

'*The Mermaid*,' said Christian, not meeting her eye. 'It's going to be called *The Mermaid*.'

'What a good title. How'd you come up with . . .?' Erica asked, but Christian brusquely shook his head, indicating that he didn't want to discuss it. She looked at him in surprise. That was so unlike him. She wondered if she'd said something to offend him, but couldn't think what it might be.

'Here are some articles that may interest you,' Christian then said. 'Shall I print them out for you?'

'Yes, please,' said Erica, still a bit startled. But when Christian returned a few minutes later, bringing her a stack of pages from the printer, he was back to his usual self.

'This should keep you busy for a while. Just let me know if there's anything else I can help you with.'

Erica thanked him and left the library. She was in luck. The café across the street was open, and she bought herself a coffee before she sat down and began to read. But what she found was so interesting that she left her cup untouched, and the coffee grew cold.

*　　*　　*

'All right, what have we found out so far?' Mellberg grimaced as he stretched out his legs. He was surprised that the aches and pains from exercising could last so long. At this rate, he would recover just in time for the next mangling of his body at the Friday salsa class. But strangely enough, the idea wasn't as alarming as he'd imagined. There was something about the combination of the fascinating music, the closeness of Rita's body, and the fact that by the end of the previous week's class his feet had actually started to figure out the moves. No, he wasn't planning to quit anytime soon. If there was anyone who had the potential to become the salsa king of Tanumshede, he was it.

'Sorry, what did you say?' Mellberg gave a start. He'd completely missed what Paula was saying as he lapsed into daydreams about Latin rhythms.

'As Paula said, we've managed to pin down the time frame for Erik Frankel's murder,' said Gösta. 'He was with his . . . girlfriend, or whatever you call people in that age bracket, on the fifteenth of June. He split up with her, and he was visibly drunk, which according to her was highly unusual.'

'And the cleaning woman went over to the house on the seventeenth of June, but couldn't get inside,' Martin added. 'That doesn't necessarily mean that he was dead by then, but it's a clear indication that he may have been. She'd never been unable to get into the house before. If the brothers weren't at home, they would always leave a key for her.'

'Okay, good, then for the time being we'll work on the assumption that Erik died between the fifteenth and seventeenth of June. Check with his brother to find out whether he was at home or had already left for Paris.' Mellberg leaned down to scratch Ernst behind the ears. The dog was lying under the kitchen table, having settled on top of Mellberg's feet, as usual.

'But do you really think that Axel Frankel had anything

to do with . . .?' Paula stopped in mid-sentence when she saw Mellberg's cross expression.

'I don't think anything at the moment. But you know as well as I do that most murders are committed by a family member. So let's give the brother a shake. Okay?'

She nodded. For once Mellberg was right. She couldn't let the fact that she'd found Axel Frankel so likable hinder the job she needed to do.

'What about the boys who broke into the house? Have we secured any leads from them?' Mellberg looked at his colleagues seated around the table. Everyone turned to Gösta. He fidgeted nervously.

'Ah . . . well . . . yes and no. I took shoe prints and fingerprints from one of the boys – Adam – but I haven't really had time to . . . talk to the other one.'

Mellberg opened his eyes wide. 'You've had several days to take care of this simple task, and yet you haven't – and I quote – had *time* for it. Is that correct?'

Gösta nodded, looking downhearted. 'Er, uh, yes . . . that's correct. But I'll see to it today.' Yet another glare from Mellberg.

'Immediately, ASAP,' said Gösta, looking down.

'You'd better hop to it,' said Mellberg, who then shifted his attention to Martin and Paula.

'Anything else? How's it going with Ringholm? Anything there? Personally, I think it seems like the most promising lead, and we should really turn things upside down with Sweden's Friends.'

'We've spoken to Frans, but didn't get anything more to go on. According to him, there were certain elements within the organization that had threatened Frankel, but he tried to intervene to protect Erik because of their old friendship.'

'And these "elements"' – Mellberg sketched quote marks around the words with his fingers – 'have we talked to them?'

'No, not yet,' said Martin calmly. 'But it's on the agenda for today.'

'Good, good,' said Mellberg, shoving Ernst off of his feet because they were starting to go numb. Ernst let loose an audible doggy fart, then settled more comfortably on top of his master's feet. 'All right, that leaves only one more thing to discuss. This station is not a day-care centre! Do you understand?!' He stared at Annika, who been quietly taking notes during the meeting. She stared back at him over the rims of her reading glasses. After a long pause, Mellberg began to squirm, wondering if his tone of voice might have been a bit too harsh.

Then she said, 'I took care of my work even though I was watching Maja for a little while yesterday, and that's the only thing that you need to worry about, Bertil.'

A silent power struggle was played out as Annika calmly met Mellberg's gaze. Finally he looked away, muttering, 'Well, all right, you're probably the best judge of –'

'Besides, it was thanks to Patrik dropping by that we realized we'd forgotten to check on Erik's bank accounts.' Paula winked at Annika to show her support.

'I'm sure we would have thought of it sooner or later . . . but thanks to Patrick it ended up being sooner, instead of later,' said Gösta, and he glanced at Annika before he lowered his eyes and returned to studying the tabletop.

'Okay, but I thought he was on paternity leave,' said Mellberg sullenly, well aware that he'd lost the battle. 'What are you all waiting for? Now that we have something to go on, let's get busy.' Everybody got up and put their coffee cups in the dishwasher.

At that moment the phone rang.

FJÄLLBACKA 1944

'I thought I'd find you here.' Elsy sat down next to Erik, sheltered in the cleft of a boulder.

'This is where I have the greatest chance of being left in peace,' said Erik crossly, but then his expression softened and he closed the book he was holding on his lap.

'Sorry,' he said. 'I didn't mean to take out my bad mood on you.'

'Is Axel the reason for your bad mood?' asked Elsy gently. 'How are things at home?'

'It's like he's already dead,' said Erik, gazing out over the water that was lapping restlessly at the entrance to Fjällbacka harbour. 'At least my mother is acting that way, as if he's already dead. And my father just goes around muttering, refusing to even talk about it.'

'What about you? How do you feel?' asked Elsy, studying her friend. She knew Erik so well. Better than he thought. They'd spent so many hours playing together – she and Erik, Britta and Frans. There weren't many games left for them to play, now that they were all almost grown up. But at this moment, she saw no difference between the fourteen-year-old Erik and the five-year-old boy, who even in short pants had seemed like an old man in a small body. It was as if Erik had been born a little old man who gradually grew into his proper self. As if the child's body, the boy's body, and now the young man's, were stages he had to go through before he fit into the skin that suited him.

'I don't know how I feel,' said Erik curtly, looking away. But he wasn't fast enough, and Elsy saw tears welling up in his eyes.

'Yes, you do,' she said, staring at his profile. 'Talk to me.'

'I feel so . . . split. Part of me is so scared and sad about what's happened, and is going to happen, to Axel. Just the thought that he might die makes me . . .' He searched for the right words, but found none. But Elsy understood. She didn't speak, just waited for him to continue.

'But there's another part of me that feels so . . . angry.' His voice was deeper, hinting at how the adult Erik's voice would sound. 'I'm angry because now I'm even more invisible than I was before. I don't exist. As long as Axel was at home, it was as though he could reflect on to me some of the light that shone on him. A tiny beam, every now and then. A little glint of light, of attention, would be aimed at me. And that was enough. I've never wanted more than that. Axel deserved to be in the spotlight, to have the attention. He's always been better than me. I'd never dare do what he did. I'm not brave. I don't attract attention. And I don't have Axel's ability to make the people around me feel good. Because that's what I think his secret is . . . that he can always make other people feel good. I don't have that talent. I make people nervous and uneasy. They don't really know what to make of me. I know too much. I don't laugh enough. I . . .' He was forced to stop and take a breath, after what was quite possibly the longest continuous speech he'd ever given.

Elsy couldn't help laughing. 'Be careful you don't use up all your words at once, Erik. You're usually so sparing with what you say.' She smiled, but Erik clenched his jaws before going on.

'But that's exactly what I mean. And you know what? I think I could just start walking away, go further and further, just keep walking and never come back. And nobody at home would even notice that I was gone. To my mother and father I'm just a shadow on the periphery of their field of vision, and in some ways I think they'd find it a relief if that shadow disappeared so they could focus all their attention on Axel.' His voice broke, and again he turned away in shame.

Elsy put her arm around him and leaned her head on his shoulder, forcing him to come back from that dark place where he was trying to hide.

'Erik, I know that they'd notice if you disappeared. They're just . . . caught up in dealing with what happened to Axel.'

'It's been four months since the Germans took him,' said Erik dully. 'How long are they going to be focusing on that? Six months? A year? Two years? A lifetime? I'm here right now. I'm still here. Why doesn't that mean anything? And at the same time I feel like a terrible person because I'm jealous of my brother who's presumably sitting in prison and might be executed before anyone has a chance to see him again. What a great brother I am!'

'Nobody doubts that you love Axel.' Elsy patted his back. 'But it's not so strange that you also want to be seen, want to exist. And I for one know you do exist. But you have to tell them how you feel, you have to make them see you.'

'I don't dare.' Erik shook his head. 'What if they think I'm a terrible person?'

Elsy took his head between her hands and forced him to look at her. 'Listen to me, Erik Frankel. You are not a terrible person. You love your brother and your parents. But you're also grieving. You have to talk to them about it, you have to demand a little space for yourself. Do you understand?'

He tried to look away, but she was still holding his head between her hands, staring into his eyes.

Finally he nodded. 'You're right. I'll talk to them.'

Impulsively Elsy put her arms around him and gave him a hug. She felt him relax as she stroked his back.

'What the devil . . .?' A voice behind them made them draw apart. Elsy turned around and saw Frans staring at them, his face white and his hands clenched into fists.

'What the devil . . .!' he repeated. He seemed to be having a hard time finding any other words. Else realized how it must have looked and spoke calmly in an attempt to make Frans understand what was really going on before his temper got away with him. She'd seen his anger flare as quickly as a lit match many times before. There was something about Frans that pushed him always to the verge of violence, as if he were constantly looking for reasons to lash out. And she was smart enough to know that he had a crush on her. In this situation, there might be disastrous consequences if she couldn't manage to explain.

'Erik and I were just sitting here talking.' She spoke calmly and quietly.

'Oh yeah, I can see you were just sitting and talking,' said Frans, and there was something in his eyes that made Elsy shudder.

'We were talking about Axel and how hard it's been because he's not here,' she said, keeping her gaze fixed on Frans. The wild, cold look in his eyes faded a bit. She kept on talking. 'I was consoling Erik. That's what I was doing. Why don't you sit down here and join us?'

She patted the rock. He hesitated. But his fists had unclenched and the cold expression was now completely gone. He sighed heavily and sat down.

'Sorry,' he said, without looking at her.

'That's okay,' she replied, 'but don't be so quick to jump to conclusions.'

Frans sat there in silence for a while. Then he turned to look at her. The intensity of the emotion she saw in his eyes suddenly frightened her more than his cold anger had done. She had a premonition that this wasn't going to end well.

She also thought about Britta and the infatuated looks she was always sending in Frans's direction.

No, this wasn't going to end well.

'She seems very nice.' Karin smiled as she pushed Ludde in his pushchair.

'Erica is the best,' said Patrik, a smile tugging at his lips. Of course they'd had a few quarrels recently, but that wasn't important. He counted himself a lucky man, waking up next to Erica every morning.

'I wish I could say the same about Leif,' said Karin. 'But I'm starting to get really tired of being married to a dance band musician. I knew what I was getting myself into, though, so I suppose I can't complain.'

'Things change when you have kids,' said Patrik, his remark half a statement and half a question.

'You think so?' replied Karin sarcastically. 'Maybe I was naïve, but I had no idea how much work it is, and how many demands there are on a person when you have a young child, and . . . it's not easy having to carry the entire load myself. Sometimes it feels like I'm the one who does all the hard work, getting up at night, changing nappies, playing with him, feeding him, taking him to the doctor when he's sick. And then Leif comes waltzing in the door and Ludde welcomes him home as if he were Santa Claus. And that feels so unfair.'

'But who does Ludde want if he hurts himself?' asked Patrik.

Karin smiled. 'You're right. I'm the one he wants. So I guess it means something to him after all that I'm the one who comforts him in the middle of the night. But I don't know . . . I feel duped somehow. This isn't the way things were supposed to be.' She sighed and straightened Ludde's cap, which had twisted round so that one ear was covered.

'Personally, I'm finding it much more fun than I'd ever imagined,' said Patrik, only realizing what a stupid remark it was when he caught the piercing look that Karin gave him.

'Does Erica feel the same way?' she asked sharply, and Patrik saw her point.

'No, she doesn't. Or at least she hasn't during the past year,' said Patrik. He felt a pang of guilt at the thought of how pale and joyless Erica had been during the first months after Maja was born.

'Could it be because Erica has been yanked out of her adult life to stay home with Maja, while you've gone off to work every day?'

'But I've helped out as much as I could,' Patrik protested.

'Helped out, sure,' said Karin, steering the pushchair and moving ahead as they came to a narrow stretch of road leading to Badholmen. 'But there's a huge difference between "helping out" and being the one who has to shoulder most of the responsibility. It's not so simple to work out how to calm a crying baby, or how and when he needs to eat, or how to keep yourself and the child busy for at least five days a week, usually without any type of adult companionship. It's a whole other matter to be the CEO of Baby Incorporated, compared with just being an assistant standing on the sidelines, taking inventory.'

'But you can't just lump all fathers together like that,' said Patrik as he manoeuvred the pushchair up the steep hill. 'Often the mothers don't want to relinquish control, and if the husband does change a nappy, she'll say he's done it wrong, or if he feeds the baby, she'll say he's not holding the bottle properly, and so on. It's not always so easy for the fathers to participate in that CEO role you're talking about.'

Karin didn't say anything for a few minutes. Then she looked at Patrik and said, 'Was Erica like that, when she stayed home with Maja? Refusing to let you participate?' She waited for his answer.

Patrik thought hard for a moment and then was forced to admit: 'No, she wasn't. I think I was actually glad not to have the major responsibility. When Maja was unhappy and I tried to comfort her, it was nice to know that, no matter how much she cried, I could always hand her over to Erica if I couldn't get her to calm down. And Erica would take care of things. And it was great to go off to work every morning, knowing I'd come home to a big welcome from Maja in the evening.'

'And in the meantime you got your dose of the adult world,' said Karin drily. 'So how are things now that you do have the major responsibility? Everything okay?'

Patrik thought for a moment and then had to shake his head. 'Well, I haven't exactly received top marks as a stay-at-home dad. But it's not easy. Erica works at home, you see, and she knows where everything is and . . .' He shook his head again.

'That sounds so familiar. Every time Leif comes home, he stands there shouting: "Karin! Where are the nappies?!" Sometimes I wonder how you men manage to do your jobs at all, since at home you can't remember where anything's kept.'

'Oh, come on now,' said Patrik, giving Karin a poke in the side. 'We're not that helpless. Give us a little credit, okay? Only a generation ago men would never have changed their kids' nappies, and we've come a long way since then. But you can't make these kinds of transformations overnight. Our fathers were our role models, they're the ones who influenced us, and it takes time to adapt. But we're doing the best we can.'

'Maybe *you* are,' said Karin, and again she sounded bitter. 'That's definitely not the case with Leif.'

Patrik didn't reply. There was really nothing to say. And when they parted in Sälvik at the intersection near Norderviken Sailing Club, he felt both sad and pensive. For a long time he'd harboured bad feelings towards Karin because of the way she'd betrayed him. Now he just felt enormously sorry for her.

The phone call to the station had them jumping into a police car immediately. Mellberg, as usual, had muttered some excuse and hurried to his office, but Martin, Paula, and Gösta had raced off to Tanumshede secondary school. On arrival, they'd been directed to the principal's office and since this wasn't their first trip to the school, Martin had no trouble finding the way.

'What's happened here?' He glanced around the room; a surly-looking teenager sat on a chair, flanked by the principal and two men, whom Martin guessed were teachers.

'Per beat up one of our students,' said the principal grimly as he sat down behind his desk. 'I'm glad you got here so fast.'

'How is the student doing?' asked Paula.

'It doesn't look good. The school nurse is with him, and an ambulance is on the way. I've phoned Per's mother. She should be here soon.' The principal glared at the boy, who responded with an indifferent yawn.

'You'll have to come down to the police station with us,' said Martin, signalling for Per to stand up. He turned to the principal. 'See if you can reach his mother before she gets here, otherwise you'll just have to ask her to meet us at the station. My colleague, Paula Morales, will stay here and interview any witnesses to the attack.'

'I'll get started right away,' Paula said, making for the door.

Per was still sporting the same indifferent expression as he sauntered down the corridor with the police officers. A large crowd of curious students had gathered, and Per reacted to the attention by grinning and giving them the finger.

'Fucking idiots,' he muttered.

Gösta gave him a sharp look. 'Keep your mouth shut until we get to the station.'

Per shrugged but obeyed. As they drove back to the squat building that housed both the police and the fire brigade, he sat staring out of the window in silence.

When they reached the station, they put the boy in an interview room and waited for his mother to arrive. Martin's mobile rang. He listened with interest and then turned to Gösta, a pensive look on his face.

'That was Paula,' he said. 'Do you know who Per beat up?'

'No, is it somebody we know?'

'You bet. Mattias Larsson, one of the boys who found Erik Frankel. They're taking him to the hospital now. So we'll need to interview him later on.'

Gösta received this information without comment, but Martin saw that his face had turned pale.

Ten minutes later Carina came running through the front door into the reception area, out of breath and asking for her son. Annika calmly brought her to Martin's office.

'Where's Per? What has he done?' She was fighting back the tears and sounded on the verge of hysteria. Martin shook hands with her as he introduced himself. Formalities and familiar routines often had a calming effect. As they did now. Carina repeated her questions, but in a more subdued tone of voice, and then she sat down on the chair that Martin offered her. He grimaced as he sat down at his desk, recognizing a familiar smell emanating from the woman across

210

from him. Stale booze. Maybe she'd been to a party the day before. But he didn't think so. Her slightly bloated features were one of the tell-tale signs of alcoholism.

'According to the report from the school, Per assaulted a fellow pupil.'

'Oh, dear God,' she said, gripping the armrests of her chair. 'How . . .? The boy, is he . . .' She couldn't finish the sentence.

'He's being taken to the hospital. Apparently he was severely beaten.'

'But why?' She swallowed hard, shaking her head.

'That's what we aim to find out. We have Per in one of the interview rooms here, and we need your permission to ask him some questions.'

Carina nodded. 'Yes, of course.' She swallowed hard again.

'All right then. Let's go and have a talk with Per.' Martin led the way. He paused in the corridor to knock on the door jamb of Gösta's office. 'Come with us. We're going to have a talk with the boy.'

Carina and Gösta shook hands, and then all three of them went into the room where Per was waiting, trying to look as if the whole business bored him. But he lost his composure the minute he saw his mother come in. Not entirely, but there was a slight twitch at the corner of his eye. A trembling in his hands. Then he forced himself to resume the indifferent expression and turned his gaze towards the wall.

'Per, what have you done now?' Carina's voice rose in pitch as she sat down next to her son and went to put her arm around him. He shook her off and refused to answer.

Martin and Gösta sat across from Per and Carina, and Martin switched on the recorder. From habit, he had also brought along a pen and notepad, which he placed on the table. Then he rattled off the date and time for the sake of the recording and cleared his throat.

'All right, Per, can you tell us what happened? By the way, Mattias has been taken to the hospital. In case you were wondering.'

Per merely smiled.

'Per!' His mother poked him in the side with her elbow. 'You need to answer the question. And of course you were worried about the boy! Right?' Her voice was shrill, and her son still refused to look at her.

'Let's give Per time to answer,' said Gösta, winking at Carina to calm her down.

They sat in silence, waiting for the fifteen-year-old to respond. Finally he tossed his head and said, 'That Mattias talks a load of shit.'

'What kind of "shit"?' said Martin, keeping his voice friendly. 'Could you be a little more precise?'

Another lengthy pause. Then: 'He was chatting up Mia, bragging about how fucking brave he was when he and Adam broke into that old guy's house and found his body and how nobody else would have dared! I mean, what the fuck was that about? They only got the idea because I'd already been inside. Their ears were as big as satellite dishes when I told them about all the cool stuff he had. Everybody knows they weren't the first to break in. Those fucking nerds.'

He threw back his head and laughed, while his mother stared shamefaced at the tabletop.

'Are you talking about Erik Frankel's house?' said Martin, incredulous.

'Yeah, the guy that Mattias and Adam found dead. The one with all the Nazi stuff. Really cool stuff,' said Per, his eyes shining. 'I was hoping to pick up a few nice pieces, but then the old guy showed up and locked me in and called my father and . . .'

'Whoa – hold on,' said Martin, holding up his hands. 'Slow down a bit. Are you saying that Erik Frankel caught

212

you when you broke into his house? And that he locked you up?'

Per nodded. 'I didn't think he was home, so I went in through a basement window. But he came downstairs while I was in that room with all the books and shit, and he closed the door and locked it. Then he made me give him my father's phone number so he could call him.'

'Did you know about this?' Martin turned to Carina, giving her a sharp look.

She nodded reluctantly. 'I only found out yesterday. Kjell, my ex-husband, didn't tell me about it before, so I had no idea. And I can't understand why you didn't give him *my* number, Per, instead of getting your father mixed up in this!'

'You wouldn't have been able to handle it,' said Per, looking at his mother for the first time. 'You just lie around drinking all the time and don't give a shit about anything else. You reek of booze, by the way. Just so you know!' Per's hands started shaking, his composure cracking again.

Tears rolled down Carina's cheeks. 'Is that the only thing you have to say about me, after all I've done for you? I gave birth to you, fed you, dressed you, and took care of you all those years when your father didn't want anything to do with us.' She turned to Martin and Gösta. 'One day he just up and left. Packed his suitcases and took off with some twenty-five-year-old tart that he'd got pregnant. He walked out on me and Per without so much as a backward glance. Got on with starting a new family while we were left behind like yesterday's rubbish.'

'It's been ten years since Pappa left,' said Per wearily. He suddenly looked much older than his fifteen years.

'What's your father's name?' asked Gösta.

'My ex-husband is Kjell Ringholm,' replied Carina tensely. 'I can give you his phone number, if you like.'

Martin and Gösta exchanged glances.

'Would that be the same Kjell Ringholm who writes for

213

Bohusläningen?' said Gösta, the pieces falling into place in his mind. 'The son of Frans Ringholm?'

'Frans is my grandfather,' said Per proudly. 'He's so cool. He's even been to prison, but now he does political work instead. They're going to win the next council election, and then those black fuckers are going to be driven out of the district.'

'Per!' exclaimed Carina, shocked. Then she turned to the officers. 'He's at that age when he's testing things. And Frans isn't a good influence on him. Kjell has forbidden Per to see his grandfather.'

'As if that would stop me,' muttered Per. 'And that old man with the Nazi stuff? He got what he deserved. I heard the way he talked to my father when he came to get me. All that shit about how he could give my father good material for the articles he was writing about Sweden's Friends, and especially about Frans. They didn't think I was listening, but I heard them make an appointment to meet again. Fucking traitors, the pair of them. I can understand why Grandpa is ashamed of my father,' said Per hostilely.

Smack! Carina slapped her son, and in the ensuing silence mother and son stared at each other with both surprise and hatred. Then Carina's expression softened. 'I'm sorry, sweetheart, I'm really sorry. I didn't mean to . . . I . . . I'm sorry.' She tried to give her son a hug, but he pushed her away.

'Get away from me, you fucking drunk. Don't you dare touch me!'

'Okay, everybody, calm down.' Gösta rose from his chair, glowering at Carina and Per. 'I don't think we're going to get much further at the moment. You can leave now, Per. But . . .' He looked at Martin, who nodded almost imperceptibly. 'But we're going to have to contact the social services office about this. We've seen enough to cause concern, and we will recommend that social services take a closer look. In the meantime we'll be carrying on our own investigation.'

'Is that necessary?' asked Carina, her voice quavering, but her question lacked any real force. Gösta had the impression she was relieved that somebody was going to take control of their situation.

After Per and Carina left the station, walking side by side without looking at each other, Gösta followed Martin to his office.

'Well, that certainly gave us something to think about,' said Martin as he sat down.

'It certainly did,' said Gösta. He bit his lip, rocking back and forth on his heels.

'You look like you have something to say. What is it?'

'Hmm . . . well, it might not be important.' Then Gösta made up his mind. It was something that had been gnawing at his subconscious for a few days, and during the interview with Per, he'd realized what it was. Now the question was how he should put it into words. Martin was not going to be happy.

Axel stood on the porch for a long time, hesitating. Finally he knocked. Herman opened the door almost immediately.

'So, it's you.'

He nodded. He stayed where he was, making no attempt to enter.

'Come in. I didn't tell her you were coming. I didn't know if she'd remember.'

'Is she that bad?' Axel looked with sympathy at the man standing in front of him. Herman looked tired. It couldn't be easy.

'Is this the whole clan?' asked Axel, nodding at the photos in the hall as he stepped inside.

Herman's face lit up. 'Yes, that's everybody.'

Axel studied the photographs, hands clasped behind his back. Midsummer and birthday celebrations, Christmas get-togethers and ordinary days. A swarm of people, including

215

children and grandchildren. For a moment he allowed himself to reflect on how his own wall of photos would have looked, if he'd had one. Pictures from his days at the office. Endless piles of documents. Countless dinners with politicians and others with the power to wield influence. Few, if any, would be pictures of friends. There weren't many who had the energy to keep up with him, who could stand the constant drive to track down yet another war criminal who'd managed to live an undeservedly comfortable life. Another former Nazi with blood on his hands who was free to enjoy the privilege of using those soiled hands to pat the heads of his grandchildren. How could family members, friends, or an ordinary life compete with that quest? For long periods of his life he hadn't even allowed himself to consider whether he was missing out on anything. And the reward when his efforts bore fruit, when those years of searching archives and interviewing survivors with failing memories finally resulted in exposing the guilty and bringing them to justice, the reward at such times was so great that it pushed aside any longing for an ordinary life. Or at least, that was what he'd always believed. But now, as he stood in front of these family photographs, he wondered whether he'd been wrong to put death ahead of life.

'They're wonderful,' said Axel, turning his back on the pictures. He followed Herman into the living room, stopping abruptly when he saw Britta. Even though he and Erik had never abandoned their home in Fjällbacka, it had been decades since he'd last seen her. There had been no occasion for their lives to intersect in all that time.

Now the years fell away with cruel force, and he felt himself reeling. She was still beautiful. She'd actually been much lovelier than Elsy, who could better be described as pretty. But Elsy had possessed an inner glow, a kindness that Britta's outward beauty could never match. Though he could see now that something about her had changed with the years. There was no trace of Britta's former haughty demeanour; now she radiated a warm maternal glow, a maturity that the years must have bestowed on her.

'Is that you?' she said, getting up from the sofa. 'Is that really you, Axel?' She held out both hands towards him, and he took them. So many years had passed. Such an unbelievable number of years. Sixty years. A lifetime. When he was younger, he never would have imagined that time could pass so quickly. The hands he held in his own were wrinkled and covered with brown age spots. Her hair was no longer dark but a lovely silvery-grey. Britta looked calmly into his eyes.

'It's good to see you again, Axel. You've aged well.'

'Funny, but I was just thinking the same thing about you,' said Axel with a smile.

'Well now, let's sit down and have a little chat. Herman, could you bring us some coffee?'

Herman nodded and went into the kitchen to make coffee. Britta sat down again, still holding Axel's hands as he took a seat next to her.

'To think we'd ever be so old, Axel. I never dreamt that would happen,' she said, tilting her head to look at him. Axel noted with amusement that she had retained some of the coquettishness of her younger days. 'You've done a lot of good, over the years, from what I've heard,' she said, studying him intently. He looked away.

'I'm not sure what you mean by "doing good". I've done what I had to do. Certain things just can't be swept under the rug,' he said, and then fell silent.

'You're right about that, Axel,' said Britta solemnly. 'You're certainly right about that.'

They sat next to each other in silence, looking out at the bay, until Herman came back with the coffee service on a floral-painted tray.

'I've made you some coffee.'

'Thank you, dear,' said Britta. Axel felt a pang in his heart when he saw the look they gave each other. He reminded himself that through his work he'd been able to contribute a sense of peace to scores of people, giving them the satisfaction of seeing their tormentors brought before a court of law. That was also a form of love. Not personal, not physical, but still a kind of love.

As if she could read his thoughts, Britta handed him a cup of coffee and said, 'Have you had a good life, Axel?'

The question encompassed so many dimensions, so many levels, that he didn't know how to answer it. In his mind he pictured Erik and his friends in the library of their house, light-hearted, carefree. Elsy with her sweet smile and gentle demeanour. Frans, who made everybody around him feel like they were tiptoeing around the edge of a volcano, yet beneath it all there remained something fragile and sensitive about him. Britta, who had seemed so different from the way she was now. Back then, she had carried her beauty like a shield, and he had judged her to be nothing more than an empty shell, with no substance worthy of notice. And maybe that's how she was back then. But the years had filled up the shell, and now she seemed to glow from within. And Erik. The thought of Erik was so painful that his brain wanted to push it away. But as he sat there in Britta's living room, Axel forced himself to picture his brother as he was back then, before the difficult times commenced. Sitting at his father's desk, with his feet propped up. His brown hair tousled as always, wearing that absent expression that made him look much older than he was. Erik. Dear, beloved Erik.

Axel realized that Britta was waiting for his reply. He forced himself back from the past and tried to find an answer in the present. But as always, the two were hopelessly intertwined, and the sixty years that had passed merged in his memory into a muddle of people, encounters, and events.

His hand holding the coffee cup began to tremble, and finally he said, 'I don't know. I think so. As good as I deserved.'

'I've had a good life, Axel. And I decided a long time ago that I deserved it. You should do the same.'

His hand trembled even more, making coffee splash on to the sofa.

'Oh, I'm so sorry . . . I . . .'

Herman leapt to his feet. 'Don't worry, I'll get a dishcloth.' He went out to the kitchen and quickly returned with a damp blue-checked kitchen towel, which he cautiously pressed over the upholstery.

Britta gave a little shriek, making Axel jump. 'Oh, now Mamma is going to be cross with me. Her fancy sofa. This is bad.'

Axel cast an enquiring glance at Herman, who responded by rubbing on the stain even harder.

'Do you think you can get it off? Mamma is going to be so cross with me!' Britta rocked back and forth, anxiously watching Herman's efforts to wipe up the coffee. He straightened up and slipped his arm around his wife. 'It will be fine, sweetheart. I'll get rid of the stain. I promise.'

'Are you sure? Because if Mamma gets mad, she might tell Pappa, and . . .' Britta wrung her hands and nervously chewed on her knuckles.

'I promise that I'll get rid of it. She won't even notice.'

'Oh, good, That's good,' said Britta, relaxing. Then she gave a start and stared at Axel. 'Who are you? What do you want?'

He looked at Herman for guidance.

'It comes and goes,' he said, sitting down next to Britta and patting her hand. She studied Axel intently, as if there was something annoying or baffling about his face, something that kept eluding her. Then she grabbed Axel's hand and moved her face close to his.

'He's calling to me, you know.'

219

'Who?' said Axel, fighting an urge to withdraw his face, his hand, his body.

Britta didn't reply at first. Then he heard the echo of his own words.

'Certain things just can't be swept under the rug,' she whispered, her face only centimetres away from his own.

He tore his hand out of her grip and looked at Herman over Britta's silvery-grey hair.

'So now you can see for yourself,' said Herman wearily. 'What do we do next?'

'Adrian! Cut that out!' Anna was struggling so hard that she broke into a sweat with the effort of getting her son dressed. Lately he'd turned his wriggling into an art form, making it impossible to get him into his clothes. She'd managed to hold on to him just long enough to pull up a pair of under-pants, but then he tore loose and started running all over the house.

'Adrian! Come on now! Please. Mamma doesn't have time for this. We're going to drive with Dan to Tanumshede to do some shopping. You can go look at the toys in Hedemyr's,' she said, desperate to win his cooperation, for all that she knew bribes probably weren't the best way to handle the getting-dressed problem. But what else could she do?

'Aren't you ready yet?' asked Dan when he came down-stairs and saw her sitting on the floor next to a pile of clothes while Adrian continued to race around like crazy. 'My class starts in half an hour. I've got to leave.'

'Fine. Do it yourself then,' snapped Anna, tossing Adrian's clothes at Dan. He looked at her in surprise. She certainly hadn't been in the best of moods lately, but maybe that wasn't so strange. Merging two families was turning out to be much harder than either of them had anticipated.

'Come on, Adrian,' said Dan, grabbing the boy by the scruff of the neck as he dashed past. 'Let's see if I still know how to do this.' He got socks on the boy with relative ease, but that was it. Adrian resumed his wriggling and flat-out refused to put on his trousers. Dan made a couple of attempts, but then he too lost patience. 'Adrian, sit still NOW!'

Looking astonished, Adrian stopped instantly. Then his face turned bright red. 'You're NOT my pappa! Get out of here! I want my pappa! PAPPA!'

That was too much for Anna. All the memories of Lucas and that terrible time when she'd lived like a prisoner in her own home came flooding back, and she started to cry. She rushed upstairs and threw herself on to the bed, where she gave into wrenching sobs.

Then she felt a gentle hand on her back. 'Sweetheart, what's wrong? It's not that bad. He's not used to the situation, and he's testing us, that's all it is. You should have seen how Belinda was at his age. He's a rank amateur compared to her. One time I was so sick and tired of her making such a fuss about getting dressed that I set her outside the door in nothing but her knickers. Pernilla was furious – it was December, after all. But I only left her outside for a minute.'

Anna didn't laugh. Instead she cried even harder, and she was shaking all over.

'Sweetie, what is it? You're making me really worried. I know that you've been through a lot, but we can make this work. Everybody just needs a little time, and then things will calm down. You . . . you and I . . . together we can make this work.'

She raised her tear-stained face to look at him and then propped herself up on the bed.

'I-I know . . .' she stammered as she tried to stop crying. 'I know that . . . and I don't understand . . . why I'm reacting . . . this way.' Dan stroked her back and the sobs began to subside. 'I'm just a little . . . oversensitive . . . I don't understand. I usually only act this way when I'm . . .' Anna stopped in mid-sentence and stared at Dan, open-mouthed.

'What?' he said, looking puzzled. 'You usually only act this way when what?'

Anna couldn't bring herself to reply, and after a moment she saw a light go on in his eyes.

Then she nodded. 'I usually only act this way when I'm . . . pregnant.'

There was utter silence in the bedroom. Then they heard a little voice from the doorway.

'I'm dressed now. I did it all by myself. I'm a big boy. Can we go to the toy shop now?'

Dan and Anna looked at Adrian standing in the doorway, beaming with pride. His trousers were on backwards, and his shirt was inside out, but it was true: he had put on his clothes. All by himself.

Even out in the hallway it smelled good. Filled with anticipation, Mellberg went into the kitchen. Rita had phoned just before eleven o'clock to ask whether he'd like to come over for lunch since Señorita had expressed a desire to play with Ernst. He hadn't asked how her dog had communicated this desire. Certain things should just be accepted like manna from heaven.

'Hi there.' Johanna was standing next to Rita, helping her chop vegetables. Clearly it was a bit of an effort, for her stomach forced her to keep some distance from the counter.

'Hi. It smells so good in here,' said Mellberg, sniffing at the air.

'We're making chilli con carne,' said Rita, coming over to give him a kiss on the cheek. Mellberg resisted an impulse to raise his hand and touch the spot where her lips had been. Instead, he sat down at the table, which was set for four.

'Is someone else joining us?' he asked, looking at Rita.

'My partner is coming home for lunch,' said Johanna, rubbing her back.

'Shouldn't you sit down?' said Mellberg, pulling out a chair. 'It must be hard to carry all that weight around.'

Johanna complied and sat down next to him, breathing heavily. 'Oh, you have no idea. Hopefully it won't be long now. It's going to feel great to get rid of this.' She ran her hand over her belly. 'Would you like to feel?' she asked Mellberg when she saw his expression.

'Could I?' he asked sheepishly. He hadn't discovered his own son's existence until Simon was a teenager, so this part of parenthood was a mystery to him.

'Here, the baby's kicking.' Johanna took his hand and placed it on the left side of her belly.

Mellberg gave a start as he felt a strong kick against his hand. 'Good heavens! That's amazing. Doesn't it hurt?' He stared at her abdomen as he kept feeling solid kicks against the palm of his hand.

'Not really. Sometimes it's a little uncomfortable when I'm trying to sleep. My partner thinks the baby is going to be a football player.'

'I'm inclined to agree with him,' said Mellberg, not wanting to take his hand away. The experience stirred strange feelings inside him that he could hardly define. Longing, fascination, regret . . . He wasn't really sure. 'Does his father have a talent for football that the baby might inherit?' he said with a laugh. To his great surprise, his question was greeted with silence. He looked up to meet Rita's astonished expression.

'But Bertil, don't you know that . . .'

At that moment the front door opened.

'How good it smells, Mamma,' they heard from the hall. 'What are you making? Your special chilli?'

Paula came into the kitchen, and her look of surprise was even greater than Mellberg's.

'Paula?'

'Boss?'

Thoughts whirled through Mellberg's mind until the pieces fell into place. Paula, who had moved here with her mother. Rita, who had recently moved here. And the dark eyes. To think he hadn't noticed earlier. They had exactly the same eyes. There was just one thing that he didn't really . . .

'So, I see that you've met my partner,' said Paula, putting her arm around Johanna's shoulders. She stared at Mellberg, waiting to see his reaction. Challenging him to say the wrong thing, do the wrong thing.

Out of the corner of her eye Rita was watching him tensely. She held a wooden spoon in one hand, but she'd stopped stirring as she too waited for his reaction. A thousand thoughts raced through Mellberg's head. A thousand prejudices. A thousand things that he'd said over the years that might have been better not said. But suddenly he realized that this was the moment in his life when he had to say the right thing, do the right thing. Too much was at stake, and with Rita's dark eyes fixed on him, he said calmly:

'I didn't know you were about to become a mother. And so soon. I see that congratulations are in order. Johanna was kind enough to let me feel that wildcat inside there, so I tend to agree with your theory that she's going to give birth to a future football player.'

Paula didn't move for a few more seconds, her arm around Johanna and her eyes riveted on his, trying to determine if there was any veiled sarcasm in what he'd said. Then she relaxed and smiled. 'It's amazing to feel all that kicking, isn't it?' The whole room seemed to implode with relief.

Rita went back to stirring the chilli as she said with a laugh: 'That's nothing compare to how you kicked, Paula. I remember that your father used to joke about it, saying it felt like you were looking to find a different way out than the usual exit.'

Paula kissed Johanna on the cheek and sat down at the table. She couldn't hide the fact that she was staring at Mellberg with astonishment. He, in turn, was feeling enormously pleased with himself. He still thought it was strange that two women would live together, and the fact that one of them was pregnant seemed especially bewildering. Sooner or later he'd be forced to satisfy his curiosity about that. And yet, he'd said the right thing. To his great surprise, he'd also meant what he'd said.

Rita set the pot of chilli on the table and urged them to help themselves. The look she gave Mellberg was the final proof that he'd done well.

He could still feel Johanna's bulging skin under his hand, and the child's foot kicking against his palm.

'You're just in time for lunch. I was about to give you a call.' Patrik tasted a spoonful of the tomato soup and then set the saucepan on the table.

'Now that's what I call service. What's the occasion?' Erica came into the kitchen and kissed him on the back of the neck.

'You think this is all? Do you mean that I could have impressed you just by making you lunch? Jeez, that means that I've done the laundry, cleaned up the living room, and changed the light bulb in the bathroom all for nothing.' Patrik turned around and kissed her on the lips.

'Whatever drug you're on, I'd like some too,' said Erica, looking at him in surprise. 'Where's Maja?'

'She fell asleep about fifteen minutes ago. So we'll be able to eat lunch in peace and quiet, just you and me. And after that, you can zip back upstairs to work while I wash the dishes.'

'Okay . . . Now it's getting to be a little too much,' said Erica. 'Either you've embezzled all our money, or you're about to tell me that you have a mistress, or that you've been accepted into NASA's space programme and you'll be spending the next year circling the planet in a spaceship . . . Or has my husband been kidnapped by aliens,

225

and you're some sort of android, half human and half robot?'

'How did you know about NASA?' said Patrik with wink. He put a few slices of bread in a basket and sat down at the kitchen table across from Erica. 'No, the truth is I had a little epiphany when I was out walking with Karin today, and . . . well, I just thought I should help you out more. But don't think you'll get this sort of treatment every day. I can't guarantee that I won't have a relapse.'

'So the only thing I need to do to get my husband to help out more around the house is to send him on a date with his ex-wife? I'll have to tell my women friends about this.'

'Oh, I don't know about that,' said Patrik, blowing on a spoonful of hot soup. 'It wasn't really a date, you know. And she's not having a very easy time of it.' He briefly recounted what Karin had told him, and Erica nodded. Even though Karin seemed to be getting considerably less support at home than she'd had, it still sounded very familiar.

'So how was your morning?' asked Patrik, slurping a bit as he ate his soup.

Erica's face lit up. 'I found a lot of good stuff. You wouldn't believe the things that happened in Fjällbacka during the Second World War. All kinds of smuggling went on, both to and from Norway – food, news, weapons, and people. Both German defectors and Norwegian resistance fighters came here. And later there were the mines to contend with. A number of fishing boats and cargo ships were lost, along with their crews and everything on board, when they ran into mines. And did you know that in 1940 a German fighter plane was shot down by the Swedish air force just outside of Dingle? All three crewmen were killed. I've never heard anyone mention any of this. I always had the impression the war had hardly any impact in these parts, aside from the food and petrol rationing.'

'It sounds as though you're getting really interested in the subject,' said Patrik as he served Erica some more soup.

'I haven't told you the half of it. I asked Christian to dig out anything that might mention my mother and her friends, never thinking he'd get anywhere with it, given that they were so young back then. But wait until you see this –' Erica's voice shook with excitement as she got up to fetch her briefcase. She set it on the kitchen table and took out a thick wad of papers.

'Wow, that's quite a stack you've got there.'

'I've spent three hours reading it all,' said Erica, leafing through the documents, her fingers trembling. Finally she found what she was looking for. 'Here! Look at this!' She pointed to an article with a big black-and-white photograph.

Patrik studied the article she handed him. The picture was the first thing that drew his attention. Five people, standing next to each other. He squinted to make out the caption, recognizing four of the names: Elsy Moström, Frans Ringholm, Erik Frankel, and Britta Johansson. But the fifth person he'd never heard of before. A boy, about the same age as the others, by the name of Hans Olavsen. Patrik silently read the article as Erica fixed her eyes on his face.

'So? What do you think? I don't know what it means, but it can't be a coincidence. Look at the date. He came to Fjällbacka on almost the same day that my mother seems to have ended her diary. That can't be a coincidence! It must mean something!' Erica paced back and forth in the kitchen.

Patrik bent his head to examine the photo again. He studied the images of the five young people. Elsy had died in a car crash four years ago. Now one more of them was dead, murdered sixty years after this picture was taken. He had a gut feeling that Erica was right. It must mean something.

Paula's thoughts were in turmoil as she walked back to the station. Her mother had mentioned that she'd met a nice

227

man who had been keeping her company on her walks, and that she'd then persuaded him to take her salsa class. But Paula never would have dreamed that the man would be her new boss. And it was no exaggeration to say that she wasn't exactly pleased. Mellberg was just about the last man on earth that she would have chosen for her mother. Mind you, she had to admit that he had handled the news about her and Johanna rather well. Surprisingly. Narrow-mindedness had been her foremost argument for not moving to Tanumshede. It had been hard enough for her and Johanna to be accepted as a family in Stockholm. And in a little town like this . . . Well, it could be disastrous. But she'd talked over everything with Johanna and her mother, and they had all agreed that if things didn't work out they could simply move back to Stockholm.

So far, everything had gone much better than expected. She liked her job at the station, her mother had settled in with her salsa classes and a part-time job at the Konsum supermarket, and even though Johanna was on sick leave at the moment and would then have a lengthy maternity leave, she'd talked to a number of local businesses who'd shown interest in enlisting her help with their finances. Yet the minute Paula saw Mellberg's expression when she put her arm around Johanna, it had felt as though everything might fall apart like a house of cards. At that moment, their whole life could have collapsed. But Mellberg had surprised her. Maybe he wasn't as hopeless as she'd assumed.

Paula exchanged a few words with Annika in the reception area. Then she knocked on Martin's door and went in.

'How are things going?' she asked when he looked up from his paperwork.

'With the assault case? Well, the boy admitted to doing it – not that he had much choice in the matter. His mother took him home, but Gösta has informed social services. It doesn't appear to be a very stable home situation.'

228

'That's often the case,' said Paula, sitting down.

'But what was really interesting was the reason for the assault in the first place. It turns out that Per broke into Erik Frankel's house in early June.'

Paula raised an eyebrow but let Martin continue without commenting. After he'd told her the whole story, they were both quiet for a moment.

'I wonder what Erik had that would have interested Kjell,' said Paula. 'Could it have it been something about Frans ?'

Martin shrugged. 'That's what the boy said. I thought it might be worth asking Kjell. We still have to go to Uddevalla to interview some of the members of Sweden's Friends, and *Bohusläningen* has its main editorial office there. And we can call in on Axel on the way.'

'No sooner said than done,' said Paula, getting up.

Twenty minutes later they were again standing outside the front door of the Frankel brothers' house.

Axel looks older than last time, Paula thought. Thinner, almost transparent in some way. He gave them a friendly smile as he let them in. He didn't ask why they had come, just led the way to the veranda.

'Have you made any progress?' he asked as they sat down. 'With the investigation, that is,' he clarified unnecessarily.

Martin glanced at Paula but then said, 'We have several leads that we're following. Most importantly, we've managed to pinpoint the probable time when your brother died.'

'Well, that's a major development,' said Axel, smiling, although the smile didn't dislodge any of the grief or fatigue from his eyes. 'So when do you think it was?'

'He went to see his . . . woman friend, Viola Ellmander, on the fifteenth of June; that seems to be the last time he was seen alive. On the seventeenth of June, the cleaning woman . . .'

'Laila,' said Axel, seeing that Martin was struggling to recall the name.

'Laila, right. She came here on the seventeenth to clean the house, as usual, but no one came to the door when she rang, and no one had left her a key, as the two of you were in the habit of doing if you weren't going to be at home.'

'Yes, Erik was very meticulous about leaving a key for Laila. As far as I know, he never forgot to do that. So if he didn't open the door, and there was no key, then . . .' Axel fell silent and rubbed his eyes, as if he were seeing visions of his brother that he'd prefer to dismiss at once.

'I'm so sorry,' said Paula gently, 'but we have to ask you where you were between the fifteenth and seventeenth of June. I assure you, it's just a formality.'

Axel waved away her attempt to reassure him. 'No need to apologize. I know you're only doing your job. And besides, don't the statistics say that most murders are committed by someone in the family?'

Martin nodded. 'True. But we need to gather information for the investigation and it will help if we can rule you out as a suspect.'

'Of course. I'll get my calendar.'

Axel was gone a few minutes. He returned carrying a thick diary. 'Let's see now . . .' He sat down again and began leafing through it. 'I left Sweden and went directly to Paris on the third of June, and I didn't come back here until you . . . were kind enough to collect me at the airport. But from the fifteenth to the seventeenth . . . ah, here we are: I had a meeting in Brussels on the fifteenth, went to Frankfurt on the sixteenth, and then returned to the head office in Paris on the seventeenth. I can get you photocopies of my tickets if you like.' He handed the diary to Paula.

She studied it closely, but after casting an enquiring glance at Martin, who shook his head, she pushed the diary back across the table.

'No, I don't think that will be necessary. Do you remember anything about these dates that might have significance with regard to Erik? Anything specific? A phone conversation? Something he may have mentioned?'

Axel shook his head. 'No, I'm sorry. As I said, my brother and I weren't in the habit of phoning each other very often when I was abroad. Erik would only have called me if the house was on fire.' He laughed but then abruptly fell silent and again rubbed his eyes. 'So, was that all? Is there anything else I can help you with?' he asked, carefully closing the diary.

'Actually, there is one other thing . . .' said Martin, fixing his eyes on Axel. 'We've interviewed a young man named Per Ringholm in connection with an assault case today. He told us that he broke into your house a few months ago. And that Erik caught him, locked him up in the library, and rang his father, Kjell Ringholm.'

'Frans's son,' said Axel.

Martin nodded. 'Exactly. And Per overheard Erik and Kjell making arrangements to meet later. It seems Erik had some information that he thought would interest Kjell. Does any of this ring a bell?'

'No, it doesn't,' said Axel, vigorously shaking his head.

'What about the information that Erik wanted to pass on? Do you have any idea what that might have been?'

Axel was silent for a while, as if considering the question. Then he shook his head again. 'No, I can't imagine what it could have been. Erik spent a lot of time studying the period leading up to the Second World War, and of course he'd personally experienced what Nazism was like during that period. Kjell, on the other hand, has devoted himself to writing about the resurgence of Nazism in Sweden today. So maybe Erik had found some kind of connection, something of historical interest that would give Kjell background material. But why don't you just ask Kjell?'

'We're on our way to Uddevalla to see him now. But why don't I give you my mobile number, just in case you happen to think of something.' Martin wrote the number on a piece of paper and handed it to Axel, who slipped it inside his diary.

Paula and Martin got back in the car and continued their journey without speaking. But they were both thinking the same thing: What was it they were not seeing?

'We can't put it off any more. She won't be able to stay here at home much longer.' Herman looked at his daughters with such deep despair that they could hardly stand to return his gaze.

'We know that, Pappa. You're doing the right thing. There's no other option. You've taken care of Mamma for as long as you could, but now others will have to step in. We'll find a really great place for her.' Anna-Greta went to stand behind her father's chair, wrapping her arms around him. She shuddered to feel how gaunt his body felt under his shirt. Their mother's illness had taken a heavy toll on him. Perhaps more than they'd known. Or wanted to see. She leaned forward and pressed her cheek against Herman's.

'We're here to help you, Pappa. Birgitta and Maggan and our families. You know we're here for you. You never need to feel alone.'

'Without your mother, I do feel alone. But there's nothing to be done about it,' said Herman listlessly, quickly wiping away a tear with his shirtsleeve. 'Still, I know that this is best for Britta. I know that.'

His daughters exchanged glances over their father's head. Herman and Britta had been the centre of all their lives, a solid rock that they could always depend on. Now the very foundation of their lives was crumbling, and they reached out as if to steady each other. It was frightening to watch their mother shrink, becoming more and more diminished until she seemed smaller than themselves. Now it was necessary for them to step in and be the adults, taking on the burden of the ones they had always regarded, throughout their entire childhood and adolescence, as infallible, indestructible. Of course, they had long since ceased to look upon their parents as godlike creatures who had the answer to everything, but it was still painful to watch Britta and Herman fading this way.

Anna-Greta hugged her father's gaunt form a few more times and then sat down at the kitchen table again.

'Will she manage all right while you're here?' asked Maggan, looking worried. 'Should I run over and look in on her?'

'She had just fallen asleep when I left,' said Herman. 'But she usually doesn't sleep more than an hour, so I'd better go back home.' Wearily he got to his feet.

'Why don't we go over there and stay with her for a couple of hours? Then you can take a rest,' said Birgitta. 'Pappa could lie down in your guest room, couldn't he?' she asked Maggan, since it was at her house they had gathered in to talk about their mother.

'That's an excellent idea,' said Maggan, nodding eagerly at her father. 'Go in and rest for a while, and we'll nip over to be with Mamma.'

'Thank you, girls,' said Herman, as he headed for the hall. 'But your mother and I have taken care of each other for over fifty years, and I'd like to continue to take care of her for the short time that we have left. Once she's settled in the nursing home, then . . .' He didn't finish his sentence but instead rushed out the door before his daughters could see his tears.

Britta smiled in her sleep. The lucid moments that her brain denied her when she was awake became all the more frequent when she slept. Then she saw everything clearly. Some of the memories were not welcome but forced themselves upon her nevertheless. Like the sound of her father's belt striking a child's bare behind. Or the sight of her mother's tear-stained cheeks. Or the cramped confines of the little house on the hill, where the shrill cries of a child echoed in the space, making her want to clap her hands over her ears and scream too. But there were other things that were more pleasant to recall. Like the summers when they played merrily, racing over the rocks warmed by the sun. Elsy in one of the floral dresses that her mother had made by hand. Erik in his short pants, with his solemn face. Frans with his curly blond hair. She had always longed to run her fingers through his curls, even back when they were so young that there seemed no significant difference between boys and girls.

A voice forced its way through the memories as she slept. A voice that was all too familiar. It had been speaking to her more and more often lately. Not allowing her any peace, whether she was awake, asleep, or wrapped in a haze. The voice that penetrated through everything, wanted everything, insisted on taking a place in her world. The voice that denied her respite, refused to let her forget. The voice that she thought she'd never hear again. Yet here it was. So strange. And so frightening.

She rolled her head from side to side in her sleep, trying to shake off the voice, shake off the memories that were disturbing her rest. Finally she succeeded. Happy memories came to the fore. The first time she saw Herman. The moment when she knew that the two of them would spend their lives together. Their wedding, walking down the aisle in her white gown, giddy with happiness. The labour pains and then the love when Anna-Greta was born. And Birgitta and Margareta, whom she loved just as much. Herman taking care of the children, doing it out of love, not out of duty or obligation. She smiled. Her eyelids fluttered. This was where she wanted to stay. Here, with these memories. If she had to choose a single memory to fill her mind for the rest of her life, it was the image of Herman bathing their youngest daughter in the little bathtub. He was humming as he carefully supported her small head with his hand. With infinite gentleness he rubbed her chubby body with a washcloth, looking into his daughter's eyes as she followed his every move. Britta saw herself standing in the doorway, watching without drawing her husband's attention. Even if she forgot everything else, she would fight to hold on to that memory. Herman and Margareta, his hand under her head, the tenderness and closeness.

A sound forced her out of her dreams. She wanted to go back. Back to the sound of water splashing as Herman dipped the flannel in the basin. The sound of Margareta's contented prattling as the warm water sloshed around her. But a new sound was forcing Britta closer to the surface. Closer to the fog that she wanted at all costs to avoid. Waking up meant risking being enveloped in the grey, confusing haze that took over her mind and had begun swallowing up more and more of her time.

At last she reluctantly opened her eyes. Somebody was leaning over her, looking at her. Britta smiled. Maybe she wasn't yet fully awake. Maybe she could still fend off the fog with the memories that came to her in her sleep.

'Is that you?' she asked, staring up at the person leaning over her. Her body felt loose-jointed and heavy with sleep, which hadn't yet completely left her. She didn't have the strength to move. For a moment neither of them spoke. There wasn't much to say. Then a sense of certainty forced its way into Britta's brain. Memories rose to the surface. Feelings that had been forgotten now flashed and awakened to life. And she felt terror take hold. The fear from which she'd been released because of her gradual loss of memory. Now she saw Death standing beside her bed, and her entire being protested at having to leave this life, leave everything that was hers. She gripped the sheet in her hands, but her parched lips could manage only a few guttural sounds. Terror spread through her body, making her roll her head rapidly from side to side. Desperately she tried to send thoughts to Herman, as if he might hear her through the telepathic waves. But she knew it was in vain. Death had come to get her, the scythe would soon fall, and there was no one who could help her. She would die alone in her bed. Without Herman. Without the girls. Without saying farewell. At that moment the fog was gone and her mind was clearer than it had been in a long time. With fear racing like a wild animal in her chest, she managed at last to take a deep breath and utter a scream. Death didn't move. Just kept staring at her as she lay in bed, staring and smiling. Not an unfriendly smile, but that made it all the more frightening.

Then Death leaned down and picked up the pillow from Herman's side of the bed. Terrified, Britta saw the white shape getting closer. The final fog.

Her body protested for a moment. Panicked from the lack of air. Tried to take a breath, bring oxygen into her lungs. Her hands let go of the sheet, clutched wildly at the air. Struck resistance, struck skin. Tore and scratched, fighting to live another second.

Then everything went black.

GRINI, OUTSIDE OSLO, 1944

'Time to get up!' The guard's voice echoed through the barracks. 'Five minutes, fall in for inspection.'

Axel opened his eyes with an effort. For a second he was totally disoriented. It was dark in the barracks; at this early hour almost no light came in from outside. But it was still an improvement over the cell where he'd sat in isolation for the first few months. He preferred the cramped quarters and stench of the barracks to the long days of solitude. He'd heard that there were 3,500 prisoners at Grini. That didn't surprise him. No matter where he turned, he saw men, all with the same resigned expression that he assumed matched his own.

He sat up on his bunk and rubbed the sleep from his eyes. Orders to stand in formation were issued several times a day, whenever the guards felt like it, and pity the man who didn't move fast enough. But today he was having a hard time getting out of bed. He'd been dreaming of Fjällbacka. Dreaming about sitting up on Veddeberget, looking at the water and watching the seagulls shrieking as they circled above the masts of the boats. It was actually quite an ugly sound, but it had somehow become part of the town's soul. He'd been dreaming of the way the wind felt as it enveloped him, warm and mild in the summertime. And of the smell of seaweed carried on the wind, even all the way up to the top of the hill, where he greedily breathed it in.

But reality was far too raw and cold for him to be able to cling to his dream. Instead, he felt the rough fabric of the blanket against his skin as he threw it off and swung his legs over the side of the rickety bunk. Hunger was tearing at him. Of course they were given food, but not enough and not very often.

'Time to get yourselves out there,' said the younger guard, who was now walking among the prisoners. He stopped in front of Axel.

'It's cold today,' he said in a friendly tone.

Axel avoided looking at him. It was the same boy who'd been on duty when he first arrived, the one he'd regarded as friendlier than the others. And that had turned out to be true. He'd never seen the young man abuse or denigrate anyone in the same way that most of the other guards did. But the months that Axel had spent in prison had drawn a clear boundary between the two of them. Prisoner and guard. They were two very distinct entities. They lived such different lives that he could hardly bear to look at the guards when they came within sight. The Norwegian Guard uniform Axel wore marked him out as belonging to a lower class of humanity. From the other prisoners he'd learned that the uniform had been instituted after a prisoner had escaped in 1941. He wondered how the man had found the strength to flee. He himself felt listless, emptied of all energy from the combination of hard labour, too little food, too little sleep, and too much anxiety for those back at home. And too much misery in general.

'You'd better get moving,' said the young guard, giving him a shove.

Axel did as he said and hurried out of the barracks. The consequences were harsh for anyone who showed up late for the morning inspection.

As he went down the stairs to the yard, he suddenly stumbled. He felt his foot lose its hold on the step, and he pitched forward, falling against the guard who was right in front of him. He flailed his arms to regain his balance, but instead of air, he felt his hands touching the guard's uniform and body. With a dull thud he landed on the man's back, and the impact knocked the air out of Axel's lungs. At first there was only silence. Then he felt hands hauling him to his feet.

'He attacked you,' said the guard who had a firm grip on him. His name was Jensen, and he was one of the most ruthless of the guards.

'I don't think –' said the young guard hesitantly as he got up, brushing dirt off his uniform.

'I said he attacked you!' Jensen's face was bright red. He took every opportunity to abuse the men who were in his power. Whenever he walked through the camp, the crowds would part like the Red Sea had parted for Moses.

'No, he –'

'I saw him do it!' shouted the older guard, taking a step forward. 'Are you going to teach him a lesson, or should I?'

'But, he . . .' The guard, who was no more than a boy, gave Axel a desperate look before turning back to his colleague.

Axel watched the scene with indifference. He had long ago stopped reacting, stopped feeling. Whatever happened would happen. Those who struggled against their fate were doomed to perish.

'All right then, I'll –' The older guard moved towards Axel, raising his rifle.

'No! I'll do it! That's my job,' said the boy, his face pale as he stepped between them. He looked Axel in the eyes, and it almost looked as if he were pleading for forgiveness. Then he raised his hand and slapped Axel.

'Is that supposed to be his punishment?' Jensen bellowed

hoarsely. A group of onlookers had now gathered, and a bunch of guards were laughing as they waited expectantly. Anything that broke the monotony of the prison's daily routines was welcome.

'Hit him harder!' yelled Jensen, his face even redder than before.

The young guard looked again at Axel, who still refused to meet his eyes. Then the guard drew back his fist and punched Axel in the jaw. His head flew back, but he remained on his feet.

'Harder!' Now more of the guards had joined in, and sweat was gleaming on the boy's forehead. He no longer tried to look at Axel. His eyes had a glazed look to them as he bent down and picked up his rifle from the ground, raising it high to strike.

Axel turned away, out of pure reflex, so the blow struck his left ear. It felt as if something broke inside him, and the pain was indescribable. When the next blow fell, he took it in the face. After that he remembered very little. All he felt was pain.

There was no sign on the door to indicate that these premises were occupied by Sweden's Friends. Just a piece of paper over the letter box stating 'No soliciting' and the name 'Svensson'. Martin and Paula had been given the address by their colleagues in Uddevalla, who kept a close eye on the organization's activities.

They hadn't phoned ahead. Instead, they'd taken a chance that someone would be there during office hours. Martin pressed the doorbell. A shrill tone was heard inside, but at first nothing happened. He was just about to press the bell again when the door opened.

'Yes?' A man in his thirties gave them an enquiring look and then frowned when he saw their uniforms. The furrow on his face deepened when he saw Paula. For several seconds he looked her up and down in a way that made her want to knee him hard in the groin.

'So. What can I do to help the government today?' he asked snidely.

'We'd like to have a few words with someone from Sweden's Friends. Have we come to the right place?'

'Sure. Come in.' The man, who was blond, tall, and big in that slightly muscle-bound way, backed away to let them in.

'Martin Molin. And this is Paula Morales. We're from the Tanumshede police.'

'Is that right? A long way to come,' said the man, leading the way to a small office. 'My name is Peter Lindgren.' He sat down behind the desk and pointed to two visitor's chairs.

Martin made a note of the name. He was going to check Lindgren against their database as soon as they got back to the station. Something told him that the man sitting in front of them would have a string of arrests to his credit.

'So, what do you want?' Peter leaned back, clasping his hands in his lap.

'We're investigating the murder of a man named Erik Frankel. Is that name familiar to you?' Paula forced herself to speak calmly. There was something about these types of men that gave her the creeps. No doubt Peter Lindgren felt the same way about people like her.

'Should it?' he replied, looking at Martin instead of Paula.

'Yes, it should,' said Martin. 'Your organization has had some . . . contact with him. Threatening contact. But I don't suppose you'd know anything about that?' Martin said sarcastically.

Peter Lindgren shook his head. 'No, that doesn't ring a bell. Do you have any proof of these . . . threats?' he asked with a smile.

Martin felt as if the man were inspecting him inside and out. After a pause he said, 'At the moment it's irrelevant what we have or don't have. We know that your organization threatened Erik Frankel. And we also know that one of your members, Frans Ringholm, knew the victim and warned him about these threats.'

'I wouldn't take Frans very seriously,' said Peter, a dangerous glint in his eyes. 'He enjoys great respect within our . . . organization, but he's getting on in years and, well . . . we live in different times, things have changed, and men like Frans don't always understand the new rules of the game.'

'But someone like you does?' said Martin.

Peter threw out his hands. 'It's important to know when to follow the rules and when to break them. What matters is doing what serves our cause in the long run.'

'And your cause in this case is . . . what?' Paula could hear how hostile she sounded, confirmed by a warning glance from Martin.

'A better society,' said Peter calmly. 'The people who have been running this country haven't made a good job of it. They've allowed . . . foreign forces to take up too much space. Allowed what is Swedish and pure to be pushed out.' He cast a belligerent look at Paula, who swallowed repeatedly in order not to react. This was not the right place or time. And she was all too aware that he was goading her. 'But all that's going to change. The Swedish people have become more and more aware that we'll be heading towards the abyss if we continue in this manner, if we allow those in power to keep tearing down what our ancestors built up. Our organization can offer a better society.'

'And in what way – theoretically speaking – would an elderly, retired history teacher represent a threat to a . . . better society?'

'Theoretically speaking . . .' Peter again clasped his hands in his lap. 'Theoretically speaking, of course he wouldn't pose any real threat. But he contributed to spreading a false image, an image that the victors of the war have worked hard to promote. And naturally that could not be tolerated. Theoretically speaking.'

Martin was about to reply, but it seemed Peter wasn't finished.

'All the images, all the accounts from the concentration camps and the like are pure fabrications, exaggerated lies that after the fact have been hammered into truths. And do you know why? In order to completely suppress the original message, the correct message. The victors of the war are the

243

ones who write the history books, and they decided to drown the truth in blood, distort the image that the world would see, so that no one would dare stand up and question whether the right side won. And Erik Frankel was part of that blackout, that propaganda. And that's why – hypothetically speaking – Erik Frankel stood in the way of the society we want to create.'

'And yet, to your knowledge, your organization never issued any threats against him?' Martin studied the man intently. He knew what the answer would be.

'No, we didn't. We work within the laws of a democracy. Ballots. Election manifestos. Acquiring power through votes. We would view anything else as untenable.' He glanced at Paula, whose hands were clasped tightly in her lap. She was picturing the soldiers who had come and taken away her father. They'd had the same look in their eyes.

'Well, we won't disturb you any longer,' said Martin, getting up. 'The Uddevalla police gave us the names of the other board members, so of course we'll be talking to them about this matter too.'

Peter stood up and nodded. 'Of course. But no one else is going to tell you anything different. And as for Frans . . . well, I wouldn't pay much attention to an old man who lives in the past.'

Erica was finding it hard to concentrate on her writing. Thoughts of her mother kept getting in the way. She took out the stack of articles and put the one with the photograph on top. It was so frustrating. Staring at those faces, without being able to get any answers. She leaned down, putting her face close to the picture and studying the five individuals in detail, one after the other.

First Erik Frankel. A serious expression as he looked at the camera. Rigid posture. There was something sad about him, and without knowing whether she was right or not, she came to the conclusion that it was his brother's imprisonment that had left its mark on Erik. But he'd had the same aura of solemnity and sorrow when she'd met with him in June to ask about the medal.

Erica shifted her gaze to the person standing next to Erik. Frans Ringholm. He was handsome. Very handsome. Blond hair curling a bit longer over his collar than his parents probably would have liked. A big, charming smile for the camera. He had his arms slung casually over the shoulders of those standing on either side of him. Neither of them seemed pleased about it.

Erica studied the person to the right of Frans. Her mother: Elsy Moström. Her expression was certainly gentler than Erica could recall having seen. But there was a slight strain to her delicate smile, signalling that she didn't care for Frans's arm around her shoulders. Erica couldn't help musing about how sweet her mother looked. The Elsy she'd known had been cold and unapproachable. There was no hint of that side to her nature in the photo. Erica gently touched the image of her mother's face. How different everything would have been if her mother had been like the girl pictured here. What had happened to her? What had stripped away all the gentleness? What had caused indifference to replace that wistful gaze? Why hadn't she ever been able to put those soft arms of hers, visible under the short sleeves of her floral-print dress, around her daughters, hugging them close?

Erica shifted to the next person in the photo. Britta was not looking into the camera. Instead, she had turned to look at Elsy. Or at Frans. It was impossible to tell. Erica reached for the magnifying glass on the desk. She held it over Britta's face and squinted to make the image as sharp as possible, but she still couldn't tell for sure. Britta was frowning, and there was something harsh and resolute about her jaw. And her eyes. Erica was almost positive. Britta was looking at one of them – Elsy or Frans – or maybe both.

Then the last person in the photo. About the same age as the others. Also blond, like Frans, but his curly hair was shorter. Tall and quite slender, with a meditative expression on his face. Not happy, but not sad either. Meditative was the closest word Erica could think of to describe the way he looked.

She read the article again. Hans Olavsen was a Norwegian resistance fighter who had fled Norway on board the fishing boat *Elfrida*, based in Fjällbacka. He'd been given refuge by the boat's captain, Elof Moström. According to the reporter who had written the article, Hans was now celebrating the end of the war along with his friends in Fjällbacka.

Erica returned the article to the top of the stack of papers. She had a gut feeling that there was something about the dynamics of that group of young people, something that felt . . . She couldn't quite put her finger on it. The one thing she knew for certain was that the key to understanding her mother lay in a deeper understanding of the relationships between these friends, and perhaps the Norwegian resistance fighter, Hans Olavsen. And there were only two people she could ask: Axel Frankel and Britta Johansson.

She really didn't want to go back there and bother the confused old woman, but how else would she find out what lay behind that angry look in her eyes? Maybe if she could explain to Britta's husband why she needed to talk to his wife, he would understand. Tomorrow, Erica decided. Tomorrow she would grab the bull by the horns and go back there.

If she could just catch Britta in one of her more lucid moments she was convinced she would fine the answers she needed.

FJÄLLBACKA 1944

It had taken its toll on Elof Moström, the war. All those trips across the water, which was no longer his friend but his enemy. He'd always loved the sea off Bohuslän. Loved the way it moved, the way it smelled, the way it sounded when it surged against the bow of his boat. But ever since the war started, he and the sea had not had the same sort of friendship. The sea had become hostile. It hid dangers beneath the surface, mines that at any moment could explode, blowing him and his entire crew sky high. And the Germans who patrolled the area weren't much better. He never knew what they might be up to. The sea had become unreliable in a whole different way than it used to be. Storms, shoals – those were things they had learned to handle, that they could deal with after generations of experience. And if nature sometimes got the better of them, it was accepted with equanimity and composure.

This new capriciousness was much worse. If they survived the crossing, there were other dangers when they docked to unload their cargo. Every time he pulled into harbour, he was reminded of how they'd lost Axel Frankel to the Germans. He stared out at the horizon, allowing himself to think about the boy for a few minutes. So brave. Seemingly so invincible. Now nobody knew where he was. He'd heard rumours that the boy had been taken to Grini, but he didn't know whether that was true. And even if it was, there was no way of knowing whether he was still there. He'd heard that they had started shipping prisoners to Germany. Maybe that was where the boy was now. Or maybe he was no longer alive. Six months had gone by since the Germans had taken him, and there'd been no word of him in all that time. So it was hard not to think the worst. Elof sighed heavily. Occasionally he ran into the boy's parents, Dr and Mrs Frankel. But he never dared meet their gaze. He would cross to the other side of the street, and hurry past with his eyes averted. He felt that he should have been able to do something. But what? Maybe he should have refused to take the boy along in the first place.

His heart ached whenever he saw Axel's brother. That small, serious boy named Erik. Not that he'd ever been much of a talker, but since his brother had disappeared he'd grown even quieter. Elof had thought of having a word with Elsy. He didn't like her spending so much time with Erik and the other boy – Frans. Not that he had anything against Erik. Frans was a different story; 'hooligan' was the word that came to mind when he tried to describe that boy. But neither of them was suitable company for Elsy. The Moströms just weren't in the same class as the Frankels and the Ringholms. They might as well have been born on a different planet, and nothing good would ever come of their two worlds meeting. Maybe it was all right back when they were kids playing tag and capture the flag. But they were older now. And nothing good would come of it.

Hilma had pointed this out to him on numerous occasions. Asked him to talk to the girl. But so far he hadn't had the heart to do so. The war had made everything more difficult. Friends were practically the only luxuries the young people had left, and who was he to rob Elsy of her friends? But sooner or later he'd be forced to do it. Boys will be boys, after all. Games of tag and capture the flag would soon turn to secret embraces. He knew that from personal experience. He'd been young once himself, even though that now seemed so very long ago. The time had come for the two worlds to be separate once more; that was how things were, and how they would always be. It was impossible to change the natural order of things.

'Captain! You'd better come and have a look.'

Startled out of his musings, Elof turned towards the source of the interruption. One of his crew was urgently motioning for him to come over. Elof frowned in surprise and then went to join him. They were in open water and still had a few hours left before arriving at Fjällbacka harbour.

'We've got a stowaway,' said Calle Ingvarsson, pointing at the cargo hold. Elof looked where he was pointing. A young boy was huddled behind the sacks of cargo. Now he crept out from his hiding place.

'I discovered him when I heard a sound coming from inside there. He was coughing so hard, it was a wonder we didn't hear him up on deck,' said Calle, sticking a pinch of snuff in his mouth. He grimaced. The snuff available during the war years was a poor substitute for the real thing.

'Who are you? And what are you doing on my boat?' asked Elof brusquely. He considered calling for reinforcements from his crew up above.

'My name is Hans Olavsen, and I came on board in Kristiansand,' said the youth, speaking a lilting Norwegian. He stood up and held out his hand. After a moment of hesitation, Elof shook hands with him. The boy looked him in the eye and said, 'I was hoping to go to Sweden with you. The Germans have . . . well, let's just say that if I value my life, I can no longer remain on Norwegian soil.'

Elof was silent for a long time, thinking about what the boy had said. He didn't like being tricked in this manner. But on the other hand, what else could the boy have done? It wasn't as if he could approach the boat openly, in full

249

view of all the Germans patrolling the harbour, and ask for transport to Sweden.

'Where are you from?' he asked at last, looking the boy up and down.

'Oslo.'

'And what have you done that makes it impossible for you to stay in Norway?'

'People don't talk about what they've been forced to do during the war,' said Hans, a dark shadow passing over his face. 'Let's just say that the underground movement no longer has any use for me.'

He probably took people over the border, thought Elof. It was a dangerous job, and once the Germans were on to you, it was wise to get out while you still could. Elof felt himself relenting. He thought about Axel, who'd made the trip to Norway so many times without ever thinking about his own safety. And he'd paid the price. Could he do less than the doctor's nineteen-year-old son? He made up his mind then and there.

'All right, we'll take you along. We're heading for Fjällbacka. Have you had anything to eat?'

Hans shook his head and swallowed hard. 'No. Not since the day before yesterday. The trip from Oslo was . . . difficult. I couldn't take a direct route.' He looked down.

'Calle, get the boy some food. I need to get back on deck – it's my job to see that we get home in one piece, which means navigating round those damn mines the Germans insist on spreading all over these waterways,' he explained as he started up the companionway. When he glanced back, he met the boy's eyes. The sympathy he felt surprised him. How old could he be? Eighteen, no more than that. And yet Elof could read so much in his eyes that shouldn't be there. Lost youth and the accompanying innocence. The war had undeniably claimed many victims. And not just those who had died.

Gösta felt somehow to blame. If he'd been doing his job, maybe Mattias wouldn't have ended up in the hospital. Possibly it wouldn't have made any difference, but he might have found out that Per had broken into the Frankels' house a few weeks before the boys did, and that could have changed the course of events. When Gösta had gone to Adam's house to take his fingerprints, the boy had actually mentioned that someone at school had talked about the cool stuff the Frankels owned. That was what had been eating at Gösta's subconscious, teasing him, eluding him. If only he'd paid more attention. Been more careful. In short, done his job properly. He sighed. It was that special sigh that Gösta had perfected after years of practice. Now it was time for him to put things right as best he could.

He went out to the garage and took the one remaining police vehicle. Martin and Paula had taken the other one to Uddevalla. Forty minutes later he parked outside Strömstad hospital. The receptionist told him that Mattias was in stable condition and then explained how to find the patient's room.

Gösta took a deep breath before entering the room. No doubt there would be family members with the boy. Gösta didn't like meeting relatives. It was always so emotional, making it so hard to stick to the task at hand. Yet at times

251

he'd actually surprised both his colleagues and himself by displaying a certain sensitivity when talking to people in traumatic situations. If he'd had the energy and the will-power, he might have been able to utilize that talent in his job and turn it into an asset. Instead, it rarely made an appearance these days, and for him it wasn't a particularly welcome guest.

'Did you get him?' A tall man wearing a suit and tie stood up when he entered the room. He'd had his arms around a sobbing woman. Gösta assumed this must be the mother, judging by her resemblance to the boy in the hospital bed. Or rather, her resemblance to the boy Gösta had interviewed outside the Frankels' house; the Mattias he was looking at now was unrecognizable. His face was like a swollen, inflamed wound with emerging bruises. His lips were twice the normal size, and he seemed able to use only one eye. The other was swollen shut.

'When I get hold of that . . . bastard,' swore Mattias's father, clenching his fists. He had tears in his eyes, but despite Gösta's qualms about dealing with family members he resolved to press on and do his job, especially since his feel-ings of guilt had intensified at the sight of Mattias's pummelled face.

'Let the police handle it,' said Gösta, sitting down in a chair next to them. He introduced himself and then gave Mattias's parents a stern look to make sure they were listening.

'We took Per Ringholm down to the station to interview him. He admitted to beating up your son, and he will defi-nitely suffer the consequences. At the moment, I don't know what they may be; that's up to the prosecutor to decide.'

'But you've got him locked up, right?' said Mattias's mother, her lips quivering.

'Not right now. It's only in exceptional cases that the prosecutor will take a minor into custody. So he was sent

252

home with his mother while we conduct an investigation. We've also brought social services into the picture.'

'So he was allowed to go home to his mother, while my son lies here and . . .' said Mattias's father, his voice breaking. In disbelief he looked from Gösta to his son.

'For the time being, yes. As I said, there will be consequences, I can promise you that. But I need to have a few words with your son, if possible, to make sure we've covered everything.'

Mattias's parents looked at each other and then nodded.

'Okay, but only if he feels up to it. He's not fully conscious all the time. They've got him on pain medication.'

'We'll let him decide how long he wants to talk,' said Gösta soothingly as he moved his chair over to the bed. He had some trouble understanding the boy's slurred words, but in the end he had the whole story confirmed. His account matched what Per had told them.

When he was done questioning Mattias, he turned to the boy's parents.

'Is it all right if I take his fingerprints?'

Once again the parents exchanged glances. And again it was Mattias's father who spoke. 'All right, go ahead. If it's necessary to . . .' He didn't finish the sentence, just looked at his son with tears in his eyes.

'It'll only take a minute,' said Gösta, getting out the fingerprinting equipment.

A short time later he was back in his vehicle, looking at the box displaying Mattias's fingerprints. They might not have any significance to the case. But he'd done his job. At last. That was some small consolation, at least.

'The final stop for today, okay?' said Martin as he climbed out of the police car in front of the editorial offices of *Bohusläningen*.

'Sounds good. It's about time to head for home,' said

Paula, looking at her watch. She hadn't said a word after their visit to the offices of Sweden's Friends, and Martin had let her ruminate in peace. He understood how hard it must be for her to be confronted by that type of person. The sort that judged her before she even had time to say hello, who saw only the colour of her skin, nothing else. He found it unpleasant too, but with his chalk-white complexion and fiery red hair, he was never subjected to the kind of stares that Paula had to endure. He'd suffered a certain amount of teasing in school because of his hair, but that was long ago, and it wasn't the same thing at all.

'We're looking for Kjell Ringholm,' said Paula, leaning over the reception desk.

'Just a minute and I'll tell him you're here.' The receptionist picked up the phone to let Ringholm know that he had visitors.

'Please have a seat. He'll be right out.'

'Thank you.' They sat down on two armchairs next to a coffee table. After a few minutes a rather pudgy man with dark hair and a dark beard came towards them. Paula thought that he looked a lot like Björn from ABBA. Or Benny. She could never tell which was which.

'Kjell Ringholm,' he said, shaking hands with them. His handshake was firm, bordering on painful, and Martin couldn't help grimacing.

He led the way to his office and invited them to sit, then said, 'I thought I knew all the police officers in Uddevalla, but I must say that you're both new faces to me. Who do you work for?' Kjell sat down behind his desk, which was cluttered with papers.

'We're from the Tanumshede station, not Uddevalla.'

'Is that so?' said Kjell, looking surprised. Paula thought she caught a momentary flash of something else, but it vanished instantly. 'Well, what's on your mind?' He leaned back, clasping his hands over his stomach.

'First of all, we have to tell you that today we brought your son down to the station after he assaulted one of his classmates,' said Martin.

The man behind the desk sat up straight. 'What? Are you telling me you've arrested Per? Who was it he . . .? How is . . .?' He stumbled over the words pouring out of his mouth, and Paula waited for him to pause so they could answer his questions.

'He beat up a student named Mattias Larsson. The boy was taken to hospital, and the latest report is that he's in stable condition, but he has sustained serious injuries.'

'What?' Kjell seemed to be having a hard time taking in what they were telling him. 'Why didn't you phone me earlier? It sounds as though this must have happened hours ago.'

'The school phoned Per's mother, so she came to the station and was present when we interviewed him. Then he was allowed to go home with her.'

'It's not exactly an ideal home situation, as you may have guessed,' said Kjell, looking at both Paula and Martin.

'From the interview we understood that there were certain . . . problems.' Martin hesitated. 'So we've asked social services to look into the situation.'

Kjell sighed. 'I should have dealt with the matter sooner. But other things kept coming up. I don't know . . .' He stared at a photograph on his desk, showing a blonde woman and two children who looked to be about nine years old. For a moment nobody spoke. Then Kjell asked, 'What happens now?'

'The prosecutor will look over the case and then decide how to proceed. But it's a serious matter.'

Kjell waved his hand. 'I understand. Believe me, I don't take this lightly. I can see how serious it is. You've experience in these cases, what do you think will . . .' He glanced at the photo again, but then turned his gaze to the police officers.

255

It was Paula who answered. 'It's hard to say. My best guess is a home for troubled youth.'

Kjell nodded wearily. 'That actually might be for the best. Per has been . . . difficult for a long time, so maybe this will force him to understand how serious it is. But it hasn't been easy for him. I haven't been much help, and his mother . . . Well, you could see what the situation is. But she wasn't always like that. It was the divorce that . . .' His voice faded, and he glanced again at the photograph on his desk. 'It was really hard on her.'

'There's something else we need to talk to you about.' Martin leaned forward to study Kjell.

'What's that?'

'During the interview it came out that Per had broken into a house in early June. And that the owner of the house, Erik Frankel, caught him. From what we understand, you know about this incident. Am I right?'

For a second Kjell didn't say a word, then he nodded.

'That's right. Erik Frankel phoned me after locking Per in his library, and I drove over there.' He smiled wryly. 'It was actually kind of funny to see Per locked up with all those books. It was probably the only time he's ever been in such close contact with a library.'

'There's nothing funny about breaking into somebody's house,' said Paula drily. 'It could have ended very badly.'

'Sure, I know that. I apologize. It was an inappropriate joke,' said Kjell. 'But both Erik and I agreed not to make a big deal out of the matter. Erik thought the whole episode would serve as a good lesson for the boy. He thought Per would think twice before doing something like that again. That was all. I went over, picked up Per and read him the riot act, and . . .' He shrugged.

'But apparently you and Erik Frankel talked about something besides Per breaking into the house. He heard Erik say that he had information for you, something that might interest you, in your capacity as a journalist, and then the two of you agreed to meet at a later date. Does that ring a bell?'

The question was met with silence. Then Kjell shook his head. 'No, I have to say I don't recall anything like that. Either Per made it up, or he misinterpreted what he heard. Erik simply said that I could contact him if I needed any help with background material regarding Nazism.'

Martin and Paula looked at him sceptically. Neither of them believed a word of it, but they couldn't prove he was lying.

'Do you know whether your father and Erik had any contact with each other?' asked Martin at last.

Kjell's shoulders relaxed slightly, as if he were relieved that they'd changed the subject. 'Not as far as I know. On the other hand, I have no interest in my father's activities – except when they become the subject of one of my articles.'

'Doesn't that feel a little strange?' said Paula. 'Publicly criticizing your father like that?'

'You of all people ought to understand the importance of actively fighting anti-foreigner sentiment,' said Kjell. 'It's like a cancerous tumour in society, and we have to combat it any way we can. And if my father chooses to be part of that cancer . . . well . . . that's his decision,' said Kjell, throwing out his hands. 'And by the way, my father and I have no real ties to each other, except for the fact that he happened to impregnate my mother. When I was growing up, the only time I saw him was in prison visiting rooms. As soon as I was old enough to think for myself and make my own decisions, I realized that he was not someone that I wanted in my life.'

'So you've had no contact with each other? Is Per in contact with him?' asked Martin, more out of curiosity than because it had any relevance to the investigation.

'No, I have no contact with him. Unfortunately, my father has managed to feed my son a lot of stupid ideas. When Per was younger, we made sure they didn't see each other, but now that he's a teenager, well . . . we haven't been able to stop them from meeting, as much as we've tried.'

'All right. I don't think there's anything more. At least for the time being,' said Martin, getting to his feet. Paula did the same. On their way out the door, Martin stopped and turned round.

'You're positive that you don't have any information either about or from Erik Frankel that we might find useful?'

Their eyes met, and for an instant Kjell hesitated. Then he shook his head and said tersely, 'No, nothing. Nothing at all.'

They didn't believe him this time either.

Margareta was worried. No one had answered the phone at her parents' house since Herman had come over yesterday. It was odd, and disturbing. They usually told her if they were going somewhere, but lately they seldom left home. And every evening she was in the habit of ringing her parents for a chat. It was a ritual they'd had for years, and she couldn't remember a single time when her parents hadn't answered the phone. But this time, it rang and rang, echoing into the void, and no one picked up at the other end. She'd wanted to go over and look in on them last night, but her husband Owe had persuaded her to wait until morning, saying that they had probably just gone to bed early. But this morning there was still no answer.

Convinced that something must have happened to them, Margareta put on her shoes and jacket and set off for her parents' house. It was a ten-minute walk, and the whole way there she cursed herself for letting Owe talk her out of going over earlier. She just knew something was wrong.

When she was only a few hundred metres away, she saw

a figure at her parents' front door. She squinted to see who it was, but before she got any closer she realized it was that writer, Erica Falck.

'Can I help you with anything?' Margareta asked, trying to sound friendly, but even she could hear the worry in her voice.

'Er . . . yes, I was looking for Britta. But nobody seems to be at home.' The blonde woman looked uncomfortable as she stood there on the porch.

'I'm their daughter. I've been ringing them since yesterday, but they don't answer the phone. So I came over to make sure everything is all right,' said Margareta. 'You can come in with me and wait in the hall.' She reached up to the rafters of the little roof over the door and took down a key. Her hand was shaking as she unlocked the door.

'Come on in. I'll just go and have a look,' she said, suddenly feeling grateful to have the company of another person. She really should have called one or both of her sisters before heading over, but then she'd have been forced to admit how serious she thought the situation might be, how worry was eating her up inside.

She walked through the ground-floor rooms, looking around. Everything was nice and tidy and looked the same as always.

'Mamma? Pappa?' she called, but no one answered. Now she was feeling truly frightened, and she was having a hard time breathing. She should have phoned her sisters. She really should have done that.

'Stay here. I'm just going upstairs to look around,' she said to Erica. She didn't rush up the stairs, but instead moved slowly, trembling all over. Everything seemed unnaturally quiet. But when she reached the top step, she heard a faint sound. Like someone sobbing. Almost like a little child. She stood still for a moment, trying to pinpoint where the sound was coming from. Then she realized it was coming from her parents' bedroom. With her heart pounding, she rushed over and opened the door. It took a few seconds for her to comprehend what she was seeing. Then, as if from far away, she heard her own voice screaming for help.

It was Per who opened the door when Frans rang the bell.

'Grandpa,' Per said, looking like a puppy that needed a pat on the head.

'What have you got yourself mixed up in?' said Frans brusquely, stepping inside.

'But I . . . he . . . he was talking a lot of bullshit. Was I just supposed to take it, or what?' Per sounded hurt. He thought that if anyone would understand, it would be his grandfather. 'Besides, it was nothing compared to what you've done,' he added defiantly, though he didn't dare look Frans in the eye.

'That's exactly why I know what I'm talking about!' Frans took the boy by the shoulders and gave him a shake, forcing his grandson to look at him.

'Let's go in and sit down and have a talk, then maybe I can knock some sense into that stubborn head of yours. Where's your mother, by the way?' Frans looked around for Carina, ready to fight for his right to talk to his grandson.

'Probably sleeping it off,' said Per, slouching into the kitchen. 'She started drinking as soon as we got home yesterday and was still at it last night when I went to bed. But I haven't heard anything from her in a while.'

'I'll just go in and say hello. In the meantime make us some coffee,' said Frans.

'But I don't know how to make . . .' Per began in a whiny tone of voice.

'Then it's time you learned,' snapped Frans, heading for Carina's bedroom.

'Carina,' he said loudly as he went into her room. The only sound was a loud snoring. She lay halfway off the bed, one arm touching the floor. The room smelled of stale booze and vomit.

Taking a deep breath, Frans went over to her. He placed his hand on her shoulder and shook her.

'Carina, time to get up.' No reaction. He glanced around. The door to the bathroom opened right off her bedroom. He went in and turned on the taps to run her a bath. As the water poured into the tub, he began undressing her, unable to hide his disgust. It didn't take long, since she was wearing only her bra and underwear. He wrapped her in a blanket, carried her to the bathroom, and without further ado put her in the tub.

'Jesus Christ!' snorted his former daughter-in-law in a daze. 'What are you doing here?'

Frans didn't reply. Instead, he went over to her wardrobe, opened the door, and selected some clean clothes for her. He set them on the toilet next to the tub.

'Per is making coffee. Dry yourself off, get dressed, and come out to the kitchen.'

For a moment it looked like she might refuse. Then she nodded submissively.

'So, have you figured out the art of using the coffeemaker?' he asked Per, who was sitting at the kitchen table examining his cuticles.

'It's probably going to taste like shit,' Per grumbled. 'But at least I tried.'

Frans studied the pitch-black liquid that had started trickling into the glass pot. 'It looks plenty strong, at least.'

For a long time, he and his grandson sat at the table across from each other, not speaking. It was such a strange feeling to see his own history in somebody else. He could glimpse traces of his own father in the boy. Traces of the father that he still regretted not killing. Maybe everything would have been different if he'd done that. Summoned up all the rage boiling inside of him and directed it at the one person who truly deserved it. Instead, his anger had seeped out in a totally different direction, without any purpose. And it was still there. He knew that. He just didn't let it run riot as he had when he was younger. Now he was in control of his fury, and not the other way around. That was what he had to make his grandson understand. There was nothing wrong with his anger, but he needed to make sure that he was the one who decided when to let it loose. Anger was an arrow to be released in a controlled manner, not an axe to be swung wildly. Frans had tried that method and as a result he'd spent much of his life in prison, and his only son couldn't bear to be in the same room with him. He had no one else. The men in the organization were not his friends. He'd never made the mistake of assuming that they were, or tried to make them friends. They were all too consumed with their own rage to establish that sort of a relationship with each other. They shared a goal. That was all.

He looked at Per and saw his father. But he also saw himself. And Kjell. He'd done his best to get to know his son during the brief family visits to the prison and those short periods when he was actually at home. But it was an endeavour doomed to failure. If he was honest with himself, Frans didn't even know whether he really loved his son. Maybe he had once. Maybe his heart had once leapt when Rakel brought along their son to see him in prison. But he no longer remembered.

The strange thing was that as he sat there at the kitchen table with his grandson, the only love he could ever recall feeling was for Elsy. A love that was sixty years old, but it was still etched in his memory. Elsy and his grandson. They were the only people he'd ever felt any affection for. They had managed to elicit some sort of emotion from him. But it was dead now. His father had killed everything else. Frans hadn't thought about it in a long time. About his father. Or all the rest. But recent events had made the past come alive for him. And now it was time to think about it again.

'Kjell will be furious if he finds out that you came here.' Carina stood in the doorway. She swayed a bit, but she was clean and dressed. Her hair was dripping wet, and she'd draped a towel over her shoulders so her shirt wouldn't get wet.

'I don't care what Kjell thinks,' said Frans drily. He got up to pour some coffee for Carina and himself.

'This doesn't look drinkable,' she said as she sat down and stared at her cup, filled to the brim with the pitch-black brew.

'Drink it,' said Frans, opening cupboards and drawers.

'What are you looking for?' asked Carina, taking a sip and making a face. 'Leave my cupboards alone!'

Frans didn't reply as he pulled out one bottle after another and methodically poured the contents down the sink.

'You have no right to interfere!' she shouted at him. Per got up to leave.

'Sit down,' said Frans, pointing at his grandson. 'We're going to get to the bottom of this.'

Per obeyed at once, sinking back on to his chair.

An hour later, after all the booze had been dumped out, only the truth was left.

Kjell stared at his computer screen. Feelings of guilt had been gnawing at him ever since the police had come to see him yesterday. He knew he should go and see Per and Carina, but he just couldn't bring himself to do it. He had no idea where to start. What scared him was the realization that he was starting to give up. He could fight external enemies. He could direct all his energy to combatting the power-mongers and neo-Nazis and wage battles with windmills, no matter how big they were. But when it came to his former family, when it came to Per and Carina, it was as if he had no strength left. It had been sapped by a guilty conscience.

263

He looked at the photo of Beata and the kids. Of course he loved Magda and Loke, and he wouldn't want to live without them. But at the same time, it had all happened so fast, gone so wrong. He'd landed in a situation that had swept him away, and sometimes he still wondered if it had caused more harm than good. Maybe it was just the timing that had been unfortunate. Maybe he'd been going through some sort of midlife crisis, and Beata came along at just the wrong moment. At first he couldn't believe it: an attractive young girl like her, interested in someone like him. But it had turned out to be true. And he hadn't been able to resist sleeping with her, touching her firm, naked body, seeing the admiration in those eyes. It was nothing short of intoxicating. He couldn't think clearly, couldn't take a step back and make any sort of rational decision. Ironically enough, he'd just begun to show the first signs of coming to his senses when he'd lost all control of the situation. He had started to tire of the fact that she never offered any counter-arguments in their discussions, that she knew nothing about moon landings or the revolt in Hungary. He was even growing tired of the feeling of her smooth skin under his fingers.

He could still remember the moment when everything fell apart. It seemed like only yesterday, that she'd looked at him with those big blue eyes and told him that he was going to be a father, that now he would finally have to tell Carina, as he'd long promised to do.

It was at that moment he realized what a mistake he'd made. For a second he considered getting up and leaving her there in the café, going home to lie down on the sofa next to Carina to watch the news on TV while five-year-old Per slept soundly in his bed. But his male instinct told him that there was no going back. There were mistresses who wouldn't dream of telling the wife, and there were mistresses who would delight in revealing every last detail of the affair. He had no doubt which category Beata fell into. She wouldn't care who or what she crushed if he dared to crush her first. She would stomp on his life, destroy his very existence without looking back. And he would be left behind with the pieces.

And so he had chosen the coward's way out. Terrified of ending up alone in some shitty bachelor's flat, staring at the walls and wondering what to do with his life, he'd taken the only way remaining to him. Beata's way. She had won. And he'd walked out on Carina and Per. Cast them aside like rubbish on the side of the road, even he could see that. In the process he had destroyed Carina. And he'd lost Per. That was the price that he'd paid for the touch of youthful skin under his fingertips.

Maybe he could have held on to Per if he'd been able to ignore the guilt that settled like a heavy stone on his chest every time he so much as thought about the two he'd left behind. But he wasn't capable of doing that. He'd made sporadic attempts, played the authority figure, played the father on rare occasions, with miserable results.

Now his son was a stranger to him. And Kjell didn't have the energy to try again. After a lifetime spent hating the father who had abandoned him and his mother in favour of a life in which they had no part, he had done the same thing to his own son. He had turned into his father, and that was the bitter truth.

He pounded his fist on the table, trying to replace the pain in his heart with a physical pain. It didn't help. Then he opened the bottom desk drawer to look at the only thing that could distract his mind from this torture.

There had been a moment when he had considered handing the material to the police, but at the last second the professional journalist in him had put on the brakes. Erik hadn't given him much. When he came up to Kjell's office, he'd spent quite a while talking in circles, obviously uncertain how much he wanted to divulge. At one stage he'd seemed about to turn on his heel and leave without having revealed anything at all.

Kjell opened the folder. He wished he'd managed to ask Erik more questions, to get some pointers as to where he ought to look. All he had were a few newspaper articles that Erik had given him, without comment or explanation.

'What do you expect me to do with this?' Kjell had asked, throwing out his hands.

'That's your job,' was Erik's reply. 'I know it might seem strange, but I can't give you the whole answer. I don't dare. So I'm giving you the tools – you can do the rest.'

And then he'd gone, leaving Kjell sitting at his desk with a folder containing three articles.

Kjell scratched his beard and opened the folder. He'd already read through the material several times, but other things kept coming up that had prevented him from giving his full attention to the task. If he were to be completely honest, he had also questioned the wisdom of devoting any time to it. The old man might just be senile. And if he was really in possession of material as explosive as he'd intimated why hadn't he explained things better? But with Erik Frankel's murder, he began to look at the folder in a different light. He was ready to give it his all now. And he knew exactly where to begin: with the common denominator in all three articles. A Norwegian resistance fighter by the name of Hans Olavsen.

FJÄLLBACKA 1944

'Hilma!' Something in Elof's tone of voice made both his wife and daughter dash out to meet him.

'Heavens, how you're shouting. What's going on?' exclaimed Hilma, but her voice trailed off when she saw that Elof was not alone. 'Are we having guests?' she asked, nervously wiping her hands on her apron. 'I was just in the middle of washing the dishes.'

'Don't worry,' Elof assured her. 'The boy won't mind how things look in the house. He came on the boat with us today. He was fleeing from the Germans.'

The boy held out his hand to Hilma and bowed when she shook it.

'Hans Olavsen,' he said in his lilting Norwegian. Then he held out his hand to Elsy, who shook it awkwardly, giving a little curtsey.

'He's had a hard time on the way here, so maybe we could offer him some refreshment,' said Elof. He hung up his peaked cap and handed his coat to Elsy, who held it in her arms without moving.

'Don't just stand there, girl. Hang up your father's coat,' he said sternly, but then he couldn't resist stroking his daughter's cheek. Considering the dangers that now accompanied every voyage, it always felt like a gift when he was able to come back home and see Elsy and Hilma again. He cleared his throat, embarrassed to have succumbed to such emotion in the presence of a stranger. Then he motioned with his hand.

'Come in, come in. I'm sure Hilma will find something nice for us,' he said, sitting down on one of the kitchen chairs.

'We don't have much to offer,' said his wife, her eyes lowered. 'But what little we have, we will gladly share.'

'I'm sincerely grateful,' said the boy, sitting down across from Elof as he hungrily eyed the plate of sandwiches that Hilma was setting on the table.

'All right, help yourself,' she said, and then went over to the cupboard to pour a little dram of aquavit for them both. Liquor was scarce, but this seemed a proper occasion for it.

They ate in silence. When there was only one sandwich left, Elof pushed the plate towards the Norwegian boy, urging him with a glance to take it. Elsy watched surreptitiously as she stood next to the counter, helping her mother. This was all so exciting. In their very own kitchen was somebody who had fled from the Germans, coming all the way here from Norway. She couldn't wait to tell the others. Then a thought occurred to her, and she almost couldn't stop the words from spilling out. But her father must have had the same thought, because he asked the very question that was on her mind.

'There's a boy from here in town who was taken by the Germans. That was more than a year ago, but maybe you . . .' Elof threw out his hands, fixing his eyes on the boy across the table.

'Well, it's not likely that I'd know anything about him. There are so many people coming and going. What's his name?'

'Axel Frankel,' said Elof. But the hope in his eyes turned to disappointment when the boy, after thinking for a moment, shook his head.

'No, I'm afraid not. We haven't come across him. At least I don't think so. You haven't heard anything about what happened to him? Nothing that would supply a little more information?'

'Unfortunately, no,' said Elof, shaking his head. 'The Germans took him in Kristiansand, and since then we haven't heard a peep. For all we know, he might be –'

'No, Pappa. I don't believe it!' Elsy's eyes filled with tears, and feeling embarrassed she ran upstairs to her room. She couldn't believe that she'd humiliated herself and her parents that way. Crying like a baby in front of a complete stranger.

'Does your daughter know this . . . Axel?' asked the Norwegian, looking concerned as he stared after her.

'She's friends with his younger brother. And it's been hard for Erik. For Axel's whole family,' said Elof with a sigh.

A shadow passed over Hans's eyes. 'Many people have been sorely tested by this war,' he said.

Elof could tell that this boy had seen things that no one his age ought to have witnessed.

'What about your own family?' he asked cautiously. Hilma was standing at the counter drying a plate, but she stopped what she was doing.

'I don't know where they are,' said Hans at last, his eyes fixed on the table. 'When the war is over – if it's ever over – I'll go back to look for them. Until then, I can't return to Norway.'

Hilma met Elof's eyes over the boy's blond head. After carrying on a silent conversation, based solely on an exchange of glances, they reached an agreement. Elof cleared his throat.

'Well, you see, we usually rent out our house to summer visitors and live in the basement room ourselves while they're here. But the room is empty the rest of the year. Maybe you'd like to . . . stay here for a while and rest up, before you decide what to do next. I can probably find you some work too. Maybe not full-time, but at least enough so you'd

269

have money in your pocket. First I'll have to report to the district police that I've brought you into the country, but if I promise to look after you, there shouldn't be any problem.'

'Only if you let me pay rent with the money that I earn,' said Hans, looking at him with a mixture of gratitude and guilt.

Elof glanced at Hilma again and he nodded.

'That would be fine. Any contribution is welcome during these times of war.'

'I'll go downstairs and put things in order for you,' said Hilma, putting on her coat.

'I can't thank you enough. I really can't,' said the boy in his lilting Norwegian as he bowed his head, but not fast enough. Elof managed to catch a glimpse of the tears in his eyes.

'It's nothing,' he said, embarrassed. 'It's nothing.'

'Help!'

Erica gave a start when she heard the scream from upstairs. She rushed towards the sound, taking the stairs in a few bounds.

'What's wrong?' she cried, but stopped short when she caught sight of Margareta's face as she stood in the doorway to one of the rooms. Erica went closer and then inhaled sharply when a big double bed came into view.

'Pappa,' said Margareta with a whimper, and then went into the room. Erica stayed in the doorway, uncertain what she was looking at or what she should do.

'Pappa,' repeated Margareta.

Herman lay on the bed, staring up at the ceiling, and he didn't react to his daughter's cries. Next to him on the bed was Britta. Her face was pale and rigid, and there was no doubt that she was dead. Herman lay close to her, with his arms wrapped tightly around her lifeless body.

'I killed her,' he said in a low voice.

Margareta gasped. 'What are you saying, Pappa? Of course you didn't kill her!'

'I killed her,' he repeated dully, hugging his dead wife even harder.

His daughter walked around the bed and sat down next

to him. Cautiously she tried to loosen his grip, and after a few attempts she succeeded. She stroked his forehead as she spoke to him.

'Pappa, it's not your fault. Mamma wasn't well. Her heart must have given up. It's not your fault. You need to understand that.'

'I was the one who killed her,' he repeated, staring at a spot on the wall.

Margareta turned to Erica. 'Could you please ring for an ambulance?'

Erica hesitated. 'Should I call the police too?'

'Pappa's in shock. He doesn't know what he's saying. We don't need the police,' said Margareta sharply. Then she turned back to her father and took his hand.

'I'll take care of everything, Pappa. I'm going to call Anna-Greta and Birgitta, and we'll all help you. We're here for you.'

Herman didn't reply, just lay there motionless, letting her hold his hand, but without squeezing it in return.

Erica went downstairs and took out her mobile. She paused for a moment before punching in a phone number.

'Hi, Martin. It's Erica. Patrik's wife. Well, I think we need your help here. I'm at the home of Britta Johansson, and she's dead. Her husband says that he killed her. It looks like death by natural causes, but . . . Oh, okay. I'll wait here. Will you ring for an ambulance, or should I? Okay.'

Erica ended the conversation, hoping that she hadn't done something stupid. Of course it looked as if Margareta was right, that Britta had simply died in her sleep. But then why did Herman keep saying that he'd killed her? And besides, it was an odd coincidence that yet another one of her mother's childhood friends was suddenly dead, only a few months after Erik was killed. No, she'd done the right thing.

Erica went back upstairs.

'I've called for help,' she said. 'Is there anything else I can do?'

'Could you make some coffee? I'll see if I can get Pappa to come downstairs.'

Margareta gently pulled Herman into a sitting position.

'All right, Pappa, come on now. Let's go downstairs and wait for the ambulance.'

Erica went into the kitchen. She searched the cupboards for what she needed and then set about making a big pot of coffee. A few minutes later she heard footsteps on the stairs and then saw Margareta escorting Herman into the room. She led him over to a kitchen chair, and he dropped on to it like a sack of flour.

'I hope the medics have something they can give him,' said Margareta, sounding worried. 'He must have been lying next to her since yesterday. I don't understand why he didn't phone one of us.'

'I've also . . .' Erica hesitated, but then started over. 'I've also notified the police. I'm sure you're right, but I felt I had to. I couldn't just . . .' She failed to find the right words, and Margareta stared at her as if she'd lost her mind.

'You phoned the police? Do you think my father was serious? Are you crazy? He's in shock after finding his wife dead, and now he's going to have to answer questions from the police? How dare you!' Margareta took a step towards Erica, who was holding the coffee pot, but just then the doorbell rang.

'That must be them. I'll go and open the door,' said Erica, keeping her eyes lowered as she put down the coffee pot before she dashed out to the hall.

When she opened the door, Martin was the first person she saw.

He nodded grimly. 'Hi, Erica.'

'Hi,' she replied quietly, stepping aside. What if she was wrong? What if she was subjecting a grieving man to unnecessary torment? But it was too late now.

'Britta's upstairs, in the bedroom,' she said, and then

273

nodded towards the kitchen. 'Her husband is in there. With the daughter. She was the one who found . . . It looks like she's been dead for a while.'

'Okay, we'll take a look,' said Martin, motioning for Paula to come inside along with the ambulance medics. He quickly introduced Paula to Erica and then went into the kitchen. Margareta had her arm around her father's shoulders.

'This is absurd,' she said, staring at Martin. 'My mother died in her sleep, and my father is in shock. Is all this really necessary?'

Martin held up his hands. 'I'm sure it happened just as you say. But now that we're here, we'll just have a look, and then it will be over with. And may I offer my condolences.' He gave her a resolute look, and reluctantly she nodded her assent.

'She's upstairs. Could I phone my sisters? And my husband?'

'Yes, of course,' said Martin and then headed upstairs.

Erica hesitated but then fell in behind him and the medics. She stood to one side and said to Martin in a low voice:

'I came over to talk to her about a few things, including Erik Frankel. It might be just a coincidence, but it seems a little strange, don't you think?'

Martin glanced at Erica as he allowed the doctor in charge to enter the room first. 'You think there's some kind of connection?'

'I don't know,' said Erica, shaking her head. 'But I've been researching my mother's past and, when she was young, she was friends with Erik Frankel, and with Britta. There was also somebody named Frans Ringholm in their group.'

'Frans Ringholm?' said Martin, looking startled.

'Yes. Do you know him?'

'Er, well . . . we've run into him in our investigation of Erik's murder,' said Martin, the wheels turning in his head.

'Then isn't it a little strange that Britta should also die

274

suddenly? Less than three months after Erik Frankel was killed?' Erica persisted.

Martin was still looking hesitant. 'We're not talking about youngsters here. I mean, at their age, a lot could happen. Stroke, heart attack, all sorts of things.'

'Well, I can tell you right now that this was not a heart attack or a stroke,' said the doctor from inside the bedroom. Martin and Erica looked round in surprise.

'Then what was it?' asked Martin. He went into the room and stood behind the doctor at Britta's bedside. Erica chose to remain in the doorway, but craned her neck to see better.

'This woman has been suffocated,' said the doctor, pointing at Britta's eyes with one hand as he used the other to lift one of her eyelids. 'Look – petechiae.'

'Petechiae?' Martin repeated, uncomprehending.

'Red spots in the whites of the eyes that occur when tiny little blood vessels burst as a consequence of increased pressure in the blood system. Typical with suffocation, strangulation, and the like.'

'But couldn't she have had some sort of attack that made it hard for her to breathe? Wouldn't that produce the same symptoms?' asked Erica.

'Yes, that's possible. Absolutely,' said the doctor. 'But upon first inspection I noticed a feather in her throat, so I'd bet that this is the murder weapon.' He pointed to a white pillow lying next to Britta's head. 'Petechiae can also indicate that pressure was applied directly to the throat, for example if someone used their hands to choke her. But the post-mortem will give us a definitive answer. One thing is certain, though. I won't be writing this up as "death by natural causes" unless the ME can convince me that I'm wrong. We need to consider this a crime scene.' He straightened up and cautiously exited the room.

Martin did the same, then pulled his mobile out of his

pocket to ring for the techs, so they could make a thorough examination of the room.

After ushering everyone downstairs, he went back to the kitchen and sat down across from Herman. Margareta glanced at him, and a frown appeared on her face as she saw that everything wasn't as it should be.

'What's your father's name?' Martin asked.

'Herman,' she told him. Her concern grew.

'Herman,' said Martin. 'Can you tell me what happened here?'

At first the man didn't answer. The only sound was the medics talking quietly to each other out in the living room. Then Herman looked up and said very clearly:

'I killed her.'

Friday arrived, and with it came glorious late summer weather. Mellberg stretched out his legs, taking big strides, as he let Ernst pull him along. Even the dog seemed to appreciate the warm day.

'Hey, Ernst,' said Mellberg, waiting for the dog to lift his leg on a shrub. 'Tonight your pappa is going out dancing again.'

Ernst tilted his head and gave him a quizzical look for a moment, but then returned to his toilet activities.

Mellberg found himself whistling as he thought about the evening's class and the feeling of Rita's body close to his own. One thing was certain: he could get used to this salsa dancing.

His expression darkened as thoughts of hot rhythms slipped away to be replaced by thoughts of the investigation. Or rather, investigations. Why was it that they never got to enjoy a bit of peace and quiet in this town? Why did people have to go on killing each other? Well, at least one of the cases seemed straightforward. The husband had confessed. Now they were just waiting for the ME's report to confirm that it was murder, and then that case would be solved. Martin Molin was going around muttering that it was a bit strange that someone with connections to Erik Frankel should also have been murdered, but Mellberg didn't give much credence to that. Good Lord, from what he'd understood, the victims had been friends when they were kids. And that was more than sixty years ago, which was an eternity, so it couldn't have anything to do with the murder investigation. No, the idea was absurd. But just in case, he'd given his permission for Molin to check things out, go through phone lists, et cetera, to see if he could find a link. Most likely he wouldn't find anything. But at least it would shut him up.

Suddenly Mellberg saw that his feet had carried him to Rita's building while he was lost in thought. Ernst was standing at the door, eagerly wagging his tail. Mellberg glanced at his watch. Eleven o'clock. The perfect time for a little coffee break, if she was at home. He hesitated for a moment, then rang the intercom. No answer.

'Hello there.'

The voice behind him made Mellberg jump. It was Johanna. She swayed a bit from side to side, holding one hand pressed to the small of her back.

'Hard to believe it could be so damn hard just to go out for a short walk,' she said, sounding frustrated as she stretched out her back with a grimace. 'I'm going nuts just staying at home waiting, but my body doesn't really want to do the same thing as my mind.' She sighed, running her hand over her huge stomach. 'I assume that you're looking for Rita?' she said, giving him a coy smile.

'Er, well, yes . . .' said Mellberg, suddenly embarrassed. 'We . . . that is, Ernst and I, are just out for a little walk, and Ernst wanted to come over to see . . . er . . . Señorita, so we . . .'

'Rita's not home,' said Johanna, the smile still on her lips. She apparently found his confusion amusing. 'She's visiting

277

a friend of hers this morning. But if you'd like to come upstairs for some coffee . . . I mean, if Ernst would like to come upstairs, Señorita is home.' She gave him a wink. 'And you can keep me company. I'm feeling a bit down in the dumps.'

'Oh, ah, of course,' said Mellberg and followed her in.

Once inside the flat, Johanna sat down on a kitchen chair to catch her breath.

'Why don't you just relax?' said Mellberg. 'I saw where Rita keeps everything, so I'll make the coffee. It's better if you rest.'

Johanna looked at him in surprise as he began opening cupboards, but she gratefully remained seated.

'That must be awfully heavy,' said Mellberg, casting a glance at her stomach as he poured water into the coffee-maker.

'Heavy is just one word for it. I have to say that being pregnant is highly overrated. First you feel like shit for three or four months and have to stay near the toilet in case you need to throw up. Next there are a couple of months when you feel okay, and occasionally even quite good. But then it's as if overnight you turn into Barbapapa in the French kids' books. Or maybe Barbamama.'

'And after that?'

'Don't even go there,' said Johanna sternly, shaking her finger at him. 'I haven't dared think that far ahead. If I start thinking about the fact that there's only one way out for this kid, I'm really going to panic. And if you tell me "women have been giving birth to children for eons and survived and even wanted to have more, so it can't be all that bad," then I may have to punch you.'

Mellberg held up his hands in protest. 'You're talking to somebody who has never even been close to a maternity ward.'

He served the coffee and then sat down at the table.

'It must be nice to eat for two, at any rate,' he said with a grin as she stuffed the third biscuit in her mouth.

'That's one benefit I'm enjoying to the hilt,' Johanna

laughed, reaching for another. 'Although it looks like you've adopted the same philosophy, without having pregnancy as an excuse,' she teased, pointing at Mellberg's sizable paunch.

'I'll be dancing this off in no time.' He patted his stomach.

'I'd like to come over and watch you sometime,' said Johanna, giving him a friendly smile.

For a moment Mellberg was amazed that someone actually seemed to appreciate his company – he wasn't used to that. But then he realized to his great surprise that he was enjoying spending time with Rita's daughter-in-law. After taking a deep breath he dared to ask the question that had been nagging at him ever since their lunch, when all the pieces had fallen into place.

'What about . . . the father? Who . . .?' He could hear that this might not be the most articulate moment in his life, but Johanna seemed to have no trouble understanding what he meant. She gave him a sharp look and for several seconds considered how to answer him. Finally her expression softened as she seemed to decide that it was only curiosity that had prompted his question.

'A clinic. In Denmark. We've never met the father. So I didn't pick up some guy in a pub, if that's what you were thinking.'

'Er, no . . . I wasn't thinking that,' said Mellberg, but he had to admit to himself that the thought had definitely occurred to him.

He glanced at his watch. He was going to have to leave for the station. It was almost time for lunch, and he didn't want to miss it. He got up to carry the cups and plate over to the counter. Then he paused for a second. Finally, he took out his wallet from his back pocket, got out a business card, and handed it to Johanna.

'If you . . . should need any assistance, or . . . Well, I assume that Paula and Rita are on standby for you until . . . but, ah . . . just in case . . .'

279

Johanna accepted the card with a surprised expression, and then Mellberg dashed for the door. He didn't really know why he'd given Johanna his card. Maybe it had to do with the fact that he could still remember how it felt when the baby had kicked against his hand when he placed it on her stomach.

'Ernst, come here,' he called brusquely, herding the dog ahead of him. Then he closed the door behind them, without saying goodbye.

Martin was staring at the phone lists. They revealed nothing to confirm his gut feeling, nor did they contradict it. Right before Erik Frankel was murdered, someone had phoned the Frankel house from the home of Britta and Herman. Two calls to the number were on the list. And another one from only a couple of days ago, indicating that either Britta or Herman must have called Axel. There was also a phone call to Frans Ringholm's number.

Martin stared out the window, then shoved back his chair and propped his feet up on his desk. He'd devoted the morning to going through the documents, the photos and all the other material that they'd gathered during the investigation into Erik's death. He had decided not to give up until he found some connection between the two murders. But so far, there was nothing. Except for this: the phone calls.

Frustrated, Martin tossed the lists on to his desk. It felt as though he'd come to a dead end. And he knew that Mellberg had only given him permission to look into the circumstances surrounding Britta's death in order to shut him up. Like everyone else, Mellberg seemed convinced that the husband was guilty. But they hadn't yet been able to interview Herman. According to the doctors, he was still in a state of deep shock, and he'd been admitted to the hospital. So they would have to wait until the doctors thought he was strong enough to tolerate an interrogation.

The whole thing was such a mess, and Martin had no idea what direction to take. He stared at the case file containing the investigation documents, as if beseeching them to speak, and then he had an idea.

Of course. Why hadn't he thought of it before?

Twenty-five minutes later, he drove up to Patrik and Erica's house. He'd phoned ahead to tell Patrik he was coming and to make sure his colleague was at home. Patrik opened the door after the first ring, holding Maja in his arms. She immediately began waving her hands when she saw who was standing on the doorstep.

'Hi, sweetie,' said Martin, waving back. She replied by stretching out her arms to him, and since she refused to let go of him, he soon found himself sitting on the sofa with Maja on his lap. Patrik sat in the armchair, leaning over the papers and photographs and pensively stroking his chin.

'Where's Erica?' asked Martin, looking around.

'Hmm?' said Patrik absentmindedly. 'Oh, she left for the library a couple of hours ago. More research for her new book.'

'I see,' said Martin. Then he went back to entertaining Maja so that Patrik could read through everything undisturbed.

'So you think Erica is right?' he asked at last, looking up. 'You agree that there may be a connection between the two murders?'

Martin paused for a moment before nodding. 'Yes, I do. I don't yet have any concrete proof, but if you're asking me what I think, I have to say that I'm practically convinced there's a connection.'

Patrik nodded. 'Well, it's undeniably a strange coincidence.' He stretched out his legs. 'Have you asked Axel Frankel and Frans Ringholm about the phone calls they received from Britta and Herman's house?'

'No, not yet.' Martin shook his head. 'I wanted to talk to

281

you first, make sure I wasn't crazy because I'm looking for some other solution when we actually have a suspect who has confessed.'

'Her husband, right . . .' said Patrik. 'The question is: why would he say that he killed her if he didn't do it?'

'I have no idea. Maybe to protect somebody else?' Martin shrugged.

'Hmm . . .' Patrik continued leafing through the docu-ments on the coffee table.

'What about the investigation of Erik's murder? Are you making any progress?'

'Well, I wouldn't exactly call it progress,' said Martin, sounding discouraged as he bounced Maja on his knee. 'Paula is working on finding out more about Sweden's Friends, and we've talked to all the neighbours, but no one remembers seeing anything out of the ordinary. The Frankel house is in such a secluded location that we didn't really have much hope that anyone would have noticed anything, and unfor-tunately that seems to be the case. Otherwise, that's all we have.' He pointed to the documents spread out like a fan on the table in front of Patrik.

'What about Erik's finances?' He shuffled through the papers, pulling out some from the very bottom. 'Anything seem odd?'

'No, not really. Mostly just the usual bill payments, some small withdrawals, that sort of thing.'

'No large sums moved in or out?' Patrik studied the columns of figures.

'No. The only thing that caught our eye was a monthly transfer that Erik made. The bank says that he'd been making the transfer payments regularly for almost fifty years.'

Patrik gave a start and stared at Martin. 'Fifty years? Did he transfer the money to a person or a company?'

'A private individual in Göteborg, apparently. The name is on one of the pieces of paper in the folder,' said Martin.

'We're not talking large sums of money. Of course, the amounts increased over the years, but the most recent payments were around two thousand kronor, and that doesn't sound like anything major. I mean, it couldn't be blackmail or anything like that, because who would keep making payments for fifty years?'

Martin could hear how lame that sounded, and he felt like slapping his hand to his forehead. He should have checked up on those transfers. Well, better late than never. 'I can call him today and find out what it was about,' he said, moving Maja on to his other knee.

Patrik was silent for a moment. Then he said, 'You know what? I need to get out of the house and take a drive.' He opened the case file and took out the piece of paper. 'Wilhelm Fridén. Apparently he's the one who received the money. I can go over there tomorrow and talk with him in person. This address –' he waved the piece of paper – 'is it current?'

'Yes, that's the address I got from the bank. So it should be up to date,' said Martin.

'Good. I'll go over there tomorrow. It may be a sensitive matter, so I think that would be better than phoning.'

'Okay. If you're willing to do that, I'd be really grateful,' said Martin. 'What about . . .?' He pointed at Maja.

'I can take her with me,' said Patrik, giving his daughter a big smile. 'Then we can drop by and see Aunt Lotta and the cousins too, all right, sweetheart? It'll be fun to see your cousins.'

Maja gurgled in agreement and clapped her hands.

'Could I keep this for a few days?' asked Patrik, pointing at the folder. Martin paused to think about it. He had copies of most of the documents, so it shouldn't be a problem.

'Okay, keep it. And let me know if you discover anything else that you think we should look into. While you're checking on things in Göteborg, I'll have a talk with Frans and Axel to find out why Britta or Herman phoned them.'

'Let's not ask Axel about the payments for the time being. Not until I have a little more information.'

'Of course.'

'Don't be discouraged,' said Patrik as he and Maja walked Martin to the door to say goodbye. 'You know from experience how it goes. Sooner or later a little piece will slide into place and end up solving the whole puzzle.'

'Sure, I know that,' said Martin, but he didn't sound convinced. 'I just think that it's a hell of a time for you to be on leave right now. We could have used your help.' He smiled to take away the sting of his words.

'Believe me, you'll be in the same boat someday. And when you're washing nappies, I'll be back at the station, working my head off.' Patrik winked at Martin before closing the door behind him.

'So, we're off to Göteborg tomorrow, you and I,' he said to Maja, dancing around with his daughter in his arms.

'We just have to sell the idea to your mother first.'

Maja nodded her agreement.

Paula felt exhausted. Exhausted and disgusted. She'd been surfing the Internet for hours, looking for information about Swedish neo-Nazi organizations, and Sweden's Friends in particular. It still seemed likely that they'd had something to do with Erik Frankel's death, but the problem was that the police had nothing concrete to go on. They hadn't found any threatening letters. All they had were the hints in the letters from Frans Ringholm, saying that Sweden's Friends didn't appreciate Erik's activities and that Frans could no longer shield him from these forces. Nor was there any technical evidence linking any of them to the crime scene. All the board members had voluntarily, albeit without disguising their contempt, provided their fingerprints, with the kind assistance of the police in Uddevalla. But the National Crime Lab had concluded there were no matches

284

with any of the fingerprints found in the Frankel library. The matter of alibis hadn't given them any leads either. None of the board members could offer an airtight alibi, but most had one that wouldn't be worth challenging unless the police found evidence that pointed in their direction. Several of them had confirmed that Frans had been visiting a sister organization in Denmark during the relevant days, and that gave him an alibi too. Another problem was that the organization was so big, much bigger than Paula had imagined, and they couldn't very well check up on the alibis and take fingerprints of everyone associated with Sweden's Friends. That was why they had decided, for the time being, to focus their attention on the board members. But so far without results.

Annoyed, Paula continued her search on the Internet. Where did all these people come from? And where did their hatred come from? She could understand hatred that was directed at specific individuals, at people who had wronged them in some way. But to hate others simply because they were from a different country, or because of the colour of their skin? No, she just didn't get it.

She herself hated the thugs who had murdered her father. Hated them so much that she wouldn't hesitate to kill them if she ever had the chance, assuming they were still alive. But her hatred stopped there, even though it could have reached upwards, outwards, expanded further. She had refused to succumb to that much hatred. Instead, she had limited her animosity to the men who held the guns that fired the bullets into her father's body. If she hadn't limited her hatred, it would have eventually made her hate her native country. And how could she do that? How could she hate the country where she'd been born, where she'd taken her first steps, where she'd played with friends, sat on her grandmother's lap, listened to songs in the evening, and danced at fiestas? How could she hate all that?

But these people . . . She scrolled down, reading one column after another proclaiming that people like herself should be eradicated, or at least sent back to their homelands. And there were pictures. Plenty of them from Nazi Germany, of course. The black-and-white photos that she'd seen so many times before – the heaps of naked, emaciated bodies that had been tossed aside like trash after the people had died in the concentration camps. Auschwitz, Buchenwald, Dachau . . . all the names that were so horribly familiar, for ever associated with the worst of all evil. But here, on these websites, they were hailed and celebrated. Or denied. For there were also the deniers, like Peter Lindgren. He insisted the holocaust had never happened. That six million Jews had not been expelled, killed, tortured, gassed to death in the concentration camps during the Second World War. How could anyone deny something like that when there was so much evidence, so many witnesses? How had the twisted minds of these people managed to deny history?

She jumped when a knock on the door interrupted her.

'Hi, what are you working on?' Martin was standing in the doorway.

'I'm checking up on all the background information I can find about Sweden's Friends,' she said with a sigh. 'But it's enough to scare the shit out of you, poking around in this stuff. Did you know that there are approximately twenty neo-Nazi organizations in Sweden? Or that the Sweden Democrat Party won a total of 281 seats in 144 municipalities? Where the hell are we headed in this country?'

'I don't know, but it makes you wonder,' said Martin.

'Well, it's fucking awful,' said Paula, angrily throwing down her pen, which slid off the desk and landed on the floor.

'Sounds like you need a break from all this,' said Martin. 'I was thinking of having another talk with Axel.'

'About anything in particular?' asked Paula, getting up to follow Martin out to the garage.

'Not really. I was just thinking that it might be good to check in with him again. After all, he had the closest relationship with Erik and knew him best. But there is one thing I do want to ask him about.' Martin paused. 'I know that I'm the only one who thinks there's some connection with the murder of Britta Johansson, but someone recently made a phone call from their house to Axel, and another one back in June, although it's impossible to know if the call was intended for Erik or Axel. I've just looked through the Frankels' phone records, and in June someone from that house called Britta or Herman. Twice. Before they'd called the Frankels.'

'It's worth checking out, at any rate,' said Paula, fastening her seatbelt. 'As long as I can get out of reading about all those Nazis for a while, I'll go along with any theory, no matter how much of a long shot it is.'

Martin nodded as they drove out of the garage. He could totally understand Paula's feelings. But something told him this wasn't really such a long shot.

She'd been in a daze all week. Only on Friday did Anna feel like she could even begin to take in the information. Dan had handled it much better. After the initial shock had subsided, he'd gone around humming to himself. He'd blithely dismissed all her objections, saying, 'Oh, it'll work out. This is going to be so great! A baby of our own – this is fantastic!'

But Anna couldn't really go along with 'fantastic'. Not yet. She found herself touching her stomach, trying to imagine the tiny lump inside. So far unidentifiable, a microscopic embryo, which in only a few months would become a baby. Even though she'd been through it twice before, it still seemed unfathomable. Maybe even more so this time

287

around, because she hardly remembered being pregnant with Emma and Adrian. Those memories had disappeared into a haze, where the fear of being beaten had dominated her every waking hour, even encroaching on her sleep. All her energy had been directed at protecting her stomach, protecting their lives, from Lucas.

This time that wasn't necessary. And absurdly enough, that frightened her. This time she could be happy. Was allowed to be happy. Should be happy. She loved Dan, after all. Felt safe with him. Knew that he would never even think of harming her or anyone else. Why should that frighten her? That was the question she'd spent the last few days trying to fathom.

'What do you think? Boy or girl? Any feelings one way or the other?' Dan had slipped behind her, wrapping his arms around her and patting her still flat stomach.

Anna laughed and carried on stirring the food, even though Dan's arms were hindering her efforts.

'I'm probably in my seventh week. Isn't that a bit early to know whether it's a boy or a girl?' Anna turned to face him, looking concerned. 'I hope you won't be too disappointed if you don't have a son, because you know that it's the father who determines the sex of the baby, and since you've already had three girls, the statistical probability is . . .'

'Shhh,' Dan laughed as he pressed his finger to Anna's lips. 'I'll be thrilled no matter what. If it's a boy, that will be great. If it's a girl, that's great too. And besides . . .' His expression turned serious. 'As I see it, I already have a son: Adrian. I hope you realize that. I thought you knew how I felt. When I asked all of you to move in with me, I didn't just mean into this house. I meant in here too.' He put his fist to his chest, right over his heart, and Anna fought to hold back her tears, though without success, as one tear rolled down her cheek and, to her annoyance, her lips began to quiver. Dan wiped away the tear, then took her face in his hands and looked into her eyes, forcing her to meet his gaze.

'If it's a girl, then Adrian and I will just have to join forces in the middle of all you women here. But don't ever doubt that I see you, Emma, and Adrian as a package deal. And I love all three of you. And I love you too, inside there. Do you hear me?' he shouted at her stomach.

Anna laughed. 'I don't think the ears develop until sometime around the twentieth week.'

'Well, all of my children develop very, very early.' Dan winked.

'Hmm, is that so?' said Anna, but she couldn't help laughing again. They stood there kissing, but moved apart when they heard the front door open and then slam shut.

'Hello? Who is it?' called Dan.

'It's me,' said a sullen voice. Belinda came in, peering at them from under her fringe.

'How did you get here?' asked Dan, staring at her angrily.

'How the hell do you think I got here? The same damn way I left here. By bus.'

'Speak to me politely, or not at all,' said Dan tensely.

'Oh, okay, then I choose . . .' Belinda pressed her finger to her cheek and pretended to think. 'Right. Now I know. Then I choose NOT TO TALK TO YOU AT ALL!' And she stormed up the stairs to her room, slamming the door behind her with a bang, then turning up the stereo as loud as it would go, making the whole house shake.

Dan sank on to the bottom step, pulled Anna close, and began talking to her stomach, which was at exactly the same level as his mouth.

'I hope you covered your ears inside there. Because your father is going to be way too old for that kind of language when you're her age.'

Anna stroked his hair, offering him her sympathy. Above them the music pounded.

289

FJÄLLBACKA 1944

'Did he have any news about Axel?' Erik couldn't hide his excitement. The four of them had gathered in their usual place on Rabekullen, right across from the cemetery. They all wanted to know what Elsy could tell them about the news that had spread like wildfire through the town – that Elof had brought home a Norwegian resistance fighter who had fled from the Germans.

Elsy shook her head. 'No, Pappa asked him, but he said he hadn't heard anything about Axel.'

Disappointed, Erik stared down at the granite rock, kicking his boot against a patch of grey lichen.

'Maybe he doesn't know him by name, but if we told him more about Axel, he might remember something,' said Erik, renewed hope gleaming in his eyes. If only there were some indication that his brother was still alive. Yesterday his mother had said for the first time what they all feared. She'd wept, her sobs more heartrending than ever, and said that they should light a candle for Axel in church on Sunday, because he was probably dead by now. His father got angry and swore at her, but Erik had seen the resignation in his eyes. Not even his father believed that Axel was among the living.

'Let's go talk to him,' said Britta eagerly, getting up and

brushing off her dress. She raised her hand to smooth down her plaits.

'Oh right, I can see that it's your concern for Erik that's making you stand there primping,' said Frans scornfully. 'I didn't know you were sweet on Norwegians. Aren't there enough Swedish boys to satisfy you?'

Britta's face turned bright red. 'Shut up, Frans. You're making a fool of yourself. Of course I care about Erik. And finding out about Axel. But there's no harm in looking decent.'

'Then you'll have to make a real effort – if you want to look *decent*,' was Frans's vulgar reply as he tugged at Britta's dress. Her face got even redder, and she looked as if she might burst into tears when Elsy said sharply:

'Stop that, Frans. Sometimes you say such stupid things. Just cut it out!'

He stared at her and his face blanched. Abruptly he stood up and ran off with a furious expression.

Erik poked at some loose stones. Without looking at Elsy, he said in a low voice, 'You should watch what you say to Frans. There's something about him . . . Something simmering underneath. I can tell.'

Elsy looked at him in surprise, wondering where that strange comment had come from. But she knew instinctively that he was right. She'd known Frans since they were little, but something was growing inside of him, something uncontrollable, something untamable.

'Oh, don't be ridiculous,' giggled Britta. 'There's nothing wrong with Frans. We were just . . . teasing each other.'

'You're blinded by the fact that you're in love with him,' said Erik.

Britta slapped him on the shoulder.

'Hey, why'd you do that?' he said, holding his shoulder.

'Because you're talking such nonsense. So, do you want to go and ask the Norwegian about your brother, or not?'

291

Britta started off as Erik and Elsy exchanged glances.

'He was at home when I left,' she said. 'I suppose it wouldn't hurt to have a few words with him.'

A short time later Elsy knocked discreetly on the basement door. Hans looked a little embarrassed when he opened the door and saw the three of them standing outside.

'Yes?' he said.

Elsy glanced at the others before she spoke. Out of the corner of her eye she noticed Frans come sauntering towards them, his expression now much calmer and his hands casually stuck in his trousers pockets.

'Well, ah, we were wondering if we could come in and talk to you for a moment.'

'Sure,' said the Norwegian, stepping aside. Britta gave him a coy wink as she moved past. The boys shook his hand and introduced themselves. There was very little furniture in the small room. Britta and Elsy sat down on the only chairs, Hans perched on the bed, and Frans and Erik sat down on the floor.

'It's about my brother,' said Erik. There were flickers of hope in his eyes. 'My brother has been helping your people during the whole war. He went with Elsy's father on his boat, the same one you came here on, and transported things back and forth to your side. But a year ago the Germans captured him at Kristiansand harbour, and . . .' He winced. 'We haven't heard anything from him since.'

'Elsy's father asked me about him,' said Hans, looking Erik in the eye. 'But I'm afraid I don't know that name. And I can't remember hearing anything about a Swede who was captured in Kristiansand. But there are lots of us. And quite a few Swedes have been helping us, for that matter.'

'You might not know his name, but maybe you'd recognize him.' Erik spoke eagerly, clasping his hands in his lap.

'It's not likely, but go ahead and tell me what he looks like.'

292

Erik described his brother as best he could. It wasn't really that difficult, because even though Axel had been gone a whole year, Erik could still picture him very clearly. At the same time, there were plenty of others who looked like Axel, and it was hard to come up with distinctive features that would set him apart from other Swedish boys his age.

Hans listened closely but then shook his head. 'No, he doesn't sound familiar. I'm really sorry.'

Erik sank back in disappointment. For a while nobody spoke. Then Frans said:

'So, tell us about your adventures in the war. You must have had some exciting experiences!' His eyes shone.

'There's not much to tell, actually,' said Hans, sounding reluctant to say more, but Britta refused to believe him. She fixed her eyes on him and urged him to tell them something, anything at all, about what he'd been through. After a few more protests, the Norwegian finally relented and began telling them about what it was like in Norway. About the German occupation, about the suffering of his countrymen, about what they'd done to fight back. The four young people listened to him, open-mouthed. It all sounded so exciting. Of course they noticed the sorrowful look in Hans's eyes, and they realized that he must have witnessed a great deal of misery. And yet . . . they couldn't help thinking that it was exciting.

'Well, I think it was terribly brave of you,' said Britta, blushing. 'Most boys would never dare do things like that. Only people like Axel – and you – are brave enough to fight for what they believe.'

'So we wouldn't dare? Is that what you think?' snapped Frans. He was even more annoyed by the fact that Britta kept casting admiring glances, usually reserved for him, at the Norwegian. 'Erik and I are just as brave, and when we're as old as Axel and . . . How old are you, by the way?' he asked Hans.

'I just turned seventeen,' said Hans, who seemed uncomfortable with all the attention directed at him and his activities. He turned to look at Elsy. She hadn't said a word as she listened to everybody else, but now she picked up on his signals.

'I think we should let Hans rest. He's been through a lot,' she said gently, motioning to her friends. Reluctantly they all got up and thanked him before backing out of the room. Elsy was the last to leave, and she turned around just before she closed the door.

'Thanks,' said Hans, giving her a faint smile. 'But it was nice to have company, so you're all welcome to come back. It's just that right now I'm a little . . .'

She smiled at him. 'I understand perfectly. We'll come back another time, and we'd be happy to show you around town too. But get some rest now.'

She closed the door. But strangely enough, she kept seeing his face in her mind, and it refused to go away.

Erica was not at the library as Patrik thought. She'd been on her way over there, but just as she parked the car an idea had occurred to her. There was another person who'd been close to her mother. And who'd been her friend much more recently than sixty years ago. Actually, she was the only friend that Erica could remember her mother ever having when she and Anna were growing up. Strange that she hadn't thought about her earlier. But Kristina had such a strong presence as her mother-in-law that Erica had forgotten she'd also been her mother's friend.

Having made up her mind, she started up the car again and drove towards Tanumshede. This was the first time she'd ever decided on impulse to visit Kristina at home. She glanced at her mobile, considering whether she ought to ring first. No, to hell with it. If Kristina could barge in on them unannounced, she could do the same to her.

Erica was still feeling annoyed when she arrived, and out of sheer contrariness, she touched the doorbell only once before opening the door and stepping inside.

'Hello?' she called.

'Who is it?' Kristina's voice came from the kitchen, and she sounded a bit alarmed. A moment later she appeared in the hall.

'Erica?' she said in surprise, staring at her daughter-in-law. 'You're here? Did you bring Maja with you?' She glanced behind Erica but didn't see her granddaughter anywhere.

'No, she's home with Patrik,' said Erica. She took off her shoes and set them neatly on the shoe rack.

'Well, come on in,' said Kristina, still looking startled. 'I'll make us some coffee.'

Erica followed her out to the kitchen, regarding her mother-in-law with surprise. She hardly recognized her. She'd never seen Kristina look anything but well groomed, and she always wore a good deal of make-up. Whenever she came to their house, she was a bundle of energy, talking non-stop and in constant motion. Right now she was like an entirely different woman. Kristina had on an old, worn-out nightgown even though it was late in the morning, and she wasn't wearing a trace of make-up. That made her look considerably older, with obvious lines and wrinkles on her face. She hadn't done anything with her hair, either, and it looked flattened from lying in bed.

'I must look a mess,' said Kristina, as if she'd read Erica's mind. She ran her hand through her hair. 'It just doesn't seem worth it to get all dressed up if I'm not doing anything special and don't have to be anywhere.'

'But it always sounds a though you have such a busy schedule,' said Erica, sitting down at the table.

At first Kristina didn't say anything, just set two cups on the table along with some Ballerina biscuits.

'It's not easy to be retired after working all your life,' she said at last as she poured coffee into their cups. 'Everyone is so busy with their own lives. I suppose there are things I could do, but I just haven't felt like . . .' She reached for a biscuit, avoiding Erica's eye.

'But why did you tell us that you have so much going on all the time?'

'Oh, you young people have your own lives. I didn't

want you to feel that you had to be bothered with me. Lord knows I don't want to be a burden to you. And I can tell that my visits aren't always that welcome, so I thought it was best if . . .' She fell silent, and Erica stared at her in astonishment. Kristina looked up and went on: 'If you must know, I live for the hours that I spend with you and with Maja. Lotta has her own life in Göteborg, and it's not always so easy for her to come here, or for me to go there, for that matter, since they don't have much room in their house. And as I said, I know that my visits with you aren't always so welcome.' Again she looked away, and Erica felt ashamed.

'That's mostly my fault, I have to admit,' she said gently. 'But you are always welcome. And you and Maja have so much fun together. The only thing we ask is that you respect our privacy. It's our home, and you're welcome to come over as our guest. So we, I, would appreciate it if you'd phone ahead to check if it's a good time to visit before you come over. Please don't just walk into the house with no warning, and for God's sake please don't tell us how we should run our household or take care of our child. If you can respect those rules, then you're welcome to come over. I'm sure Patrik would appreciate it if you could lend him a hand while he's on paternity leave.'

'Yes, I think he would,' said Kristina with a laugh that now made her eyes sparkle. 'How is he doing?'

'It was a bit touch-and-go at first,' said Erica. She told Kristina about Patrik taking Maja along to a crime scene and to the police station. 'But I think we're now in agreement as to what's important.'

'Men,' said Kristina. 'I remember when Lars was going to stay home alone with Lotta for the first time. She was about a year old, and I was going out to do the shopping on my own. It took only twenty minutes before the shop manager came to find me, saying that Lars had phoned. He had some sort of crisis and I had to go home. So I left all my groceries and rushed home. And it certainly was a crisis.'

'Really? What happened?' asked Erica, wide-eyed.

'Well, just listen to this. He mistook my menstrual pads for Lotta's nappies. And he couldn't figure out any sensible way to fasten them, so when I got home he was trying to put them on with duct tape!'

'You're kidding!' said Erica, and they both laughed.

'He learned after a while. Lars was a good father to Patrik and Lotta when they were growing up. I can't complain. But those were different times.'

'Speaking of different times,' said Erica, seizing the opportunity to turn the conversation to the reason for her visit. 'I'm doing a little research into my mother's life, her childhood, and so on. I found some old things in the attic, including several old diaries, and well, they got me to thinking.'

'Diaries?' said Kristina, staring at Erica. 'What was in them?' she asked in a sharp tone of voice. Erica looked at her mother-in-law in surprise.

'Nothing especially interesting, unfortunately. Mostly teenage musings. But the funny thing is that there's a lot about her friends from back then. Erik Frankel, Britta Johansson, and Frans Ringholm. And now two of them, Erik and Britta, have both been murdered within a few months of each other. It could just be a coincidence, but it seems strange.'

Kristina was still staring. 'Britta's dead?' she asked, and it was obvious that she was having a hard time taking in the news.

'Yes, didn't you hear about it? I thought you would have heard it on the grapevine by now. Her daughter found her dead two days ago, and it seems that she died from suffocation. Her husband claims that he killed her.'

'So both Erik and Britta are dead?' said Kristina. Thoughts seemed to be churning in her head.

'Did you know them?' asked Erica.

'No.' Kristina shook her head. 'I knew only what Elsy told me about them.'

'What did she tell you?' asked Erica, eagerly leaning forward. 'That's exactly why I've come over here. Because you were my mother's friend for so many years, I thought that you, of all people, would know things about her. So what did she tell you about those years? And why did she stop writing in her diary so abruptly in 1944? Or are there more diaries somewhere? Did Mamma ever tell you about them? In the last diary she mentions a Norwegian who had come to stay with them, a Hans Olavsen. I found a newspaper clipping that seems to indicate that all four of them spent a lot of time with him. What happened to him?' The questions came pouring out so fast that even Erica could barely keep up with them. Kristina sat across from her, not saying a word, with a shuttered expression on her face.

'I can't answer your questions, Erica,' she said at last. 'I can't. The only thing I can tell you is what happened to Hans Olavsen. Elsy told me that he went back to Norway right after the war ended. After that, she never saw him again.'

'Were they . . .' Erica hesitated, not sure how to formulate her query. 'Did she love him?'

Kristina didn't speak for a long time. She plucked at the pattern of the oilcloth on the table, weighing what she wanted to say. Finally she looked at Erica.

'Yes,' she said, 'she loved him.'

It was a splendid day. Axel hadn't thought about such things for a very long time. The fact that certain days could be nicer than others. But this one truly was. Right on the cusp between summer and autumn, with a warm, gentle breeze. The light had lost the glare of summer and started to assume the glow of autumn. A truly splendid day.

He went over to the bay window and looked out, his hands clasped behind his back. But he didn't see the trees outside. Or the grass that had grown a bit too tall and was starting to wither as cooler weather approached. Instead he saw Britta. Lovely, lively Britta, whom he'd never regarded as anything but a little girl back then, during the war. One of Erik's friends, a sweet but rather vain girl. She hadn't interested him. She'd been too young. He'd been preoccupied with everything that needed to be done, with what he needed to do. She'd had only a peripheral place in his world.

But he was thinking about her now. The way she was when he saw her the other day. Sixty years later. Still beautiful. Still slightly vain. But the years had changed her. Turned her into a different person than she'd been back then. Axel wondered if he had changed just as much. Maybe. Maybe not. Perhaps the years he'd been imprisoned by the Germans had changed him enough for a whole lifetime, so that afterwards he hadn't managed to change any more. All the things he'd seen, the horrors he'd witnessed – maybe that had changed something deep inside of him which could never be healed or redeemed.

Axel pictured other faces in his mind. Faces of the people he'd hunted and helped to capture. It didn't happen the way they showed it in the movies, with thrilling high-speed chases. Just hours of laborious work, sitting in his office and indefatigably following up five decades of paper trails, calling into question identities, payments, passenger lists, and possible cities of refuge. And so they'd brought them in, one by one. Made sure that they were punished for their sins, which were receding further and further into the past.

They would never catch them all. He knew that. There were still so many of them out there, and more and more of them were now dying. But instead of dying in prison, in degradation, they were dying the peaceful death of old age, without having to confront their deeds. That was what drove him. That was what made him refuse to give up; he was constantly searching, hunting, going from one meeting to the next, combing through archive after archive. He refused to rest as long as there was a single one of them out there that he might help to catch.

Axel stared unseeing out the window. He knew that it had become an obsession with him. The work had consumed everything. It had become a lifeline that he could grab hold of whenever he doubted himself or his humanity. As long as he was engaged in the hunt, he didn't need to question who he was. As long as he was working to serve the cause, he could slowly but surely chip away at his guilt. Only by refusing to stand still was he able to shake off everything that he didn't want to think about.

He turned around. The doorbell was ringing. For a moment he couldn't tear himself away from all those faces flickering before his eyes. Then he blinked them away and went to open the door.

'Oh, so it's you,' Axel said when he caught sight of Paula and Martin. For a second he felt overwhelmed by fatigue. Sometimes it seemed this would never end.

'Could we come in and talk to you for a few minutes?' asked Martin in a kindly tone of voice.

'Of course. Come in,' said Axel, again leading the way to the veranda. 'Is there any news? I heard about Britta, by the way. Dreadful business. I saw her and Herman just a couple of days ago, you know. It's so hard for me to imagine that he would . . .' Axel shook his head.

'Yes, it's really tragic,' said Paula. 'But we're not about to jump to any hasty conclusions.'

'But from what I heard, Herman has confessed. Isn't that true?' asked Axel.

'Well, yes,' said Martin hesitantly. 'But until we're able to interview him . . .' He threw out his hands. 'That's actually why we've come to talk to you.'

301

'All right. Although I don't really see how I can help.'

'We've taken a look at the phone records – calls that were made from Britta and Herman's house – and your number appears on three occasions.'

'Well, I can tell you about at least one of them. Herman phoned me a few days ago and asked me to come over to see Britta. We haven't had any contact for years and years, so it was a little surprising. But from what I understood, she had been diagnosed with Alzheimer's. And Herman seemed to want her to see someone from the old days, in case that might help.'

'And that's why you went over there?' asked Paula, studying him intently. 'So that Britta could see someone from the old days?'

'Yes. At least, that's the reason Herman gave me. Of course, we weren't exactly close back then. She was actually my brother Erik's friend, but I didn't think it would do any harm. And at my age, it's always pleasant to talk about old memories.'

'So what happened while you were there?' Martin leaned forward.

'She was quite clear-headed for a while, and we chatted a bit about the old days. But then she got confused, and, well, it didn't make any sense for me to stay, so I excused myself and left. Incredibly tragic. Alzheimer's is a horrible illness.'

'What about the phone calls in early June?' Martin looked at his notes. 'First one from your phone on the second, then an incoming call from Britta or Herman on the third, and finally another one from their phone on the fourth.'

Axel shook his head. 'I don't know anything about that. They must have talked to Erik. But it was probably the same sort of request. And it was actually more natural for Britta to want to see Erik if she'd started regressing into the past. They used to be friends, as I said before.'

'But the first call was made from your house,' Martin persisted. 'Do you know why Erik might have phoned them?'

'As I also said before, my brother and I may have lived under the same roof, but we didn't interfere in each other's business. I have no idea why Erik would have wanted to contact Britta. But maybe he wanted to renew their friendship. People get a little strange in that way, the older they get. Things from the distant past suddenly seem to get closer and assume greater importance.'

Axel realized how true this was as soon as he'd said it. In his mind's eye he saw jeering people from the past come bounding towards him. He took a firm grip on the armrests of his chair. This wasn't the right time to allow himself to feel overwhelmed.

'So you think it was Erik who wanted to see them, for the sake of old friendship?' asked Martin sceptically.

'As I said,' replied Axel, relaxing his grip on the armrests, 'I have absolutely no idea. But that seems the most logical explanation.'

Martin exchanged a glance with Paula. It seemed unlikely that they'd get any further. Yet he still had a nagging feeling that he was being given only tiny crumbs of something much bigger.

After they left, Axel went back to stand at the window. The same faces began dancing in front of him.

'Hi, how did it go at the library?' Patrik's face lit up when he saw Erica come in the front door.

'Er . . . I . . . didn't actually go to the library,' said Erica, with a strange expression on her face.

'Where did you go then?' asked Patrik. Maja was taking her afternoon nap and he was cleaning up after their lunch.

'To see Kristina,' she said, coming into the kitchen to join him.

303

'Kristina who? Oh, you mean my mother?' said Patrik, astonished. 'Why did you do that? I'd better check to see that you're not running a fever.' He went over to Erica and pressed his hand to her forehead. She waved him away.

'Hey, it's not all that odd. She's my mother-in-law, after all. Why shouldn't I go over to visit her on the spur of the moment?'

'Oh, right,' said Patrik, laughing. 'Okay, out with it. Why did you want to see my mother?'

Erica told him about the sudden brainwave she'd had outside the library about Kristina's friendship with her mother. And then she told him about Kristina's peculiar reaction, and how she'd revealed that Elsy had had a love affair with the Norwegian who had fled from the Germans. 'But she refused to tell me anything else,' said Erica, sounding frustrated. 'Or maybe that's all she knew. I'm not sure. But it seemed that Hans Olavsen abandoned my mother in some way. He left Fjällbacka and, according to Kristina, Elsy told her that he'd gone back to Norway.'

'So what are you going to do now?' asked Patrik, putting the lunch leftovers in the refrigerator.

'I'm going to track him down, of course,' said Erica, heading for the living room. 'By the way, I think we should invite Kristina over on Sunday. So she can spend some time with Maja.'

'Now I'm positive that you must have a fever,' laughed Patrik. 'But all right, I'll ring Mamma later and ask her if she'd like to come over for coffee on Sunday. But she may not be able to. You know how busy she always is.'

'Uh-huh,' he heard Erica say from the living room in a strange tone of voice. Patrik shook his head. Women. He would never understand them. But maybe that was the whole point.

'What's this?' called Erica.

Patrik went to see what she was talking about. She was

pointing at the folder on the coffee table, and for a second Patrik wanted to kick himself for not hiding it away before she came home. But he knew her well enough to realize that it was too late to keep it from her now.

'That's all the investigative material from the Erik Frankel murder case,' he told her, raising an admonitory finger. 'And you're not to tell anybody about what you happen to read in that file. All right?'

'Okay, okay,' said Erica with amusement as she waved him away like an annoying fly. Then she sat down on the sofa and started leafing through the documents and photographs.

An hour later she'd gone through all the material in the folder and started over again. Patrik had looked in on her several times, but eventually gave up any attempt to get her attention. Instead, he sat down with the morning newspaper, which he hadn't yet had time to read.

'You don't have much physical evidence to go on,' said Erica, running her finger over the techs' report.

'No, it seems pretty scanty,' said Patrik, putting down the newspaper. 'In their library there were no fingerprints other than those belonging to Erik and Axel and the two boys who found the body. Nothing seems to be missing, and the footprints don't belong to anyone else either. The murder weapon was under the desk. A weapon that was already on the scene, so to speak.'

'Not a premeditated murder, in other words. Most likely committed on impulse,' mused Erica.

'Right, unless, of course, somebody knew about the stone bust on the window sill.' Patrik was again struck by an idea that had occurred to him a couple of days ago. 'Tell me again, when exactly did you go see Erik Frankel to show him the medal?'

'Why do you want to know?' asked Erica, still sounding as if she were far away.

'I'm not sure. It might not be important at all. But it would be good to know.'

'It was the day before we went to visit Nordens Ark wild animal park with Maja,' said Erica, still looking through the documents. 'Wasn't that on the third of June? In that case, it was on the second that I visited Erik.'

'Did you ever get any information about the medal? Did he say anything while you were there?'

'I would have told you as soon as I got home if he had,' said Erica. 'No, he just said that he wanted to do some more checking before he told me anything about it.'

'So you still don't know what kind of Nazi medal it is?'

'No,' said Erica, giving Patrik a meditative look. 'But that's definitely something I need to find out. I'll figure out tomorrow where I should start looking.' She turned her attention back to the folder and studied the photos from the crime scene. She picked up the picture on top and squinted.

'It's impossible to . . .' she muttered, then got to her feet and headed upstairs.

'What is it?' asked Patrik, but she didn't reply. A moment later Erica returned, brandishing a magnifying glass.

'What are you doing?' he asked, peering at his wife over the top of his newspaper.

'I'm not sure. It's probably nothing, but . . . it looks like somebody scribbled something on the notepad on Erik's desk. But I can't really see . . .' She bent closer to the photo, putting the magnifying glass on top of a little white patch, which was the notepad in the picture.

'I think it says . . .' She squinted again. 'I think it says *"Ignoto Militi"*.'

'Really? And what's that supposed to mean?' said Patrik.

'I don't know. Something to do with the military, I imagine. It's probably nothing. Just scribbles,' she said, sounding disappointed.

'Erica . . .' Patrik put down his newspaper and tilted his

306

head. 'I had a little talk with Martin when he brought that folder over here. And he asked me to do him a favour.' Okay, to be honest, he was the one who had offered to help out, but he didn't need to tell Erica that. He cleared his throat and went on. 'He asked me to check up on somebody in Göteborg who was receiving regular bank payments from Erik Frankel. Every month for fifty years.'

'Fifty years?' said Erica, raising her eyebrows. 'He'd been paying somebody for fifty years? What was it? Blackmail?' She couldn't hide the fact that she found the idea rather exciting.

'Nobody knows. And it's probably nothing, but . . . Well, Martin wondered if I could go to Göteborg and check it out.'

'Of course. I'll go with you,' said Erica enthusiastically.

Patrik stared at her. That wasn't exactly the reaction he'd been expecting.

'Er, well, maybe . . .' he stammered as he pondered whether there was any reason why he shouldn't take his wife along. After all, it was just a routine assignment, checking on some bank payments, so there shouldn't be any problem.

'Okay, come with me. Then we'll drop by and visit Lotta afterwards so Maja can see her cousins.'

'Great,' said Erica. She liked Patrik's sister. 'And maybe I can find somebody in Göteborg who can tell me about the medal.'

'That seems possible. Make a few calls this afternoon and see if you can find anyone who knows about that sort of thing.' He picked up the newspaper and went back to reading. Best to make good use of his time before Maja woke up.

Erica picked up the magnifying glass and took another look at the notepad on Erik's desk. *Ignoto Militi*. Something was stirring in her subconscious.

This time it took only half an hour before he got the hang of the steps.

'Good, Bertil,' said Rita appreciatively, giving his hand an extra little squeeze. I can feel that you're getting into the rhythm now.'

'Not bad, huh?' said Mellberg modestly. 'I've always had a talent for dancing.'

'Indeed you do,' she said with a wink. 'I heard that you and Johanna had coffee together.' She smiled as she looked up at him. That was something else he found attractive about Rita. He'd never been particularly tall, but since she was so petite, he felt like a giant.

'I just happened to walk past your block of flats . . .' he said, embarrassed. 'And then I saw Johanna, and she asked if I'd like to come upstairs for coffee.'

'Ah, I see. You just happened to be walking past,' laughed Rita, as they continued to sway in time to the salsa music. 'It's too bad I wasn't home when you happened to walk past. But Johanna said you had a very nice time.'

'Yes, well, she's a sweet girl,' said Mellberg, again recalling the feel of the baby's foot kicking against his hand. 'A really sweet girl.'

'It hasn't always been easy for them.' Rita sighed. 'And I had a hard time getting used to the idea in the beginning. But I probably knew even before Paula brought Johanna home to meet me. And now they've been together for almost ten years, and, well, I can honestly say that there's nobody else I'd rather see Paula with. They're perfect for each other, so the fact that they're both female doesn't really seem to matter.'

'But it must have been easier in Stockholm. Being accepted, I mean,' said Mellberg cautiously. Then he swore as he stepped on Rita's foot. 'It's more common there, I mean. When I watch TV, I sometimes get the impression that every other person in Stockholm is gay.'

'Oh, I wouldn't say that,' Rita laughed. 'But of course we were a little nervous about moving here. I have to say that

I've been pleasantly surprised. I don't think the girls have run into any problems so far. Or maybe people just haven't noticed. But we'll cross that bridge when we come to it. What are they supposed to do? Stop living? Decide not to move where they want to? No, sometimes a person has to dare to take a leap into the unknown.' She suddenly looked sad, as if she were staring at something far away over Mellberg's shoulder. He thought he knew what she was thinking about.

'Was it hard? Having to flee?' he asked cautiously. Usually he did his best to avoid sensitive questions, or he would ask them only because it was expected of him, and he never cared what the answer might be. But right now he really wanted to know.

'It was both hard and easy,' Rita told him, and in her dark eyes he could see that she'd been through experiences that he couldn't even imagine. 'It was easy to leave what had become of my country. But hard to leave the country that it once had been.'

For a moment she lost the rhythm of the dance and stopped, her hands still in Mellberg's. Then her eyes flashed, and she pulled her hands away and clapped loudly.

'So, now it's time to learn the next step. The twirl. Bertil, help me demonstrate.' She took his hands again and slowly showed him the steps he needed to do in order to twirl her under his arm. It wasn't simple, and he got his hands and feet all tangled up. But Rita didn't lose patience. She just kept at it, over and over, until Bertil and the other couples figured it out.

'It'll be fine,' she said, looking up at Mellberg. He wondered whether she meant only the dance. Or something else as well. He hoped it was the latter.

It was starting to get dark outside. The sheet on the hospital bed rustled faintly whenever he moved, so he tried to stay still. He preferred absolute silence. He could do nothing to control the sounds outside – the sound of voices, of people walking past, of trays clattering. But in here he would make sure that it was as quiet as possible. That the silence wasn't disturbed by rustling sheets.

Herman stared out of the window. As it grew darker, he was gradually able to see his own image reflected in the pane, and he noted how pitiful the figure in the bed looked. A small, grey old man with thinning hair and furrowed cheeks, wearing a white hospital gown. As if Britta had been the one who had lent him any air of authority. She had given him a dignity that filled him. She had given his life meaning. And now it was his fault that she was gone.

His daughters had come over to see him today. Fussed over him, hugged him, stared at him with worried eyes and talked to him in concerned voices. But he hadn't had the energy even to look at them. He was afraid they would see the guilt in his eyes. See what he had done. What he had caused.

They had kept the secret for a long time. He and Britta. Shared it, concealed it, atoned for it. That was what he'd thought, at any rate. But when she fell ill and her defences started to crumble, he'd realized in a moment of clarity that it was hopeless to try to atone for anything. Sooner or later, time and fate caught up with a person. It was impossible to hide. It was impossible to flee. They had foolishly believed that it was enough to live a good life, to be good people. To love their children and raise them so they would be capable of giving love, in turn. And finally, they had convinced themselves that the good they'd created had overshadowed the bad.

He had killed Britta. Why couldn't they understand that? He knew that they would talk to him, ask him about things, question him. Why couldn't they just accept the situation?

He had killed Britta. And now he had nothing left.

* * *

310

'Do you have any idea who this person is? Or why Erik paid him money for all those years?' asked Erica as they were approaching Göteborg. Maja had behaved beautifully, sitting on the back seat, and since they'd left home just before eight thirty, it was only ten o'clock by the time they drove into the city.

'No, the only information we have is what you've already seen.' Patrik nodded at the document in the plastic sleeve that Erica was holding on her lap.

'Wilhelm Fridén, Vasagatan 38, Göteborg. Born third of October 1924,' Erica read aloud.

'That's all we know. I talked briefly to Martin last night, and he hadn't found any connections to Fjällbacka, and no criminal record. Nothing. So it's really a shot in the dark. Speaking of which, what time is your appointment to see that guy about the medal?'

'At noon, in his antique shop,' said Erica, touching the pocket in which she had put the medal for safekeeping, wrapped in a soft piece of cloth.

'Do you and Maja want to stay in the car while I talk to Wilhelm Fridén, or would you rather take a walk?' asked Patrik as he pulled into a parking place on Vasagatan.

'What do you mean?' said Erica, sounding insulted. 'I want to go with you, of course.'

'But you can't. What about Maja?' Patrik replied awkwardly, even though he could already tell how this conversation was going to go. And how it would end.

'If you can take her along to crime scenes and the police station, then she can come with us to talk to a man who is over eighty years old,' she said, her tone of voice making it clear that there was no room for discussion.

'Okay,' said Patrik with a sigh. He knew when he was beaten.

The flat was on the third floor of a turn-of-the-century apartment building. The doorbell was answered by a man

311

in his sixties. He gave them an enquiring look as he opened the door. 'Yes? Can I help you?'

Patrik held out his police ID. 'My name is Patrik Hedström, and I'm from the Tanumshede police. I have a few questions regarding a man named Wilhelm Fridén.'

'Who is it?' They heard a faint female voice from inside the flat. The man turned around and shouted, 'It's the police. They want to ask some questions about Pappa!'

He turned back to Patrik. 'I can't imagine why on earth the police would be interested in Pappa, but come on in.' He stepped aside to let them in and then raised his eyebrows in surprise when he saw Maja in Erica's arms.

'The police are starting them young these days,' he remarked with amusement.

Patrik smiled, embarrassed. 'This is my wife, Erica Falck, and our daughter Maja. They . . . er . . . my wife has a personal interest in the case that we're investigating, and . . .' He stopped. There didn't seem to be any good way to explain why a police officer would drag along his wife and child to an interview.

'I'm sorry, I should have introduced myself. I'm Göran Fridén, and it's my father that you're asking about.'

Patrik studied him with curiosity. He was of medium height with grey, slightly curly hair and friendly blue eyes.

'Is your father at home?' asked Patrik as they followed Göran Fridén down a long hall.

'I'm afraid you're too late if you want to ask my father any questions. He died two weeks ago.'

'Oh,' said Patrik, surprised. That wasn't the answer he'd expected. He had been convinced that the man, in spite of his age, was still alive, since his name wasn't on the list of deceased in the public registry. But that was no doubt because he'd died so recently. It was common knowledge that it took time before information was entered into the registry. He felt extremely disappointed. Had this lead, which his intuition told him was important, already gone cold?

'But you could talk to my mother, if you like,' said Göran, motioning them towards the living room. 'I don't know what this is about, but after you've told us, maybe she'll be able to help.'

A small, frail woman with snow-white hair got up from the sofa and came across to shake hands.

'Märta Fridén.' She studied them quizzically and then broke into a big smile when she saw Maja. 'Hi, there! Oh, what an adorable little girl! What's her name?'

'Maja,' said Erica proudly, taking an instant liking to Märta Fridén.

'Hi, Maja,' said Märta, patting her cheek. Maja beamed happily at all the attention, but then started kicking to get down when she caught sight of an old doll sitting on the sofa.

'No, Maja,' said Erica sternly, trying to restrain her daughter.

'It's all right. Let her take a look at it,' said Märta, with a wave of her hand. 'There's nothing here that she shouldn't touch. Since Wilhelm passed away, I've realized that we can't take anything with us when we die.' Her eyes took on a sorrowful expression, and her son stepped close to put his arm around her.

'Sit down, Mamma. I'll make our guests some coffee while you have a talk with them in peace and quiet.'

Märta watched him as he left the room, heading for the kitchen. 'He's a good boy,' she said. 'I don't want to be a burden to him; children should be allowed to live their own lives. But sometimes he's too nice for his own good. Wilhelm was so proud of him.' She seemed to get lost in her memories for a moment, but then turned to Patrik.

'So, why would the police want to talk to my Wilhelm?'
Patrik cleared his throat. He felt that he was treading on

313

thin ice. Maybe he was about to bring a lot of things into the light which this sweet old lady would rather not know about. But he had no choice. Hesitantly he said:

'Well, the thing is, we're investigating a murder up north in Fjällbacka. I'm from the Tanumshede police station, you see, and Fjällbacka belongs to the Tanum police district.'

'Oh, good heavens. A murder?' said Märta, frowning.

'Yes, a man by the name of Erik Frankel was killed,' said Patrik, pausing to see whether the name would prompt any reaction. But from what he could tell, Märta didn't seem to recognize it.

'Erik Frankel? That doesn't sound familiar. What led you to Wilhelm?' She leaned forward, looking interested.

'Ah, er . . . you see,' Patrik hesitated. 'The thing is, for almost fifty years this Erik Frankel has been making monthly payments to Wilhelm Fridén. Your husband. And of course we're wondering why he did that, and what sort of connection there was between the two men.'

'Wilhelm got money from . . . from a man in Fjällbacka by the name of Erik Frankel?' Märta looked genuinely surprised. At that moment Göran came back, carrying a tray with coffee cups. 'So what's this all about?' he asked, giving them an enquiring look.

His mother was the one who replied. 'These officers say that a man by the name of Erik Frankel, who was found murdered, was paying your father money every month for the past fifty years.'

'What's this?' exclaimed Göran as he sat down on the sofa next to his mother. 'To Pappa? Why?'

'Well, that's what we'd like to find out,' said Patrik. 'We were hoping that Wilhelm could answer the question himself.'

'Dolly,' said Maja with delight as she held out the old doll towards Märta.

'Yes, it's a doll,' said Märta, smiling. 'It was mine when I was little.'

Maja gave the doll a tender hug. Märta could hardly take her eyes off the girl.

'What an enchanting child,' she said, and Erica nodded enthusiastically.

'What kind of sums are we talking about?' asked Göran, staring at Patrik.

'Not large sums of money. Two thousand kronor a month during the past few years. But it had gradually increased over time, apparently keeping pace with inflation. So even though the amount changed, the actual value seems to have remained constant.'

'Why didn't Pappa ever tell us about this?' Göran asked his mother. She shook her head.

'I have no idea. But Wilhelm and I never discussed financial matters. He took care of all those sorts of things while I took care of the house. That was customary for our generation. It was how we divided up the work load. If it weren't for you, Göran, I'd be completely lost trying to take care of bank accounts and loans and that sort of thing.' She squeezed her son's hand.

'I'm happy to help you, Mamma, you know that.'

'Do you have any financial statements that we might have a look at?' asked Patrik, sounding a bit discouraged. He'd been hoping to get answers to all his questions about these strange monthly payments, but he seemed to have reached a dead end.

'We don't have any documents here at home. Our lawyers have everything,' said Göran apologetically. 'But I can ask them to make copies and send them to you.'

'We would really appreciate that,' said Patrik, feeling more hopeful. Maybe they'd still be able to get to the bottom of this.

'Oh, forgive me, I completely forgot about the coffee,' said Göran, getting up from the sofa.

'We need to get going anyway,' said Patrik, glancing

at his watch. 'So please don't go to any trouble for our sake.'

'I'm sorry we couldn't be of more help.' Märta tilted her head and smiled at Patrik.

'Don't worry, that's how things go sometimes. And again, please accept my condolences,' said Patrik. 'I hope we haven't caused you too much distress by coming here to ask questions so soon after . . . Well, we didn't know . . .'

'That's quite all right, my dear,' she replied, waving away his apologies. 'I knew my Wilhelm inside and out, and whatever these payments were for, I can guarantee that there was nothing criminal or unethical involved. So ask all the questions you want, and as Göran said, we'll make sure the documents are sent over to you. I'm just sorry that I couldn't help you.'

Everyone got up and went out to the hall. Maja was still holding the doll, hugging it to her chest.

'Maja, sweetie, you need to leave the doll here.' Erica steeled herself for the inevitable outburst.

'Let the child keep the doll,' said Märta, patting Maja on the head as she walked past. 'As I said, I can't take anything with me when I go, and I'm too old to be playing with dolls.'

'Are you sure?' stammered Erica. 'It's so old, and I'm sure you have fond memories of . . .'

'Memories are stored up here,' said Märta, tapping her forehead. 'Not in tangible objects. Nothing would make me happier than to know that a little girl will be playing with Greta again. I'm sure that poor doll has been terribly bored sitting on the sofa next to an old lady.'

'Well, thank you. Thank you so much,' said Erica, embarrassed to find herself so touched that she had to blink back tears.

'You're very welcome.' Märta patted Maja on the head again, and then she and her son escorted them to the door.

The last thing Erica and Patrik saw before the door closed

behind them was Göran gently putting his arm around his mother's shoulder and kissing her on top of her head.

Martin was at home, restlessly roaming about. Pia was at work, and since he was alone in the flat, he couldn't stop thinking about the case. It was as if his feeling of responsibility had increased tenfold because Patrik was on leave, and he wasn't quite sure that he was up to the task. He thought of it as a weakness on his part that he needed to ask Patrik for help. But he relied so heavily on his colleague's judgement, maybe even more than on his own. Sometimes he wondered if he would ever feel confident about his work. There was always a sense of doubt hovering in the background, an uncertainty that had been with him since he graduated from the police academy. Was he really suited to this job? Was he capable of doing what was expected of him?

He wandered from room to room as he brooded. He realized that his uncertainty about his profession was exacerbated by the fact that he was about to face the greatest challenge of his life, and he wasn't convinced he could handle that responsibility either. What if he didn't measure up? What if he couldn't offer Pia the support that she needed? What if he couldn't deal with what was expected of him as a father? What if, what if . . . The thoughts whirled through his mind faster and faster, and finally he realized that he had to get out and do something or he'd go crazy. He grabbed his jacket, got in the car, and headed south.

At first he didn't know where he was going, but as he approached Grebbestad, it became clear to him. It was that phone call made from Britta and Herman's house to Frans Ringholm that had been bothering him. They kept running into the same group of people in the two investigations, and even though the cases seemed to be running parallel, Martin had a gut feeling that they intersected at some point. Why

317

had Herman or Britta phoned Frans in June before Erik died? There was only one call from them on the list, from the fourth of June. It hadn't lasted very long. Two minutes and thirty-three seconds. Martin had memorized the information from the phone lists. But why had they contacted Frans? Was it as simple as Axel had suggested? That Britta's illness had made her want to renew friendships from the past? Reconnect with people who, by all accounts, she hadn't spoken to in sixty years? The brain was certainly capable of playing tricks on a person, but . . . No, there was something else. Something that kept eluding him. And he wasn't about to give up until he found out what it was.

Frans was on his way out when Martin met him at the door of his flat.

'So how can I help you today?' he asked politely.

'Just a few supplementary questions.'

'I was just going out for my daily walk. If you want to talk to me, you can come along. I don't change my walk schedule for anyone. It's how I keep in shape.' He set off towards the water, and Martin followed.

'So you don't have any problem being seen with a police officer?' asked Martin, giving him a wry smile.

'You know, I've spent so much of my life with jailers, that I'm used to your type of company,' he replied, an amused glint in his eyes. 'Okay, what was it you wanted to ask me?' he said then, all trace of amusement vanishing. Martin had to jog to keep up. The old guy set a brisk pace.

'I don't know whether you've heard, but there's been another murder in Fjällbacka.'

Frans slowed down for a moment, then picked up the pace again. 'No, I didn't know about that. Who was it?'

'Britta Johansson.' Martin studied Frans intently.

'Britta?' said Frans, turning his head to look at Martin. 'How? Who?'

'Her husband says that he did it. But I have my doubts.'

Frans gave a start. 'Herman? But why? I can't believe that.'

'Do you know Herman?' asked Martin, trying not to show how important his answer might be.

'No, not really,' said Frans, shaking his head. 'I've actually only met him once. He phoned me in June to say that Britta was ill and she'd expressed a wish to see me.'

'Didn't you think that was a bit odd? Considering that you hadn't seen each other in sixty years?' Martin made no attempt to hide his scepticism.

'Well, yes, of course I thought it was odd. But Herman explained that she was suffering from Alzheimer's, and apparently it's not uncommon for patients with that disease to revert to memories from the past, and to think about people who used to be important to them. And our little group did grow up together, you know, and spent a lot of time with each other.'

'And that little group was . . . ?'

'Me, Britta, Erik, and Elsy Moström.'

'And two of them have been murdered in a matter of months,' said Martin, panting as he trotted along next to Frans. 'Don't you think that's a strange coincidence?'

Frans stared at the horizon. 'When you get to be my age, you've witnessed enough strange coincidences to know that they actually occur quite often. Besides, you said that her husband has confessed to the murder. Do you think he was the one who killed Erik too?' Frans glanced at Martin.

'We're not speculating about anything at the moment. But it does give me pause when I think about the fact that two out of four people in a group have been murdered within such a short period of time.'

'As I said, there's nothing strange about strange coincidences. Sheer chance. And fate.'

'That sounds quite philosophical, coming from a man who has spent a great deal of his life in prison. Was that also sheer chance and fate?' A caustic tone had crept into his voice, and Martin had to remind himself to keep his personal feelings out of this. But during the past week he'd seen how Paula had been affected by the things that Frans Ringholm stood for, and he was having a hard time hiding his disgust.

'Chance and fate had nothing to do with it. I was an adult and capable of making my own decisions when I chose that particular path. And of course I can say, after the fact, that I shouldn't have done one thing or another . . . and I should have chosen a different path instead.' Frans stopped and turned to face Martin. 'But we don't have that opportunity while we're living our lives, do we?' he said, and then started walking again. 'The opportunity to see things ahead of time. No, I made the choices I made. I've lived the life I chose. And I've paid the price for it.'

'What about your opinions? Have you chosen those too?' Martin found himself genuinely curious to hear the answer. He didn't understand these people who were ready to condemn whole segments of humanity. He didn't understand how they could justify such views to themselves. And while they filled him with disgust, he was also curious about what made them tick.

Frans seemed to recognize that the question was genuine, and he spent some moments considering how to answer it.

'I stand behind my opinions,' he said finally. 'I see that something is wrong with our society, and this is my inter-pretation of what's wrong. I see it as my duty to contribute a solution.'

'But to place the blame on entire ethnic groups . . .' Martin shook his head. He simply didn't understand this way of thinking.

'You make the mistake of regarding people as individuals,' said Frans drily. 'That's not how we are. We are all part of a group. Part of a collective entity. And these groups have always fought each other, fought for a place in the hierarchy, in the world order. You might wish that things were different, but that's how it is. And even though I don't use violence to secure my place in the world, I'm a survivor. Someone who, in the end, will be a victor in the world order. And it's always the victors who write history.'

He fell silent and turned to look at Martin, who shivered in spite of the fact that he was sweating from the fast pace. There was something so unfathomably terrifying about coming face to face with such fanatical conviction. No logic in the world would ever persuade Frans and his cohorts that theirs was a distorted view of reality. It was just a matter of keeping them restrained, marginalizing them, reducing their numbers. Martin had always believed that if he could just reason with a person, he would eventually be able to reach a core that could be changed. But in Frans's eyes he saw a core that was so brutally protected by rage and hatred that it would be impossible ever to penetrate it.

FJÄLLBACKA 1944

'This is delicious,' said Vilgot, helping himself to another portion of fried mackerel. 'This is really delicious, Bodil.'

She didn't reply, just bowed her head in relief. She was always grateful when her husband was in a good mood and seemed pleased with her.

'Keep this in mind, boy.' He pointed his fork at Frans. 'When you decide to get married, make sure that the girl is good in the kitchen and good in bed!' Vilgot laughed so loudly that his whole tongue was visible in his mouth.

'Vilgot!' said Bodil, glancing at him, although she didn't dare offer more than a meek protest.

'Come on, it's best if the boy learns things like that,' he said, scooping up a huge serving of mashed potatoes. 'And by the way, you can be proud of your father today, Frans. I just had a call from Göteborg, and I found out that the company belonging to that Jew named Rosenberg has gone bankrupt, thanks to the fact that I stole so much business away from him over the past year. How about that? That's something to celebrate! That's how we need to deal with them. Force them to their knees, one after the other, both financially and with the whip!' He laughed so hard that his stomach shook. Butter from the fish trickled out of his mouth and gleamed on his chin.

'It won't be easy for him to make a living, not these days,' said Bodil, unable to stop herself. But she realized her mistake as soon as she spoke.

'What exactly are you thinking when you say that, my dear?' said Vilgot, deceptively polite as he set down his knife and fork. 'Since you're sympathetic to somebody like that, I want to know how you arrived at that point of view.'

'It's nothing. I didn't mean anything by it,' she said, staring down at her lap, hoping that such a sign of capitulation would be sufficient. But a glint had appeared in Vilgot's eyes.

'No, no, I'm interested in what you have to say. Come on, tell me.'

Frans looked back and forth, from his mother to his father, while a knot started forming in his stomach. He saw how his mother had started to tremble as Vilgot fixed his gaze on her. And how his father had that glazed look in his eyes, a look that Frans had seen many times before. He considered asking to be excused from the table, but realized that it was already too late for that.

Bodil's voice quavered and she had to swallow hard several times before she nervously said, 'I was just thinking about his family. That it must be hard to find a new means of support these days.'

'We're talking about a Jew, Bodil.' Vilgot's tone was admonitory, and he spoke slowly, as he would to a child. It was exactly that tone of voice that sparked something in his wife.

She raised her head and said, with a hint of defiance: 'Jews are also human beings. They have to provide food for their children, just as we do.'

Frans wanted to scream at his mother to shut up, not talk that way to his father. Nothing good ever came of talking like that to him. What was the matter with her? How could she say that to him? In defence of a Jew? How could that be worth the price he knew she would have to pay? Suddenly he felt an unreasonable hatred towards his mother. How could she be so stupid? Didn't she know that it never did any good to challenge Vilgot? It was best to bow her head and do as he said, not offer any opposition. Then they could get by for a while. But that stupid, stupid woman had just shown the one thing no one should ever show to Vilgot Ringholm: a spark of defiance. Frans shuddered at the thought of the powder keg that this tiny spark was about to ignite.

At first the room was utterly silent. Vilgot stared at her, seeming unable to take in what he'd heard. A vein bulged on his neck, and Frans saw him clench his hands into fists. He wanted to jump up from the table and keep on running until he couldn't run any more. Instead, he felt glued to his chair, incapable of moving.

Then the explosion came. Vilgot's fist shot out and struck Bodil on the jaw, hurling her backwards. Her chair toppled over and she landed on the floor with a loud thud. She gasped with pain, a sound that was so familiar to Frans that he could feel it in the very marrow of his bones. But instead of feeling sympathetic, he felt even more enraged. Why couldn't she have kept quiet? Why was she forcing him to witness this?

'So, you're a Jew lover. Is that right?' said Vilgot, standing up. 'Answer me! Is that what you are?'

Bodil had managed to turn over so she was now on all fours, struggling to get her breath.

Vilgot took aim and kicked her in the midriff. 'Are you? Answer me! Do I have a Jew lover in my house? In my own home? Do I?'

She didn't answer as with great effort she tried to crawl away. Vilgot followed her, then aimed another kick that landed in the same spot. She flinched and crumpled into a heap on the floor, but then managed to get up on all fours again and made another attempt to crawl away.

'You're a fucking bitch, that's what you are! A fucking Jew-loving bitch!' Vilgot spat out the words, and when Frans glanced at his father's face, he saw a look of pleasure. Vilgot took aim and kicked Bodil again as he showered curses on her. Then he looked at Frans. Excitement shone on his face, an expression that Frans knew all too well.

'All right, boy, now I'm going to teach you how to deal with bitches. It's the only language they understand. Watch and learn.' He was breathing hard as he unfastened his belt and trousers, keeping his eyes fixed on Frans. Then he took a few steps towards Bodil, who had managed to crawl a few metres away. He grabbed her hair with one hand and he pulled up her skirt with the other.

'No, no, don't . . . think about . . . Frans,' she pleaded.

Vilgot merely laughed as he yanked her head back and entered her with a loud groan.

The knot in Frans's stomach solidified into a big, cold lump of hatred. And when his mother turned her head and met his eyes, on her knees as his father thrust inside of her, Frans knew that the only thing he could do to survive was to hold on to that hatred.

Kjell spent Saturday morning at the office. Beata had taken the children and gone to visit her parents, so it had seemed the perfect opportunity to do a little research about Hans Olavsen. So far, he'd drawn a blank. There were too many Norwegians with the same name from that time period, and if he didn't find something that could eliminate some of them, it would prove to be an impossible task.

He'd read the articles that Erik had given him again and again, yet he still couldn't work out what he was supposed to make of these scraps of information. That was what surprised him the most. If Erik Frankel had wanted to hand him a story, why hadn't he just come out and told him what it was? Why this cryptic approach? Kjell sighed. The only thing the articles told him about Hans Olavsen was that he'd been a resistance fighter during World War II. For a second he considered asking his father whether he knew anything more about the Norwegian, but he immediately dismissed the idea. He would rather spend a hundred hours in some archive than seek his father's help.

An archive. That was a thought. Was there some sort of database in Norway listing people who had been part of the resistance movement? A great deal must have been written about the subject, and someone was bound to have researched the topic and attempted to chart the movement's history. Someone always did.

He opened his Internet browser and ran a series of searches using various combinations of words until he finally found what he was looking for. A man named Eskil Halvorsen had written a number of books about Norway during the Second World War, and in particular about the resistance movement. This was the man he needed to talk to. Kjell found an online Norwegian phone directory and located Halvorsen's number. He immediately reached for the phone and punched in the digits, then had to redial because in his excitement he'd forgotten to start with the country code for Norway. He wasn't concerned that he would be disturbing the man on a Saturday morning; a journalist couldn't afford to have those kinds of scruples.

After waiting impatiently for several seconds, he finally heard a voice at the other end. Kjell introduced himself and explained that he was trying to locate a man by the name of Hans Olavsen who had been part of the resistance during the war and who had subsequently fled to Sweden.

'. . . So that's not a name that you've come across in your research?' Disappointed, Kjell was drawing circles on his notepad. '. . . Yes, I realize that we're talking about thousands who were active in the resistance movement, but is there any possibility . . .?'

He continued to draw feverishly on his notepad as he listened to a long speech about the organizational structure of the Norwegian resistance. It was undeniably a fascinating subject, especially considering that neo-Nazism was his speciality, but Kjell didn't want to lose sight of his quest.

'Is there any archive that lists the name of all the resistance fighters? . . . Okay, so there is some documentation then? . . . Could you possibly help me by checking for any mention of Hans Olavsen and in particular any reference to where he might be now? I'd very grateful. And by the way, he came to Sweden in 1944, to Fjällbacka, if that's any help to you.'

Kjell put down the phone, pleased with himself. He may not have got the hot lead he was hoping for, but he was convinced that if anyone could dig up information about Hans Olavsen, it was the man he had just spoken to.

And in the meantime, there was something he himself could do. The Fjällbacka library might have more information about the Norwegian. It was at least worth a try. He glanced at his watch. If he left now, he could get there before the library closed. He grabbed his jacket, turned off his computer, and left the office.

Far away, Eskil Halvorsen had already started looking for information on the resistance fighter named Hans Olavsen.

Maja was still clutching the doll when they put her in the car. Erica was so touched by the old woman's gift, and it was endearing to see how instantly Maja had fallen in love with the doll.

'What a sweet old lady,' she said to Patrik, who merely nodded as he focused on navigating through Göteborg's traffic, with all the one-way streets and dinging trams that seemed to appear out of nowhere.

'Where should we park?' he asked, looking around.

'There's a spot –' Erica pointed, and Patrik pulled in and parked.

'It's probably best if you and Maja don't go into the shop with me,' she said, taking the pushchair out of the boot. 'I don't think antique shops are the proper setting for little miss mischief here – you know how she loves to get her hands on things.'

'You're probably right,' said Patrik, putting Maja in the chair. 'We'll go for a walk. But you'll have to tell me all about it afterwards.'

'I will, I promise.' Erica waved to Maja and then headed for the address she'd been given over the phone. The antique shop was on Guldheden, and she found it easily. A bell rang as she stepped inside, and a short, thin man with a flowing beard came out from behind a curtain.

'Can I help you with anything?' he asked politely, with an expectant air.

'Hi, I'm Erica Falck. We spoke on the phone earlier.' She went over to him and held out her hand.

'Enchanté,' he said, and to Erica's great surprise he kissed her hand. She couldn't remember the last time anyone had kissed her hand. If ever. 'So, I understand you have a medal that you'd like to know more about, is that right? Come in and we can sit down while I take a look at it.' He held the curtain aside for her and she had to duck slightly in order to go through an unusually low doorway. Then she stopped short. Russian icons covered every inch of the walls in the dark little nook, which otherwise had room only for a small table and two chairs.

'My passion,' said the man, who on the phone had introduced himself as Åke Grundén. 'I have one of Sweden's finest collections of Russian icons,' he added proudly as they sat down.

'They're beautiful,' said Erica, looking at them.

'Oh, they're much more than that, my dear, so much more than that,' he said, practically glowing with pride as he regarded his collection. 'They are the bearers of a history and a tradition that is . . . magnificent.' He stopped then and put on a pair of glasses. 'But I have a tendency to wax lyrical once I get started on that subject, so it's best if we turn to what you're here to talk about. It sounds interesting, I must say.'

'Well, I understand that you have another speciality: medals from the Second World War.'

He peered at her over the rim of his glasses. 'It's easy to

get a bit isolated when one chooses to prioritize old artefacts rather than surrounding oneself with other people. I'm not entirely certain that I've made the right choice, but it's easy to be wise with hindsight.' He smiled, and Erica smiled back. He had a quiet, ironic sense of humour that appealed to her.

She put her hand in her pocket and carefully took out the medal wrapped in cloth, as Åke turned on a high-intensity lamp that stood on the table. He watched with reverence as she removed the cloth and took out the medal.

'Ah,' he said, holding it in the palm of his hand. He studied it intently, twisting and turning it under the strong light of the lamp, squinting his eyes so as not to miss any of the small details.

'Where did you get this?' he asked at last, again peering at her over the rim of his glasses.

Erica told him about the chest that belonged to her mother and how she'd found the medal inside.

'And your mother had no connection to Germany, as far as you know?'

Erica shook her head. 'None that I've ever heard of, at least. But Fjällbacka, where my mother lived and grew up, is close to the Norwegian border. According to some research I've been doing, many local people got involved in helping the Norwegian resistance movement during the war. My maternal grandfather allowed people to smuggle goods to Norway on his boat. Towards the end of the war he even brought back a Norwegian resistance fighter and gave him lodging.'

'Yes, there was undeniably a great deal of contact between the coastal towns of our two countries during the German occupation of Norway . . .' He sounded as if he were thinking aloud as he continued to study the medal. 'Well, I have no idea how this came into your mother's possession,' he said, 'but I can tell you this much – what you have here is an

330

Iron Cross, a medal awarded for particularly valorous efforts on Germany's behalf.'

'Is there any sort of list of people who received this medal?' asked Erica hopefully. 'Whatever else one might say about the Germans, they were good administrators during the war, and surely there must be some archive . . .'

Åke shook his head. 'No, there's no list that I know of. There were various grades of Iron Cross; this is what's known as an Iron Cross First Class and it's not particularly rare. Something in the region of four hundred and fifty thousand were handed out during the war, so it would be impossible to trace the recipient.'

After all the recent setbacks Erica had been pinning her hopes on the medal. It was bitterly disappointing to come up against yet another dead end. She got up and thanked Åke, reaching to shake his hand. Instead he planted another kiss on her hand and said, 'I'm sorry, I wish I could have been more helpful.'

'That's all right,' she said, opening the door. 'I'll just have to keep searching. I'm desperate to find out why my mother had this medal in her possession.'

But when the door closed behind her, Erica felt utterly discouraged. She didn't believe she would ever solve the mystery of the medal.

SACHSENHAUSEN 1945

He was in a haze for much of the transport. What he remembered most was how his ear had festered and ached. He had sat in the train to Germany, crammed together with lots of other prisoners from Grini, unable to focus on anything other than his head, which felt like it would explode. Even when he learned that they were going to be moved to Germany, he had reacted with a dull lassitude. In a sense, the news came as a relief. He knew that Germany meant death. No one knew exactly what to expect, but there had been whispers and hints and rumours about the fate that awaited them. They had been designated NN-prisoners, from the German words *Nacht und Nebel* – night and fog. As such they would receive no court trial, no sentence would be passed, their relatives would never learn their fate: they would simply vanish into the night and the fog.

Axel had thought he was prepared for whatever might await him when he got off the train in Germany. But nothing could have prepared him for the reality. The train had delivered them to hell. A hell without fire burning under their feet, but hell just the same.

He had been here for several weeks now, and what he'd seen during that time haunted his dreams as he slept uneasily each night, and filled him with anxiety each morning when they were forced to get up at three a.m. and work without interruption until nine at night.

The NN-prisoners had it worse than the others. They were regarded as already dead, and hence were at the bottom of the pecking order. So that there would be no mistake, they all had a red 'N' on their backs. The red indicated that they were political prisoners. Criminals wore green symbols, and there was a constant battle between the red and green inmates over who was in charge. The only consolation was that the Nordic prisoners had joined forces. They were spread throughout the camp, but every evening after work they would gather to talk about what was happening. Those who could spare it would slice off a small piece of their daily ration of bread. The pieces were then collected and given to the Nordic prisoners who were ill in the infirmary. They were all determined that as many Scandinavians as possible would return home. But there were many who were beyond help. Axel soon lost track of all the prisoners who perished.

He looked at his hand holding the shovel. It was nothing but bone; no real flesh, just skin stretched over his knuckles. Feeling weak, he leaned on the shovel for a moment when the closest guard happened to look away, but then hurried to resume digging as soon as the guard turned back in his direction. Every shovelful made him pant with the effort. Axel forced himself not to glance at the reason for all the digging that he and the other prisoners were doing. He'd made that mistake only once, on the first day. And he could still see the scene every time he closed his eyes. The vast heap of corpses. Emaciated skeletons that had been piled up like rubbish and were now to be tossed into a mass grave, all jumbled together. It was best not to look. He caught only a glimpse out of the corner of his eye as he strained to shovel away enough dirt so as not to incur the guards' displeasure.

Suddenly the prisoner next to him sank to the ground. Just as gaunt and malnourished as Axel, he simply collapsed, unable to haul himself to his feet again. Axel considered going over to help the man, but as always the thought was dismissed. Right now all his dwindling reserve of energy was dedicated to his own survival. That was the way it was in the camps: each person had to fend for himself and try to survive as best he could. The German political prisoners were old hands, and he'd heeded their advice. *'Nie auffallen,'* they said: don't draw attention to yourself, don't attempt to escape. The key was to position yourself discreetly in the middle and keep your head down whenever there was any threat of trouble. And so Axel watched with indifference as the guard went over the prisoner on the ground, took him by the arm, and dragged him to the centre of the pit, the deepest section, where they'd already finished digging. The guard then calmly climbed out, leaving the prisoner behind. He wasn't going to waste any bullets on the man. Times were hard, why waste a bullet on someone who was basically dead anyway? One by one the corpses from the great heap would be tossed on top of him. If he wasn't dead yet, he would soon die from suffocation.

Axel looked away from the prisoner in the pit and carried on digging in his corner. He no longer thought about everybody back home. There was no room for such thoughts if he was going to survive.

Two days later Erica was still feeling discouraged. She knew that Patrik was equally disheartened after his attempt to find out what the monthly payments from Erik Frankel had been for. But neither of them was ready to give up yet. Patrik was hoping that something would turn up in the documents left by Wilhelm Fridén, while Erica was determined to continue her research, trying every possible angle until she turned up something.

She had retreated to her workroom to write for a while, but she couldn't concentrate on the book. Too much was whirling through her mind. She reached for the packet of Dumlekola, enjoying the cola taste as the chocolate melted in her mouth. She'd have to put a stop to this habit very soon. But so much had happened lately that she couldn't deny herself the pleasure of a little treat now and then. She'd worry about it later. She had managed to lose weight for their wedding in the springtime, relying on sheer will-power. So she was convinced she could do it again. Just not today.

'Erica!' Patrik called from downstairs. She went out to the landing to find out what he wanted.

'Karin phoned. Maja and I are going for a walk with her and Ludde.'

'Okay,' said Erica, mumbling a bit because she was sucking on the Dumlekola sweet. She went back to her workroom and sat down in front of the computer. She still hadn't decided what she thought about Patrik taking walks with Karin. She seemed nice enough, and it was a long time since she and Patrik had divorced. Erica was convinced that, for Patrik at least, the relationship was ancient history. And yet . . . It felt odd to see him going off to spend time with his ex-wife. After all, they had once shared a bed. Erica shook her head to get rid of the image that passed through her mind and then consoled herself with another sweet. She really needed to pull herself together. She never used to be the jealous type.

To get her mind off the subject, she opened her Internet browser. An idea occurred to her, and filled with anticipation she typed '*Ignoto militi*' into the search engine. It threw up plenty of hits. She chose the first one and read with interest what it said. Now she recalled why the words had sounded familiar. Long ago, on a school trip to Paris, she had been taken to visit the Arc de Triomphe. And the grave of the unknown soldier. '*Ignoto militi*' simply meant 'the unknown soldier'.

Erica frowned as she read. More questions were forming in her mind. Was it merely a coincidence that Erik Frankel had scribbled these words on the notepad on his desk? Or did they have some particular meaning for him? And if so, what? She read more of what it said on the screen but found nothing of interest, so she scrolled down for further links. With a third Dumlekola in her mouth, she propped her feet up on the desk, pondering what to do next. Then it occurred to her that there was somebody who might be able to tell her more. It was a long shot, but . . . She dashed downstairs, grabbed her car keys from the hall table, and set off for Uddevalla.

Forty-five minutes later, she was sitting in the hospital

car park, hesitating because she realized that she didn't really have a plan. It had been relatively easy to find out over the phone which ward Herman was in, but she had no idea whether she'd be allowed to see him. Well, she'd come all this way, she might as well give it a try. She would just have to improvise.

First she stopped by the shop in the lobby and bought a big bouquet. She took the lift, got out on the proper floor, and then strode confidently towards the ward. No one seemed to take any notice of her. Erica looked at the room numbers. Thirty-five: that was his room. She just hoped she would find him alone. If his daughters were with him, there would be hell to pay.

Taking a deep breath, Erica pushed open the door. What a relief. No visitors. She went in and carefully closed the door behind her. There were two beds in the room, and Herman was lying in one of them. His roommate seemed to be sound asleep. Herman, on the other hand, was awake and staring into space with his arms lying neatly on top of the sheet.

'Hello, Herman,' said Erica quietly, pulling a chair over to his bed. 'I don't know if you remember me. I came to visit Britta. And you got angry with me.'

At first she thought Herman either couldn't or didn't want to hear her. Then he slowly turned to look at her. 'I know who you are. Elsy's daughter.'

'That's right. Elsy's daughter.' Erica smiled.

'You were at our house . . . a few days ago too,' he said, staring at her without blinking. Erica was filled with a strange tenderness for him. She pictured how he'd looked, lying next to his dead wife, holding her in a tight embrace. And now he looked so small in the hospital bed, small and frail. No longer the same man who had yelled at her for upsetting Britta.

'Yes, I was at your house. With Margareta,' said Erica.

337

Herman merely nodded. Neither of them spoke for a few moments.

Finally Erica said: 'I've been doing some research into my mother's life. That was how I came across Britta's name. And when I spoke to Britta, I had the feeling that she knew more than she wanted to tell me. Or was able to tell me.'

Herman smiled oddly but didn't reply.

Erica went on: 'I also think it's a strange coincidence that two of the three people who were friends with my mother when she was young have died within such a short period of time.' She fell silent, waiting for his response.

A tear rolled down Herman's cheek. He raised his hand and wiped it away. 'I killed her,' he said, again staring into space. 'I killed her.'

Erica heard what he said, and according to Patrik, there was really nothing to contradict his statement. But she also knew that Martin was sceptical, just as she was. And there was a strange tone in Herman's voice that she couldn't interpret.

'Do you know what it was that Britta didn't want to tell me? Was it something that happened during the war? Was it something that concerned my mother? I think I have a right to know,' she insisted. She hoped she wasn't pressuring him too hard, since he was clearly in a vulnerable state, but she desperately wanted to find out what was in her mother's past that could have accounted for the drastic change she'd undergone. Receiving no answer, Erica went on: 'When Britta started to get confused when I was visiting, she said something about an unknown soldier who was whispering. Do you know what she meant by that? She thought I was Elsy, when she said it, not Elsy's daughter. An unknown soldier – do you know anything about that?'

At first she couldn't identify the sound that Herman made. Then she realized that he was laughing. An infinitely sorrowful imitation of a laugh. She didn't understand what could be so funny.

'Ask Paul Heckel. And Friedrich Hück. They can answer your questions.' He started laughing again, louder and louder, until the whole bed was shaking.

His laughter frightened Erica more than his tears, but she still asked him: 'Who are they? Where can I find them? What do they have to do with all this?' She wanted to give Herman a good shake to get him to answer her questions, jolt an explanation out of him, but just at that moment the door opened.

'What's going on here?' A doctor was standing in the doorway, his arms crossed and a stern expression on his face.

'I'm sorry, I'm in the wrong room. But the old man here said that he wanted to have a chat. And then . . .' She got up abruptly and hurried out the door, giving the doctor an apologetic look.

Erica's heart was pounding by the time she got back to her car. Herman had given her two names. Two German names that she'd never heard before, names that meant nothing to her. What did the two Germans have to do with this? Were they somehow connected to Hans Olavsen? He had fought against the Germans, after all, before he fled to Sweden.

All the way back to Fjällbacka, the two names kept whirling round in her mind: Paul Heckel and Friedrich Hück. She was positive that she'd never heard those names before. So why was it they seemed vaguely familiar?

'Martin Molin.' He answered the phone on the first ring, then listened intently for several minutes, interrupting only to ask a few questions. Then he picked up his notebook in which he'd scribbled some notes during the phone conversation and went to see Mellberg in his office. He found him sitting in the middle of the floor with his legs stretched out,

339

reaching forward in an effort to touch his toes. Without success.

'Er, sorry. Am I interrupting something?' asked Martin, who had stopped short in the doorway.

Ernst at least seemed glad to see him. He came over, wagging his tail, and began licking Martin's hand. Mellberg didn't reply, just frowned as he struggled to get up off the floor. To his great annoyance, he finally had to admit defeat and stretch out his hand to Martin, who pulled him to his feet.

'I was just doing a few stretches,' muttered Mellberg, moving stiffly over to his chair. He caught the grin on Martin's face and snapped, 'Did you want anything in particular, or were you just planning to interrupt me for no reason?'

Mellberg reached into the bottom drawer of his desk and took out a coconut marshmallow puff. Ernst sniffed at the air and swiftly homed in on the delicious and by now all too familiar scent, looking up at his master with moist, pleading eyes. Mellberg tried to give the dog a stern look, but then relented and reached for a second marshmallow, which he tossed to Ernst. It was gone in two seconds flat.

'Your dog is getting a bit pudgy around the middle,' said Martin, casting a worried look at Ernst, whose paunch was starting to resemble that of his owner.

'Oh, he's okay. A little extra weight is good for everybody,' said Mellberg contentedly, patting his own beer belly.

Martin dropped the subject and sat down across from Mellberg. 'I just had a call from Pedersen. And I also received a report from Torbjörn this morning. Their initial assumptions have been verified. Britta Johansson was indeed murdered. Suffocated with the pillow that lay next to her on the bed.'

'And how does –' Mellberg began.

'Let's see now,' Martin interrupted, consulting his notepad. 'Pedersen used slightly arcane language, as usual, but in

340

layman's terms, she had a feather from the pillow in her throat. Presumably it got there when she was gasping for breath with the pillow pressed over her face. Pedersen also looked for traces of fibre in her throat, and he found cotton fibres that matched those from the pillow. In addition, the bones in her neck had been traumatized, which shows that someone had applied direct pressure to her neck. Most likely using his hand. They checked for fingerprints on her skin, but didn't find any, unfortunately.'

'Well, that seems clear enough. From what I've heard, she was ill. A bit gaga,' said Mellberg, waving his finger at his temple.

'She had Alzheimer's,' replied Martin sharply.

'Yeah, okay, I know,' said Mellberg, dismissing Molin's annoyed reaction. 'But don't tell me you think somebody other than the old man did it. It was most likely one of those . . . mercy killings,' he said, pleased with his own deductive logic, and then he rewarded himself with yet another marshmallow.

'Er . . . well, maybe,' said Martin reluctantly, as he turned the page in his notebook. 'But according to Torbjörn, they did find a fingerprint on the pillowcase. It's usually very difficult to lift fingerprints from cloth, but in this instance the pillowcase was fastened with a couple of shiny buttons, and there was a clear thumbprint on one of them. And it doesn't belong to Herman,' said Martin quite firmly.

Mellberg frowned and gave him a worried look for a moment. Then his face lit up. 'Probably one of the daughters. Check it out, just to be sure, so you can confirm it. Then phone the doctor at the hospital and tell him to give Britta's husband whatever bloody electroshock therapy or medicine he needs in order to revive him, because before the end of the week, we want to talk to the man. Understand?'

Martin gave a sigh and nodded. He didn't like this. Not at all. But Mellberg was right. There was no proof pointing to any other perpetrator. Merely a lone thumbprint. And if he was very unlucky, it would turn out that Mellberg was right on that point too.

Martin was halfway out the door when he slapped his forehead and turned round. 'Oh, I forgot one thing. Shit, how stupid of me! Pedersen found a considerable amount of DNA under her fingernails, both skin scrapings and blood. Presumably she scratched the person who was suffocating her. Quite deeply, according to Pedersen, since she had sharp nails and she'd managed to scrape off so much skin. In his opinion, it was most likely that she scratched the murderer on the arms or face.' Martin leaned against the door jamb.

'And does her husband have any scratches?' asked Mellberg, leaning forward with his elbows propped on his desk.

'I don't know, but it certainly sounds as though we need to pay Herman a visit ASAP,' said Martin.

'It certainly does,' replied Mellberg. 'Take Paula with you,' he shouted, but Martin was already gone.

Per had been tiptoeing around the house the past few days, not believing that it would last. His mother had never managed to stay sober for even one day. Not since his father had left. Per could hardly remember how things had been before then, but the few memories he did have were quite pleasant.

Even though he was putting up a show of resistance, he was actually starting to feel hope. More and more with each hour that passed. Even for each minute. Carina looked shaky and kept giving him ashamed looks every time they ran into each other. But she was sober. He'd checked everywhere and hadn't found a single newly purchased bottle. Not one. And he knew all of her hiding places. In fact he had never understood why she bothered to hide the bottles. She could just as well have left them standing on the kitchen counter.

'Shall I make us some dinner?' Carina asked quietly, giving him a cautious look. It was as if they were padding around each other like they had just met each other for the first time and weren't sure how things might turn out. And maybe that was an accurate description. It had been such a long time since he'd seen her sober. He didn't really know who she was without any booze inside her. And she didn't know him either. How could she have kept track of what was going on when she was constantly walking around in an alcoholic fog that filtered everything she saw, everything she did? Now they were strangers to each other. But strangers who were curious, interested, and quite hopeful.

'Have you heard anything from Frans?' she asked as she took items out of the refrigerator to make spaghetti and meatballs.

Per didn't know what to say. All his life he'd been told that he was strictly forbidden to have any sort of contact with his paternal grandfather, yet it was Frans who had intervened and saved the day, or at least given them a glimpse of hope that it could be saved.

Carina noticed her son's confusion and reluctance to answer. 'It's okay. Kjell can say whatever he likes, but as far as I'm concerned, you're welcome to talk to Frans. As long as you . . .' She hesitated, afraid to say the wrong thing, something that might upset the tenuous balance that they'd spent the past few days establishing. But then she mustered her courage and went on: 'I have no problem with you contacting your grandfather. 'He . . . well, Frans said things that needed to be said. Things that made me realize . . .' She put down the knife she was using to chop onions, and Per saw that she was fighting to hold back tears as she turned to face him. 'He made me see that things have got to change, and I'm eternally grateful to him for that. But I want you to promise me that you won't hang around with . . . those people he's associating with.' She gave him a pleading look, and her lower lip began to quiver. 'I can't promise you anything in return . . . I hope you'll understand. It's so hard. Every day, every minute is hard. I can only promise you that I'll try. Okay?' Again that shameful, pleading look.

Per felt the tight knot in his chest start to loosen a little. All these years, the only thing he had wanted, especially right after his father had left them, was permission to be a child. Instead, he'd been forced to clean up her vomit, check to make sure she wouldn't burn down the house when she smoked in bed, and go out to do all the shopping. He had to do things that no young boy should have to do. All those memories flickered past in his mind. But it didn't matter. Because the only thing he heard was her voice, her soft, pleading mother's voice. And he took a step forward and put his arms around her. Nestled against her even though he was almost a head taller than she was. And for the first time in ten years, he allowed himself to feel like a child.

FJÄLLBACKA 1945

'Doesn't it feel wonderful to have a break from work?' cooed Britta, stroking Hans's arm. He merely laughed and shook off her hand. After getting to know all of them over the past six months, he was well aware when he was being used to make Frans jealous. The amused look that he received from Frans told him that he, too, knew exactly what Britta was up to. But Hans had to admire Britta's tenacity. She would probably never stop pining for Frans.

Of course Frans himself was at least partially to blame, since he occasionally encouraged her feelings for him, only to treat her with his usual chilly manner afterwards. Hans thought the game that Frans was playing bordered on cruelty, but he didn't want to get involved. What did upset him was discovering who Frans was really interested in. He glanced at her as she sat a short distance away and felt a pang in his chest because just at that moment she said something to Frans and then smiled. Elsy had such a beautiful smile. And it wasn't only her smile that was lovely. Her eyes, her spirit, her pretty arms in the short-sleeved dress she was wearing, the little dimple that appeared to the left of her mouth whenever she smiled. Everything about her, every detail, was beautiful.

They had been kind to him, Elsy and her family. He paid

a small, barely adequate amount in rent, and Elof had arranged work for him on one of the boats. He was often invited to join the family for meals – in fact, practically every evening – and there was something about their warmth, their companionship, that filled every nook and cranny of his soul. The emotions that the war had stripped away from him were slowly returning.

And then there was Elsy. Hans had tried to fight the thoughts and feelings that came over him whenever he lay in bed at night and pictured her in his mind. But finally he realized he was hopelessly in love with her. And jealousy stabbed him in the heart every time he saw Frans looking at Elsy with the same expression that he presumably had on his own face.

Britta might not be clever enough to grasp what was going on, but she instinctively understood that she was not the main focus for either Frans or Hans. He knew that this bothered her terribly. She was a shallow, selfish girl, and he really couldn't think why someone like Elsy wanted to spend time with her at all. But as long as Elsy chose to have Britta around, he would have to put up with her too.

Erik was the person Hans liked the best among his four new friends, aside from Elsy. There was something precocious, something solemn about him that Hans found reassuring. He liked sitting slightly apart from the others and talking to Erik. They discussed the war, history, politics and economics, and Erik was delighted to discover that in Hans he'd found the equal that he'd been longing for. Of course he wasn't as well-read as Erik when it came to facts and figures, but he knew a lot about the world and about history, and how various things were interconnected. They could talk for hours. Elsy used to tease them, saying that they were like two old men telling each other tall tales, but Hans could see that she was pleased they enjoyed each other's company.

The only thing they didn't speak about was Erik's brother.

Hans never broached the subject, and after that first time, Erik never did either.

'I think my mother will have dinner ready soon,' said Elsy as she stood up and brushed off her dress. Hans nodded and got up too.

'I'd better come with you, or she'll make a fuss,' he said, looking at Elsy, who merely smiled indulgently and started climbing down from the rocky hill. Hans noticed that she was blushing. He was seventeen, two years older, but she always made him feel like a foolish schoolboy.

He waved goodbye to the others, who remained where they were, and scrambled down the slope after Elsy. She looked both ways before crossing the road and then opened the gate to the cemetery. It was a shortcut home.

'It's such nice weather tonight,' he said, hearing how nervous he sounded. He cursed silently, telling himself to stop acting like an idiot. She was walking quickly along the gravel path, and he trotted behind. After a few steps he caught up and walked next to her, his hands stuffed in his trouser pockets. She hadn't replied to his comment about the weather, which was a relief because it had sounded so lame.

Suddenly he felt an intense happiness. He was walking alongside Elsy, now and then sneaking a glimpse of her profile. The wind was surprisingly warm, and the gravel on the path made a pleasant crunching sound under their feet. This was the first time in ages that he could remember feeling this way. If in fact he'd ever felt this way before. There had been so many obstacles. So much that had made his chest ache with humiliation, hatred, and fear. He had done his best not to think about the past. The moment that he sneaked on board Elof's boat, he had decided to leave everything else behind. And not look back.

But now the images came of their own accord. He walked quietly next to Elsy, trying to push them back into the caverns

347

where he had hidden them, but they were forcing their way through the barriers, into his consciousness. Maybe this was the price he had to pay for a moment of such pure happiness. That brief, bittersweet moment. If so, maybe it was worth it. But that didn't help him now, as he walked beside Elsy and felt all the faces, sights, smells, memories, and sounds descending upon him. Panic-stricken, he felt that he had to do something. His throat began to close up, and his breathing grew fast and shallow. He could no longer hold all the memories back. Nor could he allow them to take him over. He had to do something.

At that moment Elsy's hand brushed against his. Her touch made him jump. It was soft and electric, and in its simplicity it was all he needed to drive out what he didn't want to think about. He stopped abruptly on the hill above the cemetery. Elsy was a step above him, and when she turned round, the difference in their height brought her face level with his.

'What's wrong?' she asked, looking worried. And at that moment he didn't know what came over him. He stepped towards her, took her face in his hands, and kissed her gently on the lips. At first she froze, and he felt the panic rising inside of him. Then she suddenly relaxed, her lips grew soft against his, and then opened. Ever so slowly she opened her lips, and terrified but excited, he cautiously slipped his tongue in, searching for hers. He could tell that she had never been kissed before, but instinctively her tongue met his, and he felt his knees buckle. With his eyes closed, he pulled away from her, only looking up after a few seconds. The first thing he saw was her eyes. And reflected in them a mirror image of what he himself was feeling.

As they walked home together, slowly, silently, all the images from the past stayed away. It was as if they had never existed.

Christian was deeply immersed in whatever it was he was studying on his computer screen when Erica came in. She had driven straight to the library from Uddevalla and was still just as bewildered as when she'd left Herman at the hospital. She was convinced there was something familiar about those German names, and she'd written them down on a piece of paper, which she now handed to the librarian.

'Hi, Christian. Could you see if there's any information about these two people: Paul Heckel and Friedrich Hück?' she asked.

As he glanced at the names, she noticed how worn out he looked. Probably just suffering from an autumn cold, or having trouble with his children, she thought, but she couldn't help worrying about him.

'Have a seat and I'll do a search,' he said.

She sat down, mentally crossing her fingers, but her hopes faded when she saw no reaction on Christian's face as he examined the results of his search.

'I'm afraid I can't find anything,' he said at last, shaking his head apologetically. 'Nothing in our archives or databases, at any rate. But you could do a search on the Internet. I suspect, though, that these are rather common names in Germany.'

'Okay,' said Erica, disappointed. 'So there's no connection between the names and the local area?'

'Afraid not.'

Erica sighed. 'Oh, well. I suppose that would have been too easy.' Then her face lit up. 'Could you check if there's anything in the archives about a person who was mentioned in the articles that you found for me last time I was here? We didn't do a search for him in particular, just for my mother and some of her friends. It's a Norwegian resistance fighter named Hans Olavsen, and he was here in Fjällbacka . . .'

'Around the end of the war. Yes, I know,' said Christian laconically.

'You know about him?' said Erica, her eagerness somewhat deflated.

'No, but this is the second time someone has asked me about him in the past few days. Seems to be a popular guy.'

'Who else was looking for information about him?' asked Erica, holding her breath.

'I'll have to check,' replied Christian, rolling his desk chair over to a small file box. 'He left his business card in case I found out anything more about the boy. If I did, I was supposed to give him a call.' He hummed softly as he looked through the box, at last finding what he was looking for.

'Aha. Here it is. It says Kjell Ringholm.'

'Thanks, Christian,' said Erica, smiling. 'Now I know who I have to have a little chat with.'

'Sounds serious,' Christian chuckled, but his smile didn't reach his eyes.

'Not really. It's just that I'm curious why he would be interested in Hans Olavsen.' Erica was thinking aloud. 'So did you find anything out about him when Kjell Ringholm was here?'

'Just the same materials that I gave you last time. I'm afraid there's nothing more.'

'All right. Rather lean pickings today,' said Erica with a

sigh. 'Do you mind if I write down the number from his business card?'

'Be my guest,' said Christian, handing her the card.

'Thanks,' she said, giving him a wink. He winked back, though he still looked tired.

'So,' she said, 'are you continuing to make progress on your book? Are you sure I can't help you with anything? *The Mermaid* – that's the title, right?'

'Oh, sure, it's going fine,' he said, although the enthusiasm in his voice didn't sound genuine. 'And yes, it's going to be called *The Mermaid*. But if you'll excuse me now, there's something I've got to do.' He turned his back to her and began typing on the computer keyboard.

Erica was disconcerted at Christian's attitude. She'd never known him to behave like that before. Oh well, she rallied herself as she walked out of the library, there were other things she had to attend to. And top of the list was a conversation with Kjell Ringholm.

They had agreed to meet out at Veddö. There was little risk that anyone would see them there at this time of year, and if someone did happen to notice them, they would merely take them for two old men having a walk.

'Just imagine if a person was able to see what lay ahead,' said Axel as he kicked a stone that rolled away across the beach. In the summertime swimmers shared the beach with a herd of cows here, and it was just as common to find a long-haired cow cooling off in the water as children going in for a swim. But right now the beach was deserted, and the wind was picking up dried pieces of seaweed, sending them whirling through the air.

Without actually mentioning the subject, they had agreed not to talk about Erik. Or Britta. Neither of them fully understood why they had agreed to meet. It would serve no purpose. Nor would it change anything. Yet they had both felt a need to see each other. It was like a mosquito bite that needed to be scratched. And even though they knew that, just as in the case of a mosquito bite, it would only make matters worse, they had given into temptation.

'I suppose the whole point is that no one knows ahead of time,' said Frans, gazing out at the water. 'If a person had a crystal ball that revealed everything he would experience during his lifetime, he would probably never even get out of bed. People should take life in small doses. Encounter sorrows and problems in portions that are small enough to swallow.'

'Sometimes life has a way of serving up pieces that are too big to swallow,' said Axel, kicking away yet another stone.

'Perhaps that's true of others, but not you or me,' said Frans, turning to look at Axel. 'We may seem very different in other people's eyes, but you and I are alike. You know that. We never retreat. No matter how big a portion is handed to us.'

Axel merely nodded. Then he looked at Frans again. 'Do you have any regrets?'

Frans pondered the question for a long time. Then he said, 'What is there to regret? What's done is done. We all make our choices. You've made yours. And I've made mine. Do I have any regrets? No. What purpose would that serve?'

Axel shrugged. 'I suppose regret is an expression of humanity. Without regret . . . what would we be then?'

'But the question is, does regret change anything? And the same is true of the work that you've been doing – revenge. You've devoted your whole life to hunting criminals, and your only goal has been revenge. There is no other goal. Has it changed anything? Six million people still died in the concentration camps. How is that changed by your tracking down some woman who was a prison guard during the war, but who has since spent her life as a housewife in the United States? If you drag her before a tribunal and put her on trial for the crimes that she committed more than sixty years ago, what will that change?'

Axel swallowed. Mostly he believed in the meaning of the work he did. But Frans had hit a sensitive spot. He was asking the question that Axel had asked himself more than once in weak moments.

'It brings peace to the families of the victims. And it's a signal that we won't condone those acts as acceptable human behaviour.'

'Bullshit,' said Frans, stuffing his hands in his pockets. 'Do you really think it will scare anyone off, or send any sort of signal when the present is so much stronger than the past? It's human nature for people not to see the consequences of their actions, not to learn from history. And peace? If someone hasn't found peace after sixty years, he never will. It's every individual's responsibility to find his own peace – you can't expect any sort of retribution, or believe that it will be delivered some day.'

'Those are cynical words,' said Axel. The wind was getting colder, and he was shivering.

'I just want you to realize that, behind all the noble deeds you think you've devoted your life to, there is a highly primitive and fundamental human emotion: the desire for revenge. I don't believe in revenge. I believe that the only thing we should focus on is doing what we can to change the present.'

'And that's what you think you're doing?' said Axel, his voice tense.

'We stand on opposite sides of the barricades, you and I, Axel,' replied Frans drily. 'But yes, that's what I think I'm doing. I'm changing something. I'm not seeking revenge. I have no regrets. I am looking forward, and acting according to my beliefs. That's completely different from what you're doing. But we're never going to agree. Our paths diverged sixty years ago, never to meet again.'

'How did things turn out this way?' asked Axel quietly, swallowing hard.

'That's just what I'm saying: it doesn't matter how. This is the way it is. And the only thing we can try to do is to change, to survive. Not look back. Not wallow in regrets or speculations about how things might have been.' Frans stopped and forced Axel to look at him. 'You can't look back. What's done is done. The past is the past. There is no such thing as regret.'

'That's where you're wrong, Frans,' said Axel, bowing his head. 'That's where you're very wrong.'

It was with the greatest reluctance that Herman's doctor had agreed to let them speak with his patient for a few minutes. Only when Martin and Paula had agreed that two of Herman's daughters could sit in on the interview had the doctor relented.

'Hello, Herman,' said Martin, speaking gently and holding out his hand to the man lying in the bed. Herman shook his hand, but his grip was weak. 'We met at your house, but I'm not sure you'll remember. This is my colleague, Paula Morales. We'd like to ask you a few questions, if we may.' He took a seat next to Paula, beside the bed.

'All right,' said Herman, who now seemed a bit more aware of his surroundings. His daughters were seated on the other side of the bed, and Margareta was holding her father's hand.

'Please accept our sincere condolences,' said Martin. 'I understand that you and Britta were married a long time, is that right?'

'Fifty-five years,' said Herman, and for the first time since their arrival, they saw a glint of life in his eyes. 'We were married for fifty-five years, my Britta and I.'

'Could you tell us what happened? When she died?' said Paula, trying for the same gentle tone as Martin.

Margareta and Anna-Greta stared at them nervously and

were just about to protest when Herman waved his hand dismissively.

Martin, who had already noted that there were no scratches on Herman's face, was doing his best to peek under the sleeves of his hospital gown in search of tell-tale scratch marks. He couldn't see anything, but decided to wait to confirm this observation until after they had finished the interview.

'I went over to Margareta's house to have coffee,' said Herman. 'They're so sweet to me, my girls. Especially since Britta has been sick.' Herman smiled at his daughters. 'We had a lot to talk about. I . . . had decided that it would be better for Britta if she lived someplace where someone could look after her more.' He was having a hard time speaking.

Margareta patted his hand. 'It was the only thing you could do, Pappa. There was no alternative. You know that.'

Herman, seeming not to hear her, went on: 'I was worried because I'd been gone so long. Almost two hours. I'm never usually gone for more than an hour, while she's taking her afternoon nap, so she doesn't know I'm not there. I'm so afraid . . . *was* so afraid that she would wake up and set the house and herself on fire.' He was shaking, but he took a deep breath and continued. 'So I called her name when I got home. But she didn't answer. I thought: Thank heavens, she must still be asleep. So I went up to our bedroom. And there she lay . . . I thought it was strange, because she had a pillow over her face, and why would she lie in bed like that? So I went over and lifted off the pillow. And I saw at once that she was gone. Her eyes . . . her eyes were staring up at the ceiling, and she was very, very still.' Tears began trickling down his face, and Margareta gently wiped them away.

'Is this really necessary?' she pleaded, looking at Martin and Paula. 'Pappa is still in a state of shock, and –'

'It's all right, Margareta,' said Herman. 'It's all right.'

'Okay, but only a few more minutes, Pappa. Then I'm

355

going to physically throw them out if I have to, because you need to rest.'

'She's always been the feisty one,' said Herman, a wan smile appearing on his face. 'A real shrew.'

'Hush, now. You needn't be so impudent,' said Margareta, but she seemed happy that he had the energy to tease her.

'So what you're saying is that she was already dead when you went into the room?' asked Paula, surprised. 'So why did you say that you killed her?'

'Because I did kill her,' replied Herman, a closed expression on his face again. 'But I never said that I murdered her. Although I could have done that too.' He looked down at his hands, unable to meet the eyes of the police officers or his daughters.

'Pappa, what do you mean?' Anna-Greta looked bewildered, but Herman refused to answer.

'Do you know who murdered her?' asked Martin, instinctively grasping that Herman was not going to explain why he had so stubbornly insisted that he had killed his wife.

'You heard what my father said,' Margareta told Martin as she stood up. 'He's said all he's going to say. The important thing is that he was not the one who murdered my mother. As for the rest . . . that's just his grief talking.'

Martin and Paula got up. 'Thank you for allowing us to speak with you. But there is one last thing that we need to ask,' said Martin, turning to Herman. 'To confirm what you've just said, we need to take a look at your arms. We know that Britta scratched the person who suffocated her.'

'Is that really necessary? He says that . . .' Margareta's voice was getting louder, but Herman quietly pushed up the sleeves of his hospital gown and held out his arms for Martin, who studied them intently. No scratch marks.

'There, you see?' said Margareta, looking as if she would like to make good her threat to throw Martin and Paula out the door.

'We're finished now,' said Martin. 'Thank you for your time, Herman. Once again, we're very sorry for your loss.' Then he motioned to Margareta and Anna-Greta to show that he wanted to speak to them privately.

Out in the corridor, he explained the situation regarding the fingerprint on the button, and they willingly agreed to provide their prints so as to be ruled out of the investigation. Just as they were finishing up, Birgitta arrived, and she too complied so that the fingerprints of all three daughters could be sent off to the lab.

Paula and Martin sat in the car for a moment before setting off. 'Who do you think he's protecting?' asked Paula as she put the key in the ignition.

'I don't know. But I get the same impression. That he knows who murdered Britta but wants to protect that person. And that he somehow feels responsible.'

'If only he would tell us,' said Paula, now turning the key.

'Yes, I can't for the life of me . . .' Martin shook his head, annoyed, and drummed his fingertips on the dashboard.

'But you do believe him?' Paula already knew what the answer would be.

'Yes, I believe him. And the fact that he doesn't have any scratch marks proves that I'm right. But I can't understand why he would want to protect his wife's murderer. Or why he feels that he is personally to blame.'

'Well, we may never find the answer to that,' said Paula as she drove out of the car park. 'But at least we have the daughters' fingerprints. We need to send them off to the lab ASAP, then we can eliminate them and we can start trying to figure out who did leave that thumbprint.'

'I suppose that's all we can do at the moment,' said Martin, sighing heavily and looking out the car window.

Neither of them noticed when they passed Erica just north of Torp.

FJÄLLBACKA 1945

It was no coincidence that Frans saw what happened. He had kept his eyes on Elsy the whole time, wanting to look at her until she disappeared from view over the crown of the hill. And so he saw the kiss. He felt as if his blood were boiling, yet an icy cold seemed to spread through his limbs. It was so painful that he thought he would fall down dead on the spot.

'Did you see that?' asked Erik, who had also caught sight of Hans and Elsy. 'It looked like . . .' He laughed, shaking his head. The sound of Erik's laughter made a white light explode inside Frans's head. He needed some way to release all the pain, so he threw himself at Erik, gripping his neck in a stranglehold.

'Shut up, shut up, SHUT UP, you fucking stupid . . .' He gripped Erik's neck tighter, making the boy gasp for air. It made him happy to see the terror in Erik's eyes – as if that somehow diminished the size of the knot that was ever present in his stomach and seemed to have increased tenfold at the sight of the kiss.

'What are you doing!' Britta screamed, staring at the boys on the ground. Erik was on his back, with Frans on top of him. Without even thinking she rushed over and yanked at Frans's shirt, but he flailed his arm at her so hard that she toppled backwards.

'Stop it, Frans, stop it!' she yelled, sliding away from him with tears running down her cheeks. Something in her tone brought him to his senses. He looked down at Erik, whose face had taken on an odd colour, and let go of his neck.

'I'm sorry,' he muttered, rubbing his eyes. 'I'm sorry . . . I . . .'

Erik sat up and stared at him, his hands feeling his bruised throat. 'What was that all about? You just about strangled me! Are you out of your mind?' Erik's glasses were askew. He took them off and then put them on again properly.

Frans stared straight ahead, a blank look in his eyes, and didn't reply.

'He's in love with Elsy. That's why,' said Britta bitterly as she wiped the tears from her face with the back of her hand. 'And he actually thought he had a chance with her. But you're an idiot for thinking that, Frans! She has never so much as looked at you. And now she's throwing herself into the arms of that Norwegian. While I . . .' She burst into tears and started scrambling down the rocky hill.

Frans, expressionless, watched her go.

'Damn it, Frans, you're not . . . Is that true?' Erik glared at him. 'Are you in love with Elsy? I mean, if that's the case, I can understand why you went berserk. But you can't . . .' Erik stopped and shook his head.

Frans didn't reply. He couldn't. His head was filled with the image of Hans leaning forward to kiss Elsy. And of Elsy kissing him back.

Nowadays Erica always paid more attention when she saw a police car, and she thought she saw Martin in the one that passed her just before Torp, as she drove towards Uddevalla for the second time that day. She wondered where Martin had been.

There really wasn't any rush with the enquiries she was making, but she knew that she wouldn't be able to write in peace until she had followed up on the new information she'd been given. And she was curious to know why Kjell Ringholm, a journalist for *Bohusläningen*, was interested in the Norwegian resistance fighter.

Later, as she was waiting in the reception area at *Bohusläningen*, she pondered possible reasons for his interest but finally decided to stop speculating until she had the opportunity to ask him in person. A few minutes later she was escorted to his office. He looked up with a quizzical expression on his face as she came in and shook hands.

'Erica Falck? The author? Is that right?' he said, motioning her towards a visitor's chair.

'Yes, that's right,' she said, draping her jacket over the back of the chair and sitting down.

'Unfortunately, I haven't read any of your books, but I've heard that they're very good,' he said politely. 'Are you here in connection with research for a new book? I'm not a crime reporter, so I'm not sure how I can help you. Unless I'm mistaken, you write true-crime books.'

'Actually, this has nothing to do with my books,' replied Erica. 'The thing is, for various reasons I've started researching my mother's past. And she happened to be good friends with your father.'

Kjell frowned. 'When was that?' he asked, leaning forward.

'From what I understand, they were friends as children and teenagers. I've mostly been concentrating on the late war years, when they were about fifteen.'

Kjell nodded and waited for her to go on.

'They were part of a group of four teenagers who seem to have been as thick as thieves. In addition to your father, the group included Britta Johansson and Erik Frankel. And as you undoubtedly know, those two were both murdered within the last few months. Rather a strange coincidence, don't you think?'

Kjell still didn't speak, but Erica saw how tense he was, and she noticed a glint in his eyes.

'And . . .' She paused. 'There was one other person. In 1944 a Norwegian resistance fighter – he was really only a boy – came to Fjällbacka. He had stowed away on my grandfather's boat and then became a lodger in my grandparents' house. His name was Hans Olavsen. But you already know that, don't you? Because I understand that you're also interested in him, and I was wondering why.'

'I'm a journalist. I can't discuss that sort of thing,' Kjell replied evasively.

'Wrong. You can't reveal your sources,' said Erica calmly. 'But I don't see why we can't join forces to work on this matter. I'm very good at ferreting out things, and I know you are too, since you're a journalist. We're both interested in Hans Olavsen. I can live with the fact that you don't want

361

to tell me why. But we could at least exchange information – what we already know and what we find out later on our own. What do you think?' She fell silent and waited, in suspense.

Kjell considered what she'd just said. He drummed his fingers on the desk as he weighed the pros and cons.

'Okay,' he said at last, reaching for something in the top desk drawer. 'There's really no reason why we can't help each other out. And my source is dead, so I don't see why I shouldn't show you everything. Here's what I know. I came into contact with Erik Frankel because of a . . . private matter.' He cleared his throat and slid the folder towards her. 'He said that there was something he wanted to tell me, something that I might find useful and that ought to come out.'

'Is that how he phrased it?' Erica leaned forward and picked up the folder. 'That it was something that ought to come out?'

'Yes, as far as I recall,' said Kjell, leaning back in his chair. 'He called on me here a few days later. He brought along the articles in that folder and just handed them to me. But he wouldn't tell me why. I asked him a lot of questions, of course, but he refused to answer any of them. He just said that if I was as good at digging up things as he'd heard, then what was in the folder should be sufficient.'

Erica leafed through the pages inside the plastic folder. They were the same articles that she'd already got from Christian, the articles from the archives mentioning Hans Olavsen and the time he'd spent in Fjällbacka. 'Is this all?' she asked, sighing.

'That was my reaction too. If he knew something, why couldn't he just come out and tell me? But for some reason he thought it was important that I should find out the rest on my own. So that's what I've started to do, and I'd be lying if I said that my interest hadn't gone up a thousand per cent since Erik Frankel was found murdered. I've been

362

wondering if his death has anything to do with this.' He pointed at the folder that was resting on Erica's lap. 'And of course I've heard about the elderly woman who was murdered last week. But I have no idea if there's any connection . . . though it does raise a number of questions.'

'Have you found out anything more about the Norwegian?' asked Erica eagerly. 'I haven't got that far yet in my own research. The only thing I know is that he and my mother had a love affair, and that he seems to have left her behind in Fjällbacka rather suddenly. I thought my next step would be to try to locate him, find out where he went, if he really did return to Norway or go somewhere else. But maybe you already know?'

Kjell shook his head. He told Erica about his conversation with Eskil Halvorsen, the Norwegian academic who couldn't recall Hans Olavsen off the top of his head but had promised to do some further research.

'It's also possible that Hans stayed in Sweden,' said Erica pensively. 'If so, we should be able to trace him through the Swedish authorities. I can probably check that out. But if he disappeared somewhere abroad, that would be a problem.'

Kjell took back the folder. 'That's a good idea. There's no reason to assume that he returned to Norway. A lot of people stayed in Sweden after the war.'

'Did you send a picture to Eskil Halvorsen?' asked Erica.

'No, as a matter of fact, I didn't,' said Kjell, leafing through the articles. 'But you're right – I should do that. The smallest detail could prove helpful. I'll phone him as soon as you leave and see if I can send him one of these pictures. Or, even better, I could fax it to him. What about this one? It's the clearest. What do you think?' He slid across the desk the article with the group photo that Erica had studied a few days earlier.

'I agree. That would be good. Plus it shows the whole group. That's my mother there.' She pointed at Elsy.

'So you say that they spent a lot of time together back then?' Kjell cursed himself for not making the connection between the Britta in the photograph and the Britta who was murdered. But he told himself that most people would have missed the link. It was hard to see any similarity between the fifteen-year-old girl and the seventy-five-year-old woman whose picture had been in the papers.

'Yes, from what I understand, they were a close-knit group, even though their friendship wasn't entirely accepted back then. There was such a divide between the classes in Fjällbacka, and Britta and my mother belonged to the poorer social echelon, while the boys, Erik Frankel and, well . . . your father, belonged to the "upper crust".' Erica used her fingers to draw quote marks in the air.

'Oh, right, very upper crust,' Kjell muttered, and Erica sensed that there was a lot of hostility concealed below the surface of his words.

'You know, I hadn't thought about talking to Axel Frankel,' said Erica excitedly. 'He might know something about Hans Olavsen. Even though he's a bit older, he must have been around, and he might . . .' Her thoughts and expectations took off, but Kjell held up his hand to stop her.

'I wouldn't get your hopes up. I had the same idea, but luckily I did some research about Axel Frankel first. I suppose you know that he was captured by the Germans while on a trip to Norway?'

'Yes, but I don't know much about it,' said Erica, looking at Kjell with interest. 'So if you've found out anything . . .' She threw out her hands and waited.

'Well, as I said, Axel was taken prisoner by the Germans when he took delivery of some documents from the resistance movement. He was taken to Grini prison outside of Oslo, and he was held there until the beginning of 1945. Then the Germans shipped him and a lot of other prisoners to Germany. Axel first ended up in Sachsenhausen, which was where many of the Nordic prisoners were taken, and then, towards the end of the war, he was taken to Neuengamme.'

Erica gasped. 'I had no idea. So Axel Frankel was in concentration camps in Germany? I didn't know that any Norwegians or Swedes ended up there.'

Kjell nodded. 'Mostly Norwegian prisoners. And some from other countries who fell foul of a decree issued by Hitler in 1941, which stated that civilians in occupied territories who were caught participating in resistance activities against the Germans could not be tried and sentenced by a court in their homeland. Instead, they were to be sent to Germany, where they would disappear into the *Nacht und Nebel* – "night and fog". Hence they were known as NN prisoners. Some were executed. The rest were sentenced to forced labour and worked to death in the camps. At any rate, Axel Frankel was in Germany, not Fjällbacka, during the period Hans Olavsen was there.'

'But we don't know the exact date the Norwegian left Fjällbacka,' said Erica, frowning. 'At least, I haven't found any information about that. I have no idea when he left my mother.'

'Ah, but I do know when Hans Olavsen left town,' said Kjell triumphantly, and he rummaged through the papers on his desk. 'Approximately, at least,' he added. 'Here –' He pulled out an article and placed it in front of Erica, pointing to a passage in the middle of the page.

Erica leaned forward and read aloud: '*This year the Fjällbacka Association organized with great success –*'

'No, no, the next column,' said Kjell, pointing again.

'Oh, okay.' Erica started over. '*It surprised one and all to learn that the Norwegian resistance fighter who found refuge with us here in Fjällbacka has abruptly left us. Many residents of Fjällbacka regret that they were not able to say goodbye and thank him for his efforts during the war, which we have now seen come to an end.'* She glanced at the date at the top of the page and then looked up. 'Nineteenth of June 1945.'

'So he disappeared right after the war ended, if I'm interpreting this correctly,' said Kjell, taking back the article and placing it on top of the pile.

'But why?' Erica tilted her head as she pondered what she'd read. 'I still think it might be an idea to talk to Axel. His brother may have told him something. I'll give it a shot. You wouldn't by any chance be willing to talk to your father, would you?'

Kjell was silent for a moment, then he said, 'Of course. And I'll let you know if I hear anything from Halvorsen. Be sure to get in touch with me if you find out anything, okay?' He raised an admonitory finger. He wasn't used to working collaboratively, but in this case he apparently saw an advantage in having Erica's assistance.

'I'll check with the Swedish authorities too,' said Erica, getting up. 'And I promise to let you know the minute I hear anything.' She started to put on her jacket but stopped suddenly.

'By the way, Kjell, there's one other thing. I don't know if it's important, but . . .'

'Tell me. Anything could be valuable at this point,' he said, looking up at her.

'Well, I talked with Britta's husband, Herman. He seems to know something about all of this. Or at least, I'm not positive, but I got that feeling. Anyway, when I asked him about Hans Olavsen he reacted really strangely. He told me that I should ask Paul Heckel and Friedrich Hück. And I've tried to check up on the names, but couldn't find anything. But . . .'

'Yes?' said Kjell.

'Oh, I don't know. I could swear that I've never met either of them, yet there's something familiar . . .' .

Kjell tapped his pen on the desk. 'Paul Heckel and Friedrich

Hück?' When Erica nodded, he wrote down the names. 'Okay, I'll check on them too. But the names don't ring a bell.'

'Looks as if we both have something to do now,' said Erica, smiling as she paused in the doorway. 'I feel much better knowing that there are two of us working on this.'

'That's good,' said Kjell, sounding distracted.

'I'll be in touch,' said Erica.

'All right,' said Kjell, picking up the phone without looking at her as she left his office. He was eager to get to the bottom of this. His journalist's nose had picked up the unmistakable scent of rat.

'Shall we go sit down and review everything?' It was Monday afternoon, and calm had descended over the station.

'Sure,' said Gösta, getting up reluctantly. 'Paula too?'

'Of course,' said Martin. He went to get her. Mellberg was out taking Ernst for a walk, and Annika appeared to be busy in the reception area, so it was just the three of them who sat down in the kitchen with all the existing investigative materials in front of them.

'Erik Frankel,' said Martin, setting the point of his pen on a fresh page of his notepad.

'He was murdered in his home, with an object that has already been found on the scene,' said Paula, as Martin feverishly started writing.

'That seems to indicate that it was not premeditated,' said Gösta, and Martin nodded.

'There were no fingerprints on the bust that was used as the murder weapon, but it doesn't seem to have been wiped clean, so the killer must have been wearing gloves, which actually contradicts the idea that it was not premeditated,' interjected Paula. She glanced at the words that Martin was writing on the notepad.

'Can you really read what you've written?' she asked

sceptically, since his writing looked mostly like hieroglyphics. Or shorthand.

'Only if I type it up on the computer straight away,' said Martin, smiling as he continued to write. 'Otherwise I'm screwed.'

'Erik Frankel died from a violent blow to the temple,' said Gösta, taking out photographs from the crime scene. 'The perp then left the murder weapon behind.'

'Again, these are not the hallmarks of a particularly cold-blooded or calculated murder,' said Paula, getting up to pour coffee for herself and her colleagues.

'The only potential threat we've been able to identify came from the neo-Nazi organization Sweden's Friends, who targeted Frankel because he was an expert on Nazism.' Martin reached for the five letters enclosed in plastic sleeves and spread them out on the table. 'In addition, he had a personal connection to the organization through his child-hood friend, Frans Ringholm.'

'Do we have anything that might link Frans to the murder? Anything at all?' Paula stared at the letters as if she wanted to make them speak.

'Well, three of his Nazi pals claim that he was in Denmark with them on the days in question. It's not a watertight alibi, if such a thing even exists, but we don't have much physical evidence to go on. The footprints found at the scene belonged to the boys who discovered the body. There were no other footprints or fingerprints or anything else besides what we would expect to find there.'

'Are you going to pour the coffee, or are you just planning to stand there holding the pot?' Gösta said to Paula.

'Say please, and I'll give you some coffee,' Paula teased him, and Gösta reluctantly grunted 'please'.

'Then there's the date of the murder,' said Martin, nodding to Paula to thank her for filling his coffee cup. 'We've been able to establish with relative certainty that Erik Frankel died sometime between the fifteenth and the seventeenth of June. So we have three days to play with. And then his body remained there, undiscovered, because his brother was away and no one expected to hear from Erik, except possibly Viola – but as she saw it, he had broken off their relationship. And that happened just before he was killed.

'And nobody saw anything? Gösta, did you talk to all the neighbours? Did anyone see any strange cars? Any suspicious people?' Martin looked at his colleague.

'There aren't many neighbours to talk to out there,' muttered Gösta.

'Should I take that as a no?'

'I did talk to all the neighbours, and nobody saw anything.'

'Okay, we'll drop that for the moment.' Martin sighed and took a sip of his coffee.

'What about Britta Johansson? It's quite a coincidence that she had a connection to Erik Frankel. And to Frans Ringholm, for that matter. Of course it was a long time ago, but we have phone records showing that there was actually contact between them in June, and both Frans and Erik also went to see Britta around that time.' Again Martin looked to his colleagues for answers: 'Why choose that particular moment to resume contact after sixty years? Should we believe Britta's husband, who says that it was because her mental condition was deteriorating, and she wanted to recall the old days?'

'Personally, I reckon that's bullshit,' said Paula, reaching for an unopened packet of Ballerina biscuits. She removed the plastic tape on one end and helped herself to three biscuits before she offered some to the others. 'I think that if we could only work out the real reason why they met, the whole case would crack wide open. But Frans is as silent as a tomb, and Axel is sticking with the same story that Herman gave us.'

'And let's not forget about the monthly payments,' said

369

Gösta, pausing for a moment as he painstakingly removed the vanilla top layer of his biscuit and licked off the chocolate filling, then continuing: 'What do they have to do with Frankel's murder?'

Martin looked at Gösta in surprise. He didn't know that Gösta was up to speed on that part of the investigation, since his usual strategy was to sit back waiting for information to be fed to him.

'Well, Hedström tried checking out that angle on Saturday,' said Martin, taking out the notes he'd made when Patrik phoned to report on his visit to the home of Wilhelm Fridén.

'So, what did he find out?' Gösta took another biscuit and the others watched, transfixed, as he repeated his dissecting manoeuvre. Off came the vanilla top layer, then he scooped out the chocolate filling with his tongue. The remaining layers of biscuit were then discarded.

'Hey, Gösta, you can't just lick off the chocolate and leave the rest,' said Paula indignantly.

'What are you? The biscuit police?' replied Gösta, making a show of taking yet another biscuit. Paula merely snorted and picked up the packet of biscuits to put it on the counter, out of Gösta's reach.

'Unfortunately, he didn't find out much,' said Martin. 'Wilhelm Fridén died just a couple of weeks ago, and neither his widow nor his son knew anything about the payments. Of course, it's hard to say whether they were telling the truth, but Patrik seemed to think they were. At any rate, the son has promised to ask their lawyer to send over all of his father's papers, and if we're lucky we'll find something there.'

'What about Erik's brother? Did he know anything about the payments?' Gösta glanced greedily at the biscuits on the counter and seemed to be considering actually getting up off his rear to fetch it.

'We phoned Axel to ask him about the payments,' said

Paula, with a warning look to Gösta. 'But he said he had no idea what it was all about.'

'And do we believe him?' Gösta was measuring the distance from his chair to the counter. A quick lunge, and he might be able to do it.

'I don't really know. He's hard to read. What do you think, Paula?' said Martin, turning to her.

While she thought about the question, Gösta seized his chance. He jumped up and launched himself towards the packet, but Paula's left hand shot out at lightning speed and snatched it away.

'Uh-uh, no way . . .' She gave Gösta a mischievous wink, and he couldn't help smiling back. He was starting to appreciate their banter.

The packet of biscuits safely in her lap, Paula turned to Martin. 'No, I agree. I can't really make him out. So, no, I'm not sure.'

'Let's go back to Britta,' said Martin, printing BRITTA in big letters on his notepad, and then underscoring the name.

'What I judge to be our best evidence is the discovery of what is most likely the murderer's DNA under her fingernails. And the fact that she evidently managed to leave deep scratches on the face or arms of the person who was suffocating her. We were able to interview Herman briefly this morning, and he had no scratch marks. He also said that Britta was already dead when he came home. That she was lying in bed with a pillow over her face.'

'But he still claims that her death was his fault,' Paula interjected.

'So what does he mean by that?' Gösta frowned. 'Is he protecting somebody?'

'Yes, that's what we think too.' Paula relented and put the packet of biscuits back on the table, sliding it towards Gösta. 'Here, knock yourself out,' she said in English.

'What?' said Gösta, whose knowledge of that language

371

was limited to golf-related terms, although even in those instances his pronunciation left a lot to be desired.

'Never mind. Go ahead and lick off the chocolate,' said Paula.

'And then we have the thumbprint,' said Martin, listening with amusement to Gösta and Paula's friendly squabbling. If he didn't know better, he'd have said his old colleague was actually enjoying being at work.

'A single thumbprint on one button – not much to write home about,' said Gösta gloomily.

'No, not by itself, but if that thumbprint comes from the same person who left his DNA under Britta's fingernails, then I think there's cause for optimism.' Martin underscored the letters 'DNA' on his notepad.

'When will the DNA profile be ready?' asked Paula.

'The lab is estimating we'll have it by Thursday,' replied Martin.

'Okay, then we'll run a DNA sampling afterwards.' Paula stretched out her legs. Sometimes she wondered whether Johanna's pregnancy symptoms were contagious. So far she had shooting pains in her legs, strange little twinges, and a ravenous appetite.

'So do we have any candidates for DNA sampling?' Gösta was well into his third biscuit.

'I was thinking of Axel and Frans,' said Paula.

'Are we really going to wait till Thursday? It'll take a while to get the results, and scratches heal pretty fast, so we might as well take the samples as soon as possible,' said Gösta.

'Good thinking, Gösta,' said Martin, surprised. 'We'll do it tomorrow. Anything else? Anything we've forgotten or left out?'

'What do you mean, "left out"?' said a voice from the doorway. Mellberg came in with a panting Ernst in tow. The dog immediately smelled Gösta's stack of biscuit remains and lunged forward to sit at his feet. His begging had the desired result, and the biscuits were disposed of in a flash.

'We're just going over a few things, making sure we haven't overlooked anything,' explained Martin, pointing at the documents lying on the table in front of them. 'We were just saying that we need to take samples from Axel and Frans tomorrow.'

'Oh right, do that,' said Mellberg impatiently, afraid that he might get drawn into the actual work that needed to be done. 'Just carry on with what you were doing. It looks good.' He called Ernst who, tail wagging, followed him back to his office where he lay down in his usual place at his master's feet under the desk.

'I see that the idea of finding someone to adopt that dog has been put on ice,' said Paula, amused.

'I think we can consider Ernst 'taken'. Although damned if I know who's actually taking care of whom. There are also rumours that Mellberg has turned into quite the salsa king in his old age.' Gösta chuckled.

Martin lowered his voice and whispered: 'I've heard that too . . . And this morning when I went into his office, he was on the floor doing stretches.'

'You've got to be kidding!' said Gösta, wide-eyed. 'How was it going?'

'It wasn't.' Martin laughed. 'He was trying to touch his toes, but his stomach got in the way. Just to name one reason.'

'All right, you two. It's actually my mother who teaches the salsa class that Mellberg is taking,' Paula admonished them. Gösta and Martin stared at her in astonishment.

'Mamma invited him over for lunch a few days ago, and he was . . . really quite pleasant,' she told them.

Now Martin and Gösta were openly gawping at her.

'Mellberg is taking salsa classes from your mother? And he's been over to your place for lunch? Pretty soon you'll be calling him "Pappa"!' Martin laughed loudly, and Gösta joined in.

'Cut it out, you guys,' said Paula crossly as she stood up. 'We're done here, right?' She strode out of the room. Martin and Gösta exchanged disconcerted glances, but then couldn't help howling with laughter again. It was too good to be true.

The weekend had brought full-fledged warfare. Dan and Belinda had shouted non-stop at each other, until Anna thought her head was going to explode from all the ruckus. She had admonished them several times, asking them to show some consideration for Adrian and Emma, and luckily that argument seemed to have an effect on both of them. Even though Belinda would never openly admit it, Anna could tell that she liked her kids, and because of that Anna was willing to overlook some of her defiant teenage behaviour. She also thought that Dan didn't really understand what things were like for his eldest daughter, or why she reacted the way she did. It was as if the two of them had arrived at a stalemate, and neither knew what to do about it. Anna sighed as she walked about the living room, picking up toys which the kids seemed to have spread over every inch of the floor.

Over the past few days she had also been trying to come to terms with the discovery that she and Dan were going to have a child together. Her mind was still in a whirl, but she had managed to suppress the worst of her fears. She had also started feeling just as sick as she'd felt during her first two pregnancies. She didn't throw up very often, but she did go around with a queasy, seesawing feeling in her stomach, as if she were constantly seasick. Dan had noticed that she'd lost her usual appetite, and like a worried mother hen, he kept trying to tempt her with all sorts of food.

She sat down on the sofa and put her head between her

knees, focusing on her breathing in an effort to bring the nausea under control. The last time, when she was pregnant with Adrian, it had lasted until her sixth month, which had seemed like for ever. Upstairs she could hear agitated voices rising and falling to the accompaniment of Belinda's pounding music. She couldn't cope with all this. She just couldn't cope. The nausea was getting worse, and her gag reflex made sour bile rise to her mouth. She leapt up and ran for the bathroom, knelt down in front of the toilet, and tried to spit out what was surging up and down her throat. But nothing came out.

After several minutes of dry heaves, which brought her no relief, she gave up and got to her feet to wipe her mouth on a towel. As she did, she caught a glimpse of herself in the bathroom mirror. What she saw alarmed her. She was as pale as the white towel she was holding, and her eyes were big and scared. Just the way she'd looked when she was with Lucas. And yet everything was so different now. So much better. She ran her hand over her stomach, which was still flat. So much hope. And so much fear. All gathered in one little spot inside her womb. So dependent, so tiny.

Of course she'd thought about having a baby with Dan. But not now, not yet. Sometime in the far distant future. After things had calmed down, stabilized. Still, now that it had happened, it hadn't crossed her mind even for one moment to terminate the pregnancy. The connection was already there. The invisible, fragile, and yet strong connection between her and what was not yet visible to the naked eye. She took a deep breath and exited the bathroom. By now the loud voices had moved downstairs to the hallway.

'I'm going over to Linda's. Why is that so fucking difficult to understand! I have my friends, you know. Or are you going to forbid me to see my friends too?'

Anna could sense that Dan was about to launch into a scathing reply, and in that moment her patience ran out.

Steaming with fury, she strode out to the hall and bellowed: 'It's time for the two of you to SHUT UP! Do you understand? You're both acting like children, and it's going to STOP! RIGHT NOW!' She held up her finger and went on before either of them could interrupt. 'You, Dan, need to bloody well stop yelling at Belinda. You know you can't just lock her up and throw away the key! She's seventeen years old, and she needs to see her friends!'

Belinda's face lit up with a delighted smile, but Anna wasn't finished.

'And you, young lady, need to stop behaving like a brat and start acting like a grown-up, if you want to be treated like one! I don't want to hear any more rubbish about me and the kids living here, because we're staying whether you like it or not, and we'd be happy to get to know you if you'd just give us a chance!'

Anna paused to catch her breath and then continued in a tone that made Dan and Belinda stand up straight like tin soldiers, out of sheer fright. 'And just so you know, we're not going anywhere, if that's your plan, because your father and I are having a baby, so my children and you and your sisters are going to be connected by a half-brother or -sister. And I'd really like all of us to be friends, but I can't do it alone. We need to help each other! In any case, the baby will be here in the spring, whether you choose to accept me or not, and I'll be damned if I'm going to put up with all this crap until then!' Anna burst into tears, as the other two stood frozen in place. Then Belinda started sobbing. She stared at Dan and Anna for a moment before she dashed out the front door, which closed behind her with a bang.

'Anna, darling, was that really necessary?' said Dan wearily. Emma and Adrian had also witnessed the confrontation and were standing in the hall, staring at them in bewilderment.

'Oh, go to hell,' said Anna, grabbing her jacket. For a second time the front door closed with a bang.

'Hi, where have you been?' Patrik met Erica at the door, giving her a kiss on the lips. Maja wanted a kiss from her too and came toddling over, holding out her arms.

'I've had two very interesting conversations, I can tell you that much,' said Erica, hanging up her jacket and going with Patrik into the living room.

'Oh, really? About what?' he asked. He sat down on the floor and went on with what he and Maja had been doing when they heard Erica come in. They were building the world's tallest tower out of blocks.

'I thought Maja was supposed to be the one learning to use building blocks,' laughed Erica, sitting down next to them. She watched with amusement as her husband, with great concentration, attempted to place a red block on top of the tower that was now taller than Maja.

'Shh . . .,' said Patrik, sticking out his tongue as he steadied his hand to put the block on top of the rather rickety construction.

'Maja, can you give Mamma the yellow block?' Erica whispered to her daughter, pointing at a block at the very bottom. Maja's face lit up at the thought of doing her mother a favour. She leaned down and swiftly pulled out the block, causing Patrik's carefully stacked structure to collapse.

Patrik sat there, holding the red block in the air. 'Thanks a lot,' he sulked, glaring at Erica. 'Do you have any idea what skill it takes to build a tower that tall? What a steady hand it requires?'

'I see somebody is finally starting to understand what I've been saying for the past year about feeling understimulated,' laughed Erica as she leaned forward to kiss her husband.

'Hmmm, well, yes. I get it,' he said, kissing her back with a flick of his tongue. Erica returned the invitation, and what

377

had started out as a kiss developed into some light groping, which didn't stop until Maja, with perfect aim, threw a block at her father's head.

'Ow!' He put his hand to his head, and then raised his finger to warn Maja. 'What on earth do you think you're doing? Throwing blocks at Pappa just when he has a chance to do a little groping with Mamma?'

'Patrik!' Erica slapped him on the shoulder. 'Is it really necessary to teach our daughter the word "grope" at her age?'

'If she wants a little brother or sister, she'll just have to put up with the sight of her mother and father groping,' he said, and Erica saw that he had that gleam in his eye.

She stood up. 'I think we'll wait for a while with the little brother or sister. But I guess we could get in some practice tonight . . .' She winked and went out to the kitchen. They had finally managed to resume that part of their life together. It was unbelievable what a negative effect the arrival of a baby could have on a couple's sex life, but after a rather lean year in that respect, things had begun to improve. Although after spending a whole year at home, she couldn't yet imagine doing anything about a sibling for Maja. She felt as if she needed to settle into being a grown-up again before she could contemplate a return to the world of babies.

'So what were these interesting conversations you had today?' asked Patrik, following her out to the kitchen.

Erica told him about her two excursions to Uddevalla and what she'd found out.

'But you don't recognize those names?' asked Patrik, frowning after she told him what Herman had said.

'Well, that's the strange thing. I can't remember ever hearing them before, and yet there's something . . . I don't know. Paul Heckel and Friedrich Hück. Somehow they sound familiar.'

'So you and Kjell Ringholm are going to join forces to track down this . . . Hans Olavsen?' Patrik looked sceptical, and Erica could tell what he was getting at.

'Okay, I know it's a long shot. I have no idea what role Hans might have played, but something tells me it's important. And even if this has nothing to do with the murders, he seems to have meant something to my mother, and that was how I got started on all this in the first place. I wanted to find out more about her.'

'Well, just be careful.' Patrik put a saucepan of water on the stove. 'Would you like some tea, by the way?'

'Yes please.' Erica sat down at the kitchen table. 'What do you mean "be careful"?'

'According to what I've heard, Kjell is a very slick journalist, so just watch out that he doesn't exploit you.'

'I don't see how he could. The worst that could happen is that he might take the information I dig up and not give me any in return. And I'm willing to take that risk. But I actually don't think he'd do something like that. We agreed that I would talk to Axel Frankel about the Norwegian and also check whether he's listed in any official Swedish records. And Kjell is going to talk to his father. Although he wasn't exactly thrilled about the prospect.'

'No, those two don't seem to get along very well,' said Patrik, pouring boiling water into two cups, each supplied with a teabag. 'I've read a number of articles that Kjell wrote where he really let his father have it.'

'Sounds like it'll be an interesting conversation, then,' said Erica, taking the cup that Patrik handed her. She looked at him as she sipped the hot tea. They could hear Maja prattling with some imaginary playmate out in the living room. She was probably talking to the doll, which she'd refused to let out of her sight the past few days.

'How does it feel not to be part of the work they're doing at the station right now?' she asked.

'I'd be lying if I said it wasn't difficult. But I realize what an opportunity this is to stay home with Maja, and my job will still be there when I go back. That's not to say that I hope there will be more murder investigations, but, well . . . you know what I mean.'

'And how is Karin doing?' asked Erica, trying to keep her tone of voice as neutral as possible.

Patrik paused a second before answering. Then he said, 'I don't know. She seems so . . . sad. I don't think things have turned out the way she imagined, and now she's stuck in a situation that . . . no, I don't really know. I feel a little sorry for her.'

'Does she regret leaving you?' asked Erica, and then waited tensely for his reply. They hadn't ever talked about his marriage to Karin, and the few times that she had asked about it, he had given her curt, one-word answers.

'No, I don't think so. Or rather . . . I don't know. I think she regrets doing what she did, and that I caught them in the act the way I did.' He gave a bitter laugh as he pictured the scene he'd put out of his mind for so long. 'But I don't know . . . I realize now that she did what she did largely because the two of us just weren't getting along.'

'But do you think she's forgotten about that?' asked Erica. 'Sometimes we have a tendency to only remember the good stuff.'

'True, but I think she does remember how things really were. Of course she does,' said Patrik, although he sounded a bit doubtful. Eager to drop the subject, he asked: 'So what's on the agenda for tomorrow?'

Erica knew exactly what he was up to, but she let it go. 'I was thinking of having a little chat with Axel. And I'll make a few calls to the civil registry and tax authorities, see if I can dig up anything about Hans.'

'Wait a minute, don't you have a book to write too?' Patrik laughed, although he still sounded nervous.

'There's plenty of time for that, especially since I've already done most of the research. And I'm going to have a hard time concentrating on my book until I get this out of my system, so just let me . . .'

'Okay, okay,' said Patrik, holding up his hands. 'You're a big girl, and you know how to organize your time. Maja and I will take care of our own schedule, and you can take care of yours.' He got up, kissing Erica on the top of the head as he walked past.

'I've got to go and build a new masterpiece. I was thinking of a model of the Taj Mahal, built to scale.'

Erica shook her head, laughing. Sometimes she wondered if the man she'd married was completely sane. Probably not, she decided.

Anna spotted her from some distance away. A short, solitary figure at the far end of the floating docks. She hadn't intended to go looking for her. But as soon as she came down the slope of Galärbacken and saw Belinda, she knew that she would have to go out and talk to the girl.

Belinda didn't hear her approach. She was sitting on the dock, smoking, a packet of Gula Blend and a book of matches next to her.

'Hi,' said Anna.

Belinda flinched. She glanced at the cigarette in her hand and for a second seemed to consider hiding it somehow, but then she defiantly stuck it in her mouth and inhaled deeply.

'Could I have one?' asked Anna, sitting down next to Belinda.

'You smoke?' asked Belinda in surprise, but she handed over the pack.

'I used to. For five years. But my . . . former husband . . . He didn't like it.' That was a slight understatement. One time, in the beginning, when Lucas found her

381

smoking a cigarette in secret, he'd put it out on the crook of her arm. She still had a faint scar from that incident.

'You won't tell Pappa, will you?' said Belinda sullenly, waving her cigarette. But then she added a subdued: 'Please?'

'If you won't tell on me, I won't tell on you,' said Anna, closing her eyes as she took the first drag.

'Should you really be smoking? I mean because of the . . . baby?' said Belinda, suddenly sounding like an indignant old lady.

Anna laughed. 'This is going to be the first and last cigarette I smoke while I'm pregnant. I promise.'

They sat in silence for a while, blowing smoke rings out over the water. The summer heat had vanished completely, replaced by a raw September chill. But at least there was no wind, and the calm, glittering surface of the water stretched out before them. The harbour looked deserted, with only a few boats in the marina – not like in the summer when they were lined up several rows deep.

'It's not easy, is it?' said Anna, looking at the water.

'What?' asked Belinda, sounding surly and still uncertain what attitude to adopt.

'Being a kid. Although you're almost grown-up now.'

'You don't know anything about it,' replied Belinda, tossing a pebble into the water.

'No, you're right, I was born the age that I am now,' laughed Anna, giving Belinda a poke in the side to show she was teasing. She was rewarded with a tiny smile that disappeared instantly. Anna didn't say anything else. She wanted to allow Belinda to determine the pace of their conversation. Neither of them spoke for several minutes until, out of the corner of her eye, Anna noticed Belinda cautiously peering at her.

'Do you feel really sick?'

Anna nodded. 'Like a seasick polecat.'

'Why would a polecat get seasick?' asked Belinda, giggling.

382

'Why not? Can you prove that a polecat never gets seasick? If so, I'd like to see the evidence. Because that's exactly how I feel. Like a seasick polecat.'

'Oh, you're just pulling my leg,' said Belinda, but she couldn't help laughing.

'Joking aside, I feel really fat.'

'Mamma felt like shit when she was pregnant with Lisen. I was old enough then to remember it. She was . . . Oh, sorry. Maybe I shouldn't talk about when Mamma and Pappa . . .' She fell silent, embarrassed. She reached for another cigarette and cupped her hands around it to light up.

'You know, you're more than welcome to talk about your mother. Whenever you like. I have no problem with the fact that Dan had a life before he met me – he had the three of you in that life, after all. With your mother. Honestly, you needn't feel like you're betraying your father just because you love your mother. And I promise that I won't be offended if you talk about Pernilla. Not at all.' Anna placed her hand over Belinda's hand lying on the dock. At first Belinda seemed about to pull away, but then she left her hand where it was. After a few seconds Anna took her hand away, and she too reached for another cigarette. She was going to have to have two cancer-sticks during this pregnancy. But then she would stop. Cold turkey.

'I'm really good at helping out with babies,' said Belinda, meeting Anna's eye. 'I helped my mother a lot with Lisen when she was little.'

'Dan has actually told me about that. About how he and your mother practically had to force you to go out and play with your friends instead of taking care of the baby. And he said you were really good at it. So I'm hoping that I can count on a little assistance in the spring. You can take care of all the nappies.' Again she poked Belinda in the side, and this time the girl poked her back.

With a smile lighting up her eyes, she said, 'I'll only take care of the nappies that have pee on them. Deal?' Belinda held out her hand, and Anna shook it.

'Deal. The pee nappies are yours.' Then she added, 'Your father can take care of the shitty ones.'

Their laughter echoed through the deserted harbour.

Anna would always remember that moment as one of the best in her life. That moment when the ice thawed.

Axel was in the middle of packing when she arrived. He met her at the door, holding a shirt on a hanger in each hand. Behind him, she could see a garment bag hanging on a door in the hall.

'Are you going somewhere?' asked Erica.

Axel nodded as he carefully hung up the shirts so they wouldn't wrinkle.

'Yes, I need to get back to work soon. I'm leaving for Paris on Friday.'

'Can you really leave without finding out who . . .' She let the words hover in mid-air.

'I don't have a choice,' said Axel grimly. 'Of course I'll catch the first plane home if the police need my assistance in any way. But I really need to get back to my work. And it's not very constructive just to sit here brooding.' He rubbed his eyes wearily, and Erica noticed how haggard he was starting to look. He seemed to have aged several years since she last saw him.

'It'll probably do you good to get away for a while,' she said gently. Then she hesitated. 'I have a few questions, several things that I'd like to talk to you about. Could I have a few minutes of your time? If you're up to it?'

Axel nodded, looking tired and resigned, then motioned for her to come inside. She stopped at the sofa on the veranda, where they'd sat before, but this time he continued on past her, into the next room.

'What a beautiful room,' she said breathlessly, looking around. It was like stepping into a museum of a bygone era. Everything in the room dated from the forties, and even though it looked clean and tidy, the room seemed to smell old.

'Yes, well, neither our parents nor Erik and I had much interest in new-fangled things. Mother and Father never made any major changes to the house, and Erik and I didn't either. Besides, that was a period filled with many beautiful things, so I see no reason to replace the furniture with more modern pieces, which I think are much uglier,' he said, running his hand over an elegant tallboy.

They sat down on a sofa with brown upholstery. It wasn't particularly comfortable, and it forced them to sit up nice and straight.

'You wanted to ask me something?' said Axel kindly, but with a trace of impatience.

'Yes, that's right,' said Erica, suddenly feeling embarrassed. This was the second time she'd come here and bothered Axel with her questions, when he had so many other things to worry about. But as before, she decided that, since she was here, she might as well find out what she wanted to know.

'I've been doing some research into my mother's life, and also about her friends: your brother, Frans Ringholm, and Britta Johansson.'

Axel nodded, twiddling his thumbs as he waited for her to go on.

'There was one other person who was part of that group.'

Axel still didn't speak.

'Towards the end of the war, a Norwegian resistance fighter came here on my grandfather's boat . . . The same boat that I know you often travelled on.'

He looked at her without blinking, but she saw him tense up when she mentioned the trips that he'd made, crossing to the Norwegian side.

'He was a good man, your grandfather,' said Axel quietly after a moment. His hands now lay still on his lap. 'One of the best I've ever known.'

Erica had never met her maternal grandfather, and it warmed her heart to hear him described so positively.

'From what I understand, you were in prison at the time when Hans Olavsen stowed away on my grandfather's boat. He arrived here in 1944, and according to what we've found out so far, he stayed until right after the war ended.'

'You said "we",' Axel interrupted her. 'Who do you mean by "we"?' His voice sounded tense.

Erica hesitated. Then she merely said, 'By "we" I mean that I've had help from Christian at the library here in Fjällbacka. That's all.' She didn't want to mention Kjell, and Axel seemed to accept her explanation.

'Yes, I was in prison back then,' he said, tensing up again. It was as if all the muscles in his body were suddenly reminded of what they had endured and reacted by tightening up.

'So you never met him?'

Axel shook his head. 'No, he was already gone by the time I returned.'

'When did you come back to Fjällbacka?'

'In June of 1945. With the white buses.'

'White buses?' asked Erica, but then she recalled hearing something about them in her history classes.

'It was a plan initiated by Folke Bernadotte,' replied Axel, confirming what she vaguely recalled. 'He organized the transport to bring home Scandinavian prisoners who'd been in German concentration camps. The buses were white with red crosses painted on the roof and sides, so that they wouldn't be mistaken for military targets.'

'But why would there be a risk that they'd be mistaken for military targets if they were carrying prisoners after the war ended?' asked Erica.

386

Axel smiled at her ignorance and began twiddling his thumbs again. 'The first buses went to pick up prisoners as early as March and April of 1945, after negotiating with the Germans. They brought home fifteen thousand prisoners that time around. Then, after the war ended, they brought home another ten thousand in May and June. I was on one of the last buses in June 1945.' It all sounded very matter-of-fact as he explained what happened, but under the reserved tone of voice Erica could hear echoes of the horrors he had experienced.

'And Hans Olavsen disappeared from here in June 1945. Which means he must have left shortly before you arrived. Is that right?' she asked.

'It was probably only a gap of a few days,' Axel replied, nodding. 'But you'll have to forgive me if my memory is a bit muddled on that point. I was extremely . . . exhausted when I came back.'

'Of course. I understand,' said Erica, looking down. It was a strange feeling to be talking to someone who had seen the German concentration camps from the inside.

'Did your brother tell you anything about Hans? Anything you remember? Anything at all? I have the feeling that Erik and his friends spent a lot of time with Hans Olavsen during the year he was here in Fjällbacka.'

Axel stared out the window, apparently searching his memory. He tilted his head to one side and frowned.

'I recall there was something between the Norwegian and your mother, if you won't be offended by me saying so.'

'Not at all.' Erica waved her hand dismissively. 'That was a whole lifetime ago, and I found out the same thing myself.'

'How about that? I guess my memory isn't as bad as I sometimes think it is.' He smiled and turned back to look at her. 'Yes, I'm quite sure that Erik told me there was some sort of romance between Elsy and Hans.'

'How did she react when he left? Do you remember anything about her from that time?'

'Not much, I'm afraid. Of course she wasn't really herself after what happened to your grandfather. And she left very soon afterwards to start studying . . . home economics, if I remember rightly. And then we lost contact with each other. By the time she returned to Fjällbacka a few years later, I had already begun working abroad and I wasn't home very often. She and Erik didn't have any contact either, from what I remember. That's not so unusual. People can be good friends as children and adolescents, but later, when adult life and its responsibilities set in, they tend to lose touch.' He turned to look out the window again.

'I know what you mean,' said Erica. She was disappointed that Axel didn't seem to have any information about Hans either. 'And no one ever mentioned where Hans had gone? He didn't tell Erik?'

Axel shook his head apologetically. 'I'm terribly sorry. I wish I could help you, but I wasn't really myself when I came back, and afterwards I had other things on my mind. But surely it must be possible to track him down through the authorities,' he said encouragingly, getting to his feet.

Taking the hint, Erica got up too. 'Yes, that's my next step. If I'm lucky, that might solve everything. For all I know, he might not have moved very far away.'

'Well, I wish you the best of luck,' said Axel, shaking her hand. 'I know how important it is to find out about the past so that we can live in the present. Believe me, I know.' He patted her hand, and Erica smiled gratefully at his attempt to console her.

'Have you found out anything more about the medal, by the way?' he asked as she was just about to open the front door.

'No, I'm afraid not,' she told him, feeling more discouraged with each passing minute. 'I talked to an expert on

388

Nazi medals in Göteborg, but unfortunately the medal is too common to be traced.'

'I'm really sorry that I couldn't be of more help.'

'That's okay. It was a long shot,' she said, waving goodbye.

The last she saw of Axel, he was standing in the doorway, watching her leave. She felt very, very sorry for him. But something he'd said had given her an idea. Filled with determination, Erica headed back towards Fjällbacka.

Kjell hesitated before knocking. As he stood there at his father's door, he suddenly felt like a frightened little boy again. The memory transported him back to all those times he'd stood outside the prison gates clutching his mother's hand, his stomach gripped by equal parts fear and anticipation at the thought of seeing his father. Because, in the beginning, he had looked forward to the visits. He had missed Frans and longed to see him again, remembering only the good times: those brief periods when his father wasn't in prison, when he would swing Kjell through the air, or take him for walks in the woods, holding him by the hand and telling him all about the mushrooms and trees and bushes. Kjell had thought that his father knew about everything in the world. But at night he had needed to press his pillow over his ears to shut out the sounds of quarrelling, those hateful, horrid fights that never seemed to have a beginning or end. His mother and father would simply start up from where they'd left off the last time Frans had disappeared into prison, and they would keep on like that – the same arguments, the same physical abuse, over and over again – until the next time the police came and led his father away.

For that reason, Kjell's sense of anticipation dwindled with each year that passed, until he felt only fear as he stood in the visitors' room and saw his father's expectant face. And later the fear was transformed into hatred. In some ways it

389

would have been easier if he didn't have memories of those walks in the woods. Because what sparked his hatred and gave it fuel was the question that he had constantly asked himself as a child. How could his father, time after time, make the same choice to exclude everything? To exclude him? Abandoning him for a world that was grey and cold and that stripped away something in his eyes every time he had to go back.

Kjell pounded on the door, annoyed with himself for succumbing to his memories.

'I know you're in there! Open up!' he shouted and then listened tensely. Finally he heard the safety chain being lifted off and the bolt pulled back.

'Security against your pals, I assume,' snapped Kjell, forcing his way past Frans into the hall.

'What do you want now?' asked Frans.

Kjell was struck by the fact that his father suddenly looked so old. And frail. Then he dismissed the idea. The man was tougher than most people. He'd probably outlive them all.

'I want some information from you.' He went in and sat down on the sofa without waiting for an invitation.

Frans sat in the armchair across from him, but didn't say a word. Just waited.

'What do you know about a man by the name of Hans Olavsen?'

Frans gave a start but quickly regained control of himself. He casually leaned back in his chair, placing his hands on the armrests. 'Why do you want to know?' he asked, looking his son in the eyes.

'It's none of your business.'

'Why should I help you if you're going to take that attitude?'

Kjell leaned forward so that his face was only centimetres from his father's. He stared at him for a long time before he said coldly: 'Because you owe me. You owe me and need to take every little opportunity to help me if you don't want to run the risk that I'll dance on your grave when you're dead.'

For a moment something flashed through Frans's eyes. Something that had been lost. Maybe the memory of the walks through the woods and strong arms lifting a little boy towards the sky. Then it was gone. He looked at his son and said calmly:

'Hans Olavsen was a Norwegian resistance fighter who was seventeen years old when he came to Fjällbacka. I think it was in 1944. A year later he left. That's all I know.'

'Bullshit,' said Kjell, leaning back again. 'I know that you spent a lot of time together – you, Elsy Moström, Britta Johansson, and Erik Frankel. And now Britta and Erik have been murdered within months of each other. Don't you think that's a bit strange?'

Frans ignored the question. Instead he said, 'What does the Norwegian have to do with that?'

'I don't know. But I'm planning to find out,' snarled Kjell, clenching his jaws in an attempt to keep his anger in check. 'So what else do you know about him? Tell me about the time you spent together, tell me why he left. Every detail you can remember.'

Frans sighed and looked as if he was casting his mind back. 'So it's the details you want . . . Let's see if I can remember anything. Well, he lived at Elsy's parents' house, and he had come here by stowing away on her father's boat.'

'I already know that,' said Kjell. 'What else?'

'He got a job working on boats that carried cargo down the coast, but he spent his free time with us. We were actually two years younger than he was, but that didn't seem to bother him. We enjoyed each other's company. Some more than others,' he said, and sixty years hadn't erased the bitterness that he'd felt back then.

'Hans and Elsy,' said Kjell drily.

'How did you know that?' asked Frans, surprised to find that he still felt a pang at the thought of those two together. His heart definitely had a longer memory than his mind.

'I just know. Go on.'

'Well, as you say, Hans and Elsy got together, and I'm sure you also know that I wasn't happy about it.'

'I didn't know that.'

'Well, it's true. I had a crush on Elsy, but she chose him. And the irony was that Britta was infatuated with me, but I wasn't interested in her at all. Of course I sometimes imagined sleeping with her, but something always told me that it would be more trouble than it was worth, so I never did.'

'How magnanimous of you,' said Kjell sarcastically. Frans merely raised one eyebrow.

'So what happened then? If Hans and Elsy were so close, why did he leave?'

'Well, it's the oldest story in the world. He promised her the moon, and when the war ended, he said that he had to return to Norway to find his family, and then he'd be back. But . . .' Frans shrugged and smiled bitterly.

'Do you think he was just toying with her?'

'I don't know, Kjell. I honestly don't know. It was sixty years ago, and we were very young. Maybe he meant what he said to Elsy, but then was overwhelmed by commitments back home. Or maybe he intended all along to run off as soon as he got the chance.' Frans shrugged. 'The only thing I know is that he said goodbye and told us that he would be back as soon as he straightened things out with his family. And then he left. And to be honest, I've hardly given him a thought since. I know that Elsy was upset for a while, but her mother saw to it that she got into some sort of school, and I have no idea what happened after that. By then I had already left Fjällbacka and . . . well, you know what happened then.'

'Yes, I do know,' said Kjell grimly, picturing once again the big grey prison gates.

'So I don't understand why this would be of any concern to you,' said Frans. 'He came here and then he disappeared. And I don't think any of us ever had contact with him again. So why all the interest?' Frans stared at Kjell.

'I can't tell you that,' replied his son crossly. 'But if there's any mystery about his departure, I'll get to the bottom of it, believe me.' He gave his father a defiant look.

'I believe you, Kjell. I believe you,' replied Frans wearily.

Kjell glanced at his father's hand, lying on the armrest of his chair. It was an old man's hand. Wrinkled and sinewy, with age spots on the wizened skin. So different from the hand that had held his when they went for walks in the woods. That hand had been strong and smooth, and so warm as it enveloped his own small hand. So safe and secure.

'Looks like it's going to be a good year for mushrooms,' he heard himself saying.

Frans stared at him in surprise. Then his expression softened, and he replied quietly: 'Yes, it looks like it will be, Kjell. It does indeed.'

Axel packed with military precision. Years of travelling had taught him to do that. Nothing was left to chance. A pair of trousers carelessly folded might mean having to laboriously press them on the hotel's ironing board. A poorly replaced top on a tube of toothpaste might mean an even worse disaster: a caseload of laundry. So he placed everything into the big suitcase with the greatest care.

He sat down on the bed. This had been his room when he was growing up, but in later years he had chosen to change the furnishings. Model airplanes and comics didn't really belong in a grown man's bedroom. He wondered whether he would ever return here. It had been difficult to stay in the house over the past weeks. At the same time, it had seemed necessary.

He got up and headed for Erik's bedroom, a few doors down the long corridor. Axel smiled when he went in and sat down on his brother's bed. The room was filled with books. Of course. The shelves were crammed with leather-bound volumes, and there were piles of them on the floor, many with little Post-it notes stuck to them. Erik had never grown tired of his books, his facts, his dates, and the solid reality that they offered him. In that sense, things had been easier for Erik. Reality could be found in black and white. No grey zones, no political chicanery or moral ambiguities, which were everyday fare in Axel's world. Just concrete facts. The Battle of Hastings was in 1066. Napoleon died in 1821. Germany surrendered on 5 May 1945 . . .

Axel reached for a book lying on Erik's bed. A thick volume about how Germany was rebuilt after the war. Axel put it back on the bed. He knew everything about that topic. His life for the past sixty years had revolved around the war and its aftermath. But most of all, it had revolved around himself. Erik had realized that. He had pointed out the shortcomings in Axel's life, and in his own life. Recounted them as dry facts. Apparently without any emotion. But Axel knew his brother well, and he was aware that behind all the facts was more emotion than most people he'd met would ever be capable of feeling.

He wiped away the tear that was trickling down his cheek. Here, in Erik's room, things were suddenly not as crystal-clear as he'd like them to be. Axel had based his whole life on the absence of ambiguities. He had built his life around right and wrong. Presented himself as the person who could point and say which of these camps people belonged to. Yet it was Erik, in his tranquil world of books, who had known everything about right and wrong. Somewhere deep inside, Axel had always understood that. Understood that the battle to remove himself from the grey zone between good and evil would take a greater toll on his brother than on him.

But Erik had fought hard. For sixty years he had watched Axel come and go, heard him talk about the efforts he'd made in the service of good. Allowed him to construct an image of himself as the man who brought everyone to justice. In silence, Erik had watched and listened. Looked at him with those gentle eyes of his behind the glasses he wore, and let him keep his delusions. But somewhere deep inside, Axel had always known that he was fooling himself, not Erik.

And now he would have to continue to live the lie. Go back to work. Go back to the laborious hunt that had to continue. He couldn't ease up on the tempo, because soon it would be too late, soon there would be no one left who could remember, and no one left to punish. Soon there would be only history books left to bear witness.

Axel got up and glanced around the room one more time before he went back to his own bedroom. He still had a lot of packing to do.

It had a been a long time since Erica had visited the graves of her maternal grandparents. The conversation with Axel had reminded her of them, and on her way home she decided to make a detour to the cemetery. She opened the gate, hearing the gravel crunch under her feet as she walked along the path.

First she passed the gravesite belonging to her parents. It was straight ahead, on the left-hand side of the path. She squatted down and pulled out a few weeds around the headstone so that it looked tidy, reminding herself to bring fresh flowers next time. She stared at her mother's name etched into the stone. Elsy Falck. There were so many things Erica wished she could ask her. If it weren't for the car accident four years ago, she could have talked to her mother in person instead of having to fumble around, trying to find out more about why Elsy was the way she was.

As a child Erica had always blamed herself. As an adult too. She'd thought there was something wrong with her, that she had somehow failed to meet her mother's expectations. Why else had her mother never hugged her, never really talked with her? Why had her mother never said that she loved her, or even liked her? For a long time Erica had harboured the feeling that she wasn't good enough and never had been. Of course her father Tore had done his best to compensate. He had lavished so much time and love on her and Anna. He was always willing to listen, always ready to blow on a grazed knee, and his warm embrace always felt so safe and secure. But that had never been enough. Not when their mother seemed unable even to stand the sight of her daughters, let alone give them a hug.

That was why Erica was so astonished by the image of her mother that was now emerging. How could that warm and gentle girl, as everyone described her, have turned into someone so cold, so distant that she treated her own children like strangers?

Erica stretched out her hand to touch her mother's name on the headstone.

'What happened to you, Mamma?' she whispered, feeling her throat tighten. When she stood up a few minutes later, she was more determined than ever to uncover as much of her mother's story as she could. There was definitely something there, something that still eluded her and that needed to be brought to light.

And no matter what it cost her, she was going to find out what it was.

Erica cast one last look at her parents' grave and then moved on a few metres to the plot where her maternal grandparents were buried. Elof and Hilma Moström. She had never met them. The tragedy that took her grandfather's life occurred long before she was born, and her grandmother had passed away ten years after he died. Elsy had never talked about them. But Erica was happy that so far in her research she had heard them described as kind and warm. Again she squatted down and stared at the headstone, as if trying to make it speak to her. But the stone was mute. There was nothing for her to learn here. If she wanted to find out the truth, she was going to have to look elsewhere.

She walked towards the hill, heading up to the church slope to take a shortcut home. At the foot of the hill she automatically glanced to her right, towards the big, grey, moss-covered gravestone that stood off by itself, right at the base of the granite cliff that formed the border of one side of the cemetery. She took another step up the slope, but then stopped short. She backed up until she stood in front of the big, grey stone, her heart pounding hard in her chest. Disconnected facts, disconnected remarks started whirling through her head. She squinted to make sure she was seeing correctly, then took a step forward so she stood very, very close to the stone. She even ran her finger over the text, to be sure that her brain wasn't playing tricks on her.

Then all the facts fell into place in her mind with an audible thud. Of course. Now she knew what had happened, or at least some of it. She took out her mobile and punched in Patrik's number with trembling fingers. It was time for him to intervene.

Herman's daughters had just left. They came over every day, his blessed, blessed daughters. It did his heart good to see them sitting next to each other at his bedside. So alike, yet so unlike one another. And he saw Britta in all of them. Anna-Greta had her nose, Birgitta her eyes, and Margareta, the youngest, had inherited those little dimples that Britta always had when she smiled.

397

Herman closed his eyes to prevent himself from crying. He didn't have the strength to cry any more. He had no more tears left. But he was forced to open his eyes again, because every time he shut them, he pictured Britta the way she had looked when he lifted the pillow away from her face. He hadn't needed to move the pillow to know. But he had done it nonetheless. He wanted to have his suspicions confirmed. Wanted to see what he had done through his impulsive action. Because of course he had understood. The very moment he entered the bedroom and saw her lying there, motionless, with the pillow over her face, he had understood.

When he lifted it away and saw her rigid expression, he had died. At that precise moment, he too had died. He could only lie down next to her, take her in his arms and pull her close. If it had been up to him, he would still be lying there. He would have gone on holding her as her body grew colder and colder, letting the memories flood his mind.

Herman stared up at the ceiling as he thought about the past. Summer days when they took the boat out to the beach on Valö, with the girls in the cabin and Britta sitting on deck, her face tilted up towards the sun, her long legs stretched out in front of her, and her silky blonde hair hanging down her back. He saw her open her eyes, turn her head to him, and smile happily. He waved to her as he sat at the tiller, feeling in his heart how fortunate he was.

Then a shadow passed over his face. He was thinking about the first time that she told him about that unmentionable subject. A dark winter afternoon when the girls were at school. She told him to sit down because she needed to tell him something. His heart had nearly stopped, and he was ashamed to remember that his first thought had been that she was going to leave him, that she had met someone else. So what she told him had come almost as a relief. He'd listened. She'd talked. For a long time. And when it was time for them to pick up the girls, they had agreed never to speak of the topic again. What was done was done. He hadn't viewed her any differently afterwards. Hadn't felt differently about her or talked to her in a different way. How could he? How could that have forced out the images in his mind of the days that had flowed together to form their quiet, happy life, or the marvellous nights they had shared? What she had told him could never outweigh all that. And so they had agreed never to mention it again.

But her illness had changed that. Had changed everything. It had come roaring through their life like a tsunami, tearing up everything by the roots. And he had allowed himself to be swept along. He had made a mistake. One fateful mistake. One phone call that he should never have made. But he had been naïve, believing it was time to air out what was musty and rotten. He had thought that if he just showed how Britta was suffering because of what had been hidden away for so long in her mind, then it would be clear that the time had finally come. It was wrong to fight it any longer. What had happened in the past had to come out so that they might have peace of mind. So Britta would have peace of mind. Good Lord, how naïve he had been. He might just as well have put the pillow over her face himself. He knew that. And now he couldn't bear the pain.

Herman closed his eyes in an attempt to close out everything, and this time he didn't see Britta's dead face. Instead, he saw her in a hospital bed. Pale and tired, but happy. Holding Anna-Greta in her arms. She raised her hand and waved to him. Motioning for him to come closer.

With one last sigh he let go of everything that was painful and, smiling, went towards them.

Patrik was staring straight ahead. Could Erica be right? It sounded completely crazy, and yet . . . logical. He sighed, aware of what a difficult task lay ahead of him.

'Come on, sweetie. We're going out for a little excursion,' he said, lifting up Maja and carrying her out to the hall. 'And we'll pick up Mamma on the way.'

A short time later he drove up to the gate of the cemetery where Erica was waiting, so impatient to get going that she was practically jumping up and down. Patrik had started feeling equally impatient, and he had to remind himself to ease off the accelerator as they drove towards Tanumshede. He could sometimes be a rather reckless driver, but if Maja was in the car, he always drove with the utmost caution.

'I'll do the talking, okay?' said Patrik as they parked in front of the station. 'You get to come along only because I don't feel like arguing with you about it – you'd win in the end anyway. But he's my boss, and I'm the one who has done this before. Understand?'

Erica nodded reluctantly as she lifted Maja out of the car.

'Do you think we should drive over to my mother's first, and ask her to watch Maja for a while? I mean, I know how you hate it when I take Maja into the station,' Patrik teased, getting an exasperated look in reply.

'Come on, you know I want to get this over with as soon as possible. And she doesn't seem to have suffered any harm from working a shift the last time she was here,' Erica told him with a wink.

'Hi! I didn't expect to see all of you here,' said Annika, surprised, her face lighting up when Maja gave her a big smile.

'We need to talk to Bertil,' said Patrik. 'Is he in?'

'Yes, he's in his office,' said Annika, giving them an enquiring look. She let them in, and Patrik headed briskly for Mellberg's office with Erica in tow, carrying Maja in her arms.

'Hedström! What are you doing here? And I see you've brought the whole family along,' said Mellberg, sounding grumpy as he stood up to say hello.

'There's something we need to talk to you about,' said Patrik, sitting down on one of the visitor's chairs without waiting for an invitation. Maja and Ernst had now caught sight of each other, to their mutual delight.

'Is he used to being around children?' asked Erica, hesitating to set her struggling daughter down on the floor.

'How the hell should I know?' said Mellberg, but then relented. 'He's the world's nicest dog. Wouldn't hurt a fly.' His voice betrayed a certain pride, and Patrik raised one eyebrow in amusement. His boss seemed to have really fallen for that dog.

Still not entirely convinced, Erica set her daughter down next to Ernst, who enthusiastically began licking the little girl's face. Maja reacted with a mixture of alarm and delight.

'So, what is it you want?' Mellberg stared at Patrik with some curiosity.

'I want you to obtain permission to open a grave.'

Mellberg started coughing, as if something was stuck in his throat. His face turned redder and redder as he struggled to breathe.

'Open a grave! Are you out of your mind, man!' he finally managed to splutter. 'Being on paternity leave must have affected your brain! Do you know how rare it is to get permission to open a grave? And I've already done it twice in the past few years. If I ask for another one, they're going to certify me as insane and lock me up in the loony bin! And whose body are we going to exhume now, by the way?'

'A Norwegian resistance fighter who disappeared in 1945,' said Erica calmly as she squatted down next to Patrik and scratched Ernst's ears.

'What did you say?' Mellberg stared at her open-mouthed, as if he thought he must have heard wrong.

Patiently Erica recounted everything that she'd learned about the four friends and the Norwegian who had come to Fjällbacka a year before the war ended. She explained that

401

there was no trace of him after June 1945, and their efforts to track him down had got nowhere.

'Couldn't he have stayed in Sweden? Or gone back to Norway? Have you checked with the authorities in both countries?' Mellberg looked extremely sceptical.

Erica got up from the floor and sat down on the other visitor's chair. She stared at Mellberg, as if she hoped to make him take her seriously through sheer force of will. And then she told him what Herman had said to her. That Paul Heckel and Friedrich Hück should be able to tell them where Hans Olavsen was.

'I thought the names seemed vaguely familiar, but I had no idea where I might have come across them. Until today. I went over to the cemetery to visit the graves of my parents and grandparents. And that's when I saw it.'

'Saw what?' asked Mellberg, puzzled.

She waved her hand. 'I'll get to that, if you'll allow me to.'

'Sure, okay, go on,' said Mellberg, who was starting to get interested, in spite of himself.

'There's a grave in the Fjällbacka cemetery that's a little different. It's from the First World War, and ten German soldiers are buried there – seven of them were identified and are listed by name, but three of them are unknown.'

'You forgot to tell him about the scribbled note,' said Patrik, who had resigned himself to taking a back seat while his wife explained things. A good man knows when it's time to give in.

'Oh, right. There's one other piece to the puzzle.' Erica told Mellberg about the page in Erik's notebook that had caught her attention when she studied the photograph from the crime scene, and the fact that it said '*Ignoto militi.*'

'How did you happen to see photos from the crime scene?' asked Mellberg angrily, glaring at Patrik.

'We'll discuss that later,' said Patrik. 'Please, just listen to what she has to say.'

402

Mellberg grumbled but acquiesced and indicated with a wave of his hand for Erica to continue.

'Erik Frankel wrote those words on a notepad, over and over, and I found out what they mean. It's an inscription on the Arc de Triomphe in Paris, or rather on the tomb of the unknown soldier. It means: "To the unknown soldier".'

This still wasn't making any lights go on in Mellberg's head, so Erica continued:

'That note stayed in the back of my mind. Here we have a Norwegian resistance fighter who disappears in 1945, and nobody knows where he went. We have Erik scribbling about an unknown soldier. And Britta talking about "old bones", and then we have the names that Herman gave me. It was only when I walked past that grave in Fjällbacka cemetery that I suddenly realized why those names had seemed so familiar: they're etched on the headstone.' Erica paused to catch her breath.

Mellberg stared at her. 'So Paul Heckel and Friedrich Hück are the names of two Germans from the First World War who are buried in a grave in Fjällbacka cemetery?'

'That's right,' said Erica, pondering how she should go on with her story.

But Mellberg beat her to it. 'So what you're saying is . . .'

She took a deep breath and glanced at Patrik before she continued. 'What I'm saying is, it's very likely there's an extra body in that grave. I think the Norwegian resistance fighter, Hans Olavsen, is buried there. And I'm not sure how it all fits together, but I'm convinced that's the key to the murders of Erik and Britta.'

She fell silent. No one spoke. The only thing to be heard in Mellberg's office was the sound of Maja and Ernst playing together.

After a moment Patrik said softly: 'I know this sounds crazy. But I've discussed the whole thing with Erica, and I think there's a lot to be said for her theory. I can't offer any concrete proof, but all the clues we have seem to point that way. And there's also a strong chance that Erica is right, and this is what's behind the two murders. I don't know how or why. But the first step is to establish whether there really is an extra body in the grave, and if so, how he died.'

Mellberg didn't reply. He clasped his hands and sat in silence, thinking. Finally he gave a loud sigh.

'Well, I must be out of my mind, but I think you might be right. There's no guarantee that I'll get permission. As I said, we have something of a track record with this type of thing, and the prosecutor is going to go through the roof. But I will try. That's all I can promise you.'

'That's all we're asking,' said Erica eagerly, looking as though she'd like to throw her arms around Mellberg.

'Okay, take it easy. I don't think I'll be successful, but I'll do my best. And at the moment I need some peace and quiet to work.'

'We're leaving right now,' said Patrik, getting to his feet. 'Let me know as soon as you hear anything.'

Mellberg didn't answer, just waved them out the door as he picked up the phone to start on what looked set to be the most difficult test of his persuasive abilities in his entire career.

FJÄLLBACKA 1945

He had been living with them for six months, and they
had known that they were in love for three months when
disaster struck. Elsy was standing on the veranda watering
her mother's flowers when she spotted them coming up
the stairs. And she understood as soon as she saw their
grim expressions. Behind her in the kitchen she could heard
her mother washing dishes, and part of her wanted to rush
inside and make her mother leave, chase her away before
she heard the news that Elsy knew she wouldn't be able
to bear. But she realized that it was futile. Instead, she
walked stiffly to the front door and opened it, letting in
the three men from one of the other fishing boats in
Fjällbacka.

'Is Hilma at home?' asked the eldest of them. She knew
he was the captain of the boat, and she nodded, turning to
lead the way to the kitchen.

When Hilma caught sight of them, she dropped the plate
she was holding and it hit the floor, shattering into a thousand pieces. 'No, no, oh dear God, no!' she said.

Elsy barely managed to catch her mother before she fell.
She lowered her on to a chair and held her tight until it felt
as if her own heart would leap out of her body. The three
fishermen stood awkwardly next to the table, fumbling with

the peaked caps they held in their hands. Finally the captain spoke.

'It was a mine, Hilma. We saw everything from our boat, and we got there as fast as we could. But . . . there was nothing we could do.'

'Oh dear God,' Hilma repeated, gasping for breath. 'What about all the others?'

Elsy was surprised that even at a moment like this her mother was able to think of the others, but then she pictured her father's crew in her mind. The men they knew so well, and whose families were about to receive the same news.

'There were no survivors,' said the captain, swallowing hard. 'We stayed there a long time, searching, but we didn't find anyone. Only the Oscarsson boy, but he was already dead by the time we pulled him into the boat.'

Tears were running down Hilma's face, and she bit her knuckles to keep from screaming. Elsy swallowed her own sobs and willed herself to be strong. How was her mother going to survive this? How was she herself going to survive it? Her dear, sweet father. Always ready with a kind word and a helping hand. How were they going to manage without him?

A discreet knock on the door interrupted them, and one of the messengers went to open up. Hans came into the kitchen, his face grey-tinged.

'I saw . . . that you had company. I thought . . . What's . . .?' He lowered his gaze. Elsy could see that he was afraid to bother them, but she was grateful that he'd come.

'Pappa's boat ran into a mine,' she said, her voice breaking. 'There were no survivors.'

Hans's knees buckled and he wavered for a moment. Then he went over to the cabinet where Elof kept the strong drink and resolutely filled six glasses, which he set on the table.

'I think we could all use a stiff drink right now,' he said

in his lilting Norwegian, which had become closer to Swedish the longer he'd stayed with them.

Everyone gratefully reached for a glass, except for Hilma. Elsy cautiously picked up a glass and set it in front of her mother. 'Here, Mamma, try some of this.'

Hilma obeyed her daughter and raised the glass to her lips, downing the drink with a grimace. Elsy looked at Hans, her eyes filled with gratitude. It was good not to be alone right now.

Another knock at the door. This time it was Hans who opened it. The women had started to arrive. All those who knew what it was like to live under the threat of losing their husbands to the sea. They brought food and helping hands and consoling words about the will of God. And it helped. Not much, but they all knew that one day they might need the same sort of solace, and so they did their best to ease the pain of their friend who was now suffering.

Her heart hammering with grief, Elsy took a step back and watched the women flock around Hilma while the men who had brought the news bowed sorrowfully and then left to deliver the news elsewhere.

By the time night fell, Hilma had fallen asleep, exhausted. Elsy lay in bed, staring at the ceiling, empty, incapable of taking in what had happened. She saw her father's face in her mind. He had always been such a comforting presence for her. Listening to her, talking with her. She had been the apple of her father's eye. She had always known that. For him, she had been so precious, transcending all else. And she knew that he would have noticed that something was going on between her and the Norwegian boy, for whom he had developed such a fondness. But he had let them be. He had kept a watchful eye on them, giving his silent consent. Maybe he was hoping that someday he would have Hans as his son-in-law. Elsy thought he would have approved. And she and Hans had respected both him and her mother.

Limited themselves to stolen kisses and cautious embraces; nothing that would prevent them from looking her parents in the eye.

Now, as she lay in bed staring up at the ceiling, it no longer mattered. The pain in her heart was so great that she wouldn't be able to endure it alone, and she slowly sat up and put her feet on the floor. There was something in her that still hesitated, but grief was tearing at her, driving her to seek the only relief that she could find.

Quietly she crept down the stairs. She peeked in to look at her mother as she passed her parents' bedroom, feeling a pang in her heart when she saw how small Hilma looked in that big bed. But she was sound asleep, exhaustion granting her a temporary respite from reality.

The front door creaked faintly as Elsy turned the lock and opened it. The night air was so cold that it took her breath away when she stepped out on to the porch in her night-gown, and the icy chill of the stone stairs almost hurt under the soles of her feet. Quickly she padded down the steps and found herself standing outside his door, hesitating. But that lasted only a minute. Grief urged her to seek solace.

He opened the door at her first knock and moved aside to let her in without a word. She went inside and then just stood there in her nightgown, her eyes fixed on his, without speaking. His eyes silently asked a question, and she replied by taking his hand.

For a short blessed time that night she was able to forget the pain in her heart.

Kjell felt strangely agitated after the meeting with his father. For all these years he had successfully managed to hold on to his hatred. It had been so easy to see only the negative, to focus on all the mistakes that Frans had made during his childhood. But maybe things weren't really so black and white after all. He shook himself in an attempt to dismiss that idea. It was so much easier not to see any grey areas, to claim there was only right and wrong. But today Frans had seemed so old and frail. And for the first time it struck Kjell that his father wasn't going to live for ever. One day he would be gone, and then Kjell would be forced to look at himself in the mirror. Deep inside, he knew that his hatred burned as strongly as it did because he still had the possibility of reaching out his hand, of taking the first step towards reconciliation. He didn't want to do that. Had no desire to do that. But the possibility existed nonetheless, and it gave him a feeling of power. When his father died, it would be too late. Then Kjell would have only a life of hatred left. Nothing else.

His hand trembled slightly as he picked up the phone to make a few calls. Of course Erica had said that she would contact the authorities to check if there were any records on Hans, but he wasn't used to relying on anybody else. He might as well do it himself. But an hour later, his phone calls to various Swedish and Norwegian agencies had drawn a blank. Having only a name and an approximate age to go on made it difficult, but there was bound to be a way. He hadn't yet exhausted all the possibilities, and he had managed to find out enough to convince him that the boy hadn't stayed in Sweden. So it was most likely that Hans had returned to his homeland when the war ended and he was no longer in danger.

Kjell reached for the folder containing the articles and suddenly realized that he had forgotten to fax Olavsen's photograph to Eskil Halvorsen. He picked up the phone again to call the man and get his fax number.

'I'm afraid that I haven't found anything yet,' said Halvorsen as soon as he heard who was calling. He listened as Kjell explained the reason for his call, then said, 'Yes, a photo might be helpful. You can fax it to my office at the university.'

Kjell jotted down the number and faxed the article which had the clearest picture of Hans Olavsen. Then he sat down at his desk again. He was hoping that Erica's research would prove more fruitful, since he felt as if he'd come to a dead end.

Just at that moment the phone rang.

'Grandpa is here!' Per shouted towards the living room, and Carina came out to join them in the hall.

'Could I come in for a moment?' asked Frans.

Carina noticed that he didn't seem himself and it worried her. Not that she'd ever had especially warm feelings for Kjell's father, but she was grateful to him for what he had done for her and Per recently. 'Of course, come on in,' she said, leading the way to the kitchen. Noticing that he was studying her intently, she replied to his unspoken question: 'Not a drop since the last time you were here. Per can vouch for me.'

Per nodded and sat down across from Frans at the kitchen

table. The look that he gave his grandfather bordered on hero worship.

'Looks like your hair is starting to grow out,' said Frans with amusement, patting the stubble on his grandson's head.

'I guess so,' said Per, embarrassed, but then he ran his own hand over his scalp, looking pleased.

'That's good,' said Frans. 'That's good.'

Carina gave him a warning look as she spooned coffee into the filter. He nodded faintly, to confirm that he wasn't about to discuss politics.

When the coffee was ready and Carina had sat down at the table with them, she turned to him with an enquiring look. He stared down at his coffee cup. She thought again how tired he seemed. Even though she didn't approve of the causes he espoused, he had always seemed to her the epitome of strength. Right now he was not at all his usual self.

'I've opened a bank account in Per's name,' he said at last, not meeting their eyes. 'He'll have access to it when he turns twenty-five. I've already deposited a large sum in there.'

'Where did you get –' Carina started to say, but Frans held up his hand and went on.

'For reasons that I can't go into at the moment, the account and the money are not with a Swedish bank but a financial institution in Luxemburg.'

Carina raised an eyebrow, but she wasn't entirely surprised. Kjell had always claimed that his father had money stashed away somewhere, from some of the criminal activities that had landed him in prison so many times in the past.

'But why now?' she asked, looking at him.

At first Frans didn't seem willing to answer the question, but finally he said, 'If anything happens to me, I want to have this all arranged.'

Carina said nothing. She didn't want to know anything more.

411

'Cool,' said Per. 'How much dosh do I get?'

'Per!' exclaimed Carina, glaring at her son, who merely shrugged.

'A lot,' said Frans drily. 'But even though the account is in your name, there are certain restrictions. For one thing, you can't access the money until you're twenty-five.' He held up an admonitory finger. 'And I've also set it up so that you can't access it until your mother decides that you're mature enough to handle money and grants her permission. And that condition holds, even after you turn twenty-five. If she doesn't trust you to do something sensible with the funds, you won't get a cent of it. Do you understand?'

Per muttered something but accepted what Frans had said without protest.

Carina didn't know what to make of all this. There was something in Frans's manner, something in his voice, that made her uneasy. At the same time, she felt an enormous sense of gratitude towards him, on Per's behalf. She wasn't going to worry about where the money had come from. Frans must have acquired it a long time ago, and if the money could help Per in the future, she wasn't about to quibble.

'What do I do about Kjell?' she asked.

Now Frans raised his head and fixed his eyes on her. 'Kjell isn't to know anything about this until the day that Per gets the money. Promise me that you won't say anything to him! That goes for you too, Per.' He gave his grandson a stern look. 'That's my only request. That your father doesn't find out anything about this until after the event.'

'Okay. Pappa doesn't need to know about this,' said Per, delighted to be asked to keep a secret from his father.

Then Frans said in a slightly calmer voice: 'I know you're probably going to be punished for assaulting that boy. Now I want you to listen to what I'm going to tell you.' He forced Per to meet his eyes. 'You're going to accept your punishment. They'll probably send you to a home for delinquents. Stay out of trouble, don't get mixed up in any shit while you're there. Just do your time without causing any problems and afterwards don't do anything else stupid. Do you hear me?'

He spoke slowly, enunciating each word clearly, and every time Per seemed about to look away, Frans forced him to meet his gaze again.

'I'm telling you right now that you don't want to have the kind of life I've had. My life has been shit, from beginning to end. The only thing that has ever mattered to me is you and your father, even though he'd never believe that. It's true though. So promise me that you'll keep out of trouble. Promise me that!'

'Okay, okay,' said Per, squirming. But he seemed to be listening to his grandfather and taking in his words.

Frans just hoped that this would be sufficient. He knew from his own experience how hard it could be to change paths once you'd started out in a specific direction. But he hoped it wasn't too late to be giving his grandson a shove on to the right track. That was all he could do now.

'So, I've said what I came here to say.' Frans removed an envelope from his pocket and set it on the kitchen table in front of Carina. 'Here are the documents you'll need to access the money.'

'Are you sure you won't stay for a while?' she asked, still feeling uneasy.

Frans shook his head. 'I've got things to do.' He turned to leave but paused in the doorway and said quietly, 'Take care of yourselves.' Then he raised his hand to give them a little wave before he turned and headed for the front door.

Carina and Per sat at the kitchen table in silence. They had both recognized the finality of Frans's farewell.

'This is almost getting to be routine,' said Torbjörn Ruud drily as he stood next to Patrik watching the macabre business that was now under way.

413

Anna had offered to babysit, so Erica was present too, observing the digging with ill-concealed eagerness.

'It can't have been easy for Mellberg to get permission,' said Patrik. It was rare for him to praise his boss.

'From what I heard, it took ten minutes before the guy at the prosecutor's office stopped shouting at him,' said Torbjörn, without taking his eyes off the grave, where layer after layer of earth was being removed.

'Do you think we'll need to dig up the whole thing?' asked Patrik, shuddering.

Torbjörn shook his head. 'If the two of you are right, then the body we're looking for should be on top. I doubt the killer would have gone to the trouble of burying him at the very bottom, underneath the others,' he said sarcastically. 'And he's probably not in a coffin, so his clothes should tell us if your theory is correct.'

'How fast can we get a preliminary report on the cause of death?' asked Erica. 'If we find him, that is,' she added, but she seemed convinced that the exhumation would prove her right.

'I've been promised a report day after tomorrow,' said Patrik. 'I talked to Pedersen, and they're willing to move this post-mortem to the top of the list. He can start on it tomorrow and let us know the results by Friday. He stressed that it will only be a preliminary report, but it should be possible to establish cause of death, at least.'

A shout from the men working at the grave interrupted him, and they moved closer.

'We've found something,' said one of the tech guys, and Torbjörn went over to talk to him. They had a brief conversation, their heads close together. Then Torbjörn returned to Patrik and Erica, who hadn't dared go any nearer.

'It looks like someone was buried close to the surface, and not in a coffin. They're going to have go slower now so as not to destroy evidence. It will take a while to dig out the body.' He hesitated. 'But it looks as though you were right.'

Relieved, Erica nodded and took a deep breath. In the distance she saw Kjell coming towards them, but he was stopped by Martin and Gösta, who were there to prevent anyone from getting too close. She hurried over to them.

'It's okay. I'm the one who told him about what's going on here.'

'No reporters or other unauthorized individuals. Mellberg gave us specific orders to that effect,' muttered Gösta, his hand level with Kjell's chest.

'It's okay,' said Patrik, joining them. 'I'll take responsibility.' He gave Erica a sharp look that signified she would be the one who'd bear responsibility for any consequences. She nodded curtly and led Kjell over to the grave.

'Have they found anything?' he asked, his eyes gleaming with excitement.

'It looks that way. I think we've found Hans Olavsen,' she told him, watching with fascination as the techs cautiously attempted to uncover a bundle lying in the hole, which so far was no more than a foot and a half deep.

'So he never left Fjällbacka after all,' said Kjell, unable to take his eyes off the work going on in the grave.

'No, he didn't. So the question is: how did he end up here?'

'I presume that Erik and Britta knew he was here.'

'Yes, and they were both murdered.' Erica shook her head, as if that might make all the pieces fall into place.

'He's been here for at least sixty years. So why now? Why did he suddenly become so important?' Kjell wondered.

'You didn't get anything out of your father?' asked Erica, turning to look at him.

He shook his head. 'Not a thing. And I don't know whether that's because he doesn't know anything, or because he doesn't want to tell me.'

'Do you think he could have . . .?' She didn't really dare finish the sentence, but Kjell understood what she was getting at.

'My father is capable of just about anything. Of that I'm certain.'

'What are you two talking about?' asked Patrik, coming over to stand next to Erica.

'We're discussing the possibility that my father may have committed murder,' said Kjell calmly.

Patrik was startled by his honesty. 'And what did you decide?' he said. 'We've had our suspicions, but your father has an alibi for the time when Erik was killed.'

'I didn't know that,' said Kjell. 'But I hope you've double- and triple-checked your information, because an old jailbird like my father would have no difficulty arranging a false alibi.'

Patrik realized he was right and made a note to ask Martin how closely they had scrutinized Frans's alibi.

Torbjörn joined them, greeting Kjell with a nod of recognition. 'So, I see that the fourth estate has been granted permission to attend.'

'I have a personal interest,' said Kjell.

Torbjörn shrugged. If the police wanted to allow a journalist to be present, he wasn't going to interfere. That was their problem. 'We'll be done here in about an hour,' he said. 'And I know that Pedersen is standing by to start the post-mortem.'

'Yes, I've already talked to him,' said Patrik, nodding.

'All right then. We'll be getting him out of there, and then we'll see what sort of secrets the lad is hiding.' He turned and went back to the grave.

'Yes, let's see what secrets he has,' said Erica quietly, staring at the grave. Patrik put his arm round her shoulders.

FJÄLLBACKA 1945

The months following her father's death were confusing and painful. Elsy's mother continued to tend to her daily tasks and do was what was required of her, but something was missing. It was as if Elof had taken part of Hilma with him, and she no longer recognized her mother. In that sense, she had lost not only her father, but her mother too. The only solace she could find was in the nights that she and Hans shared. As soon as her mother had gone to bed, she would slip downstairs to his room and crawl into his embrace. She knew that it was wrong. She knew that there could be consequences she wouldn't be able to ignore. But she couldn't stay away. During those hours when she lay beside him under the covers, his arm around her, his hand gently stroking her hair – during those hours the world became whole again. When they kissed and the passion, by now so familiar and yet still surprising, overtook them, she couldn't understand how it could be wrong. In a world that could so suddenly and brutally be shattered by a mine, how could love possibly be wrong?

Hans had also been a blessing when it came to practical matters. Their finances were a big worry now that her father was dead; they only managed to scrape by because Hans took on extra shifts on the boat and gave them every krona of his wages.

Sometimes Elsy wondered whether her mother knew that she was sneaking downstairs to see him at night but decided to turn a blind eye because she couldn't afford to do otherwise.

Elsy ran her hand over her stomach as she lay in bed next to Hans, listening to his steady breathing. She had realized one week ago that she was pregnant. In spite of everything she'd been taught about shame and its consequences, a great calm had come over her. After all, it was Hans's child she was carrying, and there was no one in the world that she trusted more. She hadn't told him yet, but deep inside she knew that it wouldn't be a problem. He would be happy to hear the news. And they would help each other and somehow make things work.

She closed her eyes, leaving her hand resting on her stomach. Somewhere inside was a small creature that was the product of their love. Hers and Hans's. How could that be wrong? How could a child that belonged to them ever be wrong?

Elsy fell asleep with her hand on her stomach and a faint smile on her lips.

A tense feeling of anticipation had settled over the station following the events at the cemetery. Mellberg, of course, was taking full credit for the discovery, but nobody paid much attention to him. Even Gösta had a gleam in his eye as he joined in the speculation. Though they didn't yet know exactly how yesterday's discovery fit in with the two recent murders, everyone was certain it marked a major break-through in the investigation.

'The question is,' mused Paula, 'why start killing people over a murder that happened sixty years ago? I mean, we almost have to assume that Britta and Erik were killed because of some link to the "alleged"' – here she drew quote marks in the air – 'murder of that boy. But why now? What sparked the renewed interest?'

'I don't know,' said Martin, who'd been sitting at his desk wondering the very same thing when Paula dropped by. 'Let's hope the post-mortem will give us something concrete to go on.'

'What if it doesn't?' said Paula, voicing the thought that he'd been trying to avoid.

'Let's just take it one step at a time,' he said quietly.

'That reminds me,' said Paula, 'aren't we supposed to get back the DNA profile results today? It won't do us much good unless we've got something to compare them to.'

'You're right,' said Martin, pushing back his chair. 'Let's take care of that right now.'

'Who should we take first? Axel or Frans? Those are the two we should focus on, right?'

'Let's take Frans,' said Martin, and he put on his jacket.

With the summer tourist season over, Grebbestad was just as deserted as Fjällbacka, and they saw only a few residents as they drove through town. Martin parked the police vehicle in the small car park in front of the Telegraph restaurant, and they walked across the street to Frans's flat. No one answered when they rang the bell.

'Damn. He's not at home. We'll have to come back later,' said Martin, turning away.

'Wait a minute,' said Paula. 'The door's open.'

'But we can't just . . .' Martin's objection came too late. His colleague had already opened the door and stepped inside.

'Hello?' he heard her calling, and reluctantly he followed her down the hall. They peeked into the kitchen and the living room. No Frans. And not a sound.

'Come on, let's check the bedroom,' said Paula. Martin hesitated. 'Oh, come on,' she said. With a sigh he let her lead the way.

The bedroom was also empty, the bed neatly made up and no Frans in sight.

'Hello?' called Paula again when they returned to the hall. No answer. They made their way to the last room in the flat.

They saw him as soon as the door swung inwards. The room was a small office, and Frans had collapsed forward on to the desk, the gun still in his mouth and a gaping hole in the back of his head. Martin felt all the blood drain from

420

his face; for a moment he swayed on his feet and had to swallow hard. Paula, on the other hand, seemed totally unfazed. She pointed at Frans, forcing Martin to look, even though he would have preferred not to.

'Look at his arms,' she said calmly.

Fighting the waves of nausea rising up inside of him, Martin did his best to focus on Frans's forearms. He gave a start. They were covered in deep scratches.

It was just a matter now of waiting for confirmation from the scientific team. DNA and fingerprint analysis would no doubt prove that Frans had murdered Britta. And perhaps the techs combing through the apartment in Grebbestad would come up with a link to Erik Frankel's murder too. And then there was the preliminary report on the body found in the soldiers' grave in Fjällbacka; everybody was eager to know what fresh information that might provide.

Martin was the one who took the call from the ME. Holding the faxed post-mortem report in his hand, he then went round knocking on office doors and summoning his colleagues to a meeting.

After the others were seated, he leaned against the kitchen counter, deciding to remain standing so that everyone would be able to hear him.

'As I said, I've got the initial report from Pedersen,' Martin told them, turning a deaf ear to Mellberg's sullen mutterings that he should have been the one to take that phone call.

'Since we don't have any DNA or a dental chart for comparison, we can't positively identify the deceased as Hans Olavsen. But the age matches. And the time of his disappearance also fits, even though it's impossible to know for certain after such a long time.'

'So how did he die?' asked Paula. She was tapping her foot on the floor, eager to get on with things.

Enjoying his moment in the spotlight, Martin paused for

effect before announcing: 'Pedersen says that the body had sustained massive injuries. Stab wounds caused by a sharp instrument, as well as contusions from kicks or punches, or both. It looks as though Hans Olavsen was the victim of a frenzied attack. His killer must have been in a fit of rage. The details are all in Pedersen's preliminary report.' Martin leaned forward to put the pages on the table.

'So the cause of death was . . .?' Paula was still tapping her foot.

'It's hard to say which particular injury caused his death. According to Pedersen, there were several wounds that could have been fatal.'

'I'll bet Ringholm was the one who did it. And that's why he killed Erik and Britta too,' muttered Gösta, voicing what most of his colleagues were thinking. 'He's always been a hot-headed bastard,' Gösta added, shaking his head gloomily.

'That's one theory that we need to work on,' said Martin, nodding. 'But let's not jump to conclusions. Frans did have scratches on his arms, just as Pedersen told us to look for, but until we have the lab results we won't know whether Frans's DNA matches the skin scrapings that we found under Britta's fingernails, or whether he's a match for the thumbprint on the pillowcase button. So until we have that corroboration, we're going to keep plugging away as usual.'

Martin was surprised at how professional and calm he sounded. This was how Patrik came across whenever he reviewed a case. Martin couldn't help stealing a glance at Mellberg, to see whether his boss seemed upset by the fact that his subordinate had jumped in and taken over the role that rightfully belonged to him, as station chief. But, as usual, Mellberg seemed content to hand over all the investigative legwork. Only when the case was solved would he muster the energy to take all the credit.

'So what do we do now?' asked Paula, giving Martin a

quick wink to indicate that she thought he was doing a great job.

Even though the praise hadn't been put into words, Martin was glowing with pride. He'd been the station rookie for so long that it hadn't come easy, having to step up and take responsibility. But Patrik's paternity leave had finally given him a chance to show his true worth.

'Let's start by reviewing our investigation of Erik Frankel's death in the light of these new developments. We need to see if we can find any links to Frans. Could you do that, Paula?' She nodded. Then Martin turned to Gösta.

'Gösta, find out what you can about Hans Olavsen. Check out his background, see if anyone can give us more details about his stay in Fjällbacka, and so on. Talk to Patrik's wife, Erica. She seems to have done a lot of research on the subject, and Frans's son was on the trail. Get them to share their information with you. I don't think Erica will present any problems in that regard, but it might be necessary to press Kjell a bit harder.'

Gösta nodded, but he displayed considerably less enthusiasm than Paula had. It wasn't going to be either easy or fun to dig up information from sixty years ago. He sighed. 'All right, I'll work on it,' he said, looking as if he'd just been assigned the labours of Hercules.

'Annika, could you let us know ASAP when you hear from the lab?'

'Of course,' she said, putting down the pad of paper on which she had been taking notes while Martin talked.

'Okay. Let's get on with it then!'

Martin watched them troop out of the room, his face flushed with satisfaction at having successfully led his first investigative review.

Patrik put down the phone after finishing his conversation with Martin and went straight upstairs to see Erica.

'I'm sorry to bother you,' he said, tapping on her work-room door, 'but I think you'll want to hear this.' He sat down on the armchair in the corner and recounted what Martin had told him about Hans Olavsen – or rather, the body that they thought was Hans Olavsen's – and the terrible injuries he had suffered.

'I assumed that he'd been murdered . . . But this seems . . .' Erica was clearly upset.

'Yes, somebody really had a score to settle with him,' Patrik said. Then he noticed that he had interrupted Erica as she was once again reading through her mother's diaries.

'Have you found anything interesting?' he asked, pointing to the books.

'No, not really,' she said, frustrated. 'They stop right about the time that Hans Olavsen came to Fjällbacka, and that's really the moment when things started to get interesting.'

'And you have no idea why she stopped keeping a diary at that point?' asked Patrik.

'No, and that's the thing: I'm not sure that she did stop. It seems to have been an ingrained habit of hers to write for a while every day, so why would she suddenly stop? No, I think there must be more diaries somewhere, but God only knows where . . .' she said pensively, twisting a lock of hair around her finger, a habit that Patrik was quite familiar with by now.

'Well, you've searched the whole attic, so they can't be up there,' he said, thinking out loud. 'Do you suppose they might be in the basement?'

Erica thought for a moment, but then shook her head. 'No, I went through the whole basement when we cleaned up before you moved in. I have a hard time believing they would be here in the house, but I don't have any other ideas where they could be.'

'Well, at least you're getting some help with your research into Hans Olavsen. Kjell is working on it, and I have great faith in his ability to ferret out information. And Martin said that they're going to work on it too. He's asked Gösta to liaise with you.'

'Okay. I have no problem sharing my information with the police,' said Erica. 'I just hope Kjell has the same attitude.'

'I wouldn't count on it,' replied Patrik. 'He's a journalist, after all, and I'm sure he sees a story in all of this.'

'I still wonder . . .' said Erica, rocking her chair back and forth. 'I still wonder why Erik gave those newspaper articles to Kjell. What did he know about the murder of Hans Olavsen that he wanted Kjell to find out? And why didn't Erik just tell him what he knew? Why be so cryptic and evasive?'

Patrik shrugged. 'We'll probably never know. According to Martin, my colleagues at the station believe everything comes back to Frans. They think he murdered Hans Olavsen, and that he killed Erik and Britta in order to cover it up.'

'Okay, I suppose there's plenty of evidence that points in that direction,' said Erica. 'But there's still a lot that . . .' She let the sentence remain unfinished. 'There's so much that I still don't understand. For example, why now? After sixty years? Hans had been lying in his grave undisturbed for sixty years, why did all of this come to the surface now?' She chewed on the inside of her cheek as she pondered the question.

'I have no idea,' said Patrik. 'There could be any number of reasons. We'll probably just have to accept that the key events happened so far back in the past that we'll never have a whole picture.'

'You're probably right,' said Erica, clearly disappointed. She reached for the bag of sweets on her desk. 'Would you like a Dumlekola?'

'Sure,' said Patrik, taking one out of the bag. In silence they munched on the sweets as they thought about the mystery of Hans Olavsen's brutal death.

'So you think it was Frans? Are you positive? And is it certain that he murdered Erik and Britta too?' said Erica at last, studying Patrik's expression.

'Yes, I think so. At any rate, there's not much to indicate that he didn't do it. Martin's expecting the lab report to come through on Monday, and it sounds as though that will at least confirm that he killed Britta. I imagine, now the investigation has homed in on Frans, they will turn up evidence to link him to Erik's murder. As for Hans . . . he was murdered so many years ago that I doubt we'll ever have a complete explanation for it. The only thing is . . .' He made a wry face.

'What? Is there something that seems odd to you?' asked Erica.

'Not odd, exactly. Just that Frans had an alibi for the time when we think Erik was killed. But his pals could be lying. Martin and the others will have to look into that. That's my only reservation.'

'And there's no question about Frans's death? No doubt that it was suicide, I mean?'

'No, apparently not. It was his own gun, he was still holding it in his hand, and the barrel was still in his mouth.'

Erica grimaced as she pictured the scene in her mind.

Patrik went on: 'So, if we confirm that his fingerprints were on the gun and that he had powder residue on the hand that was holding it, then for all intents and purposes we're looking at suicide.'

'But you didn't find a suicide note?'

'No. Martin said they haven't found anything like that. But people who commit suicide don't always leave a note.' He got up and tossed the sweet wrapper into the wastebasket. 'Okay, I should let you work in peace, sweetheart. Try to get some work done on your book, otherwise the publisher is going to start breathing down your neck.' He went over and kissed her on the lips.

'Yes, I know,' sighed Erica. 'I've already made some headway today. What are you and Maja going to do?'

'Karin phoned,' said Patrik lightly. 'We'll probably go for a walk as soon as Maja wakes up.'

'You're certainly taking a lot of walks with Karin,' said Erica, surprising herself by how disapproving she sounded.

Patrik looked at her in astonishment. 'Are you jealous? Of Karin?' He laughed and went over to give her another kiss. 'You have no reason in the world to be jealous.' He laughed again, but then turned serious. 'Listen, if you really have a problem with me seeing her, please tell me.'

Erica shook her head. 'No, of course not. I'm just being silly. There aren't a lot of people you can spend time with now that you're on paternity leave, so it's good for you to have some adult company.'

'Are you sure?' Patrik studied her intently.

'Yes, I'm sure,' said Erica, waving him out of the room. 'Go now. Somebody in this family needs to be working.'

He laughed and closed the door behind him. The last thing he saw as he peeked through a crack in the door was Erica reaching for one of the blue diaries.

FJÄLLBACKA 1945

It was unbelievable. The war that had felt like it would never end was over. She was sitting on Hans's bed, clutching the newspaper and trying to make her brain understand the meaning of the headline screaming 'PEACE!'

Tears filling her eyes, Elsy she blew her nose on the apron she was still wearing after helping her mother wash the dishes.

'I can't believe it, Hans,' she said. He had his arm around her shoulders, and he replied by squeezing her tighter. He too was staring at the newspaper, and like her he seemed incapable of comprehending what they were reading. For a moment Elsy glanced towards the door, nervous that someone might catch them, now that they had thrown caution to the wind and were sitting here together in the daytime. But Hilma had run over to see their neighbours, and Elsy didn't think anyone would come here to disturb them just now. Besides, it would soon be time to tell everyone about their relationship. Her dresses were getting tighter around the waist, and this morning it was only with great effort that she had managed to fasten all the buttons. But everything was going to be fine. Hans had reacted exactly as she had anticipated when she told him a few weeks ago that she was pregnant. His eyes had sparkled and he had kissed her as he tenderly placed his hand on her stomach. Since then, he had assured her that they would manage. He had a job, after all, and was able to support her. And her mother was fond of him. Of course Elsy was young, but they could apply to the authorities for permission to marry. They would find a way to work things out.

His words had eased some of the worry she still carried in her heart, even though she thought she knew him so well, and trusted him. And he had been so calm. Assuring her that their child would be the most loved on earth, and that they would find a way to handle all the practical details. There might be a few bumps in the road for a while, but if they stuck by each other, any problems would be solved and both her family and God would offer their blessings.

Elsy leaned her head against his shoulder. Right now life was good. The news of peace spread over her like a warmth that thawed much of what had turned to ice after her father died. She just wished that he were here to experience this moment. If only he could have held on a few more months. She pushed the thought away. God was in charge, not people, and somewhere there had to be a plan to everything. That's just how things were, no matter how terrible it seemed. She trusted in God, and she trusted in Hans, and that was a gift that made her able to look to the future with confidence.

But it was different for her mother. Elsy had grown increasingly worried about Hilma over the past few months. With Elof gone, she had seemed to shrink, to withdraw into herself, and there was no longer any joy in her eyes. When they heard the news of peace today, it was the first time since her father died that Elsy had seen the trace of a smile on her mother's face. Perhaps the child she was expecting would make her mother happy – once she got over the initial shock, that is. Of course Elsy was afraid that her mother would be ashamed of her, but she and Hans had agreed to tell her as soon as possible, so that they could make all the proper arrangements before the baby arrived.

Elsy closed her eyes and smiled as she sat there, leaning against Hans's shoulder, breathing in his familiar smell.

'I'd like to go home and see my family, now that the war is over,' said Hans, stroking her hair. 'But I'll only be gone a few days, so you don't need to worry. I'm not about to run away from you.' He kissed the top of her head.

'That's good,' said Elsy, with a big smile. 'Because, if you were to do that, I'd chase you to the ends of the earth.'

'I'm sure you would,' he said and laughed. Then he turned serious. 'There are just a few things that I need to take care of, now that I can go back to Norway.'

'That sounds serious,' she said, lifting her head from his shoulder and looking at him nervously. 'Are you afraid that something has happened to your family?'

'I don't know,' he said hesitantly. 'It's been so long since I last talked to them. But I won't leave right away. Maybe in a week or so, and then I'll be back before you can even blink an eye.'

'That sounds good,' said Elsy, leaning against him again. 'Because I never want us to be apart.'

'And we won't be, either,' he said, kissing her hair again. 'We won't.' Hans closed his eyes as he drew her closer. Between them lay the open newspaper, with the word 'PEACE' covering the front page.

It was strange. It was only last week that it had first occurred to Kjell that his father was not immortal. And then on Thursday the police had rung the doorbell to give him the news of his death. He was surprised how strong his emotions were. How for a moment his heart had skipped a beat, and how, when he held out his hand in front of him, he could feel himself holding his father's hand, a small hand enclosed in a big one, and how their hands had then slowly slipped apart. At that moment he realized that something stronger than hatred had existed the whole time: Hope. That was the only thing that had been able to survive, the only thing that could coexist without being suffocated by the all-consuming hatred that he had felt towards his father. Any love between them had died long ago. But hope had hidden away in a corner of his heart, concealed even from himself.

As he'd stood there in the hall after closing the door behind the police officers, Kjell felt that last vestige of hope disappear, and in that moment a terrible pain made everything go black before his eyes. Because somewhere inside of him that little boy had been longing for his father. Hoping that there might be a way around the walls they had built up.

Now that way was closed. The walls would remain, eventually crumbling but with no possibility of reconciliation.

All weekend his brain had been trying to grasp the fact that his father was gone. Dead by his own hand. And even though it had always been in the back of his mind that this might be the way Frans would die, given how destructive his life had been, it was still difficult to comprehend.

On Sunday Kjell had called in on Carina and Per. He had phoned them on Thursday to tell them what had happened, but he hadn't had the strength to see them until his own thoughts and memories had settled a bit. He had sensed immediately that there was something different about the atmosphere in their home, but at first he couldn't put his finger on it. Then he had exclaimed in surprise: 'You're sober!' And he didn't mean just for the moment, or for a short period – because that had happened before, although not very often in the past few years. Instinctively he understood that this was something more; there was a sense of calm, a determination in Carina's eyes that had replaced the wounded look she'd had ever since he left her. It had always filled him with such guilt. Per was different too. They talked about what would happen after his trial for beating up his classmate, and Per had surprised Kjell with his composure and thoughts on how he was going to deal with the situation. After Per went up to his room, Kjell had mustered his courage and asked Carina what had changed. It was with growing amazement that he heard about his father's intervention. Somehow Frans had succeeded where Kjell had failed despite ten years of trying.

That had made everything worse. It confirmed the realization that any remaining hope would now chafe futilely inside his heart. After all, Frans was gone: what use was there in hoping now?

Kjell went over to stand at the window of his office and looked out. In a brief, naked moment of self-reflection, he allowed himself to scrutinize his own life and soul with the same critical gaze he had levelled at his father. And what he saw frightened him. Of course his betrayal of his family had not been as dramatic or as unforgivable in the eyes of society, but did that make it any more acceptable? Hardly. He had abandoned Carina and Per. And he had betrayed Beata, too. In fact, he had betrayed her even before their relationship had begun. He had never loved her. He had only loved what she represented, in a weak moment when he needed what she stood for. If he were honest, he wasn't even fond of her. There'd never been anything like the love he'd felt for Carina that first time he saw her in her yellow dress and with that yellow ribbon in her hair. And he had betrayed Magda and Loke too. Because of the shame he felt at abandoning his first child, he had put up all sorts of barriers inside of him, so he'd never again experienced that raw, deep, all-encompassing love that he had felt towards Per from the moment he saw him in Carina's arms. He had denied Beata and their children that kind of love, and he didn't think he was capable of ever finding it again. That was the betrayal he would have to live with. They would have to live with it too.

Kjell's hand trembled as he lifted the cup he was holding. He grimaced, noticing that the coffee had gone cold as he brooded, but he had already taken a big gulp and forced himself to swallow it.

He heard a voice at the door.

'Some mail for you.'

Kjell turned and nodded wearily. 'Thank you.' He reached out to take the day's post, already sorted for his personal attention, and leafed through it absentmindedly. A few adverts, some bills. And a letter. The address written in a hand that he recognized. Shaking uncontrollably, he sank back into his chair, placing the letter on the desk in front of him. For a long time he just sat there, staring at the envelope. At his name and the address of the newspaper, written in an ornate, old-fashioned script. The minutes ticked by as his brain tried to command his hand to pick up the letter and open the envelope. It was as if the signals got confused along the way and instead produced a total paralysis.

Finally the signals got through, and he began to open the letter, very slowly. There were three pages, handwritten, and it took a few sentences before he managed to decipher the words. But he managed it.

When he was finished, he set it back down on the desk. And for the last time he felt the warmth of his father's hand holding his. Then he grabbed his jacket and car keys. He carefully slipped the letter into his pocket.

There was only one thing for him to do now.

GERMANY 1945

They were picked up from the concentration camp in Neuengamme. It was rumoured that the white buses had first had to remove a lot of other prisoners, including Poles, from the camp before they could make room for the Nordic prisoners. It was also rumoured that this had cost a number of people their lives. The prisoners of other nationalities had been in much worse shape than the Scandinavians, who had received food parcels by various means and so had managed to survive the camps in relatively better condition. It was said that many failed to survive the journey, while others had endured terrible suffering during their transport from the camp. But even if the rumours were true, nobody dared think about that now. Not when freedom was suddenly within reach. Bernadotte had negotiated with the Germans and secured permission to bring home the Nordic prisoners, and now they were finally on their way.

His legs wobbling, Axel climbed on board the white bus. This would be his second journey in a matter of months, and the horrors of the last one – from Sachsenhausen to Neuengamme – still kept him awake at night. He would lie in his bunk reliving the hell of being locked in a freight car, listening to the bombs falling all around them, sometimes exploding so close that they could hear debris raining down on the roof above them. But miraculously none of the bombs had scored a direct hit. For some reason, Axel had survived even that. And now, just as he had almost lost all will to live, word had come that they were finally going home.

He was one of the few prisoners still capable of making his way unaided. Some were in such bad shape that they had to be carried on board. Carefully he settled down on the floor, drawing up his legs and listlessly resting his head on his knees. He couldn't comprehend it. He was going home. To his mother and father. And to Erik. To Fjällbacka. In his mind's eye he pictured everything so clearly. All the things he hadn't allowed himself to think about for such a long time. But finally, now that he knew it was all within reach, he allowed the thoughts and memories to pour over him. At the same time, he knew that life would never be the same. He would never be the same. He had seen things, experienced things, that had changed him for ever.

He hated how he had changed. Hated what he had been forced to do and what he had been forced to witness. And it wasn't over yet, just because he had climbed into this bus. Their journey was a long one, and along the way they saw towns reduced to smouldering rubble and a country in ruins. Two prisoners died, one of them Axel's neighbour whose shoulder he had leaned against for the brief periods when he was able to sleep. One morning Axel shifted his position on waking and the man toppled, his body stiff and cold as if he'd been dead for some time. Axel had simply pushed the body away and called to one of the people in charge of the transport. Then he had hunkered down in his place again. It was just another death. He had seen so many.

He found himself constantly raising his hand to touch his ear. Sometimes he heard a roaring sound, but most often it was filled with an empty, rushing silence. So many times he had pictured that scene in his mind. Of course he had endured things that were much worse since then, but there was something about the sight of the guard's rifle butt coming towards him that represented the ultimate betrayal. In spite of the fact that they stood on opposite sides in the war, they had established a human contact that had given him a sense of respect and security. But when he saw the boy raise the butt of his rifle and felt the pain as it struck him above the ear, all his illusions about the innate goodness of human beings had been shattered.

As he sat there in the bus, surrounded by others who had suffered as he had, many of them so sick and traumatized that they would not survive, he made a sacred vow to himself: he would never rest until he had brought to justice those responsible. He would make it his mission to see to it that the guilty did not escape punishment.

Axel put his hand up to his ear again and tried to picture the home he had left. Soon, very soon, he would be there.

Paula chewed on her pen as she read through one document after another. On the desk in front of her was a stack of papers that represented everything they had on Erik Frankel's murder, and she was reviewing the material in the hope of finding some small detail they had overlooked. Knowing the folly of trying to shape evidence to fit a theory, she set aside the suspicion that Frans Ringholm had killed Erik and concentrated on finding anything that raised questions. So far she had come up empty. But there was still a considerable amount of material left to go through.

She was having a hard time concentrating. Johanna's due date was fast approaching, and she could go into labour at any moment. When she thought about what lay ahead, Paula felt a mixture of joy and fear. A child; someone she would have to be responsible for. If she had talked to Martin, he would undoubtedly have recognized every one of the thoughts that was whirling through her mind, but she kept her concerns to herself. In her case, the worry had an extra dimension: had she and Johanna done the right thing by realizing their dream of having a baby? Would it turn out to be a selfish act, something that their child would end up paying the price for? Should they have stayed in Stockholm and raised their child there instead? Here, their little family would be more likely to draw attention. Yet something told Paula that they'd made the right decision. Everyone had been very friendly, and so far she hadn't encountered anyone who'd looked at them askance. Of course, that might change after the baby arrived. Who knew?

Sighing, she reached for the next document on the pile: the technical analysis of the murder weapon. The stone bust had stood on the windowsill for years, but after the murder it had been found, stained with blood, under the desk. Forensics had checked for fingerprints and foreign substances, but all they could identify were traces of Erik's blood, hair, and brain matter. She tossed the report aside and picked up the crime-scene photographs. She was impressed that Patrik's wife had noticed what it said on the notepad: *Ignoto militi* . . . 'To the unknown soldier.' Paula hadn't spotted it when she'd looked at the photos and, even if she had, she had to admit that she most likely wouldn't have thought to check what the words meant. Erica had not only discovered the words, she had also managed to link them to other leads and possibilities, which had led them to Hans Olavsen's body.

Paula set down the photograph and opened her notepad. Though they had narrowed it down to within a few days, they hadn't managed to pinpoint the exact time of Erik Frankel's murder. Paula wondered whether she might be able to figure out something more based on the dates that they had. She began drawing up a chronology of events, starting with Erica's visit to Erik Frankel, Erik's drunken parting with Viola, Axel's trip to Paris, and the cleaning woman's attempt to get into the house. She scanned through the documents, to find any information on Frans's where-abouts during that period, but she found only the statements from his henchmen at Sweden's Friends, all of whom swore Frans was in Denmark on the days in question. Damn it! They should have pressed Frans for more details while they had the chance. But given his criminal record he would no doubt have taken the precaution of equipping himself with documents that supported his alibi. Still, what was it Martin had said during the investigative review? There was no such thing as a watertight alibi . . .

Paula sat up with a start. A thought had occurred to her, and immediately she knew she was on to something. There was one thing that they hadn't checked.

'Patrik? Hi, it's me – Karin. Do you think you could come over and help with something? Leif left this morning, and now there's water pouring out of a pipe in the basement.'

'Well, I'm no expert,' said Patrik hesitantly. 'But I suppose I could take a look, see if I can fix it without you having to call in a plumber.'

'That's great,' she said, sounding relieved. 'Bring Maja along if you like. She can play with Ludde.'

'I'll do that. Erica's working, so I don't want to bother her if I can help it.'

Fifteen minutes later, as he turned into the driveway to Karin and Leif's house in Sumpan, he had to admit that it felt a bit strange, seeing the home where his ex-wife now lived with the man whose thrusting white backside he sometimes pictured in his mind. It wasn't easy to forget the moment he'd caught his wife and her lover in the act.

Karin opened the door, holding Ludde in her arms, before Patrik even rang the bell. 'Come in,' she said, moving out of the way to let him through.

'The rescue squad is here,' he said teasingly as he set Maja down. She was immediately joined by Ludde, who took her hand and pulled her down the hall towards what appeared to be his room.

'It's down here.' Karin opened a door leading to the basement stairs.

'Will they be okay?' asked Patrik nervously, glancing towards Ludde's room.

440

'They'll keep themselves busy for a few minutes, no problem,' said Karin, motioning for Patrik to follow her downstairs.

At the foot of the stairs she pointed to a pipe on the ceiling with a concerned expression on her face. Patrik went over to inspect it and then was able to reassure her.

'Hmm . . . I think it's an exaggeration to say that the water is pouring out. Looks more like condensation.' He pointed to a few scanty drops of water on top of the pipe.

'Oh, that's good. I got so worried when I saw that it was wet,' said Karin. 'It's really nice of you to come over. Could I offer you some coffee by way of a thank you, or do you need to get back home?'

'Sure, we're not on any schedule. Coffee would be nice.'

A short time later they were sitting in the kitchen, eating the biscuits that Karin had set on the table.

'You weren't expecting homemade biscuits, were you?' she asked, smiling at Patrik.

He reached for an 'oatmeal dream' and shook his head as he laughed. 'No, baking was never your strong suit. Or cooking in general, to be frank.'

'Hey, how can you say that?' said Karin, looking offended. 'It couldn't have been that bad. You used to like my meat loaf, at least.'

Patrik grinned wickedly and rocked his hand to indicate it had been so-so. 'I just said that because you were so proud of it. But I always wondered whether I ought to sell the recipe to the home guard so they could use it for cannon fodder.'

'Hey, watch it!' said Karin. 'Now you're going too far!' Then she laughed. 'You're right, though, cooking isn't really my forte. That's something Leif loves to point out. Of course, he doesn't seem to think I'm much good at anything.' Her voice broke and tears welled up in her eyes. Patrik impulsively put his hand over hers.

'Are things that bad?'

She nodded, wiping her tears with a napkin. 'We've agreed to separate. We had the world's worst fight this weekend and realized that this just isn't working. So he's packed his bags and he's not coming back.'

'I'm so sorry,' said Patrik, keeping his hand on hers.

'Do you know what hurts the most?' she said. 'The fact that I don't really miss him. This was all a big mistake.' Her voice broke again, and Patrik started to get an uneasy feeling about where this conversation was headed.

'Things were so good between us – you and me. Weren't they? If only I hadn't been so damn stupid.' She sobbed into the napkin as she grabbed hold of Patrik's hand. Now he couldn't very well take it back, even though he knew he should.

'I know that you've moved on. I know that you have Erica. But we had something special. Didn't we? Isn't there a chance that we could . . . that you and I could . . .' She couldn't finish the sentence but just squeezed his hand harder, pleading with him.

Patrik swallowed but then said calmly, 'I love Erica. That's the first thing you need to know. And secondly, the picture you have of what our marriage was like is just a fantasy, something you've made up after the fact because you and Leif aren't getting along. We had a good relationship, but it wasn't anything special. That was why things turned out the way they did. It was just a matter of time.' Patrik looked into her eyes. 'And you know that too, if you just think about it. We stayed married mostly because it was convenient, not because of love. So in a way you did both of us a service, even though I wish that it hadn't ended the way it did. But you're fooling yourself right now. Okay?'

Karin started crying again, largely because she felt so humiliated. Patrik understood and moved over to the chair next to her, putting his arms around her and leaning her

442

head against his shoulder as he stroked her hair. 'Shhh . . .' he said. 'There, there . . . Things will work out . . .'

'How can you be so . . . When I . . . just made such a . . . fool of myself?' Karin stammered.

Patrik calmly continued stroking her hair. 'There's nothing to be ashamed of,' he said. 'You're upset and not thinking very clearly at the moment. But you know that I'm right.' He picked up his napkin and wiped the tears from her flushed cheeks. 'Do you want me to leave, or should we finish our coffee?' he asked.

She hesitated for a moment, but then said, 'If we can overlook the fact that I just threw myself at you, then I'd like you to stay a little while longer.'

'All right, then,' said Patrik, moving back to the chair across from her. 'I have the memory of a goldfish, so in ten seconds all I'll remember are these delicious store-bought biscuits.' He winked, reaching for another oatmeal dream.

'What is Erica writing now?' asked Karin, desperate to change the subject.

'She's supposed to be working on a new book, but she's been caught up in some research into her mother's past,' said Patrik, also grateful to be talking about something else.

'How did she happen to get interested in that?' asked Karin, genuinely curious.

Patrik told her about what they'd found in the chest up in the attic and how Erica had discovered connections to the murders that the whole town was talking about.

'What she's most frustrated about is that for years her mother kept a diary, but the diaries she's found only go up to 1944. Either Elsy suddenly decided to stop writing, or there are a bunch of blue notebooks stored somewhere, but not in our house,' said Patrik.

Karin gave a start. 'What did you say those diaries look like?'

Patrik frowned and gave her a puzzled look. 'Thin blue books, a bit like the exercise books used in schools. Why?'

'Because in that case, I think I know where they are,' replied Karin.

'You have a visitor,' said Annika, sticking her head in to Martin's office.

'Really? Who is it?' he asked, but his question was immediately answered as Kjell Ringholm appeared in the doorway.

'I'm not here in my capacity as a journalist,' he said at once, holding up his hands when he saw that Martin was about to object. 'I'm here as the son of Frans Ringholm,' he said, sitting down heavily on the visitor's chair.

'I'm very sorry . . .' said Martin, not really knowing how to go on. Everybody knew what sort of relationship the Ringholms had had.

Kjell waved away his embarrassment and reached into his jacket pocket. 'This was delivered today.' His tone was expressionless, but his hand shook as he tossed the letter on to Martin's desk. Martin picked it up and opened it after receiving a nod of consent from Kjell. He read the three handwritten pages in silence, but raised his eyebrows several times.

'So your father takes the blame not only for the murder of Britta Johansson, but also the deaths of Hans Olavsen and Erik Frankel,' said Martin, staring at Kjell.

'Yes, that's what it says,' replied Kjell, looking down. 'But I expect you'd already assumed as much, so it won't come as much of a surprise.'

'I'd be lying if I told you otherwise,' said Martin, nodding. 'But Britta's murder is the only one where we have concrete proof against him.'

'Then this ought to help,' said Kjell, pointing at the letter.

'And you're sure that . . .?'

'That it's my father's handwriting? Yes,' Kjell told him.

444

'I'm quite sure. That letter was written by my father. And I'm not really surprised,' he added, sounding bitter. 'But I would have thought . . .' He shook his head.

Martin read through the letter again. 'In actual fact, he only confesses to killing Britta. The rest is rather vague: *I am to blame for Erik's death, and also for the death of the man that you've found in a grave that should not have been his.*'

Kjell shrugged. 'I don't see the difference. He was just being pretentious, phrasing it differently. I have no doubt that it was my father who . . .' He didn't finish what he was going to say, just sighed heavily, as if trying to keep all his feelings in check.

Martin went back to reading the letter aloud. '*I thought that I could handle things the way I usually do, that a single act of violence would solve everything, keep everything under wraps. But even as I lifted the pillow off her face, I knew that it wouldn't solve anything. And I understood that there was only one option left. That I had come to the end of the line. That the past had finally caught up with me.*' Martin looked at Kjell. 'Do you know what he means? What was it he wanted to keep under wraps? What does he mean by the past catching up with him?'

Kjell shook his head. 'I have no idea.'

'I'm going to have to keep this for the time being,' said Martin, waving the handwritten pages in the air.

'Of course,' said Kjell wearily. 'Go ahead and keep them. I was just planning to burn them otherwise.'

'By the way, I've asked my colleague Gösta to have a few words with you, when it's convenient. But maybe you and I could have a talk instead?' Martin carefully placed the letter inside a plastic sleeve and put it to one side.

'What about?' asked Kjell.

'Hans Olavsen. I understand that you've being doing some research –'

'What does that have to do with anything now? My father has confessed to murdering him.'

445

'That's one interpretation, yes. But there are still questions about Olavsen's death that we'd like to clear up. So if you have any information that you'd like to contribute . . . anything at all . . .' Martin threw out his hands and leaned back.

'Have you talked to Erica Falck?' asked Kjell.

Martin shook his head. 'Not yet, but we will. Since you happen to be here . . .'

'Well, I don't have much to tell you.' Kjell explained about contacting Eskil Halvorsen, the expert on the Norwegian resistance movement. He still hadn't heard back from him about Hans Olavsen, and there was a strong likelihood he wouldn't have any information to offer.

'Would you like to ring him now, to check if he's found out anything?' asked Martin, pointing to the phone on his desk.

Kjell shrugged and took a well-thumbed address book out of his pocket. He leafed through it until he found the page with the yellow Post-it note bearing Eskil Halvorsen's name and number.

'I think it will be a waste of time, but since you insist . . .' Kjell moved the phone closer and punched in the number from his address book. There was a pause before the Norwegian finally picked up. 'Hello, this is Kjell Ringholm. I'm sorry to bother you again, but I was just wondering if . . . Right, you got the photo. Good. Have you . . .'

Kjell nodded. As he listened, his expression grew more and more alert, which made Martin sit up straighter in his chair, eager to know what the man on the other end of the line was saying.

'And it's from that photograph that you . . .? But it's the wrong name? And his name is actually . . .?'

Kjell snapped his fingers to signal Martin that he needed pen and paper.

Martin reached for his pen holder and managed to knock it over so all the pens fell out, but Kjell picked up one of them, grabbed a report from Martin's inbox and began feverishly writing on the back of it.

'So he wasn't . . . Yes, I realize that this is extremely interesting. For us too, believe me.'

Martin was ready to burst with curiosity. It was all he could do to keep from grabbing the phone.

'Okay, thank you so much. This puts a new light on the whole matter. Yes. Right. Thank you. Thank you.'

Finally Kjell put down the phone and gave Martin a big smile.

'I know who he is! I'll be damned, I know who he is!'

'Erica!'

Erica heard the front door slam and wondered why Patrik was yelling like that.

'What is it? Something urgent?' She went out on to the landing and looked down at him.

'Come down here – there's something I need to tell you.' He motioned excitedly for her to come, and she complied. 'Let's sit down,' he said, going into the living room.

'Now I'm really curious,' she said when they were both sitting on the sofa. She looked at him. 'So tell me.'

Patrik took a deep breath. 'Okay. You know how you said you thought there had to be more diaries somewhere?'

'Ye-es,' said Erica, suddenly feeling butterflies in her stomach.

'Well, I ran over to Karin's place a little while ago.'

'You did?' said Erica, surprised.

Patrik waved his hands dismissively. 'Never mind that. Listen – I happened to mention the diaries to Karin. And she thought she knew where to find more of them!'

Erica looked at him in amazement. 'How could she possibly know that?'

Patrik told her, and Erica's face lit up. 'Oh, of course. But why didn't she ever say anything?'

447

'I have no idea. You'll have to go over there and ask her yourself,' replied Patrik. No sooner had he said the words than Erica was on her feet and heading for the front door.

'We'll go with you,' said Patrik, picking up Maja from the floor.

'Okay, but hurry,' called Erica, already halfway out the door with her car keys in her hand.

A short time later Patrik's mother, Kristina, opened her door, looking startled.

'Hello, what a surprise. What are you doing here?'

'We just thought we'd drop by for a moment,' said Erica, exchanging glances with Patrik.

'Sure, of course. Shall I make us some coffee?' asked Kristina, still surprised.

Erica waited impatiently for Kristina to finish making the coffee and sit down with them at the table before she blurted out:

'Remember that I told you that I'd found Mamma's diaries up in the attic? And that I've been reading through them, hoping to find out more about who Elsy Moström really was?'

'Yes, of course I remember you telling me about that,' said Kristina, avoiding her eyes.

'When I was here last time, I think I also said that I thought it was strange she stopped writing in 1944 and there were no more diaries.'

'Yes,' said Kristina, her eyes fixed on the tabletop.

'Well, today Patrik had coffee with Karin over at her place, and he happened to mention the diaries and described what they looked like. And she had a clear memory of seeing similar books here.' Erica paused to study her mother-in-law. 'According to Karin, you asked her to get a tablecloth out of the linen cabinet, and at the very back of the cabinet she remembers seeing several blue notebooks with the word "Diary" on the cover. She assumed they were your old diaries and didn't say anything, but today when Patrik mentioned Mamma's diaries, well . . . she made the connection. And so my question is,' Erica went on gently, 'why didn't you tell me?'

Kristina continued to stare down at the table. Patrik tried not to look at either of them, focusing his attention on eating buns with Maja. Finally Kristina got up without saying a word and left the room. Erica watched her go, hardly daring to breathe. She heard a cupboard door open and close, and a moment later Kristina came back to the kitchen. She was holding three blue notebooks. Exactly like the ones Erica had at home.

'I promised Elsy to take care of these. She didn't want you or Anna to see them. But I assume . . .' Kristina hesitated, then handed them over. 'I assume that there comes a time when things should be revealed. And it feels as though this is the time. I think that Elsy would have given her consent.'

Erica took the diaries and ran her hand over the cover of the one on top.

'Thank you,' she said, looking at Kristina. 'Do you know what she wrote in these books?'

Kristina hesitated, not sure what to say.

'I haven't read them. But I know a lot about the things that I assume Elsy would have put in those diaries.'

'I'm going to go into the living room and read them,' said Erica.

She was trembling as she sat down on the sofa. Slowly she opened to the first page of the top diary, and began to read. Her eyes raced over the lines, over the familiar handwriting, as she read about her mother's fate, and subsequently her own. With growing surprise and agitation, she read of her mother's love affair with Hans Olavsen, and how Elsy had discovered that she was pregnant. In the third diary she came to Hans's departure for Norway. And his promise.

Erica's hands were shaking harder now, as if she were experiencing her mother's rising panic when days and weeks passed with no word from him. And when Erica came to the last pages, she started to cry and couldn't stop. Through her tears she read what her mother had written in her elegant script:

Today I took the train to Borlänge. Mother stood at the door and waved, but didn't come with me. It's getting harder to hide my condition. And I don't want my mother to bear the shame. It's so hard for me to do this. But I have prayed to God to give me the strength to see it through. The strength to give away the child that I've never met, but already love so much, so very much . . .

BORLÄNGE 1945

He never came back. He had kissed her goodbye, told her that he would be back soon, and left. And she had waited. At first feeling confident and secure, then with a slight pang of uneasiness, which over time surged into an overwhelming panic. Because he never did come back. He broke his promise to her. Betrayed her and their child. And she had been so sure of him. She had never even questioned the promise that he'd made to her, taking it for granted that he loved her as much as she loved him. What a stupid, naïve girl she had been. How many girls had been fooled by the same story?

When it was no longer possible to hide her pregnancy, she had turned to her mother. With bowed head, unable to meet Hilma's eyes, she had told her everything. That she had allowed herself to be duped, that she had believed his promises, and that she was now carrying his child. At first her mother hadn't said a word. A dead, icy silence settled over the kitchen where they were sitting, and only then had fear truly gripped Elsy's heart. Because deep inside she had been hoping that her mother would rock her in her arms, and say: 'Dear child, everything will be all right. We'll work things out.' The mother Elsy had had before her father died would have done that. She would have possessed the strength to love her daughter in spite of the shame. But part of Hilma had died with her husand, and the part that remained was not strong enough.

Without saying a word, she had packed a suitcase for Elsy, putting in all the essentials. And then she put her sixteen-year-old daughter on a train to Borlänge, sending her off to stay with Hilma's sister who had a farm there. Hilma couldn't even bring herself to go with her to the station; they had said a brief goodbye in the hall, before she turned her back on Elsy and went into the kitchen. The story everyone in town would hear was that Elsy had gone to attend a home economics school.

Five months passed. In spite of the fact that her belly grew with each week that went by, she had worked as hard as anyone else on the farm. From morning to night she had toiled with all the tasks assigned to her, while the aching in her back got worse from the kicking in her womb. Sometimes she wanted to hate the baby. But she couldn't. It was a part of her and a part of Hans – and even now she couldn't feel true hatred towards him. So how could she hate a creature who united the two of them? But everything had already been arranged. The child would be taken away from her right after the birth, to be given up for adoption. There was no other way, said Aunt Edith. Her husband, Anton, had taken care of all the practical details, muttering all the while how shameful it was for his wife to have a niece who had slept with the first guy to come sniffing around. Elsy couldn't bring herself to contradict him. She accepted the reproaches without protest and without being able to offer any explanation. It was hard to argue with the fact that Hans had deserted her. In spite of his promise.

The labour pains started early one morning. At first she thought it was just the usual backache that had woken her. But then the pain got worse, coming and going, but growing stronger. After lying there, tossing and turning, for two hours, she finally realized what was happening and managed to roll out of bed. With her hands pressed to the small of her back, she had gone to Edith and Anton's bedroom and hesitantly awakened her aunt. That was followed by frantic activity. She was ordered back to bed, and the eldest daughter of the house was sent to fetch the midwife. Water was set to boil on the stove, and towels were taken out of the linen cupboard. Lying in bed, Elsy could feel her terror growing.

After ten hours the pain was unbearable. The midwife had arrived hours ago and rather roughly examined her. She was stern and unfriendly, making it very clear what she thought of unmarried girls who got themselves pregnant. No one had a kind word or a smile for Elsy as she lay in bed, believing she was going to die. Each time a wave of pain washed over her, she would grip the bed frame and clench her teeth so as not to scream. It felt like someone was slicing her down the middle. At first she was able to rest a bit between the contractions, to catch her breath and try to recoup her strength. But as the hours went on the contractions started coming so close together that she never had a chance to rest. The thought came again and again: Now I'm going to die.

She must have said the words out loud, because through the fog of pain she saw the midwife glare at her angrily and say: 'Stop making such a fuss. You're the one who got yourself into this mess, so you can just get through it without complaining. Think about that, my girl.'

Elsy had no strength left to protest. She gripped the bed frame so hard that her knuckles turned white, and then a new level of pain raced through her abdomen and into her legs. She had never known that such pain was even possible. It was everywhere, penetrating into every fibre, every cell of her body. And now she was starting to get tired. She had fought the pain for so long that part of her just wanted to give up, to sink down and let the pain take over and do whatever it liked with her. But she knew that she couldn't allow that to happen. It was her child, and Hans's, that wanted to come out, and she would give birth to this baby if it was the last thing she ever did.

A new type of pain started merging with the contractions, that were so familiar by now. She felt a great pressure, and the midwife nodded with satisfaction to Elsy's aunt, who stood nearby.

'It will be over soon,' she said, pressing on Elsy's stomach. 'You need to bear down with all your might when I tell you to, and that baby will be here very soon.'

Elsy didn't reply but she heard what the midwife had said and was waiting for what would happen next. The feeling that she needed to bear down increased, and she took a deep breath.

'All right, now push with all your might,' the midwife commanded, and Elsy pressed her chin to her chest and strained as hard as she could. It felt as though nothing happened, but the midwife gave her a curt nod to indicate that she was doing it right. 'Wait until the next contraction,' the woman said harshly.

Elsy felt the pressure building once more, and when it was at its worst, she was again ordered to bear down. This time she felt something loosen – it was hard to describe, but it was as if something gave way.

'The head is out now, Elsy. Just one more contraction, and . . .'

Elsy closed her eyes for a moment, but all she could see was Hans. She didn't have the strength to grieve for him right now, so she opened her eyes again.

'Now!' said the midwife as she stood between Elsy's legs. With her last ounce of strength, Elsy pressed her chin to her chest and bore down with her knees drawn up.

Something wet and slippery slid out of her, and she fell back, exhausted, on to the sweat-drenched sheet. Her first feeling was relief. Relief that all the hours of torment were over. She was worn out in a way that she'd never felt before; every part of her body was utterly exhausted, and she couldn't move even an inch – until she heard the cry. An angry, shrill cry that made her struggle to prop herself up on her elbows to see where it was coming from.

She sobbed when she caught sight of him. He was . . . perfect. Sticky and bloody, and angry at being out in the cold, but perfect. Elsy fell back on the pillows when she realized that this was the first and last time she would ever see him. The midwife cut the umbilical cord and carefully cleaned him off with a washcloth. Then she dressed him in a tiny, embroidered infant's shirt that Edith had provided. No one paid any attention to Elsy, but she couldn't take her eyes off the boy. Her heart felt as if it would burst with love, and her eyes were hungry to take in every detail of him. Not until Edith made a move to take him out of the room did she manage to speak.

'I want to hold him!'

'That's not advisable, under the circumstances,' said the midwife angrily, motioning for the aunt to go. But Edith hesitated.

'Please, just let me hold him. Just for a minute. Then you can take him away.' Elsy's tone of voice was so persuasive that her aunt came over and placed the baby in Elsy's arms. She held him carefully as she looked into his eyes. 'Hello, sweetheart,' she whispered, rocking him gently.

'You're bleeding on his shirt,' said the midwife, looking annoyed.

'I have more shirts,' said Edith, giving the woman a look that silenced her.

Elsy couldn't get enough of looking at him. He felt warm and heavy in her arms, and she stared with fascination at his little fingers with the perfect, tiny fingernails.

'He's a fine boy,' said Edith, standing next to the bed.

'He looks like his father,' said Elsy, smiling as the baby held on to her finger.

'You need to hand him over now. He has to be fed,' said the midwife, taking the boy out of Elsy's arms. Her first instinct was to resist, to grab him back and never let him go. But that moment passed, and the midwife began hastily pulling the bloody shirt off the infant and putting him into a clean one. Then she handed him to Edith, who, after a last look at Elsy, carried him out of the room.

At that moment, as she looked at her son for the last time, Elsy felt something break deep inside her heart. She did not know how she would survive such pain. And as she lay there in her sweaty, bloodied bed with an empty womb and empty arms, she decided never to subject herself to those sorts of feelings again. Never, ever. With tears running down her face, she made herself that promise while the midwife roughly helped her with the afterbirth.

'Martin!'

'Paula!'

They both shouted at the exact same time, each on their way to the other's office with urgent news. Now they stood in the corridor, staring at one another, their cheeks flushed. Martin was the first to pull himself together.

'Come with me,' he said. 'Kjell Ringholm was just here, and there's something I have to tell you about.'

'Okay, but then I've got something to tell you, too,' said Paula, following him into his office.

He closed the door behind her and sat down. She sat down across from him, but she was so eager to share what she'd found out that she could hardly sit still.

'First of all, Frans Ringholm confessed to the murder of Britta Johansson. He also hinted that he was the one who killed Erik Frankel and . . .' Martin hesitated, 'the man we found in the grave.'

'What? He confessed to his son before he died?' exclaimed Paula in astonishment.

Martin pushed across the desk the plastic sleeve containing the three-page letter. 'Afterwards, actually. Kjell got this in the post today. Read it and then tell me your immediate impressions.'

Paula picked up the letter and began reading intently. After she was finished, she put the pages back in the plastic sleeve and said with a pensive frown on her face: 'Well, his confession that he killed Britta is plain enough. But as for Erik and Hans Olavsen . . . He just writes that he's the one to blame, and that's rather an odd way of putting it, in this context, especially since he's so unambiguous about Britta. So I don't know. I'm not sure that he's saying he killed the other two. And besides . . .' She leaned forward and was about to tell Martin what she had found out, when he interrupted her.

'Wait. There's more.' He held up his hand, and she closed her mouth, looking slightly offended. 'Kjell has been doing some research on this Hans Olavsen. Trying to find out where he went and uncover more about him in general.'

'And?' said Paula impatiently.

'He's been in touch with a Norwegian professor who's an expert on the German occupation of Norway. Since the professor has so much material on the Norwegian resistance movement, Kjell thought he might be able to help locate Hans Olavsen.'

'And?' Paula repeated, starting to look annoyed since Martin couldn't seem to get to the point.

'At first he didn't find anything.'

Paula sighed loudly.

'. . . but then Kjell faxed over an article with a photograph of the "resistance fighter" Hans Olavsen.' Martin drew quote marks in the air.

'Then what?' Now Paula's interest had been sparked, and for a moment she forgot about her own news.

'The thing is, that boy was not a resistance fighter at all. He wasn't even called Olavsen – that was his mother's maiden name, which he took as his own surname after he fled to Sweden. It seems his Norwegian mother was married to a German named Reinhardt Wolf. When the Germans occupied

458

Norway, Wolf was given a high position in the Norwegian SS, thanks to the fact that his wife had taught him the language. At the end of the war the father was captured and sent to a prison in Germany. Nobody knows what happened to the mother, but the son, Hans, disappeared from Norway in 1944 and was never seen again. And we know why: he fled to Sweden, pretending to be in the resistance, and then somehow ended up in a grave in Fjällbacka cemetery.'

'That's incredible. But how does that fit in with our investigation?' asked Paula.

'I don't know yet. But I have a feeling it's important,' said Martin meditatively. Then he smiled. 'Okay, now you know what my big news is. What was it you wanted to tell me?'

Paula took a deep breath and quickly explained what she had discovered. Martin gave his colleague an appreciative look.

'Well, that certainly puts a different light on things,' he said, getting up. 'We need to do a search right away. Go and get the car while I ring the prosecutor and apply for a search warrant.'

That was all Paula needed to hear. She jumped up, the blood roaring in her ears. They were very close now, she could feel it. They were getting close.

Erica hadn't said a single word since they got back in the car. She just stared out the window, with the diaries on her lap and her mother's words and pain filling her head. Patrik left her alone, realizing that she would tell him when she was ready. He didn't know as many of the details as Erica, since he hadn't read the diaries, but while Erica was reading them, Kristina had been telling him about the son that Elsy had been forced to give away.

At first he had felt angry with his mother. How could she have kept something like that from Erica? And Anna, too. But gradually he began to see things from her point of view. She had made a promise to a friend and kept it. There had been times when she had considered telling Erica and Anna that they had a brother, but in the end she had decided to let things be. Though Patrik couldn't condone her decision, he believed her when she said that she had tried to do what she thought was best.

Now that the secret was out, he could tell that Kristina was relieved. It was down to Erica to decide what she would do with the information. And he was pretty sure he could guess what that would be. He knew his wife well enough to realize that she would do everything in her power to find her brother. As he turned his head to study her profile as she sat next to him staring vacantly out the window, it suddenly occurred to him how much he loved her. It was so easy to forget. So easy to let life just roll by, with his job and the housework and . . . all the days that simply passed, one by one. But at certain moments – like right now – it hit him with an almost terrifying force just how much the two of them belonged together. And how much he loved waking up next to her each morning.

When they got home, Erica went straight up to her workroom. Still without saying a word and with the same distracted expression on her face. Patrik tidied up a bit and then put Maja in her cot for her afternoon nap before he dared disturb Erica.

'Can I come in?' he asked, gently knocking on the door. Erica turned and nodded, still a bit pale but with a more alert look in her eyes.

'How are you feeling?' he asked, sitting down in the armchair in the corner.

'I'm not really sure, to be honest,' she told him, taking a deep breath. 'Dazed, I guess.'

'Are you angry with my mother? Because she didn't tell you, I mean?'

Erica thought for a moment but then shook her head. 'No, not really. Mamma made Kristina promise, and I can understand why she was afraid of doing more damage by telling us.'

'Are you going to tell Anna?' asked Patrik.

'Of course. She has the right to know too. But first I need to process everything myself.'

'And I suppose you've already started the search. Am I right?' asked Patrik, smiling as he nodded at the computer, with the Internet browser open on the screen.

Erica gave him a faint smile. 'I've done some checking to see what avenues are available for tracing adoptions. It shouldn't be that much of a problem to find him.'

'Does it seem scary?' asked Patrik. 'You have no idea what he's like or what sort of life he's had.'

'Super scary,' Erica agreed. 'But it seems scarier not to know. I mean, I have a brother out there somewhere. And I've always wanted a big brother . . .' She smiled.

'Your mother must have thought about him so many times over the years. Does this change your picture of her?'

'It does,' she replied. 'I can't say that I think she did the right thing by shutting us out, me and Anna, the way she did. But . . .' She searched for the right words. 'But I can understand that she didn't dare let anybody in after that. It must have been awful for her, first being abandoned by the child's father – because that's what she thought had happened – and then being forced to give up the baby for adoption. She was only sixteen! I can't even begin to imagine how painful it must have been for her. And right after losing her father, too – and in a practical sense her mother as well, from what I gather. No, I can't blame her. No matter how much I'd like to, I just can't.'

'If only she had known that Hans didn't abandon her.' Patrik shook his head.

'Yes, that's almost the worst part. He never left Fjällbacka. And he never left her. Instead, somebody killed him.' Erica's voice broke. 'But why? Why was he murdered?'

461

'Do you want me to ring Martin and find out if they've been able to discover anything more?' asked Patrik. It wasn't just for Erica's sake that he wanted to phone the station. The case fascinated him, even more so now that they had discovered the Norwegian was the father of Erica's half-brother.

'Could you do that?' said Erica eagerly.

'Sure, I'll phone the station right now.' Patrik got up.

Fifteen minutes later he was back in Erica's workroom, and she saw at once that he had news.

'They've found a possible motive for the murder of Hans Olavsen,' he told her.

Erica could hardly stay in her seat. 'What is it?' she said.

Patrik hesitated for a moment before telling her: 'Hans Olavsen was not a resistance fighter. He was the son of a high-ranking SS officer, and he himself worked for the Germans during the occupation of Norway.'

Silence descended over the room. Erica stared at him, for once utterly speechless. Patrik went on:

'Kjell Ringholm called in at the station earlier with a suicide letter from his father, which came in this morning's post. Frans confessed that he murdered Britta. He also wrote that he was to blame for the deaths of Erik and Hans. They're not sure whether to interpret that as an admission that he was the one who killed them.'

'Then why did he say that he was to blame? What could that mean?' said Erica. 'And the fact that Hans was not in the resistance after all – I wonder if my mother knew that? How . . . ?' She shook her head.

'What's your opinion, after reading her diaries? Did she know?' asked Patrik, sitting down again.

Erica thought for a moment, then shook her head. 'No,' she said firmly. 'I don't think Mamma knew. Absolutely not.'

'The question is whether Frans found out about it,' said Patrik, thinking aloud

462

'Did Martin say anything about how they were going to proceed now?'

'No, he just said that Paula had found a possible lead, and that they were on their way to check it out, and he would let me know as soon as they found out more. He sounded really elated,' Patrik added, feeling a slight pang at being left out of the action.

'I can tell what you're thinking right now,' said Erica, amused.

'Well, I'd be lying if I said that I didn't want to be over at the station, working the case,' Patrik told her. 'But I wouldn't want it any other way, and I think you know that.'

'I know,' said Erica. 'And I understand how you feel. There's nothing wrong with wanting to be part of the investigation.'

As if to confirm what they had just been talking about, they heard a loud cry coming from Maja's room. Patrik got up.

'Aha – that's the sound of my factory whistle.'

'Back to the salt mines you go,' laughed Erica. 'But first bring that little slave-driver in here so I can give her a kiss.'

'Be right back,' said Patrik. As he was on his way out the door, he heard Erica suddenly gasp.

'I know who my brother is!' she said. She laughed as the tears ran down her face, repeating: 'Patrik, I know who my brother is!'

While they were in the car, Martin got a call confirming that the search warrant had been issued. They'd been so confident the prosecutor would grant the request that they'd set off without waiting for an answer. Neither of them spoke. Both were lost in thought, trying to put together all the loose ends and work out the pattern that was starting to emerge.

There was no answer when they knocked on the door.

'The place seems empty,' said Paula.

'How shall we get in?' asked Martin, studying the solid door, which looked as though it would be difficult to force open.

Paula laughed and reached up to run her hand over one of the beams above the front door.

'With a key,' she said, holding up what she had found.

'What would I do without you?' said Martin, meaning every word.

'Probably break your shoulder while attempting to get inside,' she said, unlocking the door.

They went in. It was eerily quiet, stuffy and hot, and they hung up their jackets in the hall.

'Shall we split up?' asked Paula.

'Sure, I'll take the ground floor, you can take upstairs.'

'What exactly are we looking for?' Paula suddenly sounded uncertain. She was positive they were on the right track, but now that they were so close, she wasn't convinced they would find anything to prove their theory.

'I'm not really sure.' Martin looked equally doubtful. 'Let's just take a careful look around, and see what we can find.'

'Okay.' Paula nodded and headed upstairs.

An hour later she came back down. 'Nothing so far. Should I keep looking upstairs, or should we swap for a while? Have you found anything interesting?'

'No, not yet.' Martin shook his head. 'It's probably a good idea if we change places. But . . .' He looked pensive and then pointed to a door in the hall. 'We could check the basement first. Neither of us has been down there yet.'

'Good idea,' said Paula, opening the basement door. It was pitch black on the stairs, but she found the light switch in the hall, just outside the door, and turned it on. She went first, with Martin following, and a few seconds later she stood at the bottom of the stairs, her eyes adjusting to the dim light.

'What a creepy place,' said Martin when he joined her. He let his eyes roam over the walls, and what he saw made him gape.

'Shh . . .' said Paula, putting her finger to her lips. 'Did you hear something?'

'No,' said Martin, listening. 'No, I didn't hear a thing.'

'I thought I heard a car door slam. Are you sure you didn't hear anything?'

'Yes, I'm sure. It's probably your imagination.' Then he fell silent as they suddenly heard footsteps overhead.

'Imagination, huh? I think we'd better go back upstairs,' said Paula, putting her foot on the first step. At that moment the basement door closed with a bang, and they heard a key turn in the lock.

'What the –?' Paula was on her way up the stairs when the light went out. They were left in pitch darkness.

'Let us out of here!' yelled Paula, and Martin could hear her pounding on the door. 'Do you hear me? It's the police! Open this door and let us out!'

But when she paused to catch her breath, they clearly heard a car door slam and an engine start up.

'Shit!' said Paula as she trudged back down the stairs.

'We need to phone for help,' said Martin, reaching for his mobile just as he remembered that it was in his jacket pocket. 'We'll have to use your mobile because I left mine in my jacket, which is hanging in the hall,' said Martin.

The only reply from Paula was silence, which made him nervous.

'Don't tell me . . .'

'Yes,' said Paula miserably. 'I left my mobile in my jacket pocket too.'

'Damn it!' Martin climbed the stairs and tried to ram the door open. The only result was a sore shoulder. Discouraged, he went back down to join Paula.

'It won't budge.'

'So what do we do now?' asked Paula gloomily. Then she gasped. 'Johanna!'

'Who's Johanna?' asked Martin in surprise.

Paula didn't reply for a moment. Then she said, 'My partner. We're going to have a baby in two weeks. But you never know . . . and I promised to keep my mobile handy.'

'Don't worry,' said Martin, trying to process the information. 'Babies are usually late when it's the first one.'

'I hope so,' said Paula. 'Otherwise she's going to want my head on a platter. It's a good thing that she can always get hold of my mother. In the worst case . . .'

'Don't even think about that,' Martin told her. 'We're not going to be stuck down here for long. And as I said, if she still has two weeks to go, it's probably all right.'

'But nobody knows where we are,' said Paula, sitting down on the bottom step. 'And while we're stuck here, the murderer is getting away.'

'Look on the bright side. At least we know now that we were right,' Martin said. Paula didn't even deign to reply.

Upstairs in the entry hall, Paula's mobile began ringing frantically.

Mellberg hesitated as he stood on the doorstep. Everything had felt so right at the dance class on Friday, but since then he hadn't seen Rita, in spite of repeated walks along her usual route. And he missed her. It surprised him that his feelings were so strong, but he could no longer ignore the fact that he really and truly missed her. Ernst seemed to be thinking along the same lines, judging by the way he had tugged on his lead all the way to the building where Rita lived. While Mellberg hadn't exactly resisted the pull, he was hesitant. Partly because he didn't know if she'd be at home, partly because he felt uncharacteristically shy and afraid of seeming pushy. But he shook off this feeling and pressed the button on the intercom. No one answered, and he was just about to leave when he heard a crackling sound and a stressed voice gasping into the speaker.

'Hello?' he said, going back to the door. 'It's Bertil Mellberg.'

At first there was no answer; then came a barely audible 'Come up.' Followed by a groan. He frowned. How strange. But with Ernst in tow, Mellberg climbed the two floors to Rita's flat. The door was ajar. Surprised, he stepped inside.

'Hello?' he called. Again no answer until he suddenly heard a groan quite nearby, and when he glanced towards the sound, he caught sight of someone lying on the floor.

'I'm having . . . contractions . . .' gasped Johanna, who was curled up in a ball as she panted to ride out the pain.

'Oh, dear God,' said Mellberg, feeling sweat break out on his forehead. 'Where's Rita? I'll phone her! And Paula. We need to get hold of Paula, and an ambulance,' he said, looking around the hall for the nearest phone.

'I tried . . . couldn't get . . . hold of . . .' groaned Johanna, but couldn't go on until the contraction diminished. Then she slowly hauled herself to her feet by holding on to the handle on the nearby wardrobe. She clutched at her stomach, staring panic-stricken at Bertil.

'Don't you think I've tried to phone them? Nobody is answering! How hard could it be to . . . Oh shit . . .' Her curses were cut off by another contraction, and she dropped to her knees, breathing hard. 'Drive me to . . . the hospital,' she told Mellberg, pointing to a set of car keys lying on the bureau. He stared at them as if they might be transformed into a hissing snake at any moment, but then he saw his hand reach in slow motion for the keys. Without knowing how he did it, he found himself more or less carrying and dragging Johanna out to the car, and then shoving her on to the back seat. Ernst had to stay behind in the flat. Stomping down on the accelerator, Mellberg drove towards NÄL, the Norra Älvsborg County Hospital. He felt panic seize hold of him as Johanna started panting harder, and the drive from Vänersborg to Trollhättan seemed endless. But finally he was driving up to the entrance of the maternity ward, where he stopped and pulled Johanna out of the car. Her eyes were filled with terror as she followed him inside.

'She's going to have a baby,' said Mellberg to the nurse behind the glass window. She glanced at Johanna, her expression showing that she thought his words were hardly necessary.

'Come with me,' she told them peremptorily, showing them to a nearby room.

'I guess I'll be . . . leaving now,' said Mellberg nervously, when Johanna was told to start by taking off her trousers. But she grabbed his arm just as he was about to flee and hissed in a low voice as another contraction overtook her:

'You're not going . . . anywhere. I have no intention of . . . doing this . . . alone.'

'But . . .' Mellberg started to protest. Then he realized that he didn't have the heart to leave her there all alone. With a sigh, he sank on to a chair and tried to look in a different direction as Johanna was examined.

'Dilated seven centimetres,' said the midwife, glancing at Mellberg, whom she assumed would want this information. He nodded, although he silently wondered what that could mean. Was it good? Bad? How many centimetres were required? And with growing amazement, he realized that he was bound to find out, along with a good deal of other facts, before this whole thing was over.

He took his mobile out of his pocket and again punched in Paula's number. But he got only her voicemail. The same thing with Rita. What was wrong with them? Why didn't they have their phones with them, since they knew that Johanna could give birth at any moment? Mellberg put his mobile back in his pocket and began pondering whether he could slip out unnoticed.

468

Two hours later, he was still there. They had been taken to a birthing room, and he was being kept firmly in place by Johanna, who had an iron grip on his hand. He couldn't help feeling sorry for her. He had learned that those seven centimetres needed to be ten, but the last three seemed to be taking their time. Johanna was making good use of the nitrous oxide mask, and Mellberg almost wished he could try it himself.

'I can't take it any more,' said Johanna, her eyes glazed from the gas. Her sweaty hair was plastered to her forehead, and Mellberg reached for a towel and wiped her brow.

'Thanks,' she said, looking at him with an expression that made him forget any thought of leaving.

Mellberg couldn't help being fascinated by what was playing out right before his eyes. He had always known that giving birth was a painful process, but he had never witnessed what herculean efforts were required, and for the first time in his life, he felt a deep respect for the female sex. He could never have done it – that was one thing he knew for sure.

'Try to . . . phone them again,' said Johanna, breathing in nitrous oxide as the machine hooked up to her abdomen indicated that a major contraction was about to start.

Mellberg pulled loose his hand and again punched in the two numbers that he had been calling continuously the last few hours. Still nobody answered, and he sadly shook his head as he looked at Johanna.

'Where the hell . . .' she said, but then was overcome by the next contraction, and her words turned to moans.

'Are you sure you don't want that . . . pedisural, or whatever it was she asked you about?' said Mellberg nervously, wiping more sweat from Johanna's forehead.

'No. I'm so close now . . . It might slow down . . . And by the way, it's called an epidural.' She began moaning again, arching her back.

The midwife came into the room to see how dilated

Johanna was, and announced, 'She's all the way open now.' She sounded pleased. 'Do you hear that, Johanna? Good work. Ten centimetres. You'll be able to push soon. You're doing great. Your baby will be here very soon.'

Mellberg took Johanna's hand and squeezed it. He had a strange feeling in his chest. The closest word he could find to describe it was 'pride'. He was proud that the midwife had praised Johanna, that they had been working together, and that the baby would soon be here.

'How long will the pushing take?' he asked the midwife, and she patiently answered his question. No one had asked about his relationship to Johanna, so he assumed that they thought he was the father, albeit a rather old one. And he didn't bother to disabuse them.

'It varies,' said the midwife, 'but my guess is that we'll have the baby here within half an hour.' And she smiled encouragement at Johanna, who was resting for a few seconds between contractions. Then she contorted her face and tensed her body again.

'It feels different now,' she said between clenched teeth, reaching once more for the nitrous oxide.

'It's the bearing-down pains. Wait until you get a really strong one. I'll help you. And when I tell you to push, draw up your knees and press your chin to your chest, and then bear down with all your might.'

Johanna nodded listlessly and squeezed Mellberg's hand again. He squeezed back and then they both looked at the midwife, waiting tensely for further orders.

After a few seconds, Johanna began to pant. She cast an enquiring glance at the midwife.

'Wait, wait, wait . . . not yet . . . wait until it's really strong . . . Okay, NOW!'

Johanna did as she was told, pressing her chin to her chest, drawing up her knees, and then bearing down until she was bright red in the face and the pain subsided.

'Good! Good job! You did great! Now let's wait for the next one, and before you know it, it'll be over.'

The midwife was right. Two contractions later, the baby slid out and was immediately placed on Johanna's stomach. Mellberg stared with fascination. In theory, he knew how babies were born, but seeing it first-hand was . . . To think that a child actually came out, waving arms and legs and crying in protest, before starting to root around on Johanna's breast.

'Let's help out your little boy. He's trying to nurse,' said the midwife kindly, helping Johanna so the infant found her breast and began to suckle.

'Congratulations,' said the midwife to both of them, and Mellberg felt himself beaming like the sun. He had never experienced anything like this before. He certainly hadn't.

A short time later the baby was done nursing and the midwife cleaned him up and wrapped him in a blanket. Johanna sat up in bed with a pillow behind her back and looked at her son with adoring eyes. Then she glanced at Mellberg and said in a low voice:

'Thank you. I could never have done it on my own.'

All Mellberg could manage was a nod. He felt a big lump in his throat that stopped him from speaking, and he kept on swallowing, trying to make it disappear.

'Would you like to hold him?' asked Johanna.

Again, Mellberg could only nod. Nervously he held out his arms, and Johanna carefully handed him her son, making sure that he supported the baby's head properly. It was a strange feeling to hold that warm, new little body in his arms. He looked down at the tiny face and felt the lump in his throat getting bigger. And when he looked into the boy's eyes, he knew one thing. From that moment forward, he was hopelessly, helplessly in love.

FJÄLLBACKA 1945

Hans smiled to himself. Maybe he shouldn't be doing that, but he couldn't help it. Of course it was going to be difficult for them in the beginning. There'd be people who would voice their opinions and no doubt there would be talk about sinning before God and other admonitions in that vein. But after the worst had passed, they would be able to build a life together. He and Elsy and their child. How could he feel anything but joy at the prospect?

Yet the smile on his lips faded as he thought about what lay ahead of him. It was not going to be an easy task. Part of him just wanted to forget all about what had happened in the past, stay here and pretend that he'd never had any other life. That part of him wanted to believe that he'd been born anew, like a blank slate, on the day when he stowed away on the boat belonging to Elsy's father.

But the war was over now, and that changed everything. He couldn't move forward until he had first gone back. It was mostly for his mother's sake. He felt compelled to find out whether she was all right, and he wanted her to know that he was alive and had found a new home.

Hans reached for a suitcase and began packing enough clothes for a few days. A week at most. He had no intention of being gone any longer than that. He really didn't want to be away from Elsy. She had become such a vital part of him that he couldn't bear the thought of being separated from her. He just needed to make this trip, and then they would be together for ever. Every night they would go to bed together, and every morning they would wake up in each other's arms, without shame and without having to keep their love a secret. He had meant what he'd said about applying to the authorities for permission to wed. Then they could marry before the child was born. He wondered whether it would be a boy or a girl. He smiled again as he stood there, folding up his belongings. A little girl with Elsy's gentle smile. Or a little boy with his curly blond hair. It really didn't matter. He would happily take whatever God chose to give them.

Something hard wrapped in a piece of cloth fell out when he took a shirt from a bureau drawer. It clanged as it struck the floor, and Hans quickly bent down to pick it up. He sank down on the bed as he studied the object in his hand. It was the Iron Cross that his father had received in recognition of his services during the first year of the war. Hans stared at it. He had stolen the medal from his father, brought it along as a reminder of what he had fled when he left Norway. It was also a form of insurance in case the Germans had caught him before he managed to escape to Sweden. He should have got rid of the medal long ago, he knew that. If anybody poked around in his belongings and found it, his secret might be revealed. But he needed it. He needed it as a reminder.

He had felt no regret at leaving his father behind. If Hans had had his way, he would never have anything more to do with that man. Reinhardt Wolf stood for all that was wrong with the human race, and Hans was ashamed that at one time in his life he had been too weak to confront his father. Memories raced through his mind. Cruel, ruthless images of deeds carried out by a person with whom he no longer had anything in common. A weak person, someone who had bowed to his father's will but who in the end had succeeded in tearing himself away. Hans squeezed the medal so hard that the sharp edges cut into his hand. He wasn't going back to see his father; presumably fate had finally caught up with him, and he had been given the punishment that he deserved. But Hans did need to see his mother. She didn't deserve to suffer with all the worry that she must be feeling. She'd had no way of knowing whether her son was alive or dead. He wanted a chance to talk to her, show her that he was well, and tell her about Elsy and the baby. And in time he might even be able to persuade her to come to Sweden and live with them. He didn't think Elsy would have any objections. One of the things he loved about her was that she had a good heart. He thought Elsy and his mother would get along fine.

Hans got up from the bed. After hesitating for a moment, he put the medal back in the drawer. It could stay there until he returned, as a reminder of the person he never wanted to be again. A reminder that he would never again be a weak and cowardly boy. Now, because of Elsy and the baby, it was time to be a man.

He closed the suitcase and looked around the room where he had experienced so much happiness during the past year. His train left in a couple of hours. There was just one more thing he needed to do before leaving. One person he had to talk to. He left the room and closed the door behind him. He had a sudden fateful premonition as he heard the door close. A feeling that something was not going to go well. Then he shook off the feeling and left. He'd be back again in a week.

Erica had insisted on driving alone to Göteborg, even though Patrik had offered to go with her. This was something that she needed to do on her own.

She stood at the door for a moment, trying to make herself lift her hand to ring the bell. Finally she couldn't put it off any longer.

Märta looked at Erica in surprise when she opened the door, but then stepped aside to let her come in.

'I'm sorry to disturb you,' said Erica, feeling her throat go dry all of a sudden. 'I should have phoned ahead, but . . .'

'Oh, don't worry about that.' Märta smiled kindly. 'At my age, I'm just grateful for some company, so this is very nice. Come in, come in.'

Erica followed her down the hall to the living room, where they both sat down. She wondered, panic-stricken, how to begin, but Märta spoke first.

'Have you made any progress in the murder investigation?' she asked. 'I'm sorry that we couldn't be of more help when you were here last time, but as I said, I really knew nothing about our finances.'

'I know what the money was for. Or rather, who it was for,' said Erica. Her heart was thumping in her chest.

Märta gave her a puzzled look but didn't seem to know what she meant.

With her eyes fixed on the old woman, Erica said gently: 'In November 1945, my mother gave birth to a son who was immediately put up for adoption. She gave birth at the home of her aunt, in Borlänge. I think the man who was murdered, Erik Frankel, made the payments to your husband on behalf of that child.'

It was utterly silent in the living room. Then Märta looked away. Erica saw that her hands were shaking.

'I thought as much. But Wilhelm never said anything to me about it, and . . . well, part of me didn't want to know. He has always been our son, mine and Wilhelm's, and we never loved him any less just because I hadn't given birth to him myself. We'd wanted a child for such a long time, tried for so long, and . . . well, Göran arrived like a gift from Heaven.'

'Does he know that . . .?'

'That he's adopted? Yes, we've never hidden that fact from him. But to be honest, I don't think he's ever given it much thought. We were his parents, his family. We did talk about it on occasion, Wilhelm and I, about how we might feel if Göran wanted to find out more about his . . . biological parents. But we always told ourselves that we'd cross that bridge when we came to it. And Göran never seemed to want to find out about them, so we let it be.'

'I like him,' said Erica impulsively, trying to get used to the idea that the man she had met here last time was actually her brother. Hers and Anna's, she corrected herself.

'He liked you too,' said Märta, her face lighting up. 'And part of me reacted subconsciously to the fact that you do look a bit alike. There's something about your eyes . . . I'm not really sure, but you have similar features.'

'How do you think he would react if . . .' Erica didn't dare finish her question.

'Considering how much he always talked about having siblings when he was a child, I think he would welcome a little sister with open arms.' Märta smiled and seemed to have already recovered from the initial shock.

'Two sisters,' Erica said. 'I have a younger sister named Anna.'

'Two sisters,' repeated Märta, shaking her head. 'How about that? Life never ceases to amaze me. Even at my age.' Then she turned serious. 'Would you mind telling me something about your mother . . . his mother?' She gave Erica a searching look.

'I'd be happy to tell you about her,' said Erica, and then she recounted the story about Elsy and how she came to give up her son for adoption. She talked for a long time, for more than an hour, trying to do justice to her mother and her situation as she talked to this woman who had loved and brought up the son that Elsy had been forced to give away.

When the front door opened and a cheerful voice called from the hall, they both jumped.

'Hi, Mamma. Do you have visitors?' Footsteps approached the living room.

Erica looked at Märta, who nodded to give her consent. The time for secrets was over.

Four hours had passed and Paula and Martin were starting to despair. They felt like a pair of moles, trapped in the pitch-dark, though their eyes had now grown sufficiently accustomed to the gloom that they were able to distinguish the contours of the room.

'This really isn't how I imagined things would go,' said Paula, sighing. 'Do you think they'll send out a search party soon?' she joked, although she couldn't help sighing again.

Martin was busy rubbing his shoulder, which was throbbing after several attempts to break down the door. He was going to have some serious bruises to show for this.

'He must be long gone by now,' said Paula, feeling frustration well up inside her.

'There's a good chance you're right,' Martin agreed, which only made her feel even more frustrated.

'He certainly has a lot of creepy souvenirs down here.' Paula squinted, trying to make out the outlines of some of the things that filled the shelves in the basement room.

'They're probably mostly Erik's,' said Martin. 'From what I understood, he was the collector.'

'But all these Nazi artefacts . . . They must be worth a fortune.'

'No doubt. A person who devotes most of his life to collecting things is bound to end up with a lot of stuff.'

'Why do you think he did it?' Paula stared into the darkness, trying to wrap her head around what they now regarded as fact. To tell the truth, she had become convinced the minute she started looking into his alibi. That was when she got the idea to find out whether Axel Frankel's name appeared on any other airline passenger list. When they'd checked his alibi, they had verified only that he departed on the day he had specified; it hadn't occurred to them to see whether he had made any other trips. It was only this morning that she had learned a passenger named Axel Frankel had travelled from Paris to Göteborg on June sixteenth, and then returned on the same day.

'I don't know,' Martin replied to her question. 'It's hard to understand. The brothers seem to have had a good relationship, so why would Axel kill Erik? What was it that triggered such a strong reaction?'

'It must have something to do with the sudden renewal of contact between the four of them: Erik, Axel, Britta, and Frans. That can't be a coincidence. And somehow that's all connected to the murder of the Norwegian.'

'I agree. But how? And why? Why now, after sixty years? It just doesn't make sense.'

478

'We'll have to ask him. If we ever get out of here, that is. And if we ever manage to catch him. He's probably on his way to the other side of the world right now,' said Paula, discouraged.

'Maybe they'll find our skeletons down here sometime next year,' Martin joked, but his attempt at humour was not appreciated.

'If we're lucky, maybe some kid will break in,' said Paula drily.

'Hey! You've got something there!' Martin said excitedly, poking her hard in the side.

'Whatever it is, I sincerely hope it's worth the damage you just did to my ribs,' said Paula, probing the tender spot where he'd jabbed her with his elbow.

'Don't you remember what Per said when we interviewed him?'

'I wasn't there. You and Gösta conducted the interview,' she reminded him, but she was starting to sound interested.

'Well, he said that he broke into the house through a window in the basement.'

'I don't think there are any windows down here. If there were, it would be a lot brighter,' said Paula sceptically, squinting as she looked at the walls in the basement.

Martin got up and fumbled his way over to the outside wall.

'But that's what he said. There has to be a window. Maybe something is hanging in front of it. You said it yourself – the stuff stored in here must be worth a fortune. Maybe Erik didn't want anyone to be able to see his collection from outside.'

Now Paula got up too and headed in Martin's direction. She heard him say 'ow!' as he ran into the opposite wall, but when that was followed by 'aha!', she felt her hopes rise. And hope turned to triumph when Martin pulled aside a heavy curtain and daylight came flooding into the basement.

'Couldn't you have thought about this a couple of hours ago?' Paula complained.

'Hey, how about a bit of gratitude?' said Martin cheerfully as he unfastened the latch and pushed the window open. He reached for a chair standing a metre away and put it directly under the window.

'Ladies first!'

'Thanks,' Paula muttered as she climbed up on the chair and squirmed her way out through the gap.

Martin was right behind her. For a moment they both stood still to allow their eyes to adjust to the dazzling daylight. Then they set off running. They dashed up to the front door but found it to be locked, and this time there was no key above the door. That meant their jackets were locked in the house, with their mobiles and car keys. Martin was just about to run over to the nearest neighbour's house when he heard a loud crash. He glanced in the direction the sound came from and saw that Paula, with a satisfied expression, had hurled a rock through a window on the ground floor.

'Since we got out through a window, I thought we might as well get in the same way.' She picked up a stick and knocked out the splinters of glass from the window frame, then looked at Martin.

'Well? Are you planning to give Axel an even bigger head start, or would you like to help me get inside?'

Martin hesitated only a second before giving his colleague a leg-up and climbing through the window after her. What mattered now was catching up with Erik Frankel's killer. Axel already had a huge lead. And they had far too many questions that were still unanswered.

Axel had made it only as far as Landvetter airport. When he locked the police officers in the basement and took off

480

in his car the adrenaline had been surging through his veins, but that had ebbed away leaving only emptiness in its place.

He sat motionless, staring through the windows as the planes took off. He could have departed on any one of those flights; he had money and the contacts that would secure him a ticket to whatever destination he chose. Years of hunting had taught him everything there was to know about the art of vanishing without a trace. But he didn't want to do that. That was the conclusion he had finally reached. He could escape, but he didn't want to.

And so he was sitting here, in no-man's-land, watching the planes taking off and landing. He was waiting for fate to catch up with him. And to his great surprise, he was no longer dreading the moment. Maybe this was the way the men he'd hunted had felt on the day when someone finally knocked on their door and called them by their proper name. A strange mixture of fear and relief.

But in his case, the price had been too high. It had cost him Erik.

If only Elsy's daughter hadn't brought over the medal. That small piece of metal symbolized everything they'd spent all those years trying to forget, and when it was delivered to his door Erik had taken it as a sign that the time had come for the truth to surface.

Of course they had talked in the past about setting things right if they could, or at least accepting responsibility. Not before the law, for the law was indifferent to crimes so ancient they lay beyond its statute of limitations. But on a human, moral level. They deserved to suffer the shame and condemnation of their peers, their fellow human beings. According to Erik, it was time for them to acknowledge what they had done and stop evading the judgement they deserved. Axel had always managed to talk him out of it, telling him that it would serve no purpose. Nothing they said or did now could change the past and it would be pointless to sacrifice all the good that he'd accomplished in his work merely to exact a penance that would change nothing. Instead he would atone for his sins by continuing to devote himself to that work.

Each time, Erik had listened and given in, but the feelings of guilt kept gnawing at him until, finally, only shame remained. To Erik the world had always been black and white. He dealt in facts, and was never more comfortable than when he was submerged in his books; there dates and names, times and places were set out in black letters on a white backdrop. Yet for sixty years Axel had persuaded him to inhabit a grey world of ambiguity and deceit. And they might have gone on that way had it not been for Elsy's daughter – and Britta, whose defensive walls had begun to crumble from a disease that was slowly destroying her brain.

Axel had tried desperately to reason with Erik. Everything he was, everything he stood for, would be obliterated if he were to answer for this crime. No one would ever look at him in the same way. The work of an entire lifetime would be ruined. But this time his arguments failed to sway his brother. He was in Paris when he got the call from Erik. 'It's time,' he said. Just like that. He had sounded drunk when he called, which was especially alarming because Erik never drank in excess. And he had sobbed on the phone, saying that he couldn't take it any more, that he'd gone to see Viola to say goodbye so that she wouldn't have to endure the shame when the truth came out. Then he had muttered something about how he had already set things in motion, but that he couldn't wait any longer for someone else to air their dirty laundry in public. He was going to put an end to his own cowardice, put an end to the waiting, he had said, slurring his words as Axel gripped the phone, his hand sweating.

Axel had jumped on the first plane to Sweden, determined to make his brother see reason. He closed his eyes, heart aching as he relived that moment when he had rushed into the library and found Erik was sitting at his desk, scribbling absently on a notepad. In a dry and toneless voice he had said the words that Axel had lived in fear of for six decades. Erik had made up his mind. He couldn't live with the guilt any longer.

He had been hoping that what Erik had said on the phone was merely empty talk, and that his brother would have come to his senses when he sobered up. But now he saw that he was mistaken. Erik was standing by his decision with frightening resolve. He had already begun to take steps to ensure that the truth would come out. He talked about the child, too. For the first time he revealed how he had managed to find out where the child had been placed, and the monthly payments he had made to the little boy's adopted parents as a form of compensation for what they had taken from him. No doubt assuming that Erik was the boy's father, they had accepted the payments without demur. But that still wasn't enough for Erik. That act of penance hadn't eased the pain that was tearing him apart. If anything, it had only made the consequences of their action all the more real. It was now time for the true penance, Erik had said, looking his brother in the eye.

In that instant Axel had understood that the life he had built – a life filled with admiration and respect – would be destroyed. Images from the camp flooded his mind: the prisoner next to him who had been shoved into the pit they were digging, the hunger, the stench, the degradation. The rifle butt striking his ear so that something broke inside of him. The dead man toppling against him in the bus as they headed home to Sweden. Suddenly he was back there: the sounds, the smells, the rage that had smouldered in his heart, even when he had no strength left and could focus only on survival. He no longer saw his brother sitting in the chair in front of him. Instead, he saw all the people who had demeaned him, harmed him, and who were now jeering at him, rejoicing in the fact that this time he would be the one who was led to the scaffold. But he refused to give them that satisfaction, all those people, dead and alive, who were lined up to taunt him. He wouldn't be able to survive that. And he had to survive. That was the only thing that mattered.

There was a rushing in his ear, worse than usual, and he stopped hearing what Erik was saying; he just saw his lips moving. And then it was no longer Erik. It was the blond youth from Grini who had seemed so friendly when they talked, who had duped him into believing that he was the one human in that inhuman place. That same boy who had raised his rifle and then, with his eyes fixed on Axel's, smashed the butt down into Axel's head.

Filled with rage and pain, Axel picked up the object closest at hand. He had raised the heavy stone bust, held it high overhead as Erik continued to talk and scribble on the notepad on his desk.

Then he had let the bust fall. He hadn't exerted any force, just let gravity make the bust strike his brother's head. No, not Erik's head. The prison guard's head. Or was it Erik, after all? Everything seemed so confused. He was at home in their library, but all the smells and sounds were so vivid. The stench of corpses, boots stomping in time, German commands that could signify one more day to live, or death.

Axel could still hear the sound of the heavy stone striking skin and bone. Then it was over. Erik uttered a single groan before slumping lifeless in his chair, eyes still open.

After the initial shock and the realization of what he had done, a peculiar calm had settled over Axel. What was done was done. He had placed the stone bust under the desk, pulled off the bloody gloves he was wearing, and stuffed them in his jacket pocket. Then he had pulled down all the blinds, locked the door, and got in his car. He drove to the airport and caught the first flight back to Paris. And over

484

the weeks that followed he had tried to suppress the whole thing and throw himself into his work, until the police phoned him.

It had been difficult to return home. At first he didn't know how he would bring himself to set foot in that house again. But after the two friendly police officers had collected him at the airport and dropped him off at home, he had pulled himself together and simply done what he had to do. And as the days passed he had made peace with Erik's spirit, which he could still feel as a presence in the house. He knew that his brother had forgiven him. But Erik would never forgive him for what he had done to Britta. Axel hadn't laid hands on her himself, but he knew what the consequences would be when he had that phone conversation with Frans. He knew what he was doing when he told Frans that Britta was going to reveal everything. He had chosen his words carefully. Said what was necessary to provoke Frans into action, like a deadly bullet aimed with precision. He knew that Frans's political ambitions, his longing for power and status, would make him react. During their phone conversation Axel could already hear the ferocious anger that had always been Frans's driving force. So he bore just as much blame for her death as Frans did.

He pictured her face the last time he had seen her. Still beautiful. And Herman, looking at her with an expression of love that Axel had never even come close to. That love, that sense of togetherness, was what he had taken from them.

Axel watched yet another plane take off, bound for some unknown destination. He had reached the end of the road. There was nowhere for him to go now.

It came as a relief, after hours of waiting, to feel at last the hand on his shoulder and hear a voice speaking his name.

*   *   *

485

Paula kissed Johanna on the cheek and then kissed her son on the head. She still couldn't believe that she'd missed the whole thing. And that Mellberg had been here instead.

'I'm so, so sorry,' she repeated for the umpteenth time.

Johanna smiled tiredly. 'I have to admit that I did my share of swearing when I couldn't get hold of you, but I know it wasn't your fault that you got locked in. I'm just glad that you're all right.'

'Me too. I mean, that you're all right,' said Paula, kissing her again. 'And he is . . . amazing.' She looked at her son in Johanna's arms and could hardly believe that he was here. That he was actually here.

'Take him,' said Johanna, handing him to Paula, who sat down next to the bed, rocking the baby in her arms. 'What are the odds that this would be the day Rita's mobile would fail?'

'I know. Mamma is completely devastated,' said Paula, cooing to her newborn son. 'She's convinced that you'll never speak to her again.'

'Hey, she couldn't help it. And I did find somebody to help me, after all.' She laughed.

'I still can't get over it,' said Paula. 'You should just hear Bertil out in the waiting room with Mamma. He's sitting there boasting about what a "splendid boy" our son is, and how great you were. If Mamma wasn't in love with him before, she definitely is now. Good Lord.' Paula shook her head.

'There was a moment when I thought he was going to run away, but I have to admit that he's made of stronger stuff than I realized.'

As if he'd heard them talking about him, Bertil knocked on the door and then appeared in the doorway with Rita.

'Come in, come in,' said Johanna, motioning to them.

'We just want to see how you're all doing,' said Rita, going over to Paula and her grandson.

'Of course. It's been all of half an hour since you were here last,' said Johanna, teasing her mother-in-law.

'We just want to see if he's grown any. And if he has a beard yet,' said Mellberg, beaming, as he hesitantly approached, gazing tenderly the baby. Rita regarded Bertil with an expression that could only be interpreted as love.

'Could I hold him again?' Mellberg asked.

Paula nodded. 'Sure, I think you've earned it,' she said, handing him her son.

Then she leaned back and watched as Mellberg studied the baby, and Rita studied both of them. And she realized that, even though it had occurred to her that it might be nice for her son to have a male figure in his life, she had never really pictured Bertil Mellberg in that role. But now that she was actually facing the possibility, she thought it might not be such a bad idea after all.

FJÄLLBACKA 1945

He'd taken a chance that Erik would be at home. He thought it was important that they have a talk before he left for Norway. He trusted Erik. There was something sincere, something honest behind his rather reserved façade. And Hans knew that he was loyal. That was what he was counting on most of all. Because Hans couldn't ignore the possibility that something might happen to him. He was going back to Norway, and even though the war was over, he couldn't predict what might happen to him there. He had done things, unforgivable things, and his father had been one of the foremost symbols of the evil the Germans had done in his country. Now that he was going to be a father, Hans needed to think of all the eventualities. He couldn't leave Elsy without a protector. And Erik was the only person he could think of who might fill that role. He knocked on the door.

Erik was not at home alone. Hans sighed to himself when he found Britta and Frans in the library as well. They were listening to records on Erik's father's gramophone.

'Mamma and Pappa won't be home until tomorrow,' Erik explained as he took his usual place behind the desk. Hans stood in the doorway, hesitating.

'I was actually hoping to talk to you in private,' he said, looking at Erik.

'What sort of secrets do the two of you have?' Frans teased them, draping one leg over the armrest of the chair he was sitting on.

'Yes, what are your secrets?' Britta repeated, smiling at Hans.

Erik shrugged and got up. 'Let's step outside for a moment,' he told Hans, heading for the porch. Hans followed, carefully shutting the door behind him. They sat down on the bottom step.

'I have to go away for a few days,' Hans said, poking at the gravel with the toe of his shoe.

'Where are you going?' asked Erik, pushing up his glasses, which kept slipping down his nose.

'To Norway. I need to go home and . . . take care of a few things.'

'Okay,' said Erik, showing little interest.

'And I want to ask you a favour.'

'All right.' Erik shrugged his shoulders. From inside the house they could hear the music playing on the gramophone. Frans must have turned up the volume.

Hans hesitated. Then he said, 'Elsy is pregnant.'

Erik didn't reply. He just pushed up his glasses again.

'She's pregnant, and I want to apply to the authorities for permission to marry her. But first I need to go back home and take care of things. So, if . . . if something happens to me . . . Will you promise to look after her?'

Erik still didn't speak, and Hans waited nervously for his reply. He didn't want to leave without knowing that someone he trusted had promised to help Elsy.

Finally Erik said, 'Of course I'll look after Elsy. Even though I think it's unfortunate that you've put her in this situation. But why are you worried that something might happen to you?' He frowned. 'You should be welcomed back home as a hero. Why would anyone criticize you for fleeing when things got too dangerous?' He turned to look at his friend.

489

But Hans ignored the question. He stood up and brushed off his trousers.

'Of course nothing is going to happen. But just in case, I wanted to tell you about it. And now you've made me a promise.'

'Okay, okay,' said Erik, getting up too. 'Do you want to come inside and say goodbye to the others before you go? My brother is home too. He got back yesterday,' said Erik, his face lighting up.

'I'm so glad to hear that,' said Hans, patting Erik on the shoulder. 'How is he? I heard that he was on his way home, but that he'd had a rough time of it.'

'Yes, he did.' A shadow passed over Erik's face. 'He had a rough time. And he's very weak. But at least he's home now!' he said, his face lighting up again. 'So why don't you come inside and say hello. The two of you haven't met yet.'

Hans smiled and nodded as he followed Erik back inside the house.

For the first few minutes, the mood around the kitchen table was tense. Then their nervousness began to vanish, and they were able to have a cheerful and relaxed conversation with their brother. Anna was still looking a bit shocked at the news, but she stared in amazement at Göran, who was sitting across from her.

'Didn't you ever wonder about your parents?' asked Erica as she took a Dumlekola from the pile of sweets on the plate.

'Of course I did, once in a while,' said Göran. 'But at the same time . . . as far as I was concerned, Mamma and Pappa – I mean, Wilhelm and Märta – were enough. Occasionally I did think about it, and I wondered why my mother had given me away.' He hesitated. 'But I hear she was in a difficult situation.'

'Yes, she was,' said Erica, glancing at Anna. She'd had a hard time deciding how much to tell her younger sister, whom she'd always had a tendency to protect. But in the end she realized that Anna had survived much worse situations than she had, so Erica had told her about all the information she'd gathered, including the diaries. Anna had taken everything in stride, and now here they sat, all together, in the house belonging to Erica and Patrik. Three siblings. Two sisters and a brother. It was an odd feeling, but in a strange way it felt so natural. Maybe it was true that blood was thicker than water.

'So I assume it's too late to start filling me in on who your latest boyfriends are, and things like that,' laughed Göran, pointing at Patrik and Dan. 'Looks like that's a stage that I've missed, unfortunately.'

'Yes, I suppose it is,' said Erica, smiling and taking another Dumle.

'By the way, I heard that you caught the murderer – the victim's brother,' said Göran, turning serious.

Patrik nodded. 'Yes, he was waiting for a plane at the airport. It was strange, because he could have left at any time, and we probably never would have caught him. According to my colleagues, he was extremely cooperative.'

'But why did he kill his brother?' asked Dan, putting his arm around Anna's shoulders.

'They're still interviewing him, so I don't really know,' replied Patrik, handing a piece of chocolate to Maja, who was sitting on the floor next to him, playing with the doll that Göran's mother had given her.

'Well, I can't help wondering why the brother who died paid money to my father all those years. From what I understand, he wasn't my father. It was the Norwegian. Or do I have it backwards?' said Göran, looking at Erica.

'No, you're right. According to Mamma's diaries, your father was named Hans Olavsen, or rather, Hans Wolf. Erik and Mamma don't seem to have ever had a romantic relationship. So I don't know . . .' Erica chewed on her lip as she thought. 'We'll probably know more when we find out what Axel Frankel has to say.'

'Probably,' said Patrik, nodding agreement.

Dan cleared his throat, and everyone turned to look at him. He and Anna exchanged glances, and then Anna said, 'Well, er . . . we have some news.'

'What is it?' asked Erica, stuffing another Dumle into her mouth.

'Well . . .' Anna paused, but then the words came tumbling out of her. 'We're going to have a baby. In the spring.'

'Really! That's great!' cried Erica, getting up to run around the table and give first her sister a hug and then Dan before she sat down again, her eyes sparkling. 'So how do you feel? Is everything all right? Do you feel good?' Erica fired off questions one after the other, and Anna laughed.

'I'm fine, but I feel lousy. It was the same way when I was expecting Adrian. And I have this constant craving for rock candy.'

'Ha ha, rock candy, of all things,' laughed Erica. 'But I shouldn't talk. I remember stuffing myself with Dumlekola sweets when I was pregnant with . . .' Erica stopped in mid-sentence and stared at the heap of Dumle wrappers on the table. She looked up at Patrik, and saw by his open mouth that he was thinking the same thing. Frantically she began calculating. When was her period due? She had been so focused on everything about her mother that she hadn't even thought about . . . Two weeks ago! She should have had her period two weeks ago. She stared dumbfounded at the Dumle wrappers again. Then she heard Anna start to hoot with laughter.

FJÄLLBACKA 1945

Axel heard voices downstairs. With great effort he climbed out of bed. It would take time for him to fully recover. That was what the doctor had said when he was examined upon arriving back in Sweden. And his father had looked worried and said the same thing when Axel finally got home yesterday. It had been so blissful to be back home. For a moment it felt as if all the terror, all the horrible things he had been through, never existed. But his mother had wept at the sight of him. And she had wept even more when she put her arms around his gaunt and frail body. That had hurt. Because they weren't just tears of joy. She was also crying because he was no longer the same. And he never would be. The outspoken, daredevil, cheerful Axel no longer existed. The past years had beaten all that out of him. And he saw in his mother's eyes that she was grieving for the son she would never get back, at the same time that she rejoiced over the small part of him that had returned.

She hadn't wanted to go with her husband and be away overnight, even though the plans had been made long ago. But his father had understood that Axel needed some time alone, and so he had insisted that she accompany him.

'The boy is home now,' his father had said. 'There will be plenty of time to spend with him. He needs some peace and quiet so he can rest. And Erik will be here to keep him company.'

Finally she relented and they had left. Axel was relieved to have the chance to be alone; he was having a hard enough time adjusting to being at home again. Getting used to being Axel.

He turned his right ear towards the door and listened. The doctor had told him that he would just have to accept that he had lost the hearing in his left ear for good. He hadn't expected anything else. When the guard swung the rifle butt and struck him above the ear, Axel knew that something was destroyed. His injured ear would remain a constant reminder of what he'd been through.

With halting steps he went out into the hall. Since his legs were still so weak, his father had given him a cane to use for the time being. It had once belonged to his paternal grandfather. A solid, stout, silver-tipped cane.

Axel had to grip the banister as he slowly made his way down the stairs, but he had been resting in bed for a long time, and he was curious to see who the voices he'd heard belonged to. Even though he had been longing for solitude, right now he wanted company.

Frans and Britta were sitting in armchairs in the library, and Axel thought it strange to see them there again, as if nothing had happened. For them, life had continued along its customary path. They hadn't seen corpses piled up in heaps, or watched the man standing next to them jerk backwards and collapse with a bullet in his forehead. For a moment Axel was furious at how unfair it all was, but then he reminded himself that he had made the choice to put his life at risk, and thus had to endure the consequences. Some of his anger remained, though, smouldering inside of him.

'Axel! It's good to see you awake!' said Erik, sitting up straight in the chair behind the desk. His face lit up when he saw his brother. That was what had warmed Axel's heart the most when he came home. Seeing his brother's face again.

'Right. The old man is managing to get around with the use of his cane,' laughed Axel, raising the cane in jest to show it to Frans and Britta.

'There's somebody here I'd like to introduce you to,' said Erik eagerly. 'Hans is Norwegian. He was in the resistance movement, but he fled by stowing away on Elof's boat when the Germans were on his trail. Hans, this my brother Axel.' Erik's voice was filled with pride.

At first Axel noticed that someone was standing at the far end of the room. He had his back to the door, so Axel saw only a slender figure with curly blond hair. Axel took a step forward to say hello, and then the person turned around.

At that moment the world stood still. Axel saw the rifle butt. He relived the sense of betrayal, how it felt to trust someone he thought was on the side of the good, only to be disappointed. He saw the boy in front of him and recognized him at once. There was a rushing sound in his ear, and the blood raced wildly in his chest. Before Axel was even conscious of what he was doing, he lifted the cane high overhead and swung it right at the boy's face.

'What are you doing!' yelled Erik, rushing over to Hans, who had fallen to the floor, his hands over his face, with blood gushing out between his fingers. Frans and Britta had also jumped up and were staring at Axel in disbelief.

He pointed his cane at the boy and, his voice shaking with hatred, he said, 'He lied to you. He's not a Norwegian resistance fighter. He was a guard at Grini when I was a prisoner there. He's the one who robbed me of my hearing. He smashed his rifle butt into my ear.'

Silence descended over the room.

'Is it true, what my brother said?' Erik finally asked in a low voice as he sat down next to Hans, who was whimpering as he lay on the floor. 'Did you lie to us? Were you working for the Germans?'

'At Grini they said he was the son of an SS officer,' said Axel, still shaking all over.

'And someone like you has got Elsy pregnant,' said Erik, looking at Hans with hatred.

'What did you say?' asked Frans, his face turning white. 'He made Elsy pregnant?'

'That's what he wanted to tell me. He even had the nerve to ask me to take care of her if anything should happen to him. Because he needed to go back to Norway.' Erik was so furious that he was shaking. He kept opening and closing his fists as he stared at Hans, who was struggling to get to his feet.

'Right. I bet he did. He was probably going to run back to his father,' said Axel, raising his cane again. With all his strength, he again struck Hans, who curled up at once with a groan.

'No, I was going to . . . my mother . . .' Hans slurred his words as he pleaded with the others.

'You fucking bastard,' said Frans between clenched teeth, and he kicked Hans hard in the diaphragm.

'How could you? How could you lie to us like that? When you knew that my brother . . .' Erik had tears in his eyes and his voice broke. He stood up and backed away a few steps. Wrapped his arms around his body and began shaking even more.

'So you were planning to bolt, is that right?' yelled Frans. 'Get Elsy pregnant and then leave? Jesus Christ, you fucking pig! If it was any other girl . . . but not Elsy! And now she's going to have a German brat!' His voice rose to a falsetto.

Britta stared at him in despair. Only now did she seem to realize what deep feelings Frans had for Elsy. The pain in her heart made her collapse in a heap on the floor, sobbing uncontrollably.

Frans turned to look at her for a few seconds. Before anyone had time to react, he went over to the desk, picked up the letter opener lying there, and stabbed Hans in the chest.

The others stared at him in horror for several seconds. Erik and Britta were paralysed with shock, but the sight of the blood welling up around the letter opener released something bestial in Axel. He directed all his own fury at the motionless heap on the floor. Uttering primitive sounds, he and Frans punched, kicked, and pummelled Hans. And when they stopped, exhausted and out of breath, the boy on the floor was no longer recognizable. They looked at each other. Scared but somehow elated. The feeling of releasing all that hatred, everything inside of them that wanted to get out, was liberating and powerful, and they could see that in each other's eyes.

They stood there for a moment, sharing the emotion, drinking it in, covered with Hans's blood – on their hands and clothes and faces. It had splattered in a wide circle all around them, and a pool of dark blood was slowly spreading underneath the body. Some of it had also splashed on Erik, who still stood there, his arms wrapped around his body, shaking violently. He hadn't been able to take his eyes off the bloody heap, and his mouth was half open as he now turned to look at his brother. Britta was sitting on the floor, staring at her hands, which were also flecked with blood, and her expression was as blank as Erik's. None of them said a word. It was like the uncanny silence after a storm. Everything was quiet, but the silence still held memories of the roaring wind.

Frans was the one who finally spoke.

'We need to get rid of this,' he said coldly, poking his foot at Hans's body. 'Britta, you stay and clean up. Erik, Axel, and I will get him out of here.'

'But where should we take him?' asked Axel as he tried to wipe the blood off his face with his shirt sleeve.

Frans pondered that question for a moment and then said:

'I know what we're going to do. We'll wait until dark to carry him out of the house. We'll put him on top of something so he won't bleed all over. In the meantime, we can help Britta clean up in here and get washed up ourselves.'

'But . . .' Erik began, his voice trailing off as he sank to the floor, staring at a spot somewhere beyond Frans.

'I know the perfect place. We'll bury him with his own kind,' said Frans with a hint of amusement in his tone.

'His own kind?' repeated Axel, his voice sounding hollow. He was staring at the end of his cane, which was covered with blood and hair.

'We'll put him in the German soldiers' grave. In the cemetery,' said Frans, his smile even bigger. 'There's a poetic justice in that.'

'*Ignoto militi*,' murmured Erik as he sat on the floor, staring straight ahead. Frans gave him a puzzled look. 'To the unknown soldier,' Erik explained quietly. 'That's what it says on the grave.'

Frans laughed. 'See? It's perfect.'

None of the others laughed, but they offered no objections to Frans's plan. Moving numbly, they started doing what had to be done. Erik went to get a big paper sack from the basement, and they placed Hans's body on top of it. Axel brought cleaning supplies from the cupboard in the hall, and Frans and Britta began the laborious job of scrubbing the library clean. It turned out to be a lot harder than they'd imagined. The blood was viscous and at first just seemed to smear with each attempt to remove it. Britta cried hysterically as she scrubbed, sometimes pausing to sob some more as she knelt on the floor with a scrubbing brush in her hand. Frans snarled at her to keep going. He worked until the sweat poured down, but unlike the others, there was no sign of shock in his eyes. Erik scrubbed mechanically; he had stopped saying that they needed to report what had happened to the police, having finally realized that Frans was right. He couldn't take the chance that Axel, who had just returned home after surviving the hell of the concentration camps, might be seized by the police and thrown in jail.

After more than an hour of hard work, they wiped the sweat from their brows, and Frans made sure that no trace remained of what had played out in the library.

'We need to borrow some clothes from my parents' wardrobe for you,' said Erik in a subdued tone, and then left to get them. When he came back, he stopped to look at his brother, who was huddled up on the floor in a corner of the library, his eyes still fixed on the blood and hair stuck on the tip of his cane. Axel had said very little since venting his rage, but now he looked up and stared straight ahead. 'How are we going to get him over to the cemetery? Wouldn't it be better to bury him in the woods?'

'Your family has a moped with a platform. We'll use that,' said Frans, who refused to give up his idea. 'If we bury him in the woods, some animal will just come along and dig him up. But no one will ever guess that there's another body in the Germans' grave. I mean, there are already several corpses buried there. And if we take him over on the moped, with something covering him up, no one's going to see anything.'

'I've dug enough graves,' said Axel absently, shifting his gaze back to his cane.

'Frans and I will do it,' said Erik hastily. 'You can stay here, Axel. And Britta, you should go home. They'll start to worry if you're not home for dinner.' He spoke quickly, rattling out the words like a machine gun, without taking his eyes off his brother.

'Nobody cares whether I come or go,' said Frans dully. 'So I can stay. We'll wait until ten o'clock. There usually aren't many people out at that time of night, and it will be dark enough then.'

'What do we do about Elsy?' asked Erik. He looked down

at his shoes. 'She's expecting him to come back. And now that she's going to have a baby . . .'

'Oh right. A damn German brat. She'll just have to suffer the consequences,' snarled Frans. 'We're not telling Elsy anything! Do you hear me? She'll think that he went back to Norway and abandoned her, which is probably what he was going to do anyway. But I have no intention of wasting any sympathy on her. She'll just have to get by on her own. Does anyone have any objections?' Frans looked from one to the other. No one spoke.

'All right, then. That's decided. This whole thing will remain our secret. Go home now, Britta, so they don't start looking for you.'

Britta got up and with a trembling hand smoothed down her blood-stained dress. Without a word, she took the dress that Erik handed her and left to get washed up and change her clothes. The last thing she saw before leaving the three boys in the library was Erik's expression. All the anger that had appeared in his eyes when Hans's secret was revealed had gone. Only shame remained.

Several hours later Hans was laid in the grave where he would rest undisturbed for sixty years.

FJÄLLBACKA 1975

Elsy picked up the drawing that Erica had made and carefully placed it inside the chest. Tore had taken the girls out in the boat, and she had the house to herself for a few hours. On occasions like this, she often came up to the attic to sit for a while and think about the way things once were.

Her life had turned out so differently than she had imagined. She took out the blue diaries and absently stroked the cover of the one on top. How young she had been. How naïve. How much pain she might have spared herself if she had known back then what she knew now. That a person could not afford to love too much. The price was always too high, and that was why she was still paying for the one time, so long ago, when she had loved too much. But she had kept her promise to herself never to love like that again.

Of course she had sometimes felt tempted to give in, to let something into her heart. Especially when she looked at her two daughters, their faces turned towards her with such longing in their eyes. She saw in them a hunger for something that was expected of her, but she was incapable of giving it to them. Particularly Erica. She needed it more than Anna. Sometimes Elsy would notice Erica just sitting and looking at her with an expression that displayed all the unrequited longing that could possibly be found in a little girl's face. And part of Elsy wanted to break her promise and go over to put her arms around her daughter, to feel her own heart beating in time with Erica's. But something always stopped her. At the last moment, before she could get up, before she could hug her daughter, she always had a sensation of his tiny, warm body in her arms. His brand-new eyes looking up at her, so like Hans, so like herself. A love child that she thought they would raise together. Instead, she had given birth to him alone, in a room filled with strangers. She had felt him slide out of her body and then out of her arms when he was carried away to another mother – someone about whom she knew nothing.

Elsy put her hand inside the chest and took out the baby's shirt. The stains of her blood had faded over the years and now looked more like rust. She held the shirt up to her nose, sniffing at it to see if it still held any trace of that sweet, warm scent that he'd had when she held him in her arms. But there was nothing. The shirt had only a stuffy, musty odour. All those years in the chest had wiped away any scent of the boy, and she could no longer smell it.

Sometimes she had thought about trying to track him down. Maybe just to make sure that he was all right. But the idea had never gone any further. It was the same with the idea that she might throw her arms around her daughters, and in that way free herself from the promise that kept her heart closed.

She picked up the medal which lay at the bottom of the chest and weighed it in her hand. She had found it when she searched Hans's room, before she left to give birth to his child. That was when she still had hope that she might find among his possessions some explanation for why he had deserted her and the child. But the only thing she found, aside from a few items of clothing, was the medal. She didn't know what it meant, didn't know where he had found it or what role it had played in his life. But she sensed that it

503

was important, and so she had kept it. Carefully she wrapped the medal in the baby's shirt and put the small parcel back in the chest. Then she put in the diaries and the drawing that Erica had made for her in the morning. Because this was the only thing Elsy was capable of giving to her girls. A moment of love when she was alone with her memories. That was the only time she could allow herself to think of them not only with her mind but with her heart. As soon as they looked at her with their hungry eyes, her heart would close up in fear.

Because people who refused to love had nothing to lose.

ACKNOWLEDGEMENTS

Once again Micke has offered me a great deal of support, and so he's at the top of the list of those I would like to thank. Thanks, as usual, to my publisher, Karin Linge Nordh, who with her warmth and meticulous attention has turned my manuscript into a better book and made me a better writer. Thanks also to everyone at my Swedish publishing house, Forum, who continue to offer me encouragement. It's a great pleasure to work with all of you.

I've also had help with fact-checking and various opinions expressed in my story. The officers at the Tanumshede police station have been, as always, more than helpful, and I would particularly like to thank Petra Widén and Folke Åsberg. Martin Melin also read the manuscript and offered valuable insight regarding the police details. An extra bonus was the help I received from his father, Jan Melin, with historical details from the 1940s and wartime Sweden. And once again Jonas Lindgren at the forensic medicine lab in Göteborg was kind enough to allow me to ask him questions.

Thanks also to Anders Torevi, who again read the manuscript and corrected a number of details concerning Fjällbacka, since it has been quite a long time since I lived there. My mother, Gunnel Läckberg, has also provided information about Fjällbacka, and was tremendously helpful as a babysitter. The same applies to Hans and Mona Eriksson, and Mona also read the manuscript and offered her opinions.

This time I would also like to thank Lasse Anrell for allowing me to use him in a brief guest appearance in the book. He has promised to give me tips about growing geraniums the next time we see each other.

I was able to work in peace and quiet, as usual, at Gimo Herrgård. They always take such good care of me when I arrive with my computer and check in.

And to the girls . . . You know who you are . . . What would a writer's life be like without you? Desolate and lonely and dreary. And to all the readers and blog-readers – a huge thank you for continuing to read my books.

Finally I would like to thank Caroline, Johan, Maj-Britt, and Ulf, who led us to and helped us to get settled in the paradise where I now find myself.

Camilla Lackberg
Koh Lanta, Thailand, 9 March 2007

www.CamillaLackberg.com